I
Hunt
KILLers

I Hunt Killers

BARRY LYGA

(L)(B)
Little, Brown and Company
New York   Boston

Copyright © 2012 by Barry Lyga
Author Q&A copyright © 2013 by Hachette Book Group, Inc.

Little, Brown and Company

Hachette Book Group
1290 Avenue of the Americas, New York, NY 10104
Visit our website at www.lb-teens.com

Little, Brown and Company is a division of Hachette Book Group, Inc.
The Little, Brown name and logo are trademarks of Hachette Book Group, Inc.

The publisher is not responsible for websites (or their content) that are not
owned by the publisher.

First Paperback Edition: April 2013
First published in hardcover in April 2012 by Little, Brown and Company

Library of Congress Cataloging-in-Publication Data

Lyga, Barry.
I hunt killers / by Barry Lyga. — 1st ed.
p. cm.
Summary: Seventeen-year-old Jazz learned all about being a serial killer from
his notorious "Dear Old Dad," but believes he has a conscience that will help
fight his own urges and right some of his father's wrongs, so he secretly helps
the police apprehend the town's newest murderer, "The Impressionist."
ISBN 978-0-316-12584-0 (hc) / ISBN 978-0-316-12583-3 (pb)
[1. Serial murderers—Fiction. 2. Murder—Fiction. 3. Conduct of life—Fiction.
4. Fathers and sons—Fiction. 5. Psychopaths—Fiction. 6. Mystery and detective
stories.] I. Title.
PZ7.L97967Iah 2012
[Fic]—dc23
2011025418

10

RRD-C

Book design by Alison Impey

Printed in the United States of America

For Alvina. Literally.

It was a beautiful day. It was a beautiful field.
Except for the body.

CHAPTER 1

By the time Jazz got to the field outside town, yellow police tape was everywhere, strung from stake to stake in a sort of drunken, off-kilter hexagon.

The field was thick with cops—state troopers in their khakis, a cluster of deputies in their blues, even a crime-scene tech in jeans and a Windbreaker. That last one really impressed Jazz; the town of Lobo's Nod was too small for its own official crime-scene unit, so usually the deputies handled evidence collection at the scene. The fact that they'd actually called in a real, live tech from two towns over—and on a Sunday morning, no less—meant they were taking this seriously. Some of the deputies were down on all fours, heads down, and Jazz was amused to see a guy with a metal detector just outside the crime-scene tape, slowly pacing back and forth. One of the staties had a cheap little digital video camera and carefully paced the perimeter of the scene.

And riding herd over all of it was Sheriff G. William Tanner, standing off to one side, fists planted on his love handles, watching as his command scurried around at his bidding.

Jasper "Jazz" Dent wasn't about to let the cops see him. He belly-crawled the last fifteen yards through underbrush and tall grass, patiently making his way to a good vantage point. This part of the old Harrison farm had once been endless rows of soybean plants; it was now nothing but old bent and broken stalks, weeds, cattails, and scrub. Perfect cover, really. From here, Jazz could make out the entirety of the crime scene, helpfully demarcated by the yellow tape.

"What have we here?" Jazz murmured to himself as the videographer—about ten feet from the body—suddenly shouted out. Jazz was far enough away that he couldn't make out the words, but he knew it was something significant because everyone immediately turned in that direction, and another deputy rushed over.

Jazz went for his binoculars. He owned three different pairs, each for different purposes, each a gift from his father, who had very specific reasons for giving them to his son.

Jazz tried not to think about those reasons. For now, he was just happy that he'd brought this particular set of binocs: They were Steiner 8x30 binoculars—waterproof, rubberized grip, weighed just a tad over a pound. But their real selling point was the blue-tinted objective lenses, which reduced glare and reflection to almost nil. That meant the enemy—or, for example, a group of cops just twenty yards away—wouldn't catch a glimpse of the sun bouncing off the glass and haul you out of the woods.

Dust and assorted leftover plant pollens tickled Jazz's nose and he caught himself just before he sneezed. *When you're prospecting*, Dear Old Dad had told him, *you gotta be real quiet, see? Most people've got little noisy habits they never think of. You can't do them things, Jasper. You have to be totally quiet. Dead quiet.*

He hated most things about Dear Old Dad, but what he hated most was that Dear Old Dad was pretty much always right.

He zoomed in on the statie with the video camera, but the others were crowding around, making it impossible for him to see what had so excited everyone. Jazz watched as one of them held up a small plastic evidence bag, but before he could adjust to focus on the bag, the cop brought his arm down and the bag vanished behind his thigh.

"Someone found some evidence. . . ." Jazz chanted under his breath, then bit his bottom lip.

Most of these guys, they want to get caught, Dear Old Dad had said on more than one occasion. *You understand what I'm saying? I'm saying most of the time, they get caught 'cause they want it, not 'cause anyone figures 'em out, not 'cause anyone outthinks 'em.*

Jazz wasn't doing anything wrong, lying out here on his belly, watching the police process the crime scene, but getting caught would probably mean being taken away, and possibly a stern lecture from G. William, and he didn't want that.

He'd been at home earlier that morning, his bedroom door shut tight against one of his grandmother's periodic rants (they'd been getting worse and more frequent), when the police scanner had soberly announced a code two-two-thirteen:

An abandoned body had been found. Jazz had grabbed his pack—already stocked with everything he needed for a stakeout—and climbed down the drainpipe outside his window. (No point running into Gramma in the hallway and being delayed by her raving.)

A body was nothing new in Lobo's Nod. The last time bodies had turned up, Jazz's life had turned upside down, and it still hadn't righted itself. Even though it had been years since those days and everyone had packed that time away, there were still times when Jazz feared his life would never be right side up again.

As the cops clustered around G. William, Jazz refocused on the body. As best he could tell from so far away, there was little in the way of serious trauma—no obvious knife or gunshot wounds, for example. Nothing major jumped out at him, but he didn't exactly have the best vantage point.

He was reasonably certain of two things: It was a woman, and she was naked. Naked made sense. Naked bodies were tougher to identify. Clothes told you all sorts of things about a victim, and once you identified the victim, you were one step closer to identifying who made that person a victim.

Anything that slows them down—even if it's just by a few minutes—is a good thing, Jasper. You want them nice and slow. Slow like a turtle. Slow like ketchup.

Through the binocs, he watched as G. William mopped sweat from his forehead with a checkered handkerchief. Jazz knew from experience and observation that the handkerchief had been embroidered GWT years ago by the sheriff's late wife. G. William had a dozen of the snot rags, carefully laundered and cared for. He was the only man in town—probably the only man alive—who had his handkerchiefs professionally dry-cleaned.

The sheriff was a good guy. He came across as a sort of parody of himself when you first met him, but underneath that BBQ-infused gut and floppy, dishwater-colored mustache was some serious law-enforcement genius, as Jazz knew from personal experience. Tanner ran the entire county's sheriff's department from his office in Lobo's Nod, and he'd earned the respect of not just the county, but the entire state. Heck, the staties didn't send a guy out to videotape a field for just anyone. Tanner had pull.

Jazz swept his binocs over a bit and caught a glimpse of the evidence bag as G. William held it up in the sunshine. For a heart-stopping instant, he was sure what he saw in the bag couldn't be for real. But the sheriff's stance gave Jazz a perfect, binocular-enhanced view of what it held.

And that made Jazz's heart pound so hard he thought Tanner would hear it from where he stood. A body in a field was one thing. It happened. A drifter. A runaway. Whatever. But *this*...This portended something new. Something big. And Jazz had a sinking feeling that people would be looking at him with accusation in their eyes. *Only a matter of time*, they would say. *Had to happen sooner or later*, they would say.

So he started running down possible alibis. From the relatively pristine condition of the body, he was comfortable guessing the woman had been killed sometime in the past six hours...and he'd been home in bed all night...with Gramma the only other person in the house. Not the world's most reliable witness.

Connie. Connie would lie for him, if necessary.

This thought went through his mind for a fleeting second, but was interrupted almost immediately by the sound of a vehicle trundling up the grade.

The field was almost level, but not entirely. While it was flat where the body had been found, it sloped gently down about a hundred yards to the south, and also climbed a bit more steeply maybe twice as far to the north. The vehicle coming up the road from the south was a beat-up Ford station wagon from back when they used to put lead in gasoline. LOBO'S NOD MEDICAL EXAMINER was stenciled professionally if a bit pretentiously on the door. That meant...

Sure enough, as Jazz watched, two cops approached the corpse with a body bag hanging limp between them. The preliminary crime-scene examination was done.

Jazz watched as a tech carefully wrapped the corpse's head, then did the same to the hands and feet.

Always check the hands and feet, Dear Old Dad whispered from the past. *And the mouth and ears. You'd be surprised what gets left behind.*

He blinked away the voice and watched them maneuver the dead woman into the bag and zip it shut. As he focused on the struggle with the body bag, something caught his attention from the corner of his eye. He tried to ignore it. It was the kind of thing he didn't really want to notice, but he couldn't help it. Once he'd seen it, it wasn't something he could just unsee.

There was one cop in particular, standing off to the side. Not so far from the body that anyone would doubt he was a part of the crime scene, but far enough that no one would ask for his help with anything. He just stood there, and to anyone else observing, this cop would appear to be keeping out of the way, trying not to interfere.

Jazz thought he knew all of the Lobo's Nod cops on sight, and even most of the guys from the surrounding towns. This guy was wearing a Lobo's Nod uniform, but he was a stranger.

And he was *ready*. That was the only way Jazz could describe it: Ready. Vulnerable. Easy. He was fidgeting just a bit, two fingers on his left hand idly toying with a rough patch of scuffed leather on his gun belt, near the canister of Mace.

He would be easy to take down. Despite his training. Despite his gun and his Mace and his baton. Jazz could more than imagine doing so—he could see it right through the binoculars as if it were happening.

Jazz could read people. It wasn't something he worked at; it was just as natural as breathing. It was as ordinary as reading a billboard on the highway: You don't really think about the billboard; you just notice it and your brain processes it, and that's that.

He closed his eyes for a long moment and tried to think of Connie, of the two of them tangled together at the Hideout. Tried to think of playing basketball with Howie. Tried to think of his mother, of the last thing he could remember about her before she'd disappeared. Tried to think of anything—*anything*—other than how easy it would be to approach this cop...

Put him at ease, seduce him into complacency, and then...

Go for the belt. The Mace. The nightstick. The gun.

It would be so easy.

It *was* so easy.

Jazz opened his eyes. The body was in the station wagon. Even from this distance, he heard the doors slam.

Jazz wiped sweat from his forehead. G. William was picking his way carefully down the grade, toward the road and his car. The rest of the cops were staying on the scene for now.

The evidence bag. Jazz couldn't stop thinking about it. About what he'd seen inside it, actually.

A finger.

A severed human finger.

CHAPTER 2

Jazz backed up out of the brush and carefully made his way back to his Jeep, which he'd concealed along an old dirt path that cut through the Harrison property.

Jazz would go to G. William. He had to go. To see the body. He would confront his own past and see what impact it had on him. If any. Maybe it would have no impact. Or maybe it would have the *right* kind of impact. Prove something to the world, and to himself.

A body was one thing. That finger, though... That was new. He hadn't expected that. It meant...

Bouncing along now on the nearly nonexistent shocks in his father's old beat-up Jeep, he tried not to think of what it meant, even though the finger hovered there in his imagination, as though pointing at him. It's not that he'd never seen a dead body before. Or a crime scene. Jazz had been seeing those for as long as he could remember, thanks to Dear Old Dad. For Dear Old Dad, Take Your Son to Work Day was year-round. Jazz had witnessed crime scenes the way the cops wished they could—from the criminal's point of view.

Jazz's dad—William Cornelius "Billy" Dent—was the most notorious serial killer of the twenty-first century. He'd made his home in sleepy little Lobo's Nod and, for the most part, kept his nose clean while in town, adhering to the old adage "Don't crap where you eat." But eventually time had caught up with Billy Dent. Time, and his own uncontrollable urges. Even though he was a masterful murderer, having killed into the triple digits over the previous twenty-one years, he eventually couldn't help himself. Two Lobo's Nod bodies later, G. William Tanner tracked Billy down and cuffed him. It was a sad and ignominious end to Billy Dent's career, caught not by some FBI doctorate with a badge and the might of the federal government behind him, but rather by a local cop with a beer gut and a twang and one decent police car.

In fact... Maybe Dear Old Dad was right. Maybe all those guys—including Billy Dent—wanted to get caught. Otherwise, why hunt at home? Why crap where he ate?

Jazz pulled into the parking lot of the sheriff's office, a low, one-story cinder-block building in the center of town. Every election year, some town selectman or county commissioner would run on a promise to "beautify our dour, grim center of law enforcement," and after every election, G. William would quietly divert the money to better equipment and higher salaries for his deputies.

Jazz liked G. William, which was saying something, given that he'd been raised to respect but despise cops in general, to say nothing of the cop who finally put an end to Billy Dent's

12

legendary multidecade career of death and torture. Ever since arresting Dear Old Dad four years ago, G. William had kept in touch with Jazz, almost as if he felt bad for taking away Jazz's father. Anyone with any sense could see that taking away Dear Old Dad was the best thing that had ever happened to Jazz. Poor old G. William and his old-fashioned Catholic guilt.

Occasionally, Jazz would confide in G. William. Things he'd already told Connie and Howie, usually, but could use an adult perspective on. Two things remained unspoken between them, though understood: G. William didn't want Jazz to end up like Billy, and Jazz didn't confide *everything*.

Just about the only thing Jazz didn't like about the sheriff was his insistence that everyone call him "G. William," which constantly made the speaker sound surprised: "Gee, William!"

Inside the station, Jazz nodded to Lana, the secretary/dispatcher. She was pretty and young and Jazz tried not to think about what his father would have done to her, given the chance.

"Is G. William in?" he asked, as if he didn't know.

"Just blew through here like a tornado," Lana said, "then blew straight back." She pointed to the restroom. G. William's bladder couldn't stand being away from the office for too long.

"Mind if I wait for him?" Jazz said as calmly as he could, as though he weren't itching to get into that office.

"Help yourself," she said, waving him back toward G. William's office.

"Thanks," he said, and then—because he couldn't help it— he gave her the full-on megawatt smile. "The Charmer," Billy had called it. One more thing passed down from father to son.

Lana smiled back. Provoking her into a smile was no challenge.

The office door was open. A sheet of paper lay on the desk in the cone of sickly yellow light coming from an ancient lamp-shaped pile of rust. Jazz darted a glance over his shoulder, then flipped the paper around so he could read it. PRELIMINARY NOTES, it read at the top.

"—*to lab for pos. ID*—"

"—*excised digits*—"

The jangle of handcuffs and G. William's heavy tread alerted him. He flipped the page around again and managed to step away from the desk before the sheriff came through the door.

"Hey, there, Jazz." G. William positioned himself behind the desk and put a protective hand on the preliminary notes. He was no fool. "What can I do for you? A little busy right now."

Excised digits, Jazz was thinking. Digits, plural. Not singular. He'd seen only one finger in the evidence bag.

You'd need a knife. Not even a good one. Just sharp. Get between the lesser multangular and the metacarpal—

"Yeah," Jazz said, bouncing on the balls of his feet. "Body in the Harrison field."

G. William scowled. "Wish someone would outlaw police scanners."

"You know how that goes, G. William," Jazz said lightly. "If you outlaw police scanners, only outlaws will have police scanners."

G. William cleared his throat and sat, causing his ancient chair to complain. "Really am kinda busy. Can we banter another time?"

"I'm not here to banter. I want to talk to you about the body. Well, really, about the killer."

That earned him a raised eyebrow and a snort. G. William had a massive, florid nose, the sort of bulbous schnoz usually seen on heavy drinkers, though G. William rarely, if ever, touched booze. His nose was a combination of pure genetics and thirty-five years as a cop, being hit in the face with everything from fists to gun butts to planks of wood. "You know who the killer is? That's great. I'd love to go home, watch football like a citizen."

"No, but..." Jazz didn't want to admit that he'd been spying on the crime scene or that he'd read G. William's notes, but he didn't have a choice. "Look, a dead body is one thing. Excising multiple digits is—"

"Oh, Jazz." G. William slid his sheet of paper closer to himself, as though by taking it away now he could somehow erase Jazz's memory of reading it. "What are you doing? You need to stop obsessing about this stuff."

"Easy for you to say. You're not the one everyone thinks is gonna grow up to be Billy Dent, the sequel."

"No one thinks—"

"Plenty of people do. You don't see the way people look at me."

"It's in your head, Jazz."

They gazed at each other for a long moment. There was a pain in G. William's eyes that Jazz figured to be as intense as his own, though of a different flavor.

"Dead female Caucasian," Jazz said in a clipped voice. "Found at least two miles from anywhere in any direction. Naked. No apparent bruising. Missing fingers—"

"You get all of that from here?" G. William waved the paper in the air. "You didn't have that much time to look at it."

Busted. He'd revealed too much. Even knowing that G. William was savvy, Jazz had still tipped his hand too soon.

Oh, well. He would probably have to admit this, anyway. . . .

Jazz shrugged. "I was watching."

G. William slammed a fist on the desk and swore out loud. Something about that mustache and those big brown eyes made the swearing incongruous—Jazz felt like he'd just seen a nun do a striptease. G. William's bushy mustache quivered.

"You know how I grew up," Jazz said, his voice low and thick as they stared at each other across the desk. "The rumpus room. The trophies. It was my job to keep them organized for him. I understand these guys."

These guys. Serial killers. He didn't have to say it out loud.

G. William flinched. He was intimately aware of the details of Jazz's upbringing. After Billy and Jazz (and Jazz's missing mother), G. William knew the most about what growing up with Billy Dent had been like. He knew more than Gramma. More than Connie, Jazz's girlfriend. More than Melissa Hoover, the social worker who'd been messing with Jazz's life ever since Billy's arrest. Even more than Howie, the only kid Jazz truly thought of as a friend. It had, after all, been G. William who'd found Jazz that night four years ago, the night Billy Dent's reign of terror ended. Jazz had been in the rumpus room (a converted pantry in the back of the house, accessible only through a hidden hatch in the basement), doing as his father had commanded: gathering up the trophies so that they could be smuggled out of the house before the cops searched the place.

It should have been an easy task—Billy didn't take large or complicated trophies. An iPod from one, a lipstick from another. The trophies were well organized and easily portable. Still, G. William got there before Jazz could finish. And Jazz truly didn't know if he would have followed through with his father's orders. He'd spent his childhood obeying his father's every command, but as Billy Dent had become more and more erratic—culminating in the two Lobo's Nod bodies—Jazz had begun to shake off the chains his father had bound him with.

And so he had stood there with all but one of the trophies in a large backpack, staring at the last one, the driver's license of Heidi Dunlop, a pretty blond girl from Baltimore. And in that moment, Jazz had felt like he'd woken up for the first time in his life, as if everything else that had happened to him had been unreal, and now he was about to make his first and only true decision. As he tried to decide whether he would hide the trophies...or run and hide himself...or turn them over...fate took the decision out of his hands in the form of G. William, who came up through the hatch, puffing with exertion but pointing what looked like the biggest goddamn pistol in the entire universe right at Jazz's thirteen-year-old junk.

"Let me help you," Jazz insisted now. "Just let me look at the file. Maybe a few minutes with the body."

"I've been doing this for a while. I don't need your help. And it's a little early to go barking 'serial killer.' You're jumping the gun, kid. Serial killers have to have at least three victims. Over an extended period of time. This guy has one."

"There could be more," Jazz insisted. "Or there will be more. These guys escalate. You know that. Each victim is worse. And they experiment. Cutting off the fingers...You just have to look at things from his perspective."

The sheriff stiffened. "I did that with your dad. I didn't like doing it then. Don't like the thought of it now."

Finding Billy Dent had taken its toll on G. William, who had still been grieving for his recently deceased wife when the first of the Lobo's Nod bodies showed up. He'd thrown himself with an obsessive fervor into tracking and catching Billy Dent, and while he'd succeeded, his sanity had almost been another of Billy's victims. Jazz remembered the expression on G. William's face when the sheriff had come up through the rumpus room hatch, that huge revolver pointed at him. With all he'd seen in his life—the bodies, the trophies, what his father had done to poor Rusty—very few things could haunt Jazz, but the look on the sheriff's face that day was a regular star in Jazz's nightmares. He'd never seen a man so utterly despondent and devastated, the gun steady as a rock even though the big man's lips trembled when he shouted, "Drop it! Drop all of it! I swear to Christ I'll shoot you!" in a high lunatic's falsetto. G. William Tanner's eyes had seen too much; if that night had not ended Billy Dent's career, Jazz was certain that the next day would have seen G. William dead by his own hand.

It had been four years since then; G. William still saw a therapist every month.

Now G. William stroked his mustache with the thumb and forefinger of his left hand. Jazz imagined cutting off that forefinger. It wasn't that he wanted to hurt G. William. It wasn't that he wanted to hurt anyone at all. It's just that he couldn't. Stop. Thinking about it. Sometimes he felt like his brain was a slasher movie set on fast-forward. And no matter how many times he jabbed at the Off button, the movie just kept playing and playing, horrors assaulting him constantly.

For him, imagining cutting off that finger was an academic exercise, like a calculus problem at school. It wouldn't take much strength. An easy trophy. What did that mean about the killer? Did it mean he was weak and scared? Or did it mean he was confident and knew it was best to take something quickly?

If G. William knew the thoughts that came unbidden to Jazz's mind, he would...

"Let me help," Jazz begged. "For me."

"Go home, Jazz. Dead woman in a field. Tragic, but nothing more."

"But the fingers! Come on. That's not a woman who stumbled out there naked at night and fell and hit her head. That's not Joe-Bob McHick smacking around his girlfriend and then leaving her to die."

"We already had one serial killer in this town. Be a hell of a coincidence to have another one, don't you think?"

Jazz pressed on. "At any point in time, it's estimated there's something like thirty to forty serial killers active in the United States."

"I think," G. William said, sighing, "that I've got a lot of work ahead of me, and you're not helping any. We'll figure this body out, along with all the other usual junk we have to do around here." He gestured for Jazz to leave.

"You're at least treating this as a reportable death, right?"

"Of course I am. I've got the medical examiner coming in first thing tomorrow morning for a complete autopsy, but

19

Dr. Garvin is doing a quick work-up today. A woman's dead, Jazz. I take that very seriously."

"Not seriously enough to be going over the crime scene with tweezers. Or to cut down the vegetation to look for clues. Or to—"

G. William rolled his eyes. "Give me a break. What do you think this is? What kind of resources do you think we have here? I had to call in the staties and deputies from three towns over to do justice to that scene."

"You should be looking at bugs and soil samples, and I didn't see anyone casting footprint molds, and—"

"There weren't any footprints," G. William said, exasperated. "And the other stuff...We have to contract out to the state for forensic odontology, for botanical services, for anthropology and entomology. We're a small town in a small jurisdiction. Stop comparing us to the big boys. We'll get the job done."

"Not if you don't know what the job is in the first place."

"A serial killer," G. William said, skepticism dripping from every syllable.

"How did you find the body?" Jazz asked, desperate for something that would prove his point. "You didn't trip over it out there. Was it an anonymous call? If you got a call, that's totally a serial killer making sure you see his handiwork. You know that, right?"

He'd gone too far—G. William could take a lot of abuse, but he didn't cotton to condescension. "Yeah, Jazz. I know that. I also know that serial killers like to stick around and watch the cops work."

The words slammed Jazz full in the chest, no less powerful and painful than if G. William had drawn his service revolver and put two slugs into his center of mass. Jazz was afraid of two things in the world, and two things only. One of them was that people thought that his upbringing meant that he was cursed by nature, nurture, and predestination to be a serial killer like his father.

The second thing . . . was that they were right.

And with the discovery of this new body, who could blame them? The odds of two separate serial killers picking a tiny town like Lobo's Nod were beyond astronomical, so far beyond that it didn't even bear serious consideration. Billy Dent was locked up. Thirty-two consecutive life sentences. The joke around town was that he wouldn't even be eligible for parole until five years after he was dead. He was on total lockdown—twenty-three hours a day in a five-by-eight cinder-block cell—and had been since the moment he set foot in the penitentiary. He'd had no visitors other than his lawyer in that whole time.

When the original devil couldn't do the crime, who did you look at next? His son, of course. If Jazz didn't know for certain that he *wasn't* involved in this murder, he would have pointed the finger (*ha, ha*) at himself. It made complete sense that the son of the local serial killer would kill someone. But just because it made sense didn't make the thought any easier to bear.

"Th-that," he stammered, "is over the line. I learned a lot from Billy, and I can use that to—"

"You go skulking around a crime scene, spying on me and

my people. You march into my office and violate my privacy by reading my personal notes," G. William said, ticking points off on his fingers as he went. Jazz couldn't help thinking of the severed finger in its pristine plastic evidence bag, just sitting there like leftovers. "I could probably bring you up on some kind of charge, if I wanted to take five minutes to think about it. Demanding I let you in on a case, which would be *highly* improper, even if you weren't a kid, and even if you weren't Billy Dent's kid." He had lost track of the counting—his whole right hand was splayed out. "All those reasons, Jazz, and plenty more. All of them say I won't let you help out."

"Come on! You bring in experts all the—"

"You're an expert all of a sudden?"

Jazz leaned in and they met over the desk, almost bumping into each other. G. William's mustache and jowls quivered.

"I know things," Jazz said in his strongest voice.

"You know too much and not enough," the sheriff said, so softly that it caught Jazz off-guard.

"What are you saying?"

"I'm saying"—deep breath—"you learned a lot from him, but you want to be careful you don't act too much like your daddy, now don't you?"

Jazz glared at him, then wheeled around and stomped out of the office, slamming the door behind him as he went.

"Let me do this my way!" G. William called through the closed door. "That's my job. Your job is to try to be normal!"

"Um, Jasper," Lana said nervously as he flew past her desk. "Uh, good-bye?"

He didn't even realize he'd ignored her until he was next to the Jeep, seething. He kicked the bumper with the flat of his foot; it complained with a metallic, grinding squeal and threatened to drop off.

I'll show you what I learned from my father, he thought.

CHAPTER 3

Whenever Jazz needed to do something risky or vaguely illegal, he made sure to bring Howie along. This did not endear him to Howie's parents, but if Jazz wanted to stay as human as possible, it was necessary: Howie kept Jazz close to the line of safety and legality. That's because Howie was Jazz's best (and only) friend. And also because Howie was so fragile that Jazz had to hold back in his presence.

Howie Gersten was a type-A hemophiliac, which meant that he bled if you looked at him too hard. The two had met when they were younger, when Jazz had come across Howie being tormented by a trio of older kids who weren't quite stupid enough to cause any serious harm, but who reveled in poking at Howie's exposed arms, then chortling over the bruises that blossomed almost immediately. Howie's arms had taken on an almost lizardlike appearance, with overlapping bruises of blue and purple that looked like scales.

Jazz had been smaller than the other kids, younger, and they outnumbered him three to one, but even then—at the age of ten—Jazz had a rudimentary understanding of some of the more important weak spots in the human body. He'd sent the older kids packing with their own fine collection of bruises, including a couple of black eyes and fat lips, as well as one knee sprained just right—it would plague the kid for months. For his troubles, Jazz earned himself a bloody nose and an undying, unstinting friendship.

And the kind of friend who would come along when you had to break in to a morgue.

The police station was open twenty-four hours a day because it was a nerve center for the county's law enforcement efforts. But at night, many hours after Jazz had left in a huff, it was just a skeleton crew, consisting of a deputy on duty and a dispatcher. Lana was still at the desk, having pulled the night shift. Jazz knew that would make this easy. Lana thought he was cute. She was right out of high school and he was a junior, so only a couple of years separated them.

"I'll distract Lana," Jazz told Howie, "and then you work your magic."

"You sure you can keep her occupied?"

Jazz rolled his eyes. "Puh-lease."

"The ladies love bad boys," Howie said, striking what was supposed to be a tough-guy pose. "Gotcha. I will be your magic trick. Misdirection!" He waggled his fingers. "Abracadaver! Get it?" he added as they headed for the door. "Abra*cadaver*? Get it?"

Jazz sighed. "I got it, Howie."

Together, they walked into the police station, which was quiet this late at night. Lana looked up, then grinned a wide grin when she saw Jazz.

"Hi there!" she chirped.

Jazz sauntered over to her cubicle and leaned on the half-wall with both elbows. "Hi, Lana."

"What brings you back?" she asked, her eyes very wide and earnest. This was going to be way too easy. "You stormed out of here before."

"I just wanted to—"

Just then Howie came up to them, clearing his throat. "Okay if I get a Coke?" he asked, pointing to the back corridor, where an ancient Coke machine loomed large.

"Go ahead," Lana said, not even flicking her eyes in his direction as he walked past them.

"I just wanted to apologize for the way I went out of here before," Jazz said, pretending to give Lana all his attention. He cranked up the wattage on his smile. "I didn't even say goodbye to you."

As he chatted with Lana—who assured him that his apology wasn't necessary, all the while lapping it up—Jazz watched Howie head for the second desk in the row behind Lana. He looked up at Jazz, who nodded quickly. Howie opened the top desk drawer, fished around, then closed it. A moment later, he rejoined Jazz at Lana's cubicle.

"Done," Howie said.

"Well," Jazz said to Lana, "I guess we have to go. School tomorrow, you know. But I just knew I wouldn't be able to sleep tonight if I didn't say something to you." Another big smile.

Howie and Jazz were almost to the door when Lana called out, "Hey, Howie, I thought you were getting a Coke?"

Jazz shot a glare at Howie, who shrugged meekly. "Turns out I don't have any change."

They got outside before Lana could say anything more. "You're an idiot," Jazz told him.

"And yet, I recover well." He dug into his pocket and produced the block of wax Jazz had given him earlier. "Still an idiot?"

"Yes," Jazz said, grabbing the wax. In it was a perfect impression of the morgue key Howie had found in the desk drawer. "Just somewhat competent. Let's go."

Making a duplicate key from a wax impression was an extremely useful skill to have if you were the sort of person who liked invading other people's homes and killing them. Billy Dent felt it was important for Jazz to know how to do this, and for once Jazz was grateful for Billy's lessons. It didn't take long before he'd turned Howie's wax block into an actual key—he had a selection of blanks and cutting tools that Billy had given him on his eleventh birthday. Match up the right blank with the wax impression, then file away everything that isn't in the right place until the notches fit the wax. Simple. He'd been practicing most of his life, after all.

The police station abutted the Giancci Funeral Home on one side, the two buildings joined by the briefest of outdoor corridors. The Lobo's Nod morgue was half the basement of the funeral parlor.

With Howie at his side, Jazz strode into the morgue like he

lived there, flicking on one of the overhead lights to bathe the place in cold white light. Because there were no windows to the outside, he and Howie would be able to mill about with confidence.

"We need to move quickly," Jazz said. "There's a rent-a-cop who comes by every hour."

Howie craned his neck, gawking. "This place is nothing like on *CSI*."

"What did you expect?"

"I guess I expected *CSI*," Howie said, miffed. "Otherwise, why would I have said—"

Jazz snaked a pair of purple, powdered latex gloves from an open box on a metal tray. He threw them at Howie, who bobbled them, but managed to catch them. "Put these on. Fingerprints."

"I hope they fit...."

He watched Howie cram his oversized mitts into the gloves, which looked like they were stretched just slightly beyond their tolerance. Howie had the build of an NBA player: gangly, loose limbs, rope-thin frame, hands that seemed preternaturally grasping. But Howie's hemophilia saw to it that he would never play basketball on a team, not even Little League.

Still, Howie loved the game. He obsessed over the stats and the standings. Every March, Jazz had to tune out Howie's endless droning about the Sweet Sixteen, the Elite Eight, the Final Four, etc. Still, it was worth it—not many kids would willingly pal around with "that Dent kid." Before Billy had been arrested and exposed as the Artist (or Gentle Killer or Satan's Eye or Hand-in-Glove or Green Jack—take your pick of Billy's media-assigned nicknames), Jazz had been a pretty popular kid. Then the arrest had come, and Jazz became a pariah.

Except to Howie.

Howie had been the constant in Jazz's life, the kid he'd come to rely on to keep him grounded and sane when the world threatened to tip him over into Billy-style craziness. When he'd started dating his girlfriend, Connie, several months ago, he'd been a little worried that maybe he and Howie would become less close, but if anything, they'd become even tighter, as though Jazz doing something as amazingly normal as dating a girl made him a better, stronger friend.

The sound of Howie—now gloved—pawing around on a tray of medical instruments brought Jazz back to the present. "Stop it," Jazz said.

"Bro, I'm wearing gloves." Howie waved to prove his point.

Jazz jammed a shower cap on Howie's head. "We're not here to mess around with their stuff. Stick to the mission." He settled a cap on his own head, too.

"'Stick to the mission,'" Howie mocked, but he left the instruments alone and instead joined Jazz at a large steel door set with a surprisingly modern digital lock. The keypad was numbered 0 through 9 and also included the letters A to F. Howie frowned at it. "This isn't going to be easy," he said. "'Tonight, on *CSI: Hicksville*, Dent and Gersten encounter their toughest case yet....'"

"How much do you want to bet I can get that door open on the first try?" Jazz said.

Howie pursed his lips, thinking. "You pay for burgers next time. And we have to eat at Grasser's."

Jazz scowled. He hated the food at Grasser's, a local burger joint more appropriately nicknamed "Grosser's," but Howie loved the place with a lust that bordered on the irrational. "Okay, fine. And what if I can get it open on the first try?"

Howie thought. "We don't eat at Grasser's for a month."

Totally worth it. "Watch," Jazz said, grinning. He reached for the door handle and twisted. The steel door opened with only a tiny squeak.

"Oh, come on!" Howie protested. "Not fair! It wasn't even locked."

"A deal's a deal." They slipped into a small refrigerated room, where the bodies were stored while awaiting autopsy, reclamation, or burial. Right now, there was a single body in the freezer, zipped into a new body bag (the one on the scene had been bright yellow; this one was black) and resting on a wheeled stretcher.

"Is that her?" Howie whispered, shivering slightly.

"It," Jazz corrected. "It stopped being a 'her' a while ago."

Screwed to the wall of the freezer room was a plastic file holder, in which sat a lonely pale green folder. The tab read DOE, JANE (1), the number denoting that this was the year's first Jane Doe. Probably the only one, too. In a place like New York City, there might be upwards of fifteen hundred unidentified bodies in a year. There had been bodies in the Nod before, of course, but they'd always been identified. For this town, a single Doe broke the long-standing record of none.

Jazz plucked the file from the holder and flipped through it, scanning the report.

"Have the lambs stopped screaming, Clarice?" Howie said suddenly in a dead-on Hannibal Lecter impression.

"Stop that!"

"Well, I don't understand why you have to see the body," Howie complained, hugging himself for warmth. "She's dead. She had a finger chopped off. You knew that already."

The report was short. As G. William had indicated, it was just preliminary. Jazz went back to the first page and started reading. "Ever hear of Locard's Exchange Principle?"

"Oh, sure," Howie said. "I saw them open for Green Day last year. They rocked." He played a little air guitar.

"L-O-L," Jazz deadpanned. "Locard was this French guy who said that any time a person comes into contact with anything at all, there's a two-way trip involved. Stuff from the guy gets on the thing—hair, maybe, or skin cells, dandruff, whatever—and the thing gets stuff on the guy—like dust or paint or dirt or something. Stuff is exchanged. Get it?"

"French guy. Stuff exchanged. Got it." Howie saluted, then went back to hugging himself against the cold.

"So I thought maybe the killer left some kind of evidence," Jazz went on, then sighed. "But according to this report, nothing. No fibers, no hairs, no fluids . . . Clean."

"As clean as you can be after lying out in a field," Howie said. "Can we go now?"

There were crime-scene photos paper-clipped to the inside of the folder. Jazz stared at them. It was almost eerie, the perfect poise of that body. Unnatural. Perfect, save for the missing fingers, and even they had been neatly "excised" (the police report's antiseptic language) postmortem, with no blood loss. No pain.

If there had been some sort of savagery before death—torture, cutting, mutilation—it might somehow be easier to believe that something once living was now dead. As it was, the word *dead* seemed somehow... inaccurate.

"Earth to Jazz. Can we go?"

"Not yet." Jazz slipped the coroner's report back into its holder and started to unzip the bag.

"Oh, man!" Howie took a step back. "Totally not into checking out the corpses today."

"You can wait outside if you want." He got the zipper all the way down, and there lay Jane Doe, eyes closed, skin a waxy white. After roughly forty-eight hours, bacterial action turns skin a greenish hue, so Jazz figured it had been less than two days since the murder, and the early report agreed with him.

"Oh, man," Howie said from behind him, his voice hushed. "God. Look at her."

"It," Jazz reminded him again, staring down. He knew he was supposed to feel something here. Even coroners felt a momentary glimmer of regret when someone so young and healthy was laid out before them. But Jazz looked down at the body and felt... nothing. Exactly, precisely nothing.

Well, that wasn't completely true. A tiny part of him registered that, when alive, Jane Doe would have been an easy victim. Simple prey. To a killer's eye, the smallish frame and lack of obvious strength would have been attractive. Short fingernails meant less risk of being scratched. According to the report, Jane Doe stood no more than five foot one—

when standing was still possible. A killer's dream victim. You couldn't custom-order one better.

"Man, this sucks, doesn't it?" Howie whispered. "She was like this little bitty thing and someone just came along and—"

"Yeah, sucks," Jazz interrupted. "Now be quiet. I'm working."

No bruises, no cuts or contusions or scrapes. All he could do was a cursory examination, and the report had most of that data already. Autopsies were conducted in a specific sequence: ID the body, photograph it, remove any trace evidence, measure and weigh it, then x-ray it and examine the outside. That's as far as they'd gotten tonight, with just old Dr. Garvin on call. The real medical examiner would come in the morning to cut her open, then look at tissues under a microscope and prepare the toxicology samples. In the meantime, according to the folder, the cops thought strangulation. Jazz thought that made sense; strangling was a relatively easy way to kill someone. No weapons needed. Just hands. As long as you wore gloves, you wouldn't leave any incriminating evidence.

The report said that Jane Doe was a "Caucasian female, between 18 and 25, no distinguishing tattoos, birthmarks, scars." Jazz scanned quickly, agreeing with the assessment. He took a moment to peel open the eyelids, causing Howie to gag and take a step back. The eyes—light brown—stared out at nothing. It was possible, Jazz knew, for red blood cells in the retinal veins to keep moving hours after death, one of the last gasps of life in an already-dead body. But the dead eyes betrayed no movement, so he checked what he'd come here for, what he'd really needed to see with his own eyes: the right hand. He wanted to make certain what he'd seen in the report was accurate.

It was.

Three fingers on the right hand were missing—the index finger, the middle finger, and the ring finger. The thumb and pinky were all that remained; that hand would flash "hang loose" while the corpse rotted in the ground somewhere. But according to what Jazz had seen in the Harrison field with his own eyes and Billy's gift binocs, the cops had recovered only one finger—the one he'd seen in the evidence bag.

The killer had taken the other two with him. According to the woefully thin report, he'd taken the ring and index fingers.

Howie cleared his throat. "Man, are you sure about this? What if the whole thing was just an accident? Like, what if it was just two people out in the field? Like, having sex and stuff? And she hits her head or has a heart attack or something and the guy is scared, so he runs away."

"And what? Accidentally cuts off three fingers postmortem? 'Oops, oh, no, my girlfriend just died! Clumsy me, in trying to perform CPR, I chopped off some fingers! Guess I'll take them with me. . . . Oh, darn, where did that middle finger go?'"

Howie sniffed in offense. "Fine. Maybe an animal came along and—"

"Look at the cleavage plane here."

"Cleavage?" Howie perked up, then immediately winced and shrank back as Jazz grabbed Jane's wrist and held up the mutilated hand.

"Cleavage *plane*," Jazz said again, shaking the hand just

slightly. "The cut. It's smooth. An animal would have gnawed away at it; the wound would be ragged and chewed."

"But there's more than one finger missing. So maybe an animal ate them—"

"No. The killer took them. As a trophy."

"Why the fingers? Your pops never took body parts. Say what you want about him, but   "

"Projective identification."

"What?"

"It's when the killer projects his worst characteristics on the victim and then kills for it. So, why the fingers? Was he caught touching something he wasn't supposed to? Some*one* he wasn't supposed to? Is this his way of punishing himself?"

"Put that away," Howie said, and Jazz realized he was still holding the corpse by the wrist.

Jazz tucked the hand back into the bag, and Howie visibly relaxed. "So, fine. Why does it have to be a serial killer? It could be a onetime thing."

Jazz shook his head. "No. The fingers. Your average murderer doesn't mutilate a body like that. And he especially doesn't take trophies. But it's more than that. It's that he left one behind. He left the middle one behind."

"Are you serious?"

"Yeah. He *literally* gave the cops the finger. He's saying, 'Come and get me. Catch me if you can.' That's a serial killer."

For a moment, there was nothing but silence in the freezer, as Jazz stared at the body and Howie stared at Jazz.

Jazz gazed down at the eyes, at the lips pressed together in a pale pink line. When people saw dead bodies like this, they said it looked like the person was sleeping. Jazz thought that was crazy. He'd never seen a dead body that looked like it was sleeping. He'd never seen a dead body that didn't look like exactly what it was—a corpse. A husk. A thing.

Wrapped my hands around her throat, Billy whispered in Jazz's mind. *Just squeezed and squeezed...*

Jazz looked closely at the neck. Howie leaned in, curious despite himself, and said, "Was she choked to death?" He mimed throttling someone.

"*Strangled* is the right term," Jazz told him. "Choking is when something blocks your airway from the inside. And, yeah, I think so. Can't be sure yet." A good strangulation left few signs. The medical examiner would have to drain all the blood from the neck, then slowly and meticulously peel back layers of tissue, looking for telltale small bruises.

"Can they, like, get fingerprints from her neck? Can they catch the guy that way?"

"This guy isn't an amateur. He probably used gloves."

"How do you know he isn't an amateur, Sherlock?"

"There's bruising on the left-hand knuckles, and on the sides of both hands. Probably would be on the right-hand knuckles, too, if we had them."

"She hit him," Howie said. "She fought back."

"And that means this guy has done this before. If you're a newbie, you don't want a fight on your hands. You sneak up behind them and you knock them out and *then* you start the nasty stuff. If you confront someone while they're awake, you're a badass."

Struggling is what makes it worth doing, Billy said. Jazz

closed his eyes, trying to chase away his father's voice, but it was no good. Billy was on a roll, dispensing what he thought of as honest fatherly wisdom, baring what passed for his soul. *Sometimes I can't tell the difference between living and dead. Sometimes I look at a pretty little girlie and I think to myself, Is she a living, breathing thing? Or is she just a doll? Are those actual tears she's crying? Are those real screams coming out of her mouth? And it's like a fog in my mind, like I get all confused and frustrated and mixed up, so I start doing things. Start small at first, like maybe with the ears or the lips or the toes. And then move on to the bigger things, and there's blood, so I keep going and my hands are wet and my mouth is warm and I keep going and then something real magical happens, Jasper. It's real magical and special and beautiful. See, they stop moving. They stop struggling. All the fight just goes away and that's when it's all clear to me: She's dead. And if she's dead, then that means that she used to be alive. So then I know: This was a living one, a real one. And I feel good after that 'cause I figured it out.*

Jazz realized that his own gloved hands—

This guy isn't an amateur. He probably used gloves.

—had come to rest on either side of the neck. With just the right movement, he could have that neck in his hands—

This guy isn't an amateur.

—and he could feel the muscles and the windpipe and the—

This guy

He jerked away and grabbed the steel lip of the stretcher to steady himself. "You were right," he told Howie.

"Um, I was?"

"Yeah."

"Score for me. Beauty. But what was I right about?"

"She's a she. Not an it. She's always been a she."

"Yeah, no kidding."

"Don't ever let me call her an it again," Jazz told him. "Actually, don't ever let me call *anyone* an it, okay?"

Jazz finished his examination of the body while Howie crept into the nearby funeral home business office to make a photocopy of the anemic preliminary report. There was nothing substantial in the file, but Jazz figured it couldn't hurt to have a copy. Besides, he didn't want Howie around when he rolled the body.

The human body holds about ten pints of blood when everything is going right, and Jane still had enough of hers when she died to cause dark purplish areas, almost like bruises, when the blood pooled postmortem. Jane had been found on her back, but there was evidence of blood-pooling on her front and side, giving the flesh of her lower abdomen and left hip an almost mottled appearance. Jazz reached into the bag, slipping his hands under her, one near the shoulders, the other near her buttocks. He paused for a moment. It was so strange. He was touching a woman's *ass*. It was wrong on so many levels.

"People matter," he whispered to himself. "People matter. People are real. Remember Bobby Joe Long."

His personal mantra, whispered every morning. A reminder. His own magic spell, casting a shield against his own evil.

It was tough to turn her, as her body was still going into rigor mortis. Rigor usually started about two hours after death. It started in the face and hands—the small muscles—and spread to the entire body over about twelve hours. If her big muscles were just freezing up now . . . Jazz did some quick math, factored in the pliability he'd observed in the field when the cops moved Jane's body, and decided that she must have been killed no more than an hour or two before the cops arrived on the scene. Just before daybreak, then.

He turned her onto her left side. Her back was pale.

If she'd been killed in the field and left there on her back, all the blood in her body would have settled in her back and buttocks, making them purple and slightly swollen. But the blood had pooled elsewhere in her body. That meant she'd been killed somewhere else and then transported, her blood sloshing around in her dead body like the grains in a piece of sand art every time she was moved.

So the killer killed her . . . then moved her . . . then called the cops right away. . . .

Yeah. Definitely not a newbie.

The killer *was* a badass. Talk about supreme confidence. Jazz couldn't help it; he sort of admired the guy.

People matter. People are real. People matter. . . .

The spot in the field where Jane had been dumped wasn't just the sort of place you stumbled upon while carrying a corpse around. The killer must have scoped it out in advance. Did it have some significance to him? And why that particular spot? Moving a body was risky, but also necessary. *You want distance between you and the cops, so you have to—*

Shut up, Billy, Jazz thought fiercely.

"Uh-oh," Howie said from behind him, his voice panicked. "Jazz?"

Jazz turned and saw that Howie's face was covered in blood.

CHAPTER 4

For a split second, Jazz thought someone had attacked Howie, but then Howie tilted his head back and said, "Oh, no. Crap!"

Howie had twice-weekly shots to boost his clotting factor, but he was still prone to random nosebleeds. This one was a real flood, twin red rivulets running out of his nose, gushing over his mouth and chin. Howie had the report in one hand and the photocopy in the other, his arms spread wide to keep him from bleeding on either of them. Jazz dashed over and cupped his hand under Howie's chin to catch the blood before it could hit the floor. Even so, a few drops spattered against the cold tile, almost perfect circles of red.

Howie's blood was warm, especially in the cold freezer. *Special kinda warm*, Billy said, and Jazz grimaced, then used his free hand to pinch Howie's nose shut and stanch the flow.

"Danks," Howie said.

"How long since your last desmopressin shot?"

"Uh . . . Dursday?"

"Must have been the cold in here," Jazz said. "Back up to the other room. There were some Kleenex on the desk."

They carefully edged out of the freezer and back into the office, Jazz still pinching with one hand and cupping with the other, all while watching his feet so as not to smear and track the blood all over the place. Blood was the worst bit of evidence to leave behind: Blood is chockablock with DNA, and it's almost impossible to remove every trace from most surfaces.

Ten pints, he thought again. Ten pints. How easy to lose track of a few drops, and a few drops were sometimes enough to give you away.

Once they were in the office, Jazz had Howie drop the papers and take over pinching duty. He couldn't walk around with bloody gloves, and he couldn't just throw them away covered like this, so he stripped them off and rinsed them in the nearby sink, watching the rusty red water swirl down the drain. It was hypnotic, taking him back to a time he could scarcely remember and yet could never forget: his own childhood. His own childhood, and another time when rusty red water had swirled.

Billy Dent's fathering skills—such as they were—resembled brainwashing techniques more than parenting. As a result, Jazz mostly remembered bits and pieces, like now—a memory of blood running into a sink drain; the pungent smell of it thick in his nose; a sharp, stained knife resting in the sink. Jazz had a terror of knives left in sinks. He couldn't stand seeing them there. At home, every time he used a knife, he had to clean it and stow it in a drawer or knife block immediately; just the sight of a knife in a sink made him shiver and quake.

Nice job, son... Nice, good cut. Clean...
—just like chicken—

He forced himself back to the present, drying his hands and tossing the gloves into one of the morgue's medical-waste containers. Then he helped Howie jam some tissue between his upper lip and his gums—a big blood vessel ran through there, the one that supplied the nose with blood, so putting pressure on that would stop a nosebleed faster than anything else.

Sure enough, soon Howie's bleeding ebbed, and then stopped entirely. "Sorry," Howie said miserably, stooping to pick up the papers.

Jazz grabbed them instead. "Don't worry about it." But deep down, he was worried. Despite taking all the precautions with gloves and caps, now they risked contaminating the place with Howie's DNA. "Toss your gloves and tissues into the waste container, then take the bag. We'll take it all with us and burn it."

They put on fresh gloves and got back to business. Jazz wiped up the blood spatters in the freezer and tossed the tissues in with the rest of Howie's waste. It bothered him that he was leaving evidence behind—without some sort of oxygenated bleach, those blood spatters would still show up under Luminol. Of course, the odds of anyone deciding to spray down the morgue freezer and switch on an ultraviolet light were pretty minimal, so it's not like it was evidence that anyone would ever find or use. Still: Billy Dent's First Commandment was "Thou shalt not leave evidence."

"Stay out there," Jazz said when he saw Howie coming back to the freezer. "I'll finish up in here. I don't want you gushing again."

He replaced the report, then took one final look at the body. She'd been young. Pretty. She was, he couldn't help thinking, the kind of victim Billy had preferred. Billy wouldn't have even minded her fighting back. That just made it more fun. More challenging.

He checked that the body was in the same position he'd found it in, then zipped up the bag, returning her to the darkness.

"They don't know who she is," Howie said from the door, where he was flipping through the copy of the report. His upper lip was still stained red. "Can't they just take her fingerprints?" He paused. "Well, *most* of her fingerprints?"

"Not until she comes out of rigor. That could take a while. Might even be another day." Jazz left the freezer and shut the door, careful not to lock it, since they'd found it unlocked. Details mattered. "And it takes a while for fingerprints to come back, anyway. If there's nothing in the state database, they'll send it to the feds. And fingerprints are only good if you have something to compare them to. If she's not in the system, they won't get a hit."

Howie nodded thoughtfully. "They found her naked," he said, his voice low and serious. "Do you think whoever did this...Do you think he did stuff to her?"

Jazz swallowed hard. He knew Howie was asking about Jane, but somehow he couldn't help thinking of Billy's victims. Howie was pretty good about not asking for details of what Billy had done to his victims or what growing up with Billy had been like. But then again, if he wanted details, all he had to do was go to any of the websites devoted to Billy Dent. Or turn

44

on a random cable channel during sweeps for a two-hour documentary on "Butcher Billy" (the preferred nickname these days, it seemed). Still, it was one thing to read about hacking and slashing and beating. The other stuff—the sex stuff—was usually glossed over. *Sexual assault* was the preferred term, a conveniently neutral phrase that allowed the audience's imagination to run amok without the hair-sprayed, shiny-toothed news anchors having to sully the airwaves with actual descriptions. It covered a vast multitude of sins that would have made Howie puke.

"Not according to this," Jazz said, taking the report. "No evidence of sexual activity or anything like that."

"Well, there's that," Howie said, sounding relieved. Jazz wondered at that—was it really so much better to be unmolested, but still murdered in a horrible fashion? To die in pain and terror, stripped, left in a field, your fingers cut off? But as long as you weren't raped, well, that was all right, then? Did it really matter at that point?

"Why leave her naked, then?" Howie asked.

Jazz wondered. Not why the killer had taken her clothes, but what he'd done with them. He had his trophies—the fingers. Had he burned the clothes? Buried them?

He thought of Arthur John Shawcross, a real sick puppy if ever there'd been one. Killed a bunch of people in upstate New York. He used to fold his victims' clothes and leave them near the bodies. Sometimes he would have the victim fold her own clothes. It probably made the poor women think they would be getting dressed again as long as they cooperated. Made them more compliant, thinking they would live.

Had Jane Doe thought that? Had she willingly stripped down and put her clothes aside, thinking she would live if she could just suffer through a rape?

Those bruises on her hands...No. Not Jane. Jane had fought like hell, he knew.

"Any number of reasons," he told Howie as they moved around the morgue to make sure everything was back in place as they'd found it. "Could have been to slow the cops down. It could mean that he's trying to humiliate her. He might have hated her. Maybe she snubbed him, or maybe she looked like someone who snubbed him, so this was his revenge. Or maybe he *wanted* to do something to her but couldn't perform, couldn't get it up, so he decided to embarrass her by leaving her naked."

"That all makes sense." Howie paused. "Well, crazy sense, y'know?"

"Sure. But most likely he just didn't want to leave any evidence behind. See all these seams and linings in your clothes? They can gather trace evidence, and even if it looks clean to you, you could be carrying around all kinds of stuff. Heck, every hour three or four hairs just drop out of your head. That's a lot of evidence."

Howie put a hand to his head, as if he could hold his hairs in place. "Is that why your dad shaved his head sometimes?"

"Yeah. Well, and he thought it looked cool, too."

"Excuse me," said a new voice. Howie shrieked like a little girl, and even Jazz jumped at the sound.

The rent-a-cop! There was no way it had been an hour! How could he have—

Standing at the door was anything but a rent-a-cop. It was the real deal—the deputy Jazz had seen earlier. The one standing off to one side at the crime scene. He blocked the one door out of the morgue, his hand resting on his holster, and he looked anything but vulnerable.

Jazz and Howie sat on a bench in the hallway of the funeral home, cuffed together. The cuffs were too tight, even though Howie had immediately brought up his hemophilia, and a bruise was already forming on his wrist. Howie bore it with his usual stoicism.

"My mom is gonna kill me," he whined. "Seriously. She's gonna see this bruise and be like, 'How did you get that?' And then I'm gonna have to tell her that I let you talk me into this crazy idea and then she's gonna..."

Jazz tuned him out, instead watching the deputy, who was poking around inside the morgue, just barely within visual range. Making sure nothing was out of order or missing. He'd already confiscated the copy of the report in Jazz's possession.

How had he so misread this guy? At the crime scene, he'd seemed nervous and fidgety. Now he was just fine. He—

The deputy came out of the morgue. "You kids are in a lot of trouble," he said. "You moved the body, didn't you?"

Jazz shrugged.

"Do you know who you're talking to?" Howie demanded.

"Well, yeah," said the deputy. "I took your wallets when I cuffed you. Remember?"

"Oh. Right."

The deputy grinned. "Don't go thinking that just because your buddy is some kind of local celebrity that you're going to get off easy."

Jazz laughed. Local celebrity? That was the first time he'd ever been described that way.

"You think this is funny?" The deputy turned his attention to Jazz. "This is serious business here. Breaking and entering. Contaminating evidence. Theft. What did you think you were doing here?"

What are you *doing here?* Jazz wanted to ask. It's never a bad tactic to put someone on the defensive, if you can. No deputy should be lingering around the morgue at night.

But before Jazz could say anything, a door opened at the other end of the corridor and G. William trundled in, dressed in jeans and an old Windbreaker, his hair a bird's nest of tangles and offshoots.

"Oh, great," Howie muttered.

The deputy looked up, mingled relief and concern flashing across his face. "Sorry to get you out of bed for something like this, Sheriff. But being as it's my first day and all, I didn't want to assume too much authority right off the bat. Especially since I know you have a..." He stumbled for a moment. "Well, a relationship with one of these guys."

G. William stood before Jazz and Howie, hands on hips. "Well, well. Looks like you boys have met Deputy Erickson already. Just transferred in from out of state. Lindenberg, right, Erickson?"

"Yes, sir. Just up past the state line."

48

G. William grinned at the boys. "Grooming him to be my second-in-command. Damn good cop, wouldn't you say?"

"Lucky, more like," Jazz said.

Erickson stiffened.

"He didn't track us down," Jazz pointed out. "He didn't have an inkling that something was going on in the morgue. He just wandered in there and saw us. Speaking of which, why *was*—"

"You're missing the point here, Jazz," G. William interrupted. "The point being that I don't care how or why he got you. What matters is that you're busted. Now. I'm gonna ask you how you got in here, and if I don't like your answer, I'm gonna ask Howie, because I know Howie will tell me the truth. Won't you, Howie?"

Howie gulped.

Jazz thought quickly. There was no point getting Lana in trouble by telling G. William how they'd sneaked a copy of the key out right in front of her. "I made a dupe last month," Jazz said. "When you had that car-accident victim in here. I was curious."

G. William's eyes narrowed and he looked from Jazz to Howie and back again. Then: "Erickson, take Howie upstairs and start the paperwork on him. Be careful on account of his illness."

"Got it."

"Jazz, you and me are gonna talk." He led Jazz into the morgue as Erickson led Howie away. Jazz tried not to let the wounded-puppy look on Howie's face affect him. He had more immediate concerns.

"So, you were just curious about that body last month, eh?" G. William said once they were in the morgue. "And did you satisfy that curiosity?"

"Yes."

"Really? You got up close to it, saw everything you needed to see? Got your eyeballs nice and bloody with it?"

Sure, why not? "Yes, G. William. I saw it. I was wondering what—"

G. William laughed and slapped his thigh. "I have got to tell you, Jazz. I've been a cop for most of my life, so I've been lied to a lot. And I've been lied to by some real pros. But you, kiddo, you are the best liar I've ever had the pleasure to bust in a lie."

"I'm not—"

G. William waved a hand. "No, no, save your breath. Save it. You're busted, Jazz. You're totally convincing, and you would have had me, but for one thing. That accident victim last month? He was an orthodox Jew. In accordance with his family's wishes, we had a rabbi sitting in here with the body all night, until we could get a Jewish funeral home to take it away."

Jazz groaned.

"And Rabbi Goldstein might not be all that spry these days, but he would have noticed you skulking around the body, I think."

"Howie shouldn't get in trouble," Jazz said immediately. "I made him come along. He does whatever I tell him to do. Do what you want to me, but it's not cool to ding Howie."

At that, G. William softened. "You keep surprising me."

"Meaning what? That maybe I won't turn out like my dad?"

"I never said that," G. William barked, pointing a stubby finger at Jazz. "Don't go putting words in my mouth. You're the one who walks around town acting like you're... you're *fated* to be just like Billy when you grow up. I never accused you of that. But I have to admit," he went on, now looking around the morgue, "busting in to this place at night doesn't exactly rank high on the 'normal guy' scale."

It was time to come clean, whether Jazz liked it or not. Until G. William was satisfied, he was going to hold the threat of Howie being booked over Jazz's head, and Jazz didn't want to have to deal with Howie's mother freaking out about her baby being arrested. And, of course, he actually didn't want Howie to be arrested in the first place.

"I wanted to see if you guys missed anything with the Jane Doe," he admitted. "I needed to see for myself."

"And helped yourself to a copy of the preliminary report while you were at it."

Jazz shrugged. "It's not like it had anything important in it."

"Nope. You should have waited to break in tomorrow night, after the full autopsy was done. Got impatient, eh?"

"It's a serial killer, G. William. You have to believe me—"

"All I have to do is wake up in the morning and go to bed at night, Jazz. Everything else is optional. Come on." He gestured for Jazz to follow and led him out of the morgue, then up to the police station. Howie sat shackled to a chair next to Deputy Erickson's desk, looking miserable. Erickson was trying to figure out something on the computer; Lana stood behind him, pointing at the screen.

When Jazz walked in she looked shocked, even though Howie's presence must have clued her in. Jazz tried flashing her "The Charmer" and, sure enough, Lana responded with a smile, even though Jazz was cuffed, too.

"Hi, Lana."

"Uh, hi, Jasper."

"Enough chitchat," G. William said. "We're gonna cut these two loose—"

"Score!" said Howie.

"What?" said Erickson.

"Like I was saying," G. William repeated with ill-concealed annoyance at the interruption, "we're gonna cut these two loose. With a warning. And we're confiscating their key."

"But, Sheriff . . ." Erickson was out of his chair, practically knocking over Lana. "They were breaking and entering. They could have taken evidence or—"

"You caught 'em, Erickson. You stopped 'em. That's enough for me. Part of being a good cop is knowing when something is too much effort for its own good. We put this one's name in a police blotter"—he pointed at Jazz—"and believe me, we'll spend the next week doing nothing but answering questions about Billy Dent's kid. We don't have time for that nonsense. Not for something that boils down to the equivalent of a kids' prank. Let 'em go."

"Thanks, G. William," Jazz said quietly.

"I didn't do it for you, kid. Did it for my own sanity. I'm heading home." He paused at the door and turned back. "Oh, and Jazz? Howie? I catch you two pulling any more shenanigans and I will not be inclined to go easy on you. Hear?"

"Yes, sir," Jazz said.

"Sir, yes, sir!" Howie barked, saluting with his free hand.

Lana returned to her desk (not before stealing another look at Jazz, of course) and Erickson grumbled as he released Howie from the cuffs.

"Careful!" Howie said. "Watch it!" His wrist was mottled with bruises from the cuff and from Erickson's fingers.

"Sorry," the deputy said in a curt tone that seemed to be anything but an apology.

Erickson stalked over to Jazz, who held out his wrists to be released. Erickson stared at Jazz, and something in the deputy's eyes made Jazz want to shiver, an urge he resisted. He had the disturbing sense that Erickson was going to defy Tanner and refuse to unlock the cuffs.

How could I have been so wrong about that guy? Jazz thought. *I saw isolation and weakness, but it was really . . . what? First-day jitters? Something else?*

Their eyes locked for long seconds. Jazz had never feared another human being—other than his father—and he wasn't about to start now.

Erickson grunted at last and unlocked the cuffs. "I'm not going to forget this," he said.

Jazz flashed him a grin, just because he knew it was annoying. *I won't, either.*

CHAPTER 5

"That," Howie said as they climbed into the Jeep, "was a close call. What was that guy doing down there, anyway?"

"I don't know," Jazz said. "And right now, I don't care. Let's get out to the field, though. I want to see it at night, the way the killer—"

"Are you nuts?" Howie goggled at him. "Go by yourself. I'm not going anywhere but home. Didn't you hear Tanner? He was pretty serious."

"It's his job to be serious. I need you to come with me to—"

"Uh-uh. No way. Take me home. It's already past midnight, and I need my beauty rest."

Jazz really wanted to go back to the field and see it the way the killer had seen it—in the predawn dark. But he would need Howie's help again, so it was best to let his friend cool off first.

Jazz dropped Howie off at his house and headed home. His grandmother was sound asleep, having passed out on the couch in the living room as she often did these days. The TV was still on, blaring at full volume. Jazz had learned from prior experience that if he turned it off or down, Gramma would bolt awake and raise holy hell for his troubles, so he left everything as it was and crept past her sleeping, snoring form.

How could G. William not see what Jazz saw? How could he miss it? Were the million petty details of being a cop making G. William ignore what was right in front of him? Or was it something deeper?

Linkage blindness is the technical term for when cops refuse to acknowledge that two or more cases might be connected, despite the evidence. The idea that they might be dealing with a serial killer is so huge, so overwhelming and horrifying and depressing, that they just refuse to see it. In this case, there was only the one victim, but Jazz was certain of something: This was not the killer's first victim, nor would it be his last. If G. William didn't see that, then Jazz would have to take matters into his own hands.

And how do you know that, Jazz? he asked himself. He avoided looking at himself in the mirror as he brushed his teeth and washed up for bed. There were times when he was afraid that he would see Billy staring back from the mirror, and this was one of those times.

No. *Afraid* was the wrong word to use. Jazz wasn't afraid— he was *convinced.*

Convinced because he heard Billy's voice in his head too much these days: It grew with time, as though the longer Billy stayed in prison, the stronger his voice in Jazz's head became. Convinced because he couldn't help seeing another serial killer in the Nod, even with very little evidence.

What was the opposite of linkage blindness? What described being certain of something without any kind of evidence?

As he flopped into bed, Jazz realized: The term was *faith*.

What a thing to have faith in, he thought, and drifted off to sleep.

In his sleep, there was a knife.

A knife in a sink.

There was always a knife in a sink.

And a voice.

And a hand.

A hand on the knife.

Sometimes he thought—

(no)

—he thought—

(no don't don't don't you go and)

Easy, a voice says. *So easy. It's just like cutting chicken.*

And another voice says:

(no)

It's okay. It's okay. I want—

And sometimes he thinks

(no)

A knife.

Jazz jerked awake as though shocked with electricity, out of breath and trembling. He looked over at his clock; no more than an hour had passed since he'd collapsed into bed. Yet he was fully awake, his mind spinning. This was ridiculous. He needed to get some sleep. He had school in the morning.

The dream. The dream. The knife. And then the voices. And then the other things... At least this time he'd woken up before...

Jazz tossed and turned in bed, willing himself back to sleep, unable to get there. Images of Jane Doe drifted through his mind's eye, and Billy's voice whispered in his ear. Suggesting. Insisting. Reminding. *People matter. People are real. I will never kill*, Jazz told himself over and over, his promise to himself. He had said it to his father once—just once—and Billy had laughed and said, *You go on thinking that way, Jasper. If that's what it takes to get you through the night, you go on thinking that way.* Billy had been so sure that Jazz would someday go into the family business.

Something about Jane Doe nagged at him. Was it something in the report? No—the report had been useless. G. William was right—he should have waited another day or so for more information to come in. From the complete autopsy. From fingerprints.

He rolled over and punched his pillow, cursing under his breath. What an idiot he'd been, breaking into the morgue tonight. Another day—two at most—and the complete autopsy report would have been available to him. Just a little more time and he could have had all the information the police had.

But no. He had to be impatient. He had to rush in. Stupid. A stupid kid's mistake. And there was no way he'd ever get back in now; G. William would have the locks changed by morning, and the new keys would be watched carefully. Jazz would never see that final autopsy report, and he had only himself to blame. If he was going to do this—really *do* this—then he couldn't make any more stupid mistakes.

Jane Doe, he thought, looking at the ceiling, wasn't her real name, of course. Would her real name give him some additional clue? It wasn't the name itself that mattered—her name just identified her to people. But a name is about a person and their relations. Jane Doe wasn't important because of who she was. Classic victimology: It wasn't about what she seemed like. It wasn't even about what she really was. It was, instead, all about what she symbolized or represented for him, for the killer.

"Him," because of course the killer would be a man. Most serial killers were. Most killers were, period. And when the victim is a young, attractive woman, found naked...Plus, you had to factor in the location—there were no tire tracks anywhere in the field near the body, which meant the killer carried her. Few women have the upper-body strength to do that, even with someone as small as Jane Doe, and there'd been no drag marks.

So, a male. Probably thirties or older, because—Jazz was convinced—the guy wasn't new at this. White—serial killers tended to hunt (to *prospect*, in Billy's parlance) within their own ethnic groups. He was probably smart.

Jazz sighed. Age, race, and intelligence were all relatively easy to predict. Motive was tougher.

He would go to the field tomorrow. No question about it. He would see what the cops had missed. Because he knew they had to have missed something. He could feel it.

More faith. Jazz figured he had enough faith for an entire seminary. What he needed was some evidence.

He ran through the report in his mind, ran through what he'd seen at the crime scene. He was replaying his memory of looking at Jane Doe's mutilated hand in the morgue when sleep finally slipped up behind him, wrapped an arm around him, and carried him off, this time without dreams.

CHAPTER 6

The Impressionist—that was the name he'd settled on for himself, picking it from a list of three quite good ones—stood just across the street from Jazz's house, gazing up at Jazz's dark bedroom window. He wondered—idly, but he wondered nonetheless—how Billy Dent's son slept at night. Did Jasper Dent dream of bodies and blood, or was he like every other teenage boy, dreaming of girls and cars and the future?

The Impressionist had followed the body to the police station/morgue. There was no particular reason to do so, no imperative that compelled him. But when you've spent such intimate time with someone, when you've seen the light in her eyes glimmer and then blink out, heard the soft sigh of her last breath...Sometimes it's hard to let go. So he'd parked down the block to watch the cranky old station wagon pull into the parking lot.

And, to his amazement, he'd spotted none other than Billy Dent's Jeep in the parking lot, just like any other car. The

Impressionist recognized it from an episode of *60 Minutes*. Or maybe it was *20/20*—he kept getting them confused. Whichever one, it didn't matter. What mattered was that it was definitely Billy Dent's Jeep, which meant that the kid who then came out of the police station and kicked the bumper had to be none other than Jasper Dent.

From the police station, the Impressionist followed Jasper at a distance. To the morgue that night, then to here, home.

The "street" on which Jazz lived with his grandmother was a street in name only; it was more a long driveway to a large, grotesque McMansion half a mile away, a run of cracked pavement and loose stone. The Dent house, a rickety colonial in a state of disrepair, sat along this drive like an afterthought, equidistant between the McMansion and the main road. Everything about the house said, "Oh, that's right, now I remember...." as though the house were slowly forgetting itself into nonexistence. Unless you knew who lived within, you would never peg this house as the epicenter of Billy Dent's decades-long harrowing of America. But within those humble walls, a legacy had been born. Billy Dent had grown up there, and now his son lived there, the house and the legacy passed down like a baton going from one runner to the next. A simple house, run-down and inconspicuous. Right here in the very middle of Middle America, hell had been born and suckled and matured.

The Impressionist grinned.

A serial killer's greatest ability is the ability to blend in. Just like this house. No one driving by would guess at what had grown within, and no one would guess what was growing in there now. Billy Dent had blended in flawlessly, convincing friends and neighbors and acquaintances that he was "just one of the guys." Barbecues in the summer. Coaching a Little League baseball team for three years. Volunteering to drive the FoodMobile on alternating weekends. And no one knew. No one suspected. Idiots.

No, no. Not idiots.

Prospects.

The Impressionist blended in, too. The dead woman in the field hadn't suspected a thing when he'd first approached her at the Dairy Queen off the highway just outside Lobo's Nob. Late at night, a bland-looking man asks to borrow your cell. Car died two miles back, you see. Just need to call AAA, if you don't mind. Oh, hell (and then a quick apology for swearing in front of a lady—she ate it up), they need to call me again near the car so I can read them the VIN number. Can I borrow your phone again? Or . . . maybe you can just walk with me and then take your phone back when I'm done?

It was too easy, really.

He sighed into the cool October night air, his breath a vaporous cloud that dispersed almost immediately.

The Impressionist had known that he would, inevitably, cross paths with Dent's kid. In a perverse way, he looked forward to it, even though he had been given a rule: He was not to interact with Jasper Dent. And sure as hell, no harm was to come to Jasper Dent.

We'll see about that, the Impressionist thought. He raised his cell phone and thumbed through the photos and videos stored there. All shot today. All of Jasper Dent, caught unawares, going about his life.

As far as the Impressionist could tell, young Jasper Dent had the blending-in part down to a tee. No one suspected him of being a killer.

Even Jasper himself didn't suspect it.

CHAPTER 7

—gotta wakey, wakey, Jasper, my boy—

Jazz forced himself awake the next morning, past the shreds of his father's voice. Lay awake in the sunlight slanting through his window blinds.

—gotta wakey, wakey—

People matter, he countered. *People are real.*

And just in case he forgot, the scrolling screen saver on his computer reminded him: *Remember Bobby Joe Long.*

He dressed and headed out to the Coff-E-Shop, where he and Howie met almost every morning before school. The tables bore several generations' worth of nicks and stains, and every surface was slick with a grease that seemed to congeal from the very air, but none of that stopped the clientele from pouring in every morning.

Jazz got there first and grabbed a small table near the window for Howie and himself. He'd invited Connie to join them for their morning ritual about a month ago, but she had declined. "You guys need to have your guy time. I don't want you to start ignoring poor Howie just because you have a girlfriend now."

Helen was usually on duty this time of day, and today was no exception. She spied Jazz from across the shop, saw he was alone, and nodded to him, a nod that said, *I'll be over once Howie gets here.* One of the benefits of living in a small town.

Howie came in a few moments later. Jazz watched him make his careful way through the crowded line of people waiting for take-out coffee, gently edging bodies aside and making as little contact as possible to avoid bruises.

"Once again," Howie announced as he got to the table, "Howie the Barbarian deftly avoids the crushing throngs of heathens looking to destroy him and arrives unscathed!"

"Did your mom say anything about the bruise on your wrist?"

"Wore long sleeves today. I'm no dummy."

"What can I get you today, Howie?" Helen asked, gliding up to their table. She didn't have to ask Jazz because he always drank his coffee black with a little sugar. Howie, though, treated ordering coffee as if it were some sort of game show, where you only get points for not repeating yourself.

"Hmm..." He tapped a finger to his lips. "Hmm...What do I feel like having today?"

Jazz held up his wrist so that Howie could see his watch. "School in twenty minutes."

"You can't rush my creative genius," Howie said, "with your quotidian worries."

"*Quotidian*? Seriously?"

"I would have said *mundane*, but that word is so... mundane."

"I do have other tables...." Helen reminded them.

"I think today," Howie announced, "I'm going to try a nonfat macchiato with a double shot of caramel, lots of foam, and whipped cream on top."

Helen's pen hesitated at her order pad. "Foam *and* whipped cream?"

Howie pretended to mull it over. "Yep."

"And you want nonfat, but then you want whipped cream?"

"I'm a complicated man, with complicated taste buds."

Before Helen could move away entirely, Jazz stopped her. "Make those to go, will you?"

"Sure, Jasper."

"What the—" Howie broke off. "Oh. I see. Sleazoid alert."

He had seen what Jazz noticed moments before: Sitting at the Coff-E-Shop's counter was none other than Doug Weathers, a reporter for the county's weekly rag of a newspaper. When Billy had been caught and arrested, Weathers found himself in the catbird seat as the first reporter on the scene, and the one with all the background dirt. He knew the most recent victims' families. He knew the area. He knew Billy's friends and coworkers. He had even met Billy once, many years earlier, at some local political function.

And Weathers milked that for all it was worth when the time came. Suddenly he was in demand as a "local expert," his mug plastered all over CNN and Fox News and all the major broadcast channels. For months, you couldn't turn on a television without seeing Billy Dent...and right after Billy, you'd see Doug Weathers.

Doug was also responsible for pictures of Jazz showing up, first in the newspapers and then on TV. Jazz was sure there were people he hated more than Doug Weathers, but he was equally sure that it was a really short list. He wanted to get out of the Coff-E-Shop before Weathers could—

Too late. Weathers had turned on his stool and spied Jazz and Howie. His eyes—murky and dun-colored—widened, and he slid off the stool immediately.

"Oh, great."

"Hey, there, Jasper," Weathers said, grabbing a chair from another table to join the boys. "Fancy meeting you here."

"Yeah, real fancy," Howie growled. "Everyone knows we get coffee here. How long have you been waiting for us?"

Weathers grinned. He was in his thirties, medium build, with a face that looked sad even when he smiled. It was a bright, clear day outside, but he wore a trench coat anyway, probably because someone had once told him that reporters wore them.

"Hey, Gersten, if you want in on the fame, I can make it happen. Convince Jasper here to give me an exclusive. A one-on-one interview. Mano a mano. And I'll do a nice sidebar with you as the 'best friend who lived through the madness.' "

"Wow, Jazz." Howie whistled with false appreciation. "A sidebar. I could be a sidebar!"

"Back off," Jazz said to Weathers. "Did you not understand it the ten other times I've said it to you?"

"Check it, kid. Together we can—"

"Or the six times I e-mailed it to you?"

"—get your side of the story out there—"

"Or the dozen texts?"

"—and make a big splash with it," Weathers rattled on as if Jazz had said nothing. "C'mon. Just a single interview. Been up to the penitentiary to see your dad lately? That's even better. Good atmosphere. I'll get a photographer and we'll go together. One little interview. Won't hurt anyone, and it'll change your life." His eyes danced with excitement.

"It'll change *your* life. Put you back in the spotlight. Do you really miss being on CNN that bad?"

His eyes alight with fame-lust, Weathers laughed a modest little laugh. "Well, I'm sure there'll be some demands for my time and my insight. That's usually how the game's played...."

Just then Helen arrived with the coffees. To go. Jazz and Howie snatched theirs up.

"It's not a game, douche," Jazz said.

"Yeah, and if it were," Howie said, "you would seriously suck at it."

They scooted from the Coff-E-Shop. Jazz shot one last look over his shoulder. Weathers still sat at the table in the window, glaring out at the two of them, his eyes lifeless and burning at the same time. He'd had a glimpse of the world beyond the Nod when Billy was arrested, and would spend the rest of his life doing anything to claw his way back to it.

But he wouldn't get there by climbing up on Jazz's shoulders.

Somewhere up the street, a dog barked. Jazz thought of Rusty. Great. An encounter with Doug Weathers and now thinking of Rusty. He knew that this was going to be a bad day.

Sure enough, school was torture.

Jazz wanted nothing more than to get back out to the field. With every hour that passed—with every *minute* that passed—the field was reverting to its natural state, losing any remaining evidence. If Howie hadn't lost his nerve last night...

Well, no point thinking about that now. He wanted to get out there and poke around, ideally in the hours before sunrise. To see the field the way the killer had seen it.

But school dragged.

Jazz didn't like school, but not for the usual teen reasons. He didn't like school for the same reason that he didn't like any situation where he was surrounded by people.

"It's like this," he'd explained once to Connie. "If someone gave you a single rose, you'd be happy, right?"

They had been sitting in Jazz's Jeep at the nearby state park. Connie had feigned confusion, peering in the glove compartment, twisting to look in the backseat. "I don't see a rose. There's no happiness here."

"Okay," he went on, "now imagine someone gives you *ten thousand* roses."

"That is a whole lotta roses," she said. "That's too much."

"Right. Too much. But more than that, it makes each individual rose much less special, right? It makes it hard to pick one out and say, 'That's the good one.' And it makes you want to just get rid of all of them because none of them seem special now."

Connie had narrowed her eyes. "Are you saying when you're at school you just want to get rid of everyone?"

It wasn't that. Jazz wished he knew how to explain it. It wasn't a matter of wanting to kill people. It was simply that when there were so many people, didn't they seem, well, expendable? With fifteen hundred students at Lobo's Nod High, would anyone really notice if a few went missing? The more people there were around him, the less personal they became. The less real.

People matter. It was a tough lesson; it was the opposite of what Billy had taught Jazz all his life. *All these people, you see 'em,* Billy would say at a ball game or at the park or in a movie theater or mall. *All these people aren't real. They don't have real lives. They don't have hearts. They don't matter. Only you matter.*

"Lots of people had crappy childhoods," Connie had told him. "Some of them even grew up the same way as a serial killer, but they didn't turn into serial killers. It's not like there's a manual you can follow and it makes a kid grow up to kill people."

"If anyone would know how to custom-design a sociopath, it's Billy," Jazz had said.

"But you don't *want* to kill people," she'd said with finality, and Jazz had let the conversation die right there. Because the only honest response would have been:

It's not that I want to or don't want to. It's just...I can. I could. It's like...I imagine it's like being a great runner. If you knew you could run really fast, wouldn't you? If you were stuck walking somewhere, wouldn't you want to let loose and run like hell? That's how I feel.

Instead of saying any of that, he'd let it go and then sent Connie a dozen red roses the next day, with one rare blue rose at the center of the bouquet; money he could ill afford to spend, but it felt somehow necessary. The card read, "You'll always be my special rose." He didn't know if the sentiment was romantic or corny as hell (he strongly suspected the latter), but Connie ate it up, and since the whole point of the gesture was to make her happy, Jazz counted it as a win.

Sometimes his programming simulated human emotions pretty well. And sometimes he convinced himself that it wasn't programming at all.

On Mondays, between calculus and biology, he had five minutes to kill, five minutes when his schedule jibed with Connie's. They connected outside her history class, as they always did on Mondays. Today she was wearing jeans and a pink T-shirt that stretched across her chest, reading, CONTAINS 0% PLASTIC. He moved in for a quick kiss on the lips.

"Dent!" barked Mr. Gomez. "PDA!"

Jazz threw his arm around Connie's shoulders. "Aw, c'mon, Mr. Gomez!" he said with just the right amount of swagger in his voice. "Could *you* resist?"

Jazz could read people, and he had a pretty good suspicion that Albert Gomez entertained some R-rated—at the very least—fantasies about the girls in his class. So he didn't outright accuse him of anything, just poked right at the tender spot.

Mr. Gomez cleared his throat nervously—music to Jazz's ears—and wiped at an imaginary bead of sweat on his upper lip. "Just watch it, okay?" he said, and suddenly found something else to occupy his attention.

71

"That was mean," Connie said as they found a spot against the wall to lean and talk. "He's not a bad guy."

Yeah, right. "I was just being honest. How could anyone resist?" He moved to run a hand through her cornrows, then pulled back, remembering the one time he'd tried that— Connie had lectured him on the Eleventh Commandment: Thou shalt not touch thy black girlfriend's hair. Ever. He kissed her again instead, quickly and out of the visual range of any random teacher drones.

Hmm. Drones. Not good. *People matter.*

Especially Connie. Connie, with her soft lips, her wicked grins, her dark eyes that couldn't see into his soul, but still made him jump a little inside whenever they roamed his way. Her hair—off-limits to touch, but not to his other senses— entranced him, jet black, shoulder-length, tightly coiled like powerful springs, smelling slightly of chemicals and cinnamon, the beads at the end of each braid clicking together as she walked. It was as if she bound up limitless energy in those braids, and he couldn't imagine what it would be like to release it. Her skin was soft to the touch and the color of...

Well, who cared about color? She was the color of Connie. Beautiful.

For his part, Jazz knew he was handsome. It had nothing to do with looking in the mirror, which he rarely did. It had everything to do with the way the girls at school looked at him, the way they became satellites when he walked by, their orbits contorted by his own mysterious gravity. If attention could be measured like the Doppler effect, girls would show a massive blue shift in his presence. In the last year or so, he had even remarked the scrutiny of older women—teachers, cashiers at stores, the woman who delivered UPS packages to his house. What had once been a maternal flavor in their glances had taken on a lingering, cool sort of appraisal. He could almost hear them thinking, *Not yet. But soon.*

Despite his upbringing, despite the infamy of his father, they still watched him. Or maybe because of it. Maybe Howie was right about bad boys.

None of this mattered to him, except that it made getting his way fairly easy. Most guys were cowed by him, and most women were attracted to him. As long as he could exploit that, he had a pretty easy time of it.

Prospects are there for you and for me, Jasper. That's what they exist for, get it?

"Howie told me what you guys did last night," Connie said, shutting up Billy's voice in his head. "Not cool."

"I knew I should have killed that kid when I had the chance," Jazz said lightly, then immediately regretted it when he saw the expression on her face. "Not funny?" he asked.

"Not when you say it. You don't know how to joke like that." She thought for a moment, her warm, dark eyes searching him for...what? He didn't know. "You should probably never joke like that."

"Okay." Connie gave good lessons in being human. "But it needed to be done. We had to go in there."

Connie patted Jazz's shirtfront and frowned. "Nope. Not there. Let me see your wallet."

Mystified, he put his wallet into her outstretched hand. She flipped it open. "Well, now," she said, looking at the picture of her that he kept there, "that is one fine-looking honey, but...No. I don't see it here, either."

"See what?"

"The badge Tanner gave you when he made you a deputy," she said, shoving his wallet at his chest. "Don't do stupid things, Jazz. And don't make me go all 'psycho girlfriend' on you. I don't want to, but I will."

The bell rang and Connie darted for her class. Jazz fumbled his wallet back into his pocket and hightailed it to biology.

Jazz didn't see Connie again until the end of the day, when they met at the auditorium for rehearsal. The new drama teacher, Ms. Davis (she actually insisted that her students call her Ginny), was bringing *The Crucible* to life on the Lobo's Nod High stage, and Jazz had been "encouraged" by Connie to audition. Result: He was now stuck every afternoon rehearsing with a bunch of kids he really didn't care about, all to act out a role—Reverend Hale—that he found sort of annoying and wishy-washy. Not to mention hopelessly naive. There is a moment early in the play where Hale—an "expert" on witchcraft—haughtily brandishes his books and asserts that "Here is all the invisible world, caught, defined, and calculated." As if it could be that easy.

Connie was no longer annoyed with him by the time they connected after the last bell; they spent the fifteen minutes between the end of school and the beginning of rehearsal feverishly kissing and groping back in the wings, behind a leftover matte painting from an old production of *Grease*. Or maybe she'd never been annoyed with him at all, he thought. Sometimes he couldn't get a read on Connie's emotions. Maybe it was a guy/girl thing.

He hoped that's all it was. What if it was a predator/prey thing? A *human* thing? What if he was losing his connection to her? God, don't let that be it. Connie was one of the few anchors that kept Jazz's sanity firmly moored. Losing any one of them would be disastrous, but losing Connie in particular, he knew, would be catastrophic.

"Are you all right?" she asked, her fingers lightly stroking his cheek.

"Fine."

"'Cause it's like you're not even here. Your tongue just stopped."

"Sorry. I was thinking." He kissed her again, and this time he forced himself not to think while he did it. This was how normal people kissed. Without thinking.

"Everyone onstage!" Ginny shouted from the house. "Come on, now!"

Jazz and Connie joined the rest of the cast onstage. Today they were running through the last scenes of the play, so Connie—who was playing Tituba—didn't have to be there the whole time, but she always stayed through every rehearsal. Of the two of them, Connie was the drama geek, and would have watched rehearsals even if she didn't have a part in the play. Now she sat in the front row with Ginny and watched Jazz in a scene close to the end of the play, as Reverend Hale argues and pleads with Judge Danforth to release the heroic John

Proctor from jail and stay his execution. In the play, Hale starts out as one of the main proponents of the witch trials in Salem, but later comes to regret his part in them. As the play and John Proctor's life near their end, Hale rants in the jail, begging Danforth to reconsider and spare Proctor so that he will not join the others who've died already at the hands of the Puritans. If Proctor can live, then maybe Hale can be redeemed.

"There is blood on my head!" Hale screams at Danforth, pleading with him. *You won't just be saving Proctor's life*, he's saying. *You'll be saving my soul, too!* "Can you not see the blood on my head!!"

It was a great moment, and Jazz and Eddie Viggaro (the kid playing Danforth) turned up the volume on it this rehearsal, really clicking for the first time. Danforth stood stone-faced and immobile, glaring out at the audience as Hale, a twitchy, fidgety mass of tics and guilt-induced pacing, roamed the stage, screaming, pleading, finally crumbling in a heap at Danforth's feet.

"Really wonderful work today, Jasper," Ginny told him when they broke for the day. "I really felt that. Nicely done. Everyone else!" She cupped her hands around her mouth. "Hey! All of you! Off-book next week on this scene. Take a few pointers from Mr. Dent and get those lines memorized, okay?"

"You're awesome," Connie said later, linking her arm in Jazz's as they headed to the Jeep.

He shrugged. Pretending to be someone he wasn't...That wasn't the sort of thing he really wanted to be awesome at. But his being a part of the play with Connie seemed to make her happy.

"I can't believe you're playing Tituba," he told her. "Like Ginny couldn't have given you another role?"

"I *wanted* to play Tituba. It's a great role."

"But she's a slave." He opened Connie's door and helped her into the Jeep. "Doesn't that bother you?"

"Should it?"

"Well, you're black...."

"I am?" Connie looked at the back of her hand and feigned shock. "Holy crap! You're right! I am."

"Ha, ha." Jazz closed her door and got in on the driver's side.

"I don't care about Africa," she said suddenly.

"What?"

"Africa," she explained. "I don't care about it."

Jazz stared at her. She had that expression on her face that told him that she had thought long and hard about what she was saying. So he figured it was best just to get out of her way and let her do it.

"I mean," she went on, "I care about the people who are hurting there. The wars. The genocide. The famine. I care about that. But no more than people on any other continent who are suffering. And I don't care about slavery, either. I know I'm supposed to. I know I'm supposed to be angry about it, like my dad is. But I care about the *now*, Jazz. The now and the coming. I don't care about the past. Get it?"

He wasn't sure where she was headed with this, and the expression on her face told him that she was trying to make a point beyond the obvious one.

She waited patiently while he thought about it. Lessons in

being human. She told him something about herself and then turned it around on him, so...

"So, you're saying maybe *I* should forget about *my* past and stop thinking about my father and serial killers and just get on with my life?"

She grinned and patted his cheek. "Aw, see? And everyone told me you were just a pretty face. But you have—"

Just then, a man appeared in front of the Jeep as Jazz was about to turn the key, making him forget all about race and Connie and *The Crucible* and the blood on Reverend Hale's head. If not for his hangdog posture and the age in his eyes, Jazz would have thought him no older than forty. But the defeated, dragging stoop of his stance made him look more like sixty. He was a man crushed by the world, by life itself.

He was also right in front of the Jeep and not moving, staring at Jazz as though disbelieving his own eyes.

Jazz started the engine to give the guy a hint: *Move it, pal.*

The man put a trembling hand on the Jeep's hood and left it there as he slowly made his way around the fender to Jazz's window and grabbed hold of the side mirror.

Sighing, Jazz obeyed when the man motioned to him to roll down the window.

"You're Jasper Dent, aren't you?" the man asked, his voice hollow and quavering. "I've been looking for you."

Now that he was face-to-face with the guy, Jazz saw that his eyes—muddy brown and bloodshot—were sunken, as though they had seen too much and retreated as far into his skull as possible. Heavy bags drooped under them—the man needed a week's worth of sleep at the very least.

He wasn't a reporter; of that much, Jazz was certain. Jazz had a lot of experience with the press, far beyond bottom-feeding morons like Doug Weathers. Reporters of all kinds made their way to Lobo's Nod, interviewing residents, all of them trying to land the Holy Grail of torture-porn journalism: an interview with Billy Dent's only child. Jazz could have been rich beyond his wildest dreams by now, just by accepting the offers from the sleazier newspapers and tabloid TV shows, or the seven-figure offer from a big New York publishing house for his memoir. ("We'll get someone to ghost the whole thing for you," they had promised him. "The only writing you'll do is when you sign the check.")

"I've been looking for you," the man said again, stumbling over his words. "Just got to town today. Didn't think I'd...So soon..." As if he'd just remembered what to do when meeting someone, the man extended a hand through the window. Jazz shot a look over at Connie, who was staring at the scene unfolding before her. He sighed and shook the man's hand.

"My name's Jeff Fulton. Hello, miss," he said, as though just seeing Connie for the first time. "I'm sorry. I'm so sorry. I don't want to keep you. I just... Harriet Klein is my... *was* my daughter."

Jazz stiffened and jerked his hand away from Jeff Fulton. Harriet Klein. Billy's eighty-third victim in the official chronology (eighty-fourth in Jazz's own chronology). White. Twenty-seven years old. Pretty in an unnoticeable sort of way—you wouldn't stop to look at her on the street, but if you were in a room alone with her, you'd feel it.

Unbidden, images flashed before his eyes: the police photo

of her body, nailed naked to the ceiling of a church in Pennsylvania ("Hoo-boy, that took *all night*!" Billy had crowed, flushed with triumph and pride), her head lolling downward, her limbs bearing the weight of her body. When the reverend who found the body called the police, the skin and muscle were already coming loose; the medical examiner arrived just before her left arm pulled free from the wall. Four cops had to climb a scaffold and hold her in place so that they could get her down before the rest of her limbs shredded and dropped her amputated corpse to the floor.

It had been one hell of a piece of work.

"I don't... I can't help you," Jazz said. And he couldn't. This wasn't the first time he'd been approached by a victim's family. In the months after Billy Dent had been exposed and arrested, family members had flocked to Lobo's Nod along with the reporters, looking for a glimpse of the killer, looking for clues, looking for that most elusive factor of all: closure.

In that time, Jazz had learned how to apply Billy's lessons for hiding in plain sight—walk a certain way, dress a certain way, and people just won't notice you, especially in crowds. And Lobo's Nod had suddenly become very crowded.

Jazz was mostly successful at avoiding personal encounters like this one. The e-mails and phone calls were another matter entirely—no matter what sort of precautions he took, someone always managed to track him down, and then the harassment would start up again. Some pleading. Some just pathetic. Some of them outright threatening, like the woman who sent him detailed e-mails explaining how she wanted to kidnap Jazz and "hire some big ex-cons to do to you what your father did to my daughter, and see how you like it when no one comes to save you." Jazz had actually reported her to the police.

The incident that resonated with him, though... The worst one of them all...

Jazz had been picking up his grandmother's prescription at the drugstore when a kid he didn't recognize — an outsider — approached him, some unidentifiable emotion swirling in his eyes. Jazz took a step back, on the defensive, checking for the kid's weak spots already.

But the kid hadn't been angry. Or ready to attack. Instead, he'd started crying and begged, "Why didn't you stop him? Why didn't you stop him?" over and over until he just collapsed in a pile of anguish and tears, his family rushing over to help him to his feet and take him away.

What was I supposed to do? Jazz wanted to ask the kid, wanted to ask the whole world. *Was I supposed to kill him in his sleep? That would have been the only way to stop him. Kill my own father?*

Maybe that's what the world had wanted, though.

It bothered Jazz that he'd never done anything to stop Billy. But on that day, what bothered him more was his reaction to the kid—the way he'd immediately gone on the defensive and started looking for ways to hurt him. And all along, the kid hadn't been angry or intent on revenge. He'd been wounded and hurt and mournful.

And Jazz hadn't been able to tell the difference.

"I think you can help," Fulton said now. "I just want to talk to you."

"No. No, I'm sorry. I can't."

"Please." Fulton gripped the Jeep tightly, his knuckles whitening. "Just five minutes of your time." He gagged on his own emotions; tears welled up in his eyes. "I just want...I just want to understand...."

"Please leave him alone." Connie spoke from the passenger seat, her voice quiet but strong. "He didn't kill your daughter."

Harriet Klein. Reddish hair. Green eyes, according to the file, but they were gone when the police found the body, of course. *I was worried they'd drop out, what with her hanging upside down all night. So I took 'em out before I left her.*

(At that point in the story, Billy had paused and looked at the ceiling, tapping his chin with one finger, as he often did when thinking hard.)

Now, where did I...Oh, that's right—I fed 'em to some wild cats in an alleyway a few blocks away. Almost forgot that part.

Harriet had been taking night classes to get her law degree; her student ID had made its way into Billy's trophy collection in the rumpus room.

"I just want to understand," Fulton said, now weeping openly. "Her mother—my ex—she's just blocked it all out. Remarried now, two new kids, like you can just replace one with another, like it's that easy." He wiped his eyes with the back of one hand, keeping a death grip on the Jeep with the other. "But I have to know: Why? Why my little girl? Why did he—"

"He can't tell you," Connie said, now with some heat. "Jazz, just go. Drive."

Jazz shook his whole body as though waking from a nightmare. He'd been lost in Harriet Klein, remembering the photos, the story Billy had told, the student ID, which he'd touched so many times over the years.

He gunned the engine, a threat. "We have to go," he told Fulton, and then reeled off the line he'd so often practiced over the past four years: "I'm sorry for your loss and for everything my father did." He put the Jeep into gear.

Fulton's face fell; he knew he would get no further, and he only became more desperate and more pained. "I'm staying in town. Just for a couple days," he said, then fumbled in his pocket before bringing out a business card, which he pushed into Jazz's hand. "If you change your mind, my cell's on there. Please. Anytime. I don't care. Anytime at all."

Jazz refused to look at him again; he looked straight ahead and hit the gas. Fulton let go of the Jeep.

"That sucked," Connie said.

Jazz checked the rearview mirror as they pulled out of the school parking lot; Jeff Fulton stood in the same spot, watching them go. Then, as they turned onto the main road, he shuffled away with infinite slowness until he disappeared from Jazz's mirror.

Jazz dropped Connie off at her house. "Do you want to come in?" she asked. He saw that her father was already home, his big SUV stationed in the driveway like a blockade.

"No, that's all right." Connie's dad hated Jazz. The race

stuff that didn't matter to Jazz and Connie mattered a lot to Connie's dad. Jazz could reel off the arguments, though he could never understand them. *There's a history of white men doing what they want with black women in this country*, Connie's dad had said to him once, barely controlling a rage that wanted to come to the surface. *Go read about Thomas Jefferson. Read about what white men used to do to black women in America.*

Jazz knew all about that. *I'm not one of those guys*, he wanted to say. *I'm not a bad person. That was a long time ago.*

But who was he to talk about the past like that? Or to claim to be a good person?

Why didn't you stop him? the boy had cried.

Should have taken that knife from the sink and cut *him*, should have cut Billy. That's what the world wanted.

—good boy, good boy—

In the Jeep now, Connie mistook Jazz's silence for worry about her father. She simply shrugged when she saw him looking at the SUV. "He won't do anything stupid. You can come in."

"I just need to think," he told her. "I'm a little shaken up."

She kissed him gently on the lips, then leaned in closer for a more urgent kiss. For a moment, he couldn't help thinking of what else had happened in this Jeep. With Billy pleading guilty to so many crimes, most of the seized evidence had been returned, and Jazz couldn't afford a new car. But how many crimes had Billy planned from this seat? How many victims had he stalked behind this wheel?

But then he let himself go and surrendered to the kiss, to

the soft insistence of Connie's plush lips, to the warmth of her tongue, to the familiar tang of her hair. When they separated, she arched an eyebrow and asked in a passable Jamaican accent, "Are you sure you don't want to be comin' in, Reverend Hale?"

Jazz laughed. "Thanks, Tituba, but I have to go catch, define, and calculate the invisible world."

They kissed again—a quick peck this time—and Connie got out of the Jeep, but not before saying, "Don't do anything stupid again, okay?"

Last night's trip to the morgue flashed through him in an instant.

"Why would I do anything stupid?" he asked.

Which made her happy. But it wasn't an agreement, and it also wasn't a lie.

CHAPTER 8

On bad days, Jazz wondered if he had figuratively taken his father's place, just as he'd literally taken Billy's place behind the wheel of the Jeep. Was that his destiny? Billy Dent made no secrets of his plans for Jazz: *You'll be the greatest ever, Jasper. They'll never catch you. You'll be the new boogeyman parents use to scare their kids into behaving. You'll make everyone forget Speck and Dahmer and even Jack the Goddamn Ripper. My boy. My boy.*

But today wasn't a bad   'lay practice had gone well; Connie had forgiven him for getting caught breaking into the morgue. A part of him wished he could forget about tracking down whoever had killed Jane Doe. Just be a normal guy. Look to the future, not the past. Maybe focus on the play. On school. On being a better friend to Howie and a better boyfriend to Connie. Prove once and for all to her dad that he was a good fit for his daughter, and prove to the world that he wasn't going to grow up to be the new Billy.

That would be nice.

Yeah, right. And Howie might be starting center for the Pistons next season.

As his grandmother's house came into view on the left, a familiar sight greeted him: a late-model sedan parked in the driveway. He groaned out loud, then plastered a pleasant grin on his face. It was easy, reflexive—Jazz had been conning the sedan's owner for a while now.

He parked next to the sedan and climbed out. It was the only person who annoyed him more than Doug Weathers: Melissa Hoover, social worker, sat on the front porch step. She worked for the county, and ever since Billy had gone to prison, she'd had one goal in life: getting Jazz out of his grandmother's house and then either to a foster home or to his aunt Samantha. Samantha. Who'd never even met Jazz. Who hadn't spoken to Billy in fifteen years. Who swore she would flip the switch herself if the government ever "came to its senses" and decided to execute him.

Yeah, sure. That would be great.

Jazz would have none of it, meaning he spent his days striving to prop Gramma up just enough that she could maintain custody of him.

For a week after Billy's arrest more than four years ago, Jazz had been with social services, and he spent four of those days in a foster home. After the initial shock of Billy being arrested and of being yanked out of his home, Jazz fell back on the skills Billy had taught him—acting, conning, pretending to be normal. He'd easily fooled the social workers and the foster family into thinking he was fine. (A sneak peek at his file revealed the phrase "impressively well adjusted.") He gave them just enough that they thought he was working on his "issues," and they released him into the custody of his grandmother, his closest living relative.

But the truth was he didn't know what his "issues" were. He knew he was afraid of his own powers and prowess, but that was his demon to wrestle with. No one on earth could understand what he'd gone through, what his upbringing had been like. So how could anyone help him? He was on his own.

He might as well do that work here, in the house Billy had grown up in. Gramma's house was the only home remaining for him, quite literally: The wealthy father of one of Dear Old Dad's victims had bought the Dent house at auction and had it bulldozed, then burned the wreckage and debris to ash. Jazz watched on TV as his childhood home went up in smoke, to the cheers of the gathered crowd.

(That same wealthy father later contacted Jazz and offered to pay for him to attend the college of his choice, claiming—in a letter that went on for ten pages—that there was "no reason for Billy Dent to claim one more victim." Jazz politely declined the offer.)

Jazz sauntered over to Melissa, who stood and brushed off her skirt as he approached.

"Did Gramma pitch a fit when she saw you coming?" he asked.

"She went for the shotgun."

Gramma Dent was never all that sane to begin with, her head packed full with a rotting collection of twisted religious dogma, crackpot conspiracy theories, and just plain *wrong*, handed down from generation to generation. Now she'd gone from unpleasant to outright dangerous. She avoided doctors, so no one could be sure, but even without a diagnosis Jazz was certain she was on the road to Alzheimer's Town, an opinion he was careful not to let slip. As bad as she appeared to the outside world, Jazz knew she was actually much, much worse.

Hateful, spiteful, and crazier than a wind sock in a tornado, but family.

"Both barrels are plugged and the firing pins are popped," Jazz assured Melissa. "She's not trying to shoot you; she's just trying to scare you off. She's from that generation that doesn't trust government people, you know?"

"I know, Jasper. When she's in this kind of mood, I just steer clear."

"Probably the best move." Jazz cranked up the wattage on his smile. "You look lovely today. I like the skirt."

Melissa snorted and glared at him. "Flattery will get you nowhere."

But it had already gotten him exactly where he wanted to be. He was less than arm's length from Melissa. She was a plain woman—not unattractive, not attractive. Just plain. In her late thirties, she was unmarried and likely to remain so, a workaholic aging out of her childbearing years. Jazz knew the type. He'd studied everything he could about Melissa Hoover as soon as she'd been assigned to his case. He'd even followed her for a day or so, employing all the useful skills Billy Dent had passed down. He knew she was tough, that she took care of kids whether they wanted it or not. But he couldn't let her learn just how bad Gramma had gotten. Because then she would be able to take him away.

"I don't know why you keep coming out here," Jazz said, "but I have to admit I like seeing you."

Melissa wasn't falling for it, but she didn't say anything about how close he was to her. If he wanted to kill her, he was close enough now. Close enough that there was absolutely nothing she could do to stop him. As tough as she was, as capable as she was, her life was now in Jazz's hands, and she didn't even know it.

But people matter.... Even people mucking around in my life.

"She's a sick old woman and she's not getting any better," Melissa said. "I think she's starting to drift into senility, too." *Ha. If only you knew.* "You're a great kid—a great young man—with your whole life ahead of you."

"So I should just cut her loose?"

"I'm not saying that. But you should think of yourself."

"Thinking of myself is one of the diagnostic criteria for antisocial personality disorder," Jazz told her. "You should be glad I'm thinking of someone else. It means maybe I'm not a sociopath like Billy."

"You're staying with her because you think that maybe by caring for the woman who started all this, you can somehow redeem her and your father *and* maintain your own— Are you listening to me, Jasper?"

"Of course I am," he said smoothly. "Look, I'm seventeen. In a year, I'll be out on my own."

"Even a year in this toxic environment could—"

"Toxic?" The mask slipped, and he let his anger show. "You think *this* is toxic? Where were you on my ninth birthday, when Billy showed me how to use quicklime to dissolve body parts?"

Melissa took a step back, her eyes wide, a hand on her purse. Damn. He'd gone too far. Mace? Probably Mace. With women, it was almost always Mace. But Jazz wouldn't put it past Melissa to be packing heat. And not some little girlie derringer, either. He wouldn't be surprised to see her whip a big ol' Glock or Magnum out of that purse.

Jazz reached out and grabbed her by the wrist, widening his smile, making his eyes dance with mischief. "Aw, c'mon, Melissa. I'm just joking. If I can't joke about this stuff, what *can* I joke about? Black humor. Good for the soul."

Jazz employed his very finest lost-puppy-dog look— guaranteed to work every time.

"I'm trying to help you," she said. "I know you don't want my help, but you need it, and I'm not giving up on you. I'll go for now. But only because your grandmother's having a bad day. I'm coming back, Jasper. I'm going to help you whether you like it or not."

Jazz watched her back out of the driveway, forcing himself to wave jauntily as she pulled away, while inside he seethed. This was the worst, darkest part of the curse Billy Dent had passed down to him—women. Jazz knew that women were no better or worse than men, but he knew this at a remove, like a scientist knows that a photon moves without actually watching one in motion. His upbringing, his gut, his every screaming thought told him that women were simultaneously special and useless. That they compelled him, drove him on, but were ultimately expendable. Fungible. Good for a couple of things, but not for long.

Of Billy Dent's one hundred and twenty-three (or one hundred and twenty-four, depending on how you counted) victims, close to one hundred had been women. Of the men, half were victims of opportunity. Women—and especially certain types of women—were prospects and nothing more.

The Gospel According to Billy Dent.

Jazz hated that part of himself. He hated the part of himself that looked at a strong woman like Melissa Hoover and could think only of how to make her weak and desperate before finally...

Well, before finally making that weakness and desperation moot.

He thought of Connie. Connie was different. Connie was the one girl—woman, really—he could be himself with. "Being himself" meant a whole host of things—good, bad, grotesque. Connie accepted all of them, and most important of all, he allowed her to accept them, something he'd never done with anyone in his entire life. Did that mean there was hope for him? Hope for something beyond what Billy Dent had planned for him?

He sank to the front porch step, his legs trembling and no longer trustworthy to hold his weight. Sometimes hope could be the most frightening thing in the world.

When he'd managed to gather his wits, Jazz pulled himself to his feet and dared to go inside.

The vestibule was dark. Gramma had turned off the lights and closed all the blinds.

"Gramma?" he called. "Hey, Gramma. It's Jasper. I'm alone."

Nothing.

He flicked on a light and made his way into what Gramma insisted on calling the parlor, even though it was nothing more than a cramped little dayroom with a dusty old love seat and some side tables. His grandmother was curled into a corner on the love seat, her legs tucked up against her chest, her spindly form wrapped in a threadbare housecoat. Her thinning hair spun around her head like a whirlwind of gray cotton candy gone wrong.

She was aiming a shotgun at him, her eyes wide and wild.

"Hi, Gramma."

"I'll shoot her!" Gramma shouted. "I'll shoot her right through you if I have to!"

"She's not with me, Gramma. I'm alone. I promise." He took another step toward her.

"Don't think I won't shoot you. I will. I shoulda shot your daddy. Shoulda shot him when he came right out of me. Or maybe when he was still in me. That would have been good, too."

"Can't argue with you there, Gramma." Another step. The gun was harmless, but if she pulled the trigger, she'd learn how harmless it was. And she'd be twice as pissed.

"He wasn't always bad, you know. He grew up okay. It was when he met *her* that everything went all to hell."

Billy Dent had been torturing and killing small animals since the age of eight, but Jazz let Gramma have her delusions. She liked to believe that Jazz's mother had made Billy into a

93

sociopathic murder machine, and since Mom was long dead, there was no harm in letting her have that special, specific delusion.

"Just like *you*!" she yelled, raising the shotgun to track his head as he closed in on her. "Like *you*! I know what you been up to! Just like your pappy! Taking up with *whores*! Putting your *thing* inside them! That's where the *corruption* comes from, boy!"

Jazz bit the inside of his cheek to keep from laughing. Had he just been bemoaning his fears and constant struggles over women? Well, here was their genesis! Handed down from crazy old Gramma Dent to sociopathic Billy Dent, and from there to Jazz himself. Rarely did real life provide such immediate context for a problem. Who needed therapy when Gramma could just explain everything?

"I'm thinking of making macaroni and cheese for dinner," Jazz told her, now mere inches from the shotgun. "I'll use the garlic bread crumbs on the top, the way you like it. And if we have some Romano cheese, I'll add that to the cheddar. How's that sound?"

"I should blow your damn fool head off," Gramma snarled. "I don't want them damn elbow noodles, either."

"Right. Who would? I'll use bow ties. How's that?"

"Bow ties are good. They remind me of how I met your granddad. He was so handsome in his dress uniform." She sighed. "You think cooking me dinner means I'm not gonna shoot you?"

"Well, you can shoot me *after* dinner. If you shoot me before dinner, who's gonna cook for you?"

She squinted as if she were attempting long division somewhere behind those ice-blue eyes. They were Billy's eyes, almost exactly. Jazz's were hazel. His mother's eyes. He thought of them as "sane eyes."

"Garlic! Bread! Crumbs!" she spat, thrusting the shotgun for emphasis.

With a smooth, unhurried motion, Jazz plucked the shotgun out of her hands. "Yep. Garlic. No vampire will come within a hundred yards of you after you eat this stuff."

Gramma sniffed and crossed her arms over her chest. "No such thing as vampires. Just monsters."

Jazz couldn't argue with that. He gave the shotgun back to Gramma, who looked at it like it was a new toy and then, bored, laid it next to the love seat. If the whole scene hadn't been so routine to him by now, he would have found it hilarious or horrifying.

Probably hilarious.

He whipped up the macaroni and cheese as promised. After dinner, he was standing at the sink, washing dishes and idly gazing out the back window at the old abandoned birdbath, when Gramma suddenly marched up to him at the sink and smacked him on the back of the head.

"For back-talking me!" she shrieked.

Jazz gripped the edge of the sink and told himself not to spin around, not to strike back at her. She was a weak old woman. He was a strong young man. One blow from him would cripple, if not kill, her.

Another blow landed. Jazz kept washing the dishes. A beating from Gramma was more an inconvenience than anything else. He let her pinwheel her bony arms at him until she tired and staggered back to lean against the kitchen table, clutching her chest and breathing in ragged gasps. The chest-clutching was new. Was she about to have a heart attack, right here and now?

Jazz didn't know how he felt about that. No one would weep when Gramma died. Dead, she would be nothing more than another body on the Dent family's roster of them. Alive, though: Like Melissa said, maybe his caring for Gramma would somehow redeem her. Or his father. Or himself. Maybe in caring for her, he would observe something, learn something about his lineage, something that would give him some sort of insight into his father and his own upbringing. Anything. Something to help him figure out how to avoid a future that, on some days, felt inevitable. A future that ran thick with blood.

Or maybe, more likely—

"Just like your daddy," Gramma gasped, fumbling into a chair, having apparently decided not to die. "You're just like your daddy."

Now *that* hurt. More than a beating ever could.

After getting Gramma washed up and tucked in for the night, Jazz finally allowed himself to collapse on his bed, but not for long. He had plans to make for his excursion back to the crime scene. He scoped the area out on Google Earth, even though he knew it well already. Then he carefully packed a small duffel bag with everything he thought he and Howie would need.

Had he forgotten anything? He tilted back in his desk chair, thinking, staring at the walls. Long ago, he'd taped up images of his father's victims—one hundred twenty-three photos clipped from newspapers, printed off the Web, surreptitiously photocopied from G. William's files. He told himself it was a reminder. A reminder of what could happen if he ever lost control.

In that roster of the dead was a one hundred and twenty-fourth photo, this one taped between Billy's eightieth and eighty-first official kills. That was Jazz's best guess as to when Billy had killed the woman in the photo, Jazz's own mother.

The photo was all that remained of her. That and a few scanty memories of her from when he was much younger: the dog, Rusty, that she'd given him as a puppy; the smell of cupcakes in the oven; the tang of her homemade lemon frosting. That was it. He remembered so little about her, but based on Gramma's comments and Billy's actions, there was only one reasonable conclusion: His mother had been the one good thing in his life, and even though he had precious few memories of that good thing, he would kill or die to keep them.

The police could find no evidence that Billy had killed Mom. No one could. She was officially a missing person, and her case was colder than Popsicles on New Year's Eve. Jazz only knew that one day she'd been in his life and the next she'd been gone. He had been eight years old, and when he asked Billy, "Where's Mom?" Billy had simply shrugged and said, "She went away." That's all Billy would ever say, no matter how Jazz asked. He could beg and plead: "She went away." Weep and bawl: "She went away." Threaten and rage: "She went away."

All that remained were the half-remembered snippets of his childhood. Did anyone ever remember their childhood with perfect clarity? Jazz wasn't sure, but his own was staticky and foggy. Billy's lessons remained, of course. The day he met Howie. What had happened to Rusty. But so much else was just...muddy. A river of images and thoughts and feelings, dirtied and polluted so that no one could drink from it without gagging.

And that one memory. Or dream. Or both. He didn't know which it was. But it felt so *real*. The knife. The voice. Billy's voice, he knew, telling him to take the knife. Billy's hands, guiding his own, Billy's voice again—

A knife...

A knife and flesh and the flesh parts and he feels the resistance of it and how does he know? How does he know the resistance of flesh?

Another voice, drawn tight in pain, a gasp.

Of all his victims, Billy refused to talk at all about Janice Dent. Par for the course. Serial killers pretended to confess, but they never really told the truth, going back to olden days. Back in the nineteenth century, H. H. Holmes confessed to killing twenty-seven women during the Chicago World's Fair, but police were convinced he'd murdered more than a hundred.

Jazz knew killers. Billy had studied the serial killers of the past the way painters study the Renaissance masters. He learned from their mistakes. He obsessed over them. And he passed his knowledge down to his son. Lucky Jazz—*those* were the things he remembered from his childhood.

Killers always held something back. They couldn't help themselves.

Jazz's mom was Billy's hold-back.

Other than the one hundred twenty-four victim pictures, there was only one other photo in the room, this one of someone still living. It was a black-and-white photo of a pretty, slender teenager dressed in a prim dress, wearing a pillbox hat and carrying a small clutch purse. She was standing in front of a church, smiling at the camera.

His grandmother as a young woman. Years before she begat a monster.

Jazz followed the chronology of Billy's career, reciting the name of each victim from memory as he gazed at the pictures. "Cassie Overton," he began. "Farrah Gordon. Harper McLeod." He ended back at Gramma's old photo.

"Someday," he murmured. "Someday I could snap. I'm my father's son. It could happen. And when that day comes, when I take my first victim...it could even be you."

He surprised himself by crying, but he wasn't sure if it was for his grandmother or for himself. He didn't like thinking about killing her, but he couldn't help it; it felt good. She was a horrible person; she'd given the world the Artist, Green Jack, whichever nickname you wanted to use for Dear Old Dad. He wanted to figure out what made her tick, but he also wanted her gone from the face of the planet. Maybe then—*maybe*— he wouldn't feel so guilty.

But he knew that wasn't true. He would always feel guilty. He hadn't been able to protect his own mother. He hadn't been able to help that kid, the one at the drugstore who'd collapsed at his feet. He should have killed Billy in his sleep years ago. God knows he knew how to do it—Billy had been instructing Jazz in the fine, gory art of murder since Jazz was old enough to walk. He could handle knives, guns, hatchets, hammers.... Billy had kept an old hand drill in a kitchen cabinet, and Jazz could have drilled right into his father's brain while Dear Old Dad slept. Could have done it and saved the world the gruesome murders that followed.

People said to him: *You were thirteen. You knew right from wrong. You knew what he was doing was wrong. Why didn't you stop him?*

But what they could never understand was that killing was only wrong for *other* people. Not for Billy. And not for Jazz. That's how he'd been raised; brainwashed; duped. Whatever word you wanted to use. That was...

He rolled over in bed and stared at the wall, finding Harriet Klein's picture. Green eyes, like he remembered.

Bringing back Harriet Klein was impossible. And there was nothing he could tell Jeff Fulton that would make the poor man's sad, wretched life any better. But there was a way to atone, Jazz knew, for his father's sins, and for his own.

Jane Doe's killer was still out there.

"I'm going to catch you," Jazz whispered. "I'll track you down, no matter how crazy it is, no matter how crazy it makes me."

Because ultimately, he would rather be *that* kind of crazy than his grandmother's.

CHAPTER 9

He called Howie, keeping his voice low so as not to waken Gramma, who slept one thin wall away.

"We're on," Jazz said when Howie answered. He checked his bedside clock: 11:20. Plenty of night left.

"Are you kidding me?" Howie complained. "Colbert's on in, like, ten minutes. Besides, after the morgue, I figured you'd stop being Supercop."

"First of all, we're going in a few hours, not right now. To see it closer to when the killer was there. Second of all, not a chance. Third of all, if you want me to forgive you for ratting out our field trip to the morgue to Connie, you'll do this."

"Oh, come on!"

"I can't believe you told her. Whatever happened to bros before hos?"

"There's a little-known corollary to bros before hos, which states that if Bro One is terrified because Bro Two's girlfriend can make his nose bleed just by looking at him the wrong way, he's allowed to put hos before bros. I chose to implement that corollary because your girlfriend is a total badass."

"Howie, I want you to think about this carefully: Who are you really more afraid of, Connie or me?"

Howie went silent for a moment. "Honestly? Some days it's about even. But hey, if you want to go back to the field, I'm there for you. On one condition."

Jazz groaned. He could tell from Howie's tone of voice what that condition would be.

Jazz caught a few hours' sleep, then sneaked out of the house. Howie was no slouch at sneaking away from his overprotective mother, either; he was already waiting for Jazz at their usual meeting spot, a goofily tall shadow in the moonlight.

"Left shoulder this time," Howie said as he climbed into the Jeep. "It's gonna be a flaming basketball. I mean, like, one that's actually on fire, you know? Wait, wait," he said before Jazz could interrupt. "Let me see what we've got so far so I can be sure."

"Now?" Jazz asked. "Here?"

"You want my help or not?"

Jazz grumbled, but he shifted the Jeep into park and then slipped off his T-shirt, revealing three tattoos—on his right shoulder a stylized CP3, for Chris Paul, Howie's favorite basketball player; across the broad sweep of his back a Yosemite Sam with both pistols drawn; and around his right biceps a black string of Korean characters that Howie swore translated to "I am strong and mighty in the wind," but which Jazz feared actually translated to "Another dumbass white kid with Asian tats. LOL."

Howie had wanted the first tat—the Paul number—last year, but his parents and his doctor thought it was too risky, given Howie's particularly persnickety flavor of hemophilia. Jazz in a moment of weakness he now regretted—had stepped in and told Howie that *he* would get the tattoo on his behalf, and Howie could look at it whenever he wanted.

One thing had led to another.

"Yeah," Howie said as Jazz swiveled in the seat so that he could see the tats better. "Left shoulder. A basketball on fire. I drew a sketch."

He fumbled in his pocket for a piece of paper, but Jazz pushed his hands away. "I don't want to see it. I don't care what it looks like. We'll go to the guy who doesn't check IDs next week and get it done, okay?"

"Sweet." Howie beamed like a kid on a Halloween sugar high. "But if that Erickson guy shows up out of nowhere again to arrest us, I'm gonna be totally pissed."

"Yeah, well, me, too." The thought of Erickson popping up again made Jazz think of the way the deputy had glared at him the night before, leaving just the slightest impression that he wouldn't unlock the handcuffs. Erickson had enjoyed that moment, Jazz knew—Billy had always said that there was only a hairbreadth of difference between cops and killers.

As they drove to the field, Howie said, "You know what?"
"What?"
"I think I would follow you onto the battlefields of hell."

"That's nice."

"But I would still ask you why we were going to the battle-fields of hell."

"Right." Sometimes talking to Howie was an exercise in extreme patience. It was patience as Olympic sport. He talked circles and circles and circles until the conversation was a whirlpool.

"What I'm saying is, I'm going tonight. I'm there for you. But I still have to ask: Why are you so obsessed with this?"

"I told you yesterday: I think this is a serial killer."

"So? If it is, the cops will eventually figure it out."

"And a lot of other people might die in the meantime."

"People are dying all over the world. Right now. Everywhere. And you *know* they're dying; it's totally not theoretical. So why are you so focused on this totally imaginary, maybe-not-real serial killer?"

Jazz pressed his lips together tightly, as if he could physically prevent himself from speaking. But some part of him needed to say what came next, and that part overrode the rest of him.

"Because," he said quietly, "if I *catch* killers, then maybe that means I'm not a killer."

Howie snorted. "You are so totally *not* a serial killer. I can prove it."

"This should be good. Go ahead, Dr. Freud."

Howie rushed on, his gestures animated. "Lookit. Serial killers tend to go after the weak, right? The ones who can't fight back. Well, who's weaker than me, man? I bleed at the *sight* of a knife. I could hemorrhage to death by being hit with a spoon."

All true.

"But you're my best friend, and you'd never hurt me. That should tell you everything you need to know." Howie crossed his arms over his chest and nodded, as if he'd just solved cold fusion.

It was a nice thought, and Jazz really, truly wished it meant what Howie wanted it to mean. But even serial killers could form attachments. There was a couple he'd read about in England, where the husband tortured and killed all sorts of women, including his own daughters, but never harmed his wife.

It was another twenty minutes to the field where Jane Doe was found; they were silent for the rest of it. Howie leaned against his window, staring out at the darkness as they pulled onto an access road without street lamps. Only the moon offered any light, its luminescence shredded and blotched by the trees overhead. As Jazz parked along the road—they would have to walk the mile to the spot where Jane Doe was found, so as not to leave tire tracks—Howie spoke up.

"What's your middle name again?"

"What?"

"Your middle name. I don't remember it."

"Why do you want to know?"

"Starts with an *F*, right?"

"What's the big deal?" Jazz asked as they got out. He opened the back of the Jeep to haul out the small, stuffed duffel bag.

"Serial killers all have three names," Howie said. "I'm checking to see what yours is like."

"I think that's assassins. John Wilkes Booth. Lee Harvey Oswald."

"Serial killers, too," Howie insisted. They began walking toward the crime scene. "Like John Wayne Gacy. Bobby Joe Long. Jeremy Bryan Jones."

"You've spent way too much time with me, to know all those guys."

"And more! William Cornelius Dent. The Boston Strangler."

"Now you're being ridiculous. Boston isn't his middle—"

"I can be ridiculous all night long."

"Fine. Francis. It's Francis."

"Jasper Francis *Dent*," Howie mused. He said it several more times, giving it different inflections and different emphases: "*Jasper* Francis Dent. Jasper *Francis* Dent." Finally, he shook his head. "Nah, it doesn't work. Doesn't sound right. I don't think you're a serial killer."

Carefully stepping through tall weeds and dead stalks of soybean plants, Jazz muttered, "Well, that's a relief." But deep down, he was surprised by how grateful Howie's pronouncement made him feel.

They finally crested the hill that overlooked the site where Jane Doe's body had been found. The crime-scene tape still staked out a lopsided hexagon. Forgotten and flicking in a slight breeze, a single plastic flag marked where the severed finger had been found near the body. Stakes ran in rows up the hill, twine strung between them in both directions to form a series of tight, adjoining squares. So, G. William at least ordered his men to perform a rudimentary grid search. That was good.

Before they went any farther, Jazz pulled out shower caps and gloves.

"Here we go again," Howie grumbled, slipping them on. "Why do I have to be here?"

Jazz chuckled; they were two miles in any direction from civilization, and Howie was whispering.

"I might need to measure some things. And it can never hurt to have a lookout."

"For what?" Howie looked around. In the moonlight, the field had gone dull silver, with spots of black, like tarnish. "Afraid gophers are going to show up and interfere?"

"Nah. But this guy might not know yet that the cops took her. A lot of them like to come back and see the body where they left it. To relive it."

"Oh, that's gross."

Jazz grinned. "Sometimes they even jerk off."

Howie mimed shoving a finger down his throat. "T-M-I. You have so totally ruined masturbation for me. Why couldn't you have brought Connie instead?"

"Connie doesn't like it when I go all Billy."

"Oh, and I do?"

"You tolerate it. Just keep an eye out, man." Jazz hunkered down on the hill, scanning the grade that rolled gently down to the spot where Jane Doe had been left and then found. Howie fell silent behind him, standing tall and still, like the world's least effective scarecrow.

He didn't tell Howie the other reason he hadn't invited

Connie: When it came to this sort of skulduggery, "bros before hos" stopped being a cute motto and became a rule to live by—he'd been dating Connie for only a few months, but he'd been friends with Howie for years. Howie might spill his guts to Connie, but he would never tell an adult about this trip. He couldn't be certain that the same applied to Connie.

It wasn't that he didn't trust her; it's just that his trust for Howie bordered on psychotic. Howie had been there all along, always a friend. He was Jazz's friend when Billy was still home, pretending to be just another single dad juggling his child with his job. And Howie was there when Billy got arrested, and in the shocking days right after the arrest.

Most important of all, Howie remained his friend in the dark days afterward—during the hearings and the trials; after the reporters swarmed Lobo's Nod; when the TV specials aired. Back when no one else even wanted to look in Jazz's direction. Jazz had felt guilty that he'd never told Howie about his father's true occupation, that he'd never managed to reveal the dark secret of his upbringing before the rest of the world found out. But like the children of alcoholics and the victims of abuse, Jazz had been a master at compartmentalizing. That, combined with Billy's persistent brainwashing and total control, meant Jazz had never uttered a peep to anyone.

Howie never let that get between them. That meant something. For Jazz it meant everything.

He stared into the moonlit murk of the field. The moon was only a tiny bit smaller than it would have been when the killer dumped Jane Doe here. Jazz was seeing the scene the way the killer had, which was important.

No one but us ever sees it like this, Billy said. The occasion was Jazz's seventh birthday, and Dear Old Dad had decided to take his son to work. Jazz sat in the Jeep while Billy finished killing his thirty-ninth victim—a schoolteacher named Gail Clinton—in an abandoned restroom in a public park in Madison, Wisconsin. Then, when he'd finished disjointing her corpse (for victims thirty-five through forty-two, Billy went through a phase where he liked repositioning the body with the limbs in interesting and varied positions that required separating them at the joints), he brought Jazz in and walked him through the crucial steps necessary to remove evidence that would lead the cops ("the bastard cops," Billy always called them) back to him. *No one ever sees it like this,* he'd explained. *They try to imagine how we see it, but we can't let them. So we leave false clues sometimes. And we never let 'em into our heads. Got it? 'Cause our heads belong to us, to us and no one else. Now go hand Daddy that garbage bag like a good boy, will ya?*

There were no false clues here. No clues at all. The cops had walked at least half a mile in a grid pattern to search for evidence. They'd come up empty-handed. Locard was a smart guy, but out in a field like this, the exchange of evidence could mean a thread from the killer's pants clinging to and blending in with a tall weed. It was worse than looking for a needle in a haystack.

"Mind telling me what we're looking for?" Howie asked. "Maybe I can help."

"I'm trying to think like the killer," Jazz admitted after a moment, a bit frustrated that he was having trouble doing just that. "The most important thing is to figure out how the guy entered or left the scene. If he was smart, he did both the same way. Easier to keep from leaving evidence that way."

"Look!" Howie's voice broke with excitement and he pointed. "A footprint! And oh my God—there's another one!"

Jazz shook his head. "Those are from the cops. They tried to be careful, but the ground was soft when they got here."

"So maybe the killer guy left footprints," Howie said, sulking a little bit.

"Cops didn't find any. Makes sense. He would have been here before sunup. This time of year, the ground would be too hard at night from the cold." To illustrate, he pointed to the path he and Howie had taken—there were no footprints from their own shoes.

Howie sniffed. "Well, if it's that cold, she could have been out here for days. Or weeks."

"Nah, it's not *that* cold yet. Animals and bacteria can devour every scrap of flesh in a month. She didn't even have flies on her yet. She was fresh.

"So he came here at night," Jazz went on, thinking aloud. "If you were coming here at night, which direction would *you* come from?"

Howie pointed. "Back the way we came. Duh. It's the easiest way."

"Yeah, but it's only the easiest way because we know about it. We grew up around here, so we know about the access road."

"So you're saying he couldn't have come that way?"

Jazz shrugged. "I'm saying we can't assume it. But if he *did* come that way, it means something about him. It means he's

110

either a local or he scouted Lobo's Nod and this field for a long time before he did this."

"Whoa. You think he's someone in town? Someone we know? What are the odds?"

He meant the odds of a town the size of Lobo's Nod having two resident serial killers, of course. Jazz was no math whiz, but he figured those odds to be something like a jillion to one, to be technical about it. Jazz ignored Howie for a moment and crept forward in the dark until he found the spot he was looking for. He glanced over his shoulder; only twenty yards away, in the direction he now looked, he had hidden and watched the cops the day before. He was now standing exactly where Deputy Erickson had been standing then, unaware that Jazz was observing him. Erickson, Jazz realized now, had had the best view of the entire crime scene as the investigators worked.

"Maybe he just scouted the area," Jazz said. "The access road isn't on any maps, but maybe it shows up on Google Earth or something. I didn't notice before; I'll have to check."

"No one knows her, so she's not from around here," Howie said. "He killed her somewhere else and just dumped her here in the Nod. The highway's thataway." He pointed off to their left. "And the farmhouse is thataway"—to the right now— "so you know he didn't come from *that* direction. So it makes sense he'd be driving by on the highway, see this nice empty field, and think, *Oh, cool—I'll leave the body there.* Right?"

Jazz blinked. Of course. He was an idiot. The answer was in front of him the whole time!

"He came up the hill," he whispered.

"What?"

Still crouched, Jazz pointed down the grade, past the flat spot where the body had been found, to a slightly steeper grade that rolled down to a copse of trees. "This guy is no dummy. He knew the cops would make two assumptions, just like you did. That he came from the highway or from the access road. Look—from here you can see where the cops did their grid search, and they only came *up* the hill to the left and toward you and me. Because that's where the roads are, and that's where it's easiest. Path of least resistance. When you're carrying a dead body, do you want to carry it up a hill or down a hill?"

"Me, personally?" Howie asked. "I usually carry all my corpses downhill. Easier on the back."

"Right. That's like Forensics 101—body-dumpers go downhill. But this guy..." Jazz stood up and clapped his hands together. "I guarantee you he came *up* the hill from those trees. Because he knew the cops wouldn't think to look there. Come on."

They loped down the grade in a circular pathway that avoided contaminating the crime scene. "I can't imagine carrying a body up this hill," Howie complained. "I would have just burned it up. Why didn't he just burn it?"

"Are you kidding? A crematorium gets up to fifteen hundred degrees for two hours, and bones and teeth *still* survive. Billy learned that one the hard way. Tried burning his tenth victim. Didn't go well."

"What about that lime stuff? Dissolve it."

"Quicklime? Takes a long time. And you need a lot of it. And while it's happening, the body can get dehydrated and might actually end up preserved, not dissolved. So there's no guarantee you can get rid of the body. Your best bet is to make sure you've removed all connections from it to you."

"Well, now I know who to call if I ever need to get rid of a body," Howie said. At the bottom of the hill, he paused and looked ahead at the trees. "This doesn't make sense. How would he get into the trees in the first place? There's no road. There's no—"

"I don't know how," Jazz said, his voice rising in excitement as they took off running across the field under the light of the moon. "He just did. I know he did!" His heart thrummed with something more than the exertion of running. Something deeper. More primal. He didn't know what it was, not yet, but he liked it.

In moments, they'd crossed the tree line. Jazz warned Howie to be careful, playing a flashlight beam along the ground and up the trunks of trees. Howie complained until Jazz gave him a flashlight, too, and soon the two of them were creeping along through the trees, picking out roots and moss and shrubbery with their flashlights. Suddenly, Jazz stopped dead in his tracks and motioned for Howie to stop, too, hissing, "Ssshh! Don't say anything!"

"I *didn't* say anything!" Howie argued.

"You just did."

"Yeah, because *you* said—"

"Just shut up and listen!" Jazz waved his hand manically for emphasis and Howie shut up. They both strained, leaning into the air, listening.

"Do you hear it?" Jazz whispered.

"Hear what? All I hear is the creek. What do you hear, Super-Hearing Guy?"

"Exactly. The creek." A grin split Jazz's face. He shined his light right in Howie's face so he could see the expression when the facts collided in Howie's head. "Where does the creek lead?"

"Lead?" Howie frowned. Like most kids in the Nod, he'd played in and around these fields when he was younger. "Doesn't *lead* anywhere. It cuts through the farm and goes west to ... Oh." Howie's jaw dropped. "Holy ... It goes to the highway!"

The creek in question—no more than thirty yards from where they stood—ran across the farm property east to west, passing under the highway and then petering out to a trickle. The killer could have left his car along the highway late at night when no one from Lobo's Nod would be on the roads, then carried Jane Doe through the creek to the trees, then up the hill to dump her body. The water was no more than a foot high at the creek's greatest depth. Would it be easy work? Not at all. But serial killers tended to be dedicated types, real overachievers. Wading the creek would leave less of a scent for dogs (if the cops ever got this far), and trace evidence would just be washed away or dissolved. Put Jane Doe in a plastic bag, and she would even bob along in the water a little without getting wet. When it was time to leave, he would go back the same way he'd come. It was a pretty decent plan.

"This guy is a hell of an organized killer," Jazz said as they walked. "He thought of everything. Didn't leave anything behind he didn't want found."

"So we can't learn anything about him."

"We can always learn something. Even if there's nothing there, that still tells us something. Disorganized killers go nuts and leave all kinds of evidence. So we can assume things about them. Organized killers don't leave evidence, but that tells us something about their personalities. Like our guy. He's highly organized. Probably firstborn or an only child. Probably had a decent relationship with his father. Stable. Did well in school, but most likely dropped out."

"He's starting to sound like your dad," Howie said.

Jazz laughed. "Pretty sure Dear Old Dad is still locked up. I think we would have heard if he was out." Jazz refused to communicate with Billy, but G. William made a point of calling once a month and confirming that—yes—Billy was still locked up in the penitentiary.

They reached the creek and rushed to explore its borders. Jazz wasn't so naive as to hope for footprints in the softer ground near the water, but he did see two or three spots that looked as though they'd been swept and brushed with leaves or branches. Had the killer entered or exited the water at one or more of these points, then covered up his tracks?

The faster thud of Jazz's heart told him yes. Yes, he had.

But there was nothing else to see. Jazz knew that—despite what Billy had taught him—there was really no such thing as a perfect crime or a perfect crime scene. Everyone left some clue, some trace, some trail to follow. Something. Maybe the cops would miss it, but that didn't mean it wasn't there. Jazz had something the cops didn't have, though. It went beyond just being able to think like a killer, though that was a big part of it.

Most natural thing in the world, his father's voice whispered from the past. *Cain slew Abel, all under God's eye.* One of those memories that wouldn't go away, no matter how much Jazz tried to make it. Rusty—poor Rusty—was long dead. Mom—poor Mom—was long gone. It was just Jazz and Billy and regular lessons in how to murder. Twelve years old, and Jazz was learning very well, learning blood-spatter patterns, learning anatomy, learning knives and garrotes and hammers and screwdrivers and more.

Standing perfectly still, he drew in a deep breath and tried to see the scene the way the killer would have. Tried to see it the way Billy would have. It wasn't difficult.

Good cover. Even during the day, you combine the tree cover with the remote location, and the odds of being seen are slim. A pain to haul her up that hill—even as tiny as she was, she was still dead weight—but worth it, to throw the cops off the trail. And before you go, you drop the middle finger there, you stick it to the cops, but you keep the other two because . . . Because they're small. Portable. Stick a finger in your pocket and no one will notice. "Say, is that a severed finger in your pocket, or are you just happy to see me?" Ho ho ho. But why keep two of them? Why—

"Hey, Jazz?" Howie said, a note of curiosity in his voice.

Jazz turned and aimed his flashlight at the sound. Howie was balanced precariously on some wet rocks jutting from the creek, stooping low to gaze into the water at his feet. Jazz bit his bottom lip and tried not to picture Howie slipping and cracking his skull. "Hey, be careful, okay?" He didn't want to imagine how quickly Howie would bleed out.

"When you said clues," Howie went on, ignoring him, "did you mean something like this?"

With that, Howie did the worst, stupidest thing he could do, reaching out between two rocks even as Jazz shouted, "Don't touch anything!"

But it was too late.

A moment later, Howie, with a puzzled expression on his face, offered a glittering *something* in one outstretched hand. "What? What did I do wrong?" he asked.

"It doesn't matter anymore," Jazz said, a little more grumpily than was probably necessary. Even seasoned cops occasionally screwed up and forgot or just plain ignored proper evidence-handling procedures. He picked his way through the soft dirt and wet rocks to Howie's side and shined his flashlight on Howie's hand. It was a ring. Jazz consoled himself that the water would probably have washed away any evidence or fingerprints, anyway. Still, it sucked that his first actual break in the case was now irrevocably contaminated.

"It looks like a kid's ring," Howie said. "It's so small."

"Not a kid's ring," Jazz said. He held out his hand and let Howie drop the ring into his palm. "It's hers. I bet it's a toe ring."

Howie growled. "Sexy!" Then he remembered who had owned the toe ring. "Oh, gross! Gross. Forget I said that."

Jazz held the flashlight at a new angle. The ring, a slender circle of slightly dull gold, had two channel-set stones adorning it. They might have been rubies or garnets...or just chips of red plastic. There was no way to tell right now.

"What does red mean?" Howie asked excitedly. "You said we need to understand the victim, right? So what does red tell us?"

"Probably nothing. Might be her birthstone. Or the birthstone of someone important to her. Or maybe she just liked the color red." He resisted the urge to throw the thing back into the creek. It was a clue, yes, but so far useless.

"There's some writing in it," Howie said, pointing. He had a different angle on the ring.

Sure enough, there were letters engraved along the inside of the band. Together, Jazz and Howie recited them as they tilted their flashlight beams back and forth in order to pick out the details of the engraving:

"Four-F-G-dash-D-R."

They looked at each other and then back down at the ring:

4FG-DR

"Well," Howie said after a long silence. "*That* explains everything, doesn't it?"

CHAPTER 10

The Impressionist unfolded the sheet of paper he kept in his pocket at all times. Right front pants pocket. All the time. That way, he always knew where it was.

He didn't really need the paper anymore. He had long since memorized its contents, not merely the words in the correct order, but also the particulars of the handwriting itself—the loops of the Os, the jagged slashes of the Fs and Ts. He was certain that, if called upon, he could reproduce the contents of the paper right down to the tiny stutter in the word *field*, the stutter where the pen had clogged for an instant and made a slight skip and an almost-imperceptible blotch on the paper before once again giving a smooth line.

The paper held the Impressionist's instructions. They were sacred to him. No matter how well he knew those instructions, he would never throw away that paper.

So far, he had followed his instructions precisely to the letter. With one exception, of course.

The boy.

Jasper Dent.

The next morning—Tuesday morning—the Impressionist sat in the Coff-E-Shop on Main Street in Lobo's Nod, thinking of wolves and sheep and sheep's clothing. Thinking of the Trojan horse.

Thinking, too, of his next victim.

He wondered—idly, for it did not matter greatly one way or the other—if the boy had found the ring yet. He had followed Jasper enough to puzzle out that the boy was running his own investigation beyond the sheriff's. The Impressionist wasn't particularly worried about either of them actually catching him. That just wouldn't happen. But he knew that the sheriff would never find the ring. Tanner was burned out after catching one serial killer and didn't have the chops to catch a second. Jasper might find the ring, but then what? Would he be able to decipher its meaning in time?

In the meantime, his next victim lived here in town. In fact, he could summon her now, easily, and did so with a single raised finger.

The waitress came to him, flashing him a quick, practiced smile. HELEN, her nametag read. Helen, he was sure, was thinking of nothing more than refilling his coffee. And then maybe retreating into the kitchen for a moment's respite before taking the orders of three college-age kids who'd just stumbled through the door with the air of demanding, hungover hunger.

"Thank you," the Impressionist said to her with great earnestness.

Her practiced smile widened into something a bit more

genuine—maybe this guy would be worth more of a tip than the usual cheapskates left.

The Impressionist, for his part, returned her smile, then watched her refill his coffee, watched the tendons in her forearm go taut, watched the bend of her wrist.

Watched her slender, elegant fingers on the handle of the carafe.

Her fingers.

Just noticing.

CHAPTER 11

That same morning, Jazz, running on only five hours' sleep, blew off both coffee with Howie and homeroom to return to the sheriff's office. It wasn't quite eight, and Lana hadn't come in yet for the morning shift. A lone deputy sat at a desk in a corner, mousing around on a website. Deputy Erickson was nowhere to be seen, which made Jazz gladder than he'd like to admit.

He walked past the empty receptionist's desk and straight back to G. William's office. G. William, an early riser, was always the first person in the office, and today was no exception.

"Where's the new guy?" Jazz asked as he barged in without knocking. "Figured he'd be an early bird, catching the worm, all that stuff."

"Even deputies get days off, Jazz," G. William said. "I'm willing to bet you're not here to check the man's time card, though."

"I figured it out," Jazz announced. He tossed a plastic sandwich bag on G. William's desk—he'd taped it shut and stuck a label on it recording where and when he'd found the toe ring.

G. William flicked a glance at the ring and then pushed it aside. "Little early in the morning for shenanigans, Jazz. Okay with you if I get my coffee first?"

"I figured out who Jane Doe is," Jazz said in disbelief, following G. William to the office's ancient coffee machine. It reeked of years of burned coffee. "Don't you care?"

G. William said nothing as he poured the day's first coffee into his cup. He said nothing as he took his first sip, winced so much his mustache quivered, then marched back into his office and planted himself behind his desk. And he *still* said nothing as he nursed a swallow of more coffee and finally held up the makeshift evidence bag, squinting at the ring within.

"I don't want to hear you tell me you went to the crime scene," G. William said. "In fact, if I hear you tell me that, I'll have to do official things, you read me?"

Jazz fidgeted for a moment, then said, "I was at the creek. On the Harrison property. That's not technically the crime scene. Although it should have been from the start." He couldn't keep a note of haughty disdain out of his voice.

The sheriff's eyes narrowed.

"Her initials are F.G.," Jazz said, determined to prove to G. William that he knew what he was doing. "The ring's inscription. It took me a while, but I figured it out. It looks like a code—Howie said it looks like a robot's name—but it's a dedication. 'For F.G., from D.R.' Weird to get a toe ring engraved, I guess, but it takes all kinds, right? You can do a cross-check on national databases for missing persons with the initials—"

"Her name's Fiona Goodling," G. William said in a flat tone.

123

"Went missing two weeks ago outside Atlanta. Boyfriend's name is Doug Reeve. Occasionally—if you let us use both hands *and* a flashlight—we poor, pathetic cops can find our own asses."

Jazz felt a shameful blush burn across both cheeks and touch as far back as his ears. "Oh," was all he could think of to say.

"She spent her summers teaching swim classes for kids at the YMCA, so she had to have a background check, finger-printing, the whole nine yards. I got the call from IAFIS last night at home. Was just about to call her family."

Jazz could still think of nothing to say. He'd been so convinced that he knew better than the cops what was going on, that he was the only one who could crack this case.

And now he felt... *withered* under G. William's glare. It was one thing to defy the sheriff, breach a crime scene, and inter-fere with an investigation if you were the only hope. It was another thing entirely when all you did was confirm what the cops already knew.

G. William stared at him, as if daring him to speak.

And Jazz decided that he wasn't afraid of G. William.

"Is Atlanta PD going to set up a task force? You'll need to be involved. You—"

"Jazz," G. William said in a not-unkind tone of voice. "You got serial killers on the brain, kid, and I understand that, but this isn't a serial killer."

"Cutting off the fingers—"

"Serial killers," G. William went on as if he hadn't been interrupted, "have well-defined comfort zones that they kill in. Jeopardy surfaces. No serial killer is going to kill a woman in

Atlanta and then drive her body all the way here to dump it. It's too far out of his home turf."

"Billy had a comfort zone the size of the country," Jazz snarled. "The size of the world. You should know that. You of all people."

The sheriff's expression hardened. Whatever reservoir of sympathy he had for Jazz, it wasn't deep enough to put up with that kind of back talk. "Her family will appreciate getting this back." He gestured to the toe ring. "And I'm warning you: Stay the hell out of my crime scenes."

"You have to go public. You have to leak that someone saw something that night. Force the guy to come in and give some excuse for why he was seen there. That's how you—"

"Don't tell me my business!" G. William thundered, rising from his chair. His face went from white to red to purple in less than a second. "Don't you dare tell me! Not when it comes to this!"

Jazz backed up to the door. "There will be more killings," he said as darkly as he knew how.

For Billy Dent's son, that was pretty dark. G. William seemed visibly shaken. "I gave you a warning. Heed it. And isn't today a school day?"

Jazz opened his mouth to speak, but knew that whatever he said would be lost on G. William, so instead he left.

Jazz got to school halfway through first period and tried to persuade the assistant principal that he'd had car trouble and couldn't make it on time. Usually he could charm his way into or out of just about anything, but this morning he was rattled and off his game. And the bags under his eyes gave him away—the assistant principal gave him a "Nice try" and sent him off to second period (the bell had rung by then) with an admonition not to "stay up partying all night." If only she'd known what Jazz had really been doing the night before.

He saw Howie in the hallway and told him what G. William had said, but now that they had the victim's name, "Jane Doe" was old news to him. "I just wanna know when my new tattoo happens, man."

Oh. Right. Jazz's skin was already crawling at the thought of it. "I'm sorta busy right now, Howie. Maybe next week."

He grumbled and growled his way through school. Connie tried to soothe him, but he was having none of it. "I got out-investigated by G. William," he told her at lunch. They were outside on the front lawn of the school, huddled under a tree together for shade from the fall sun. It was late October, just chilly enough that the lawn was sparsely populated and they had privacy. "That's bad enough. But he still doesn't believe me when I say it's a serial killer."

"First of all," she told him, offering him a grape, which he accepted, "look at it this way: He's got the whole world of law enforcement behind him, and you just had Howie, but you still kept up with him. Second of all, I am still going to kick your butt for going out and doing something that stupid after you said you wouldn't. Third of all, maybe he's right— maybe you're too quick to think it's a serial killer. Which makes perfect sense," she added. "And fourth of all," she finished, "I'm going to kick your butt for going out like that last night after you said you wouldn't."

"You said that twice."

"Then I will kick your butt twice."

But she really got angry when he told her that he couldn't come to play practice. The school had a very strict policy: Students who missed a day or part of a day without an excuse could not participate in extracurricular activities that same day. Jazz was forbidden to attend rehearsal.

Ginny found him in the hallway just as school was ending and cornered him. She was a tiny thing, barely five feet tall, but her acting training gave her an outsized presence. "Jasper! Do you remember the first day of auditions?"

"Uh, yes." He looked around for a way out. There was none. "I guess Connie ratted me out?"

"Don't try to distract me. Do you remember when I said that being in this play was a commitment, that it was a commitment to me and to your fellow actors and to yourself?"

"Sure do." He had a vague recollection.

"Then why are you letting me down today? Why are you letting your castmates down? Most important of all, why are you letting yourself down?"

Jazz groaned inside. Guilt trips rarely worked on him, but he knew what was expected of him, so he played his part.

"I'm really sorry," he said. "But look—I've been off-book longer than anyone else. I'm not going to lose anything between today and tomorrow."

"It's not about that, Jasper. It's about you living up to your word. It's about you being there for the other people in the play, who are counting on you."

"I'm really sorry," Jazz said again, this time ramping up the sincerity. He had more important things to do than bang swords with Ginny Davis and her teeny, tiny anger. She was such a comical figure that Jazz almost wanted to pick her up by the waist and bob her up and down in the air, cooing, *Who's angry? Who's the angriest widdle one?*

"It won't happen again," he promised, throwing out the most earnest, defeated, wounded expression in his arsenal.

She melted in an instant, holding out her arms. Jazz froze. There was just no way in the world he would let her hug him.

And then Ginny took advantage of his paralysis and threw her arms around him, squeezing him tight.

And he felt...

Everything.

He was acutely aware of the pressure and the presence of her body, of the tickle of her curly hair just under his nose, of the small, firm, outthrust breasts against his lower rib cage.

Of the smell of her.

More than that, though, he was aware of the fragility of her. Of her breakability. He thought of his gloved hands at Fiona Goodling's neck, of the killer's gloved hands, of Billy's gloved hands, of trophies and fingers and knives.

He was terrified of sex.

Like every teenage boy, he was obsessed with it, of course, and wanted to have as much of it as humanly possible as soon as humanly possible, but unlike every teenage boy, he couldn't let himself. The very thought of it absolutely petrified him. Sex was like lighter fluid for people like him. Connie was safe because...

Well, Connie was safe, but Ginny felt warm and perfect and *vulnerable*—

"I'm sorry I had to be so rough on you," she said, backing away, utterly unaware of what she'd done to him. "Don't be late tomorrow, okay?"

Escaping school—and Ginny Davis's clutches—Jazz stood in the parking lot for a few minutes, clearing his head before he dared get behind the wheel. As he headed home, he ran down a mental to-do list. He had to find a way to prove to G. William that Fiona Goodling (and how strange it felt not to think of her as Jane Doe any longer) was the victim of a serial killer. He couldn't explain how or why he was so sure—he just was. Those missing fingers... Leaving the middle finger. Taking the others... It sounded like something Billy might have come up with. It was impertinent. It was rude.

Jazz suddenly slammed on the brakes. Fortunately, he'd turned down a side street with no traffic, so no one was around. Except for the guy lurking on the street corner.

Jeff Fulton.

Jazz couldn't believe it was a coincidence and, sure enough, Fulton came running up to the driver's side of the Jeep, waving his hands like he was trying to land a jet with semaphore flags. Take off? Stick around? Jazz kept his foot on the brake, but left the Jeep in drive so he could make a quick getaway.

He rolled down the window to the sound of Fulton gasping for breath.

"I'm glad I caught you," he managed. "Been waiting there,

figuring you'd drive by on your way from school. I know how this must look—"

"Are you stalking me, Mr. Fulton?" The idea both amused and horrified Jazz.

"What? No! God, no." Fulton's whole face twisted into a freakish paroxysm of guilt and shock, as though the very thought of such a notion had made him relive every lemon he'd ever bitten into in his life. "I just need to talk to you. Please, Jasper. I'm begging you."

"Mr. Fulton, I really can't help you."

"But there's a website out there. For your father's victims. And on the discussion board, someone said that there's a rumor that your father used to tell you everything. And I just have one question, just a single question. You don't know how much this would mean to me. Please."

Jazz's spine went rigid. He knew about the website— www.dentedlives.com—where victims' groups and families shared details, information, anger, and sympathy. As part of the deal that had spared him from the death penalty, Billy Dent had agreed to release information about his victims at rigorously specified times, though he hadn't said *which* victims he would talk about at those times. As a result, every six months the website erupted with a flurry of posts and discussion, as the newest details of Billy's depravities came to light.

Worse yet, of course, was that Billy *had* told Jazz a lot about his victims. Those stories became twisted bedtime yarns told to Jazz each night: The Sad Story of the Girl Who Tried to Get Away. The Guy Who Stopped Too Soon. The Woman with the Knife Who Didn't Use It. These tales and more—over a hundred of them—jam-packed Jazz's childhood brain like a sick volume of fairy tales. Only the pages had been shredded and then taped back together in some random, haphazard way, such that Jazz could recall a welter of vile images, conjure a lifetime's worth of gore and sickness, but most of it without context. A psychiatrist who had examined him during his brief stay with Social Services had diagnosed him with a peculiar variety of post-traumatic stress disorder. He could remember finding human teeth in his father's nightstand at the age of seven, for example, but he couldn't remember where those teeth had come from. All he remembered was finding the teeth and—with a child's innocence—playing with them like dice, not even realizing there was anything wrong with it, as though he could visit a friend's house and find the same thing in a random cupboard or drawer.

Furthermore, Billy hadn't given him all the details of his kills, particularly when it came to the deeper sexual aspects of his murderous compulsions. Make no mistake—Billy Dent did not merely kill his victims. He tormented them. Tortured them. Raped them and abused them. But he had his own notions of what Jazz needed to know. For some things, he claimed, Jazz needed no guidance: "You have to figure out what works for *you*, son. You have to find your own way."

News magazines and cable TV channels deluged him regularly with offers to tell "his story," to offer "his side" to the world. But Jazz didn't have a "side." He just had a seriously messed-up childhood and a tossed salad of memories that wouldn't help anyone.

"I can't do anything for you, Mr. Fulton. I really can't."

"Just one question. Please. Do you need money? I can give you money. Not much, but—"

"Stop it, Mr. Fulton! Please." He couldn't even look at the pathetic sight; he stared into the rearview mirror, hoping someone would pull up and honk him into action, but the side street remained empty.

"The police report said she was gagged," Fulton said, now returned to a standing position, leaning into the window so far that Jazz could feel the man's breath on his neck. "But the coroner thinks the gag had to have been removed before she died. So I'm just asking, please, did your father... Did your father ever tell you her last words? I just want to know."

Oh, God.

Jazz shut his eyes tight. Was this man insane? Did he have any idea—any idea at all—what the likely answer to that question was? That the odds favored her last words being something like *Ohgodpleasenojesuspleasenonononooooooooooo!*

"I can't help you," he whispered. It was the truth: He had no idea what Harriet Klein's last words were, and he wasn't about to guess.

"Did he keep any kind of a journal or anything? Something you kept from the police, maybe? I promise you—I promise on my daughter's grave—I won't tell anyone. I just want to look. To see."

Jazz took a deep breath and slowly blew it out. He turned to Fulton, whose eyes had become more sunken, whose face had become more creased. "Mr. Fulton, I can't help you. Please leave me alone. I'm going to hit the gas now, so please step back."

132

With a whimper of defeat, Fulton stepped back. Just as Jazz rolled the window up, though, he said one last thing, one thing that cut into Jazz like an Arctic wind: "Didn't you ever lose anything?" Fulton spat, his voice full of anguish and spite. "Someone who mattered? Even a pet? Didn't you ever care?"

Jazz slammed down on the gas and took off down the road.

The memory of Fulton's voice and enraged eyes spun and whirled in the confines of the Jeep as Jazz drove. *Didn't you ever care? Didn't you ever care?*

I care! Jazz thought fiercely. *I care!*

He cared so much that at first he'd considered getting in touch with as many victims as possible. Maybe setting up some kind of charity or fund, where he could be the figurehead and attract contributions that way. Do some sort of good deed to prove to himself and the world that he wasn't a monster waiting to happen.

But Billy had done good deeds all the time. So had John Wayne Gacy, and dozens of others. It didn't matter. It was all part of the disguise. Jazz realized that he couldn't trust even his noblest impulses. They might not be genuine. They might just be camouflage.

Even the one truly good thing he'd done in his life—rescuing Howie from those bullies all those years ago—was tainted. Billy had been outraged when the parents of the bullies complained to him about their kids' injuries: "You shoulda just killed 'em, son. We could have gotten rid of the bodies and then I wouldn't have to deal with this. Kill 'em and dump 'em. But no. You had to go and beat them up and make them go cry to their mommies, so now I gotta go and put on my civilized face and pacify these witches."

And there were the urges. The feelings. The memories. The things that he'd been taught and then forgotten, but that lurked somewhere in his brain's basement, ready to strike like stalkers in the night. The Social Services shrink had told Jazz to be prepared, to be on guard for "emergent memories"—memories thought forgotten that could, unbidden, resurface at any time, without warning.

If memories could resurface...couldn't other things, too? Needs? Drives? Desires?

Urges?

Technically, seventeen was too young to diagnose someone as a sociopath. Psychiatrists liked to wait until eighteen to make the diagnosis, so in a technical sense it was impossible for Jazz to be one. But he knew there was no magical switch that would be thrown on his eighteenth birthday to determine who and what he was. Age didn't matter—a kid named Craig Price had started a serial killing career at the age of thirteen. Thirteen years old and he was out there murdering, with a lot less preparation than Jazz had.

The dice had already been tossed, the cards shuffled and drawn. He was what he was, whether he knew it yet or not. Maybe he was just a guy with a crazy dad, like other kids with crazy dads.

Or maybe he was something else.

CHAPTER 12

He knew he should go home—Gramma would be waiting—
but Fulton had put ideas in his head that made him feel poi-
sonous. Radioactive. He couldn't abide the nearness of other
people just then, so instead he peeled off from town and
headed for the Hideout.

One of the benefits of growing up in a small town in the middle of nowhere that had seen its best days decades ago, Jazz
had learned, was that there was a lot of abandoned property
to be taken advantage of. This was, he admitted, something
he'd learned from Billy. After all, Billy had killed two natives
of Lobo's Nod and managed to stay out of G. William's sights
for six months before the sheriff finally added up the right col-
umns and arrived at the inescapable conclusions that led him
to the Dent house. Billy was no stranger to the lost byways and
forgotten vistas of the Nod, and he'd taught his son their im-
portance.

Jazz had stumbled upon the Hideout—an old, ramshackle
moonshining hut from the looks of it, eighty years old if it was

a day—a year earlier. Through good fortune, it sat in a copse of neglected spruce and pine, so it was hidden year-round even though it wasn't more than a quarter of a mile from the nearest road. It struck him as a good place to be alone and to think, so he'd made some desultory repairs and declared it his own private hideaway. Since he didn't have a cell phone, it was as isolated as he could get without hitching a dogsled and making for the North Pole.

About six months ago, he'd come to the frightening realization that this was pretty much textbook serial killer behavior. "LESSON ONE: FIND A RUN-DOWN OLD SHACK OUT IN THE WOODS WHERE YOU CAN PLAN YOUR CRIMES AND BRING YOUR VICTIMS WITHOUT ANYONE KNOWING."

So he'd told Connie about it, and she occasionally joined him there, which made him feel a little less... Billy.

He made a beeline for it now, needing to be alone. Inside, he didn't bother to turn on the lanterns or even to pull back the makeshift window blind, preferring instead to sit in the dark. The Hideout wasn't any bigger than ten feet to a side, its walls rough stone tarred over in an effort to keep out the rain and the bugs. Jazz had hauled in a pair of old barstools and a beanbag chair last summer, and now he flopped down on the latter.

He flipped open his wallet. Flipped past the picture of Connie, past the photo from the school carnival last month, Howie draping his mile-long arms over Connie's and Jazz's shoulders. They all smiled at the camera, and it shocked Jazz every time he saw himself happy.

The only other picture in the wallet was of his mother.

Yeah, Mr. Fulton. Yeah, I've lost someone. Yeah, I've cared.

This was the original—the one on his bedroom wall in the eighty-third position was a blown-up copy. After Mom had gone away/disappeared/vanished/been *murdered*, Billy had ransacked the house, gathering up every trace of her and burning it all in a massive bonfire. This picture, which Jazz had kept tucked under his pillow as a child, had survived. It was all he had.

Sociopaths don't care about anyone but themselves, or so the literature says. So if he cared about his mother (or her memory, at least), and if he cared about Connie and Howie, then didn't that mean . . . ?

But no. It wasn't that simple. Sociopaths could have pets and treat them quite well. They could even be married and carry on a facsimile of an emotional relationship. (Serial killers also tended to be pack rats, something Jazz tried not to think about when he considered the old junk piled around the Hideout.)

The question for Jazz was this: Did he really care for Connie and Howie, or did he just think he did? It was the oldest philosophical question in the book—how do I know that what I see as blue and what you see as blue are the same thing?

Answer: We don't. We take it on faith.

Would a true sociopath worry about things like this—if the caring was real? And then worry about the worrying about it? He didn't have an answer, but he also knew that sociopaths worried about all kinds of things. Billy had been obsessed with keeping his lawn neatly trimmed, convinced that the entire town of Lobo's Nod was gossiping about him if the grass became at all unruly. Why the man who'd killed one hundred and twenty-four innocents should care about small-town gossip, Jazz didn't know. But that didn't stop Billy.

Jazz sat on the beanbag chair, staring at the photo for more than an hour, time passing without his awareness. A sound outside made him jump up just in time to see Connie inch open the door and peer in.

"I thought you'd be here," she said.

"Still angry?" he asked as she came in.

"No." She hugged him. "Forgiven."

"But not forgotten."

"I don't forget anything. Don't know how."

He nodded. Fair enough. "I just wanted to help the cops. I still think it's a serial killer. G. William is wrong. And more people are going to die."

"It's not your job to take care of that. It's his. Let him do it. What *is* that?" she asked, backing away as Jazz's wallet—still out and in his hand—poked at her.

"Nothing. Just—"

She took it from him again and it fell open to the picture of his mother. Connie fixed him with her most withering stare.

He relented, not because of the stare, but because it was just easier. He told her about the second meeting with Fulton. "And it just made me think of ... things," he finished lamely.

"What things?" By now they had both sunk into the beanbag chair, Connie curled into his lap, her head resting on his chest. Her hair tickled his nose. He felt himself respond to her weight in his lap the only way a teen boy *should* respond.

"You know. The usual things."

And then, for some reason he couldn't name, he told her something he'd never told her before. He told her about the dream, the nightmare. The knife. The voices.

Most girls, Jazz knew, would have been creeped out. Creeped right out the door, in fact. Right out of his life. Connie just squeezed his hand tight and gazed at him steadily.

"It doesn't have to mean anything. It's a dream."

"I have it all the time."

"The way you grew up, I'm surprised it's that tame."

He hesitated, then told her what *really* worried him. "What if it's not just a dream?"

She looked at him blankly.

"I mean..." His jaw tightened, but he went on. "I mean, what if I'm dreaming about something that actually happened?"

"Jazz..."

"What if my father actually put a knife in my hand? What if he took it out of the sink—"

"Jazz..."

"—and put it in my hand and made me—"

"Jazz, it didn't—"

"—made me *cut* someone, told me it was like cutting *chicken*, and made me—"

"Stop doing this to yourself. Stop it."

But he couldn't. He'd held it back too long, and now it wouldn't stop gushing. He'd nicked some sort of memory artery and the blood was spraying everywhere.

"What if it was my mother? What if that was her voice, and he made me cut my own mother? Made me *kill*—"

"Stop it!" She took his face in her hands. "Stop it. That did not happen, do you hear me? It didn't."

Miserably, he said, "Then how do I know what it feels like? In the dream, I know what it feels like to cut someone. If I've never done it, how could I know what it feels like so that I could dream it?"

Connie's eyes darted back and forth as she thought. Then she said, "People dream about stuff they've never done all the time. Like flying. Or having sex with a supermodel. Or driving a race car, or whatever. Maybe it's like the voice says. Maybe it's just like cutting chicken. You're just thinking of that, is all."

It destroyed him to kill the hope in her eyes. But he said, "I don't think that's it, Con."

"And if it's not? If you *did* cut someone?" She kissed him suddenly. Hard. Savagely. As if her lips could drive out the demons. Jazz let himself be swept away by it. Connie was safe. She was safe. She wasn't like the other girls. She was safe because—

"If you did cut someone," she went on, "it wasn't your fault. It wasn't because you wanted to. Someone made you. Billy made you. It wasn't your idea. You're not a psychopath."

"Sociopath. There's a difference."

"My apologies, mon. I did not mean to offend," she said in her best Tituba accent, one eyebrow arched.

He laughed in spite of himself; she could always make him laugh. But the mood lasted only seconds. Even if he turned out *not* to be a stone-cold killer like Dear Old Dad, he still was a guy with a brain-load of problems. One day she would get tired of him, grow sick of those problems, and leave him. So what was the point in—

She broke in as if she could read his mind: "Did you think when we met that I didn't know who you were? Just because I was new to town? Did you think I had no clue? I knew who you were when we first met. I knew who you were the first time we kissed. And it's not stopping me, and it's not *going* to stop me." She adjusted herself in his lap, grinding her butt into his groin in that special pleasant/painful way only the right girl's butt can grind.

Connie is safe. . . .

"The more you obsess over things, the worse they get. Let it all out. Let it all go." She made magical fairy dust–sprinkling gestures with her long, elegant fingers.

"It's not that easy."

"You know what you should do?"

"Don't say it."

"You should go see your father."

God. "Didn't I just say not to say it?"

She locked eyes with him. "Listen to me: It's a good idea. That guy Fulton, he wants closure, right? You can't give it to him. But it's the right idea. And Billy can give you your closure. For the things he made you do as a kid. The things you saw."

Jazz hadn't given her many details of exactly what life in the Dent house had been like, but he'd told her enough that she knew it wasn't hearts and flowers. Well, except for the occasional heart cut from a chest. And the kind of flowers you send to funerals.

He dumped her off his lap as gently as he could; he'd already gone numb enough that he wasn't even hard anymore. "You don't get it," he said, walking to the Hideout's only window. There was no glass, just a sheet of scratched-up, milky-fogged plastic Jazz had staple-gunned in place. He squinted, peering through it as best he could at the trees beyond that sheltered this little oasis from the rest of the world.

"Billy doesn't give closure. That's not his thing. He only started doling out details about his victims because his lawyers convinced him that was the only way to avoid the death penalty, and there's nothing more important in this world to Billy Dent than, well, Billy Dent. He's not taking a lethal injection for anyone. But he's not going to apologize to me for what he did, or anything like that. He isn't wired that way."

"He doesn't have to apologize." She came up behind him and wrapped her arms around him. "Just telling him how he's affected you—"

"No way." Jazz shivered at the thought of it. "The last thing you want in this world is to show weakness to him. Never. I can never go see him. Just doing it would give him the upper hand. You show any weakness to a serial killer and they live inside you after that."

"He's already living inside you," she whispered in a tone of regret. "Because you can't let go."

"Let go?" He exploded, spinning around. Connie jumped back. "Let go? He killed my mother!"

"You don't know that. Not for sure."

"Oh, I know it. One day she was there. The next day: *Poof.* Gone. And all of her stuff: Gone. Pictures: Gone. Like she never existed. He *erased* her, Con. Like she was a mistake on a notepad. That's all she was to him. *Poof.*"

"They would have found—"

"They would have found *nothing*," he spat. "Trust me on that one. There are ways to make a body disappear for good, and Billy knows them. It usually takes a while, but if you have the time, you can do it. With Mom, he would have had the time. She had no family—no one to miss her, other than Billy. Billy!" he said one last time, then turned to the window again, punching it with all his strength before he realized what he was doing.

The plastic—and his staple-gun work—held. His knuckles complained in a throbbing tempo that traveled up his arm.

"You're angry," Connie said quietly. "At her."

At *her*? At his mother? At the one good thing in his life?

"No. I'm not."

"Yeah, you are," she said confidently. "You're angry at your mother because she left you."

"She was murdered."

"That's still leaving you."

He laughed, the sound bitter to his ears. "Sometimes I think she got away. Well, I don't really think it, but I like to imagine it. I imagine that one day she realized what Billy was and she ran."

"See?" Connie said triumphantly. "You *are* angry. You think she escaped without you."

"Nah. That doesn't make me angry. It makes me *proud*."

"Proud that she abandoned a little boy? Are you nuts?"

He shrugged. "If she did get away, then good for her. She's

the only one who ever did. Most serial killers who are married never turn on their spouses, but she wouldn't really know that. So she ran. And I'm seriously not angry that she didn't take me. She saw her chance. She ran. She was probably so scared.... But that's just what I imagine sometimes. Deep down, I know the truth. She's dead. She's been dead a long time." He cradled his bruised hand. "And there's nothing left of her."

"Except you," Connie said. "This is why I forgive, but I don't forget. When you forget someone, the forgiveness doesn't mean anything anymore. So, let's say she left. Fine. You forgive her for that. Good. But you'll never, ever forget her."

He knew it was true. Even though there were days when he wished he could.

CHAPTER 13

Helen blinked rapidly, coming to as a man spoke to her. She was in chains, she realized, bound upright to a post. Gagged, with a rag stuffed in her mouth. It looked like she was in some kind of barn or outbuilding; shafts of dust-speckled sunlight slanted in through breaks in the beams overhead. So it was still daylight. That was something. Really bad things—truly awful, heinous things—didn't happen to people in broad daylight.

Did they?

The man was still speaking, rising from an old, battered chair. "Are you worried?" he asked, approaching her. "Are you scared?"

She didn't know what to do. She was still disoriented—she vaguely remembered going out into the alley to take out the trash from the Coff-E-Shop. And a man...Coming close...Offering to help...

And then a little pinprick and...

"Are you scared?" he asked again, sounding genuinely concerned.

Whatever drug he'd used on her was still blurring her vision. She tried to think as quickly as she could—what, oh what, was the best answer? Her friend Marlene had once told her that you have to humanize yourself to a rapist. Make yourself a real person, and they'll stop treating you like an object. Would that work?

It was the only shot she had. She nodded once, briefly, almost afraid to admit to being afraid.

"Shh, shh, shh," he told her, now within arm's length. "Don't be afraid. Don't." He reached into his pocket and made a show of unfolding a piece of well-worn paper. He scanned its contents quickly.

"I have this memorized, you know," he told her, his tone slightly jovial. "But I want to make sure I get it right. You know how it is."

She nodded fiercely, agreeing with him. Anything to get on his good side. Now that he was closer—and now that her vision was clearing—she could see him. Average. Boringly average. Maybe a little familiar, but she saw so many faces every day at the shop....

Oh, God! She saw his face! Didn't they usually kill people who saw their faces?

"I know what you're thinking," he said soothingly. He grinned an aw-shucks grin. "You're thinking that since you've seen my face, I have to kill you, right?" He *tsk*ed. "Don't worry about *that*. I have a pretty common face. My own mother used to lose me in the supermarket all the time." He chuckled, and she wanted to chuckle along with him, *burned* to chuckle along with him. But she had a rag stuffed in her mouth.

"Now then, down to business," he said, consulting the paper once more. "Your name is Helen Myerson, right?" Before she could answer, he held up her purse by the shoulder strap. "Remember, I can check your driver's license, so no lying. Helen Myerson?"

She nodded.

"And you are, in fact, a waitress, right?"

Another nod.

"Excellent!" He smiled at her and even dropped a friendly wink, then refolded the paper and returned it to his pocket. "I'm going to pull down your gag now and take that nasty rag out of your mouth. I'm not going to do that thing where I say, 'Don't scream or you'll be sorry.' Because you know what, Helen? You go ahead and scream if you want to. It won't bother me at all, and no one will hear you, so I don't care. So if it makes you feel better, you just go ahead and do it."

She considered calling his bluff and hollering her head off as the gag came down and the rag came out, but she found herself too terrified to scream.

"Really?" he said. "Nothing? Not going to scream? Well, that's okay. Whatever works for you." He sighed and jammed his hands in his pockets and looked at her with a sort of lopsided smile on his face, as though he wasn't quite sure what he was doing there or what she was doing there or how either of them had gotten there in the first place.

"Do you know what an impressionist is, Helen?" he asked suddenly.

Her lips had gone dry and she wet them before speaking. The sound of her own voice surprised her—it sounded deep

147

and foreign. "It's . . . Isn't it . . ." She took a deep breath. Insane, but maybe if she answered his questions, he'd let her go. She'd heard crazier things. "It's someone who does impressions of other people." For a moment he said nothing, so she added, "Right?"

He grinned and clapped his hands together. "Ha! Well. Yes. Yes, I suppose so. But you know, Helen, that's sort of cheating, isn't it? 'An impressionist is someone who does impressions.' Sort of like saying, 'An actor is someone who acts.' Or 'A worker is someone who works.' Using the word to define itself. But that's all right. I'm gonna give you . . . let's say half-credit. Because that was about half the answer I wanted. And that's all right. Don't worry. Your grade on this quiz doesn't really matter."

With that, he meandered over to a table off to his left, an old rickety set of nailed-together planks that had gone halfway to rot. It was positioned just so that she couldn't quite see what he was doing over there.

"What are . . ." she started, then stopped. Was this smart? She didn't know, but she couldn't stop herself. "What are you going to do? To me?"

"You don't need to worry about that," he told her, his voice soothing again. He was rummaging around on the table; she heard a slight *clink* of metal on metal. "Remember before, how I asked if you were afraid? And you said you were?"

"Yes."

He came back from the table, his hands clasped behind his back as though he were taking a stroll. "Well, Helen, there's no need to be afraid. None at all. You know why?"

Relief washed over her. He was smiling again. *No need to be afraid. None at all.* His exact words.

"Because you're going to let me go?" she asked.

"In a sense," he told her. "But there's no reason to be afraid because in the end, it's not going to help you one damn bit." He leaned in close and brought up his hand. She saw a needle there, filled with something bright blue, and her breath left her.

"Helen, I have to be honest with you now. This is going to hurt. It's going to hurt a lot."

She went ahead and screamed. True to his word, he didn't care at all.

CHAPTER 14

After a while, Jazz knew he had to get going, no matter how tempting it was to stay in the Hideout with Connie forever. Gramma would be waiting.

He sped home, only to find his grandmother sprawled on the floor in front of the battered old TV, watching the Home Shopping Network with her chin in her hands, laughing her head off as if it were the latest sitcom.

"Four payments of $18.99 each!" she chortled. "Oh, Lord! Oh, Lordy!" She rolled to one side, held her flank, and laughed and laughed and laughed. "Supplies are limited, they say! Jasper, did you hear that? Oh, Lord!"

"This is the funniest thing I've seen in a while," he admitted as she giggled like a teenager. "How about some dinner?"

"Ate already," she said between gasps. "She brought me some of that fried chicken I like. From the Kentucky place."

She? Jazz had a sinking feeling, one that was rewarded when he went into the kitchen and found Melissa Hoover there, washing dishes in the sink.

"Hello, Jasper," she said over one shoulder. "I'll be done in a minute."

She'd come by again, and this time found Gramma in a better mood. Fried chicken—the crispier and greasier the better—was a great bribe. Smart enough to park her car down the road somewhere and walk so that Gramma wouldn't hear the engine, look out the window, and have time to go for the shotgun. Smarter than Jazz had given her credit for. He adjusted his perception of her threat level accordingly.

And that meant no more Mr. Nice Guy. He wasn't going to let Social Services kick him out of his own house, and if Melissa Hoover was tougher than he thought, then it was time for him to get tough with her.

"What the hell do you think you're doing?" he exploded, slapping a palm against the refrigerator door for good measure. Melissa, gratifyingly, jumped. She actually *jumped* in shock and fear, spinning around, the water still running, her hands covered in suds.

"You think you can just come in here?" Jazz stage-whispered, pitching his voice low and scary. "That is a sick woman in there. She's afraid of change, of people."

"She was fine," Melissa assured him. "She was so friendly—"

"Of course she was friendly. You brought her a bucketful of heart attack." He snorted scornfully and knocked over the bucket of chicken, which sat on the kitchen table. A drumstick rolled out.

"It won't hurt anything just once—"

"Where are you gonna be tonight when she's complaining about stomach cramps because you fed her that crap? Are you gonna stick around to change her sheets and wash her up when she has diarrhea?"

Melissa folded her arms over her chest. "It's that bad, then? What else are you keeping from me? Her last report indicated that her health was pretty good. Is she faking the paperwork? Are you?"

Jazz laughed as snottily as he could. "Please. She's just old. Old people have gut problems."

"You're proving my point. You need to be out of this house. You're seventeen. You should be living a life, not taking care of her."

Deep down, Jazz knew that she was right. Deeper down, he knew it didn't matter.

"Why are you so obsessed with me, Melissa? There have to be kids out there worse off than I am. Go work your mojo on them."

"I'm trying to help you, which you would see if you weren't so stubborn."

"You're wasting your time. I'm doing fine. In nine months I'll be eighteen, and then you can't stop me from taking care of her. Just because you couldn't have kids of your own doesn't mean I need you to be my mommy."

Bang. It was the meanest, cruelest thing Jazz could have said to her. He'd been keeping it in reserve for just such an occasion, when he would need Melissa blinded by sudden emotion.

And it worked. Melissa's entire demeanor changed, from hard-charging to shocked and hurt. He glared at her, then counted to ten in his head before ramping up the intensity of his stare. It was no contest; he'd learned intimidation from the best.

"Fine," she said after an unnerving moment. "Fine." She grabbed her purse from a kitchen chair. "Don't think this is over, though. I'm coming back. I know what's right for you, and it's my job to make it happen."

With a quick, angry stride, she made for the back door. Jazz grabbed her wrist before she could wrestle the old, stuck door open. "Melissa," he said as contritely as he could.

"What?" She was annoyed, a tiny bit cowed, but she wasn't shaking off his hand.

"I'm sorry I was so...overwrought. I shouldn't have raised my voice. I shouldn't have said what I said."

When she looked over her shoulder, he cast his eyes downward in shame.

Heard her inhale.

"You're going through things no one should go through. Especially not alone." She patted his hand with her free one. "Get some rest. We'll talk again soon."

He let her go and watched her wend her way through the shrubbery that shrouded the side of Gramma's house. *See, I really don't need the extra acting practice, Ginny.* When Melissa thought about this encounter later—and she would, probably home alone in her tiny little studio apartment above the dry-cleaning place over in Calverton—she wouldn't focus so much on the anger he'd shown; she'd remember the apology more than anything else. If he could crack through her toughness and make her more pliable, more manipulable, she'd be an ally. She would be able to make his life much easier. And the cost was just breaking her soul.

Gramma stumbled into the kitchen from the other room, still laughing. "I think I peed myself. A little. Maybe. I think." Her eyes lit up. "Oh, look! Chicken! From Kentucky!"

"Knock yourself out, Gramma," Jazz said, turning the bucket in her direction. She scampered back to the TV with a wing in each hand. Despite what he'd told Melissa, his grandmother had—as near as he could tell—a cast-iron gut. Her brain only worked sporadically, but her bowels were as regular as a metronome no matter what she ate. Cholesterol? Fat? Jazz figured she'd survived eighty-two years on Planet Earth, forty of them with Billy Dent as her son. She deserved some fat and cholesterol.

"Hey, look!" Gramma shouted around a mouthful of fried skin. "Your daddy's on TV!"

Jazz didn't want to look, but he knew she would pester him until he did. She must have changed the channel. Some "news" channel was running one of a million "documentaries" about Billy Dent, rolling the same footage they all had: Billy Dent in handcuffs and a crisp gray suit, walking up the courthouse steps with a phalanx of lawyers around him.

A portentous voice-over announced: "Dr. Perry Shinkeski thinks Dent is a new kind of serial killer, what he calls a 'super-serial killer.'"

The video shifted to a mousy-looking man in a tweed jacket with enormous glasses and a self-satisfied little grin on his face as he spoke from behind a desk.

"Most, ah, serial killers," Shinkeski said, "have, ah, a single identity and signature that they, ah, rely on. Dent metamorphosed from, ah, one to another to another over a period of, ah, years, each one highly organized and highly capable."

Cut to a bottle-blond reporter showing way too much cleavage. "And is this typical, Doctor?"

Back to Shinkeski. "This, ah, is a new sort of, ah, psychopathology that we're only now beginning to, ah, understand. These, ah, super-serial killers have no, ah, 'type'"—he actually made air-quotes—"but, ah, rather consider everyone to be their 'type.'"

"Did you hear that?" Gramma gasped. "Your daddy's a *superhero*!"

Jazz wanted to bang his head against the wall. Better yet—put it through the television. Instead, he left her to the chicken and the TV, slipping into what had once been the den, when his grandfather had been alive. Nowadays it was dark and dusty, stacked high and tight with boxes of Grampa's old clothes and old books, all of which Gramma refused to part with. That pack-rat gene.

The room also had a phone extension with an ancient answering machine attached to it. (Gramma refused to get voice mail, claiming that the phone company could hear those messages, then edit them into new and disturbing forms.) The light was blinking. A couple of messages from Doug Weathers— "Your experiences, my words—it's gold, Jasper! We'll both be famous. Best thing that could happen around this town, and you know it."—were mixed in with messages from Melissa, her last one ending with "Well, I'm going to come over, then." There was an excellent chance she would call back tonight, so he took the phone off the hook and then went upstairs and dropped onto his bed. He just wanted to rest for a moment, but even though it wasn't yet nine o'clock, he fell asleep almost immediately.

Only to be awakened by a ceaseless pounding on the front door and his grandmother screaming, "They're here! They're here! They found us! Billy! Jon! Get the guns! Get the guns and blow their damn heads off before they take me away!"

"Jon" was Grampa Dent, dead twenty years except to Gramma's synapses.

Jazz rolled out of bed. It was past eleven, according to his bedside clock, and that pounding from downstairs wouldn't stop. Who would be banging away so late at—

Weathers. Of course. It was the only answer.

That's it, Jazz thought darkly as he stumbled into the hall and down the stairs. *I've decided on my first victim.*

Gramma was hiding in the shadow of the old grandfather clock, her trusty shotgun at the ready and aimed at the front door. "I'm usin' *God's* ammo!" she shouted. "Wallop your ass with the hellfire o' Jesus!"

The hellfire o' Jesus. That was new.

"I've got this one," Jazz assured her.

"You be careful, Billy," Gramma said, her eyes wild, her gums slack as she talked and slobbered bits of chicken. "You gotta bring a gun. And get your daddy."

Oh, great. He just *loved* when she thought he was Billy.

"I'm good," he told her. "I'm gonna kill 'em all with my thoughts."

Gramma cackled. "You hear that?" More pounding on the door. "He's gonna kill y'all with—"

Jazz wrenched open the front door, ready to let loose at Doug Weathers with a soul-withering blast of invective. But instead, he saw G. William standing there, fist raised to knock again, his shoulders still broad, his stance still confident.

But his eyes...

Something had gone misty and cold in his eyes.

Oh, Jazz thought, and the realization hit him even as G. William said it: "You were right. It's a serial killer. We got another victim."

CHAPTER 15

Jazz ushered G. William into the house. Gramma peeked around the grandfather clock, saw it was the sheriff, and pointed her shotgun, trembling. G. William forced a grin and said, "How do, ma'am? Didn't know there was a lady present. Apologies." Then he doffed his hat.

Gramma giggled and scampered off to her bedroom.

G. William arched an eyebrow. "She's getting worse, Jazz."

"What? Nah. She's pretty stable these days. She's just off-kilter because it's late, is all."

G. William grunted.

The sheriff had come here many, many times after arresting Billy, so Jazz didn't have to show him the way to the kitchen. Jazz groaned when he saw the scattered remnants of Gramma's meal. He swept the remains into the greasy bucket and dumped it in the sink.

"Coffee?" he asked as G. William settled into a chair.

"Got enough in me to float an armada, Jazz. Thanks, no." He sighed. "I am *not* happy about this."

Jazz felt great—he'd been right. Fiona Goodling hadn't been a one-off. Someone was out there prospecting. Someone was prospecting, and Jazz had seen it—had *known* it—before anyone else. Tanner sort of reminded Jazz of Reverend Parris from *The Crucible*: so eager to do something to help the town, but completely unwilling to believe that true evil was afoot.

At first. Eventually, he came around. He had to.

Linkage blindness was common in law enforcement, but in G. William's case, it came with a dose of wishful thinking. At the time Dear Old Dad had violated his own cardinal rule and decided to prospect in Lobo's Nod, G. William Tanner was a broken man. His wife of thirty-seven years had just died after a yearlong bout with a strain of ovarian cancer so cruel and so lingering that Billy himself would have admired it. In the next election, Tanner was all but guaranteed to lose to a young upstart from Calverton who had run on a thinly disguised platform of ageism, his slogan running along the lines of "Sweep in the new!" Basically, with his wife dead and his lifelong career almost in the grave as well, G. William had had nothing better to do than to obsess over Cara Swinton, a blond cheerleader from Lobo's Nod High School who'd gone missing, some strands of her hair and a torn patch of her sweater found in a bush outside the post office. Everyone— even Cara's parents—thought she'd run off to New York (Cara dreamed of being a model), but G. William felt something different in the air.

And when Samantha Reed—another pretty young blond— turned up dead in a culvert a week later, G. William knew he had something. He tied the murders to two of Billy's other crimes, committed ten years apart and in ways that Billy had been sure could never be connected. G. William Tanner, though, made the connections and came to realize that the Artist, Green Jack, and others were all the same man, a man now operating in Lobo's Nod.

Widower. Almost voted out of office. Combined with the stresses of his personal life, the tracking of Billy Dent nearly destroyed G. William. Jazz understood why the sheriff desperately did not want to have to chase another serial killer.

"I've been tryin' to call you all night," G. William said. "Couldn't get through. Pretty much decided not to bother, but I couldn't sleep. Realized I needed to tell you that you were right."

If Jazz had been waiting for an apology, he would have waited a long time. One wouldn't be coming. As far as G. William was concerned, Jazz violating the crime scene made them even as far as not trusting each other went.

Jazz slid into a chair across from the sheriff. "So tell me what happened."

A shrug. "All started when we turned up a recent case with the same finger-removal MO."

"It's not his MO," Jazz said. "It's his signature." He bit his lip immediately, and too late; G. William didn't need to be schooled right now.

But the sheriff just nodded wearily. "Right. Right. I know," he said without reproach. "Anyhow, body turned up three days ago, up in Lindenberg, just across the state line. Two fingers removed, one of them left behind. The middle finger."

"Just two fingers? He only took one? Are you sure?"

"We pretty much have the whole count-to-ten thing down pat, Jazz."

"Do they have an ID? Was she connected to Goodling at all?"

"No. Not so's we can tell, at least. Name's..." G. William heaved his bulk to one side and slid his smartphone out of his hip pocket. He scrolled through a screen. "Name's Carla O'Donnelly. College student from State U. No connection to Goodling that we can tell." G. William replaced the phone and passed a hand over his face, as though he could work some sort of magic trick and—*ta-da!*—change the world before his eyes.

The trick didn't work.

"I don't know if I'm up to this, Jazz," he said, his voice cracking with emotion. "I'm just..." His fingers trembled as he massaged his temples. Jazz felt like he'd just walked in on someone having sex—awkward and embarrassed for G. William and ashamed of himself all at once. And maybe a little confused. Still, he couldn't help watching. Observing. Some cold and clinical part of him—maybe the same part that made him such a fit for Reverend Hale—filed away G. William's reactions, his motions, his words. *This is what it's like to be completely overwhelmed*, he thought. *This is what it's like to be at the end of your rope.* Hale's words were fitting here: "No man may longer doubt the powers of the dark are gathered in monstrous attack upon this village."

Hale... Acting...

What if it was all an act? The visit at night. The almost-breakdown. Jazz didn't want to think it, but he had to. It would be irresponsible *not* to think it.

What if the killer was none other than G. William Tanner?

Everyone said that pursuing Billy had almost driven the sheriff crazy. So what if that "almost" wasn't part of the equation? What if G. William had gone completely off his rocker and now had become the thing he hunted? Was that possible?

No.

No. Jazz wouldn't let himself believe it. *Not everyone has a killer inside. Not everyone is like me.*

The sheriff harrumphed loudly and steepled his fingers on the table in front of him. "Anyway. She wasn't strangled to death like Goodling; she was smothered. Probably with a plastic bag, according to the report we got from Lindenberg. They e-mailed the whole thing, but I haven't gone through all of it yet. We don't know why he changed the number of fingers. We don't—"

"He's counting," Jazz interrupted. It came to him like the original flash of insight that told him a serial killer had prospected Fiona Goodling, back when he only knew her as Jane Doe. "He's counting his victims. Goodling was his second. O'Donnelly was his first. He takes one finger for each victim to count. Leaves one behind to flip us off. That's his signature."

"Yeah, probably. That makes sense." *Here is all the invisible world....*

Jazz leaned forward. "You need me on this, G. William. I can help you. Let me see the report. Both of them—Goodling and O'Donnelly. I was right from the beginning, and I can help."

For a moment, Jazz thought that G. William would finally

relent, but the moment passed. A head shake, vigorous and implacable. "No. Not a chance. For one thing, you get involved and word will leak out. And then I'll have the press all over it, and that's the last thing I need right now. Especially that jackass Doug Weathers. He'll try to ride this thing to fame and fortune, just like he tried to ride your daddy."

"But—"

"No. I'm not letting you get dragged into this nonsense. Like I said the other day: Your job is to try to be normal. Your job is to be a kid, then grow up, then have a decent life. You've seen enough already."

"So have you."

The sheriff smiled a tight, grim smile. "Difference between you and me, kid? I get paid for this."

Jazz shrugged. "Okay, you talked me into it—I'll even give you a break on my salary."

G. William guffawed, slapping the table with one heavy palm. "Nice try, Jazz. Nice try. I think I've abused your grandmom's hospitality enough for one night, though. Sorry I got her all het up."

Jazz walked him to the front door. "I wouldn't know what to do with myself if there was a nice, calm, quiet night around here."

G. William snorted something noncommittal and empathetic as he opened the door. He jammed his hat on his head. "Rest easy, Jazz. And hey—good call." It was the closest thing to an apology Jazz would get, he knew.

"You know there'll be more, right?" Jazz told him. "He's counting up, not down."

G. William said nothing. He just nodded once, and when he walked out the door, Jazz thought he'd just seen a dead man go out into the night.

And a dream.
  And a knife.
  (one two)
  There was always a knife in a sink.
  And now in his hand.
  (something new)
  And a voice.
  (Billy's voice)
  And a hand.
  (my hand)
  A hand on the knife.
  Easy. So easy. It's just like cutting chicken.
  And another voice says:
  (one two)
  It's okay. It's okay. I want—
  A line of blood bubbles where the knife slices.
  Good boy. Good boy.
  (one cut, two cuts)
  Just like that. Just like—
  (one two)

For the second time that night, Jazz awoke suddenly. This time, though, it had nothing to do with anyone pounding on his door. All was silent, save for the occasional snore from Gramma through the wall.

Jazz sat upright, shifting from dead asleep to fully awake in a split second, his mind buzzing and sparking. Somehow, in his sleep, he'd made the connection. It was about the counting. The fingers. He knew.... Was it even possible?

He flipped on a light and went online, searching for information about Fiona Goodling. In an irony that Jazz enjoyed for a brief moment, he noticed that Doug Weathers had posted a story with all the pertinent information, beginning with her discovery in the field and ending with her identification. Strangled to death. Hands around her neck. Yes. Definitely. But what else? She'd had a boyfriend, he knew. What about her age?

Weathers had linked to her hometown paper's obituary, which included her age—twenty-seven. Jazz broke out in a cold sweat all at once. This just could *not* be happening....

And what about Carla O'Donnelly? College student. She was probably between eighteen and twenty. He did another search and brought up the news reports from Lindenberg, the results of the police finding her body. She'd been found by a railroad worker near a spur line. The guy had been on a smoke break. He never would have seen the body if not for the fact that he kicked a rock and was surprised by the sound it made when it landed among a tall stand of weeds. A moment later, he peered within . . . and his life changed.

Wait. Wait a second. Lindenberg? Wasn't Erickson from there? Hadn't he just transferred from there? Yes. He had.

Wonder if he was on the scene there, too.

But the paper had no names for the police officers on the scene where Carla O'Donnelly's body had been found. It did, however, have information on how she'd been killed.

Asphyxiated, the newspaper said, most likely smothered by a plastic bag tied around her neck with a cord. She was nineteen.

Oh, God, Jazz thought, wiping sweat from his upper lip. *I can't believe...*

He tossed a quick look over his shoulder at the photos of his father's victims. They seemed to glare at him. *What are you waiting for?* they said. *Why are you sitting around?* they said.

Had it just been a couple of days ago that he'd railed against G. William for suffering from linkage blindness? Ha! Jazz had had linkage blindness, too, it turned out.

The fingers—the fingers threw me off. I thought they were his signature, but they're not. They're something else entirely. He's counting, but he's not just *counting.*

Jazz fumbled for the telephone and dialed G. William's cell. He got the sheriff's voice mail. As the message rambled— "You've reached Sheriff G. William Tanner. If this is an emergency, hang up and call nine-one-one. Otherwise, you know what to do, so get to it already."—he ran through what he would say. At the beep, he drew a deep breath. He wanted to blurt out everything he knew, but instead he had to stay calm, so that G. William would understand him.

"G. William. Hey. It's Jazz." Calm. Cool. Rational. Inside, though, his blood thrummed and his soul screamed. "I figured it out. There will be more victims. Here's what I know about the next one...."

CHAPTER 16

In the crisp light of the autumn morning, Jazz was no longer as certain as he'd been the night before. He double-checked his logic and found no flaws. No flaws except for the fact that his theory was completely insane. But maybe G. William would see potential in it.

He gulped down a quick breakfast and set up Gramma in her favorite chair in front of the TV. Mornings were her best time, so she was usually okay during the day while he was at school. By three or four in the afternoon, though, she started wavering, which was one reason among many why Jazz was eager for *The Crucible* to have its debut in a couple of weeks. It was also why he'd never had—and never could have—an after-school job.

He met Howie at the Coff-E-Shop, which was more chaotic than usual for the morning rush. On this morning, his best friend was sporting a massive bruise along the left edge of his jaw. It looked like someone had smacked him in the face with a sock full of quarters.

"What happened?" Jazz asked.

"Medicine cabinets are *dangerous*," Howie said. "Those doors, man. They'll just spring on you like a ninja. Mark my words: Be careful in your bathroom or you could end up like me."

What would it be like to go through life so fragile? Jazz wondered. He was glad he would never know, but he also worried that someday Howie's sense of humor would run out. Or at least prove not broad enough to cover an ever-growing roster of bruises, abrasions, and contusions.

"Nice set of luggage," Howie said out of nowhere, and it took Jazz a moment to realize he was talking about the bags under his eyes.

"Yeah, didn't sleep much." He told Howie about G. William's late-night visit and the revelation that there was definitely a serial killer at work.

"Suh-weet!" Howie fist-pumped the air in triumph, then realized that he was celebrating a serial killer's handiwork. "I mean, you know, 'suh-weet' that you were right, not 'suh-weet' that...you were...right...." He drifted off and they stared at each other for a silent moment.

"What is taking so long today?" Howie demanded, peering around the shop. Helen was nowhere to be seen, and the rest of the staff was scrambling to keep up.

Before Jazz could answer, he saw Doug Weathers push his way through the door and the crowd. Persistent. Like hemorrhoids.

"Let's just get out of here," Jazz said, tugging Howie toward another door.

"But I need my caffeine! And today I was gonna try a double-pumpkin foamless latte with vanilla syrup, cloves, and—"

"Come on. We can grab Cokes at school."

They were already at school and in separate homerooms when Jazz realized that he'd forgotten to borrow Howie's cell phone. He wanted to call G. William and see what the sheriff thought of his theory. By the time lunch rolled around, Jazz had successfully allowed himself to be distracted by Howie's demands that they get the new tattoo this weekend.

In fact, he managed to forget about the case all day long, until about halfway through play practice, when the rear door to the auditorium suddenly clanged open with a sound like an off-key church bell. Ginny spun around in her seat in the middle of the house and shouted, "Quiet, please! Rehearsal!" at a volume hilariously at odds with her tiny frame.

"Sorry to interrupt," Deputy Erickson said in a tone that made it clear he really could not care less. He stomped halfway down the aisle to the stage, then planted his feet and pointed a steady finger right at Jazz. "You. Now."

Jazz, standing onstage between Tituba and John Proctor, looked around as if he'd just been accused of witchcraft. "Me? What?"

"I will *drag* you out of here if I have to," Erickson said.

After a hasty apology to Ginny and a quick hand-squeeze of reassurance from Connie, Jazz hopped off the stage and walked up the aisle. Erickson didn't wait for him—he turned on his heel and was out the door before Jazz was halfway there.

The hallway was empty, school having gotten out an hour

ago, and Erickson stood in front of the glass trophy case, staring at his own reflection. The extracurricular clubs would all be meeting in rooms somewhere, and Howie was probably lurking in the library, where he liked scoping out the hot college girl who was student-teaching toward her library degree and stayed late to reshelve books. (Howie had suddenly developed a yen for the work of e. e. cummings, since that was shelved with the best view of the circulation desk.)

Jazz came to a halt behind Erickson and planted his feet. "Who do you think you are—"

He didn't get any further. The deputy spun around so fast that Jazz was surprised the man didn't topple over. Erickson's eyes narrowed, and then he grabbed Jazz by the arm and marched him out to the parking lot and hustled him into the back of his squad car.

And that was enough. Jazz was done with Erickson. "I have rights, dillweed," he said. "You can't just grab me up and do whatever you want."

"Shut up," Erickson said in a flat tone.

Bail. That was Jazz's best option: Jump out before the car got up to speed. He reached for the door handle and learned a quick lesson that should have been obvious from the start: Cop cars don't *have* door handles in the backseat. Of course they wouldn't.

As Erickson cruised out of the school parking lot, a small, cold spike of fear pricked at Jazz. He was trapped. Erickson was armed and in control of the car. He could take Jazz anywhere, do anything. . . .

A thought reared up and demanded Jazz's attention. It was

a series of thoughts, actually, beginning with Erickson's positioning himself at Fiona Goodling's crime scene. And then showing up that same night in the morgue. And then... He was originally from Lindenberg, where Carla O'Donnelly had been murdered. Being groomed by G. William... Did he have access to the sheriff's voice mail? Did he know what Jazz knew, the suppositions he'd made?

No matter how much Jazz protested or questioned, Erickson said nothing as they cruised to the police station, where he let Jazz out of the car and dragged him inside, marching him past Lana, who watched, gape-mouthed.

It was the second time in less than a week that Lana had seen Jazz dragged around by the cops. Jazz threw her a smile, just to keep things on an even keel. Despite herself, Lana smiled back, but it was fleeting.

"Here he is," Erickson announced, pushing Jazz into G. William's office. The sheriff was on the phone, nodding and grunting occasionally. He shooed Erickson out with a curt wave of his hand. Jazz allowed himself to enjoy the wounded, angry expression on the deputy's face.

Erickson slammed the door on his way out—so hard that the framed pictures on the walls rattled. G. William seemed not to notice.

"Sit down," he told Jazz once he was off the phone.

"No." Jazz stood his ground, arms crossed over his chest. "What's going on here? You can't just kidnap me from school and then—"

"What the hell are you up to, Jazz?" G. William hissed. "What kind of sick game are you playing?"

"Game? I'm not playing any kind of—"

G. William whipped out his smartphone and fiddled with it for a moment. Then Jazz heard his own voice: "G. William. Hey. It's Jazz. I figured it out. There will be more victims. Here's what I know about the next one. She'll be around twenty-five years old. Brown hair. She'll be a waitress. She'll be killed by an injection of drain cleaner. The body will be posed in a kneeling position, the hands tied together at the wrists to mimic prayer. She'll be missing four fingers, but the middle one will be at the scene. And her initials will be H.M. That's all."

G. William shoved the smartphone back into his pocket and glared at Jazz. Jazz didn't know what to think. He hadn't expected the sheriff to get so upset about a stupid voice mail.

"I'm sorry, G. William. I guess I wasn't thinking—"

The sheriff pointed to a chair. This time, Jazz sat.

A moment later, G. William threw a folder at him. "Explain," he said, biting into the word like it was a worm he'd found in his apple.

Jazz's hands were trembling and he could barely get the folder turned around in his lap. The file tab read MYERSON, HELEN.

His throat went impossibly tight.

"Helen Myerson," G. William said, saving Jazz the trouble of opening the file. "Age twenty-five. Works over at the Coff-E-Shop as a waitress. You've probably sat at her table before, Jazz. You and your friends. Brown hair. Found her this morning over in the old abandoned barn on the west side. You know it?" He didn't wait for an answer. "Sure you do. Cause of death, well, we're still waiting for the labs back, but it sure looked like a heart attack to me. And there was a needle and a bottle of Drano on a table near the body, just in case we didn't get it on the first try. The body that—guess what?—was posed like she was praying. So, Jazz"—G. William sat on the edge of his desk and leaned into Jazz's space—"you got anything you want to tell me?"

Oh my God. I was right. Jazz was too shocked to say anything for a moment, and then he wondered if G. William would take his silence for guilt. "I didn't do this," he blurted out. "It wasn't me."

G. William's expression shifted from anger to cunning curiosity. "Why would you say that? I didn't accuse you of being part of it."

Even before getting caught, Billy had been questioned by the police numerous times in connection with his crimes, always as a witness or passerby. Billy had enjoyed those times, seeing the inner workings of the investigation against him, and had always cooperated as long as it didn't involve the truth. One thing he had drummed into Jazz's head: *Don't ever tell the cops more than what they ask for. Never, ever, ever!*

Jazz had broken that rule.

"It wasn't me," he said again, dug deep into a hole and not sure how to get out. He had what was called "guilty knowledge." He knew things that only the killer or an eyewitness would know, and he had to explain how he knew those things, or else the cops would think he was the killer...and Jazz couldn't really blame them. How much of a leap was it to think that the son of the world's most notorious serial killer would someday snap?

"You got something to say, now's the time for it," G. William said, shifting his bulk on the desk. "It's just me and you in here. We can figure this out together, or I can figure it out on my own."

No longer was G. William the shaky, overstressed, pathetic figure from the night before. He was confident. Sure. He was the man who'd puzzled out Billy Dent's last two murders and then bearded Dent in his own home. Jazz flashed to the first time he'd seen G. William, to the image burned irrevocably into the backs of his eyelids: the sheriff bursting into the rumpus room, the impossibly huge hand-cannon pointed Jazz's way. *Drop it! Drop all of it! I swear to Christ I'll shoot you!*

"It's not me," Jazz said again. "It's my dad. It's Billy."

CHAPTER 17

"Okay, okay. Thanks. Yeah, thanks. You, too," G. William was saying into the phone. He leaned back in his chair, gazing over the desk at Jazz, who still sat opposite him, the Helen Myerson file on his lap. Myerson. She had served him coffee a thousand times, and he'd never known her last name. He tried to remember when he'd last seen her. A couple of days ago . . . Weathers had been there, the first time Jazz had seen him in a long time. So he and Howie had gotten their coffee to go. Had Jazz left a tip? He couldn't remember, and it suddenly seemed incredibly important.

G. William finished on the phone. It had taken only a few minutes to confirm what they already knew.

"Billy's still locked up nice and tight," G. William said. "Warden says he's been exactly where he's supposed to be. All night and all day and all night again. Just like the last four years. He's not going anywhere, and he hasn't gone anywhere. So unless your dad has figured out how to teleport or split himself in two . . ."

Jazz shook his head, staring down at the Myerson file. It all made sense. It all fit. He had realized last night—looking at the O'Donnelly and Goodling murders, then looking at Billy's victims—what the pattern was. And it fit Billy Dent.

"Billy's first victim," he had explained moments earlier to G. William, "was a woman named Cassie Overton. Her life, her age, her appearance, her death—all identical to O'Donnelly. His second victim was Farrah Gordon. Same age, job, hair color as Fiona Goodling. Strangled to death and left naked in a field, just like Goodling. And now a third victim. Same initials as Helen. Harper McLeod. Waitress. Twenty-five. Brown hair. Boom. Billy started having fun at that point. Drain-cleaner injections. Causes muscle spasms. Intense pain. Arrhythmia. Eventually, heart attack. That's when he started the posing, too. Got the nickname 'the Artist.'"

"It's not your daddy," G. William said now, his tone kind.

It was meant to be reassuring, Jazz supposed, but he couldn't let himself take it that way. He wasn't sure which was worse: the idea that Billy had somehow escaped and decided to relive his greatest hits, or that...

"A copycat, maybe," G. William said, almost to himself, as though Jazz weren't even in the room. "Someone out there doing his best Billy Dent impression?"

And *there* was the "or that..." that had worried him. A copycat. Someone who knew Billy's crimes well.

But the most likely copycat, everyone would assume, would be none other than Billy Dent, Jr., also known as Jasper Francis Dent. Maybe Howie was wrong—maybe that was a good serial killer name after all.

Jazz wet his lips; it took him almost a minute to find his breath, to say the words he didn't want to say. But he had to know.

"You don't think I did this, do you, G. William?"

"I don't want to think that." The sheriff sounded like he was trying to convince someone. Himself? Or Jazz?

"That...didn't really answer my question."

G. William sat up straight and strummed a jaunty little rhythm on the desk, totally out of nowhere, completely un-suited to the moment. "Plenty of people out there know all sorts of things about your dad's crimes, Jazz. You're pretty far down on my suspect list."

Ah. "But I'm still on it."

G. William snorted. "If my mama was alive, she'd be on my list until I could clear her. You know how this goes, Jazz."

Yes, Jazz knew how it went, but it didn't make him feel any better. He couldn't allow the niceties and vagaries of police procedure to lull him into complacency. G. William's opinion was fine, but pretty soon this would be bigger than the sheriff of Lobo's Nod. There would be a task force, and reporters, and all the usual nonsense. And sooner or later—probably sooner; probably way too soon for comfort, really—someone would say, *You know what? Why are we spending all this time look-ing for some mystery man when the most likely candidate is over at the high school, dressed like a Puritan and screaming to the rafters about the blood on his head?*

Because didn't that make the most sense? That Jazz had finally cracked and decided to follow in Dear Old Dad's foot-steps?

Jazz struggled to keep his expression neutral, but something must have slipped through because G. William, again in a not-unkind tone, said, "Jazz, don't go worrying. We're gonna catch this guy. It's a done deal. He's caught, you hear me?"

"There'll be more murders," Jazz said. "Once he hit number three, Billy went on a spree and did three more in pretty rapid succession. You're going to have—"

"Listen to me," G. William interrupted. "Listen. It might not be someone following his career. Could be someone inspired, sure, but that doesn't mean they're following him to the letter. Those first two murders were pretty generic. A plastic bag. Strangling."

"It's exactly how Billy did it!" He couldn't believe G. William wasn't taking this more seriously.

"And," the sheriff said calmly, "it's exactly how a thousand other people did it, too. There's nothing unique about a plastic bag or throttling someone with your bare hands."

"But the initials...The victims...And the latest one...It's practically the same woman!"

G. William leaned back in his chair. "I know you're trying to help, but there's things worse than linkage blindness in cases like this."

"Yeah? Like what?" Jazz fought to keep a sneer out of his voice. Fought and failed.

"You have to think around corners and behind walls to catch these guys, Jazz. Nothing is ever what it appears to be. Figure you'd know that more than anyone else. Worse thing than linkage blindness is getting cocky. Thinking you get it, thinking you've got it figured out before you really do. You ever think this could all be a setup? Hmm? That this guy could be playing us?"

Jazz shrugged. Sure, it was possible.... But an obnoxious, un-ignorable tickle in the back of his mind—and a matching twist in his guts—told him that it wasn't likely.

"If I wanted to throw the cops off my scent," G. William went on, "you know what I would do? I would make it look like I was following a preset list. I would follow it to the letter. And then I would totally juke to the right when they were looking for me to go left."

"I don't know."

"You can't underestimate these guys. This guy, he's like your daddy, all right. Highly organized. Really smart, this one. You know how we found Helen? I'll tell you how: an anonymous tip. Nine-one-one call from a pay phone outside town. Same as Goodling. Now, who do you think gave us that tip?"

"The killer. Of course."

With a pleased smile, G. William said, "Right. Had to be. He's setting us up. Making it look like he's following Billy's path. And to make it look that way, he has to make sure we find every clue. So he's 'helping' us along. But you know how these guys are, Jazz. They don't give with one hand unless they got a gun loaded and cocked and pointed at your head with the other. He's trying to trick us. And I'm not gonna let that happen."

"But—"

"Look, we're gonna look into it. All the aspects, all the angles. Including this Billy angle. Probably get the feds into it, too, soon as we can fill out that damn ViCAP questionnaire and get it confirmed Goodling and O'Donnelly were killed by the same guy. So don't you worry—we're gonna get him." He nodded thoughtfully. "We're gonna get him, Jazz. This isn't gonna be a repeat of your dad's days. This guy's not even getting close to double digits, all right?"

Jazz forced himself to nod.

G. William heaved his bulk out of the chair, using the desk for support and leverage. "Let's go. I'll drive you back to school."

They rode in silence, G. William speaking only once, to apologize for Erickson yanking Jazz out of play practice so roughly.

"It's all right," Jazz told him.

"It's been a bad few days for him. He was first on the scene to find Myerson's body. And he was first on the scene for Goodling, too." G. William chuckled without mirth. "Poor guy transfers down from Lindenberg and his first couple of days are one body stacked on top of another. So he's just real upset. You know how it is."

"It's really all right."

Play practice was still in session as they pulled up—Jazz recognized some of his castmates' cars in the parking lot, as well as Ginny's beat-up old Kia.

"You're done, Jazz," G. William told him as he got out of the car. "You're out of the investigative business, got it? You got any other ideas, you run 'em past me, okay?"

"Sure."

180

He waved good-bye to G. William and headed inside, where practice was just ending. With the exception of Connie and Ginny, everyone looked surprised to see him, as though they had expected him to be behind bars by now. And maybe that wasn't such a crazy expectation. He could hardly blame them.

"I can't believe he pulled you out of here like that," Ginny fumed after rehearsal ended. The rest of the cast had drifted off to their cars, leaving Jazz onstage with Ginny and Connie. "I was going to call your grandmother, but Connie said that might not be such a great idea."

"Probably not." He squeezed Connie's hand, which hadn't left his since he'd walked through the door. "Thanks."

"But I was ready to call a lawyer. My brother knows some-one—"

"It was a misunderstanding," he assured her, pouring on the charm. He allowed his face to relax into a lazy grin, a "nothing's wrong in the whole wide world, darlin'" sort of smile that immediately put people at ease. He'd learned it from watching Billy, and it was way too effective. Also, it was far too easy to slip into.

Maybe it was just being in the auditorium, surrounded by the pieces of *The Crucible*, but Jazz couldn't help being reminded of another of Hale's bits of dialogue: "Theology, sir, is a fortress; no crack in a fortress may be accounted small." He felt the same way about his own sanity. Even the smallest crack, the smallest lapse, could lead to...

Ginny patted his arm. "You let me know if I can help. If you want me to write a letter or something..."

Jazz suppressed a snort of laughter. Write a letter. God bless Ginny Davis and her goofy curls and her millennial hippie-ism.

Connie stayed quiet until they got to Jazz's car.

"Now what?" she asked, though the expression on her face and the tension he felt in her hand told him that she already knew.

"Ignoring G. William has gotten me this far," Jazz said. "Let's see where it takes me next."

CHAPTER 18

Since his grandmother wasn't just a senile, dangerous old coot, but also a *racist*, senile, dangerous old coot, Jazz had to do some advance prep work before Connie could come over to the house. After giving it a lot of thought, he fell back on what Billy had once described to him as a "poor man's sedative," to be used only when nothing else was at hand. He ground up some Benadryl in Gramma's soup and fed her dinner in front of the TV. It took only minutes for her head to droop, then go slack against the threadbare recliner that had been old since before Billy was born. Her spoon clattered into the bowl and she nearly spilled the remaining soup all over herself, but Jazz—who'd been watching—darted in just in time and grabbed the bowl as it slipped from her liver-spotted hands.

He checked her pulse. She was fine. She would sleep soundly for hours. He easily gathered her in his arms; Gramma was made up of skin and bones and hate and crazy—and hate and crazy don't weigh anything. He laid her out on the sofa, then called Howie with the all clear.

Within twenty minutes, he was in his bedroom with Howie and Connie, Howie lounging at the desk, Connie sitting cross-legged on the bed, Jazz's head in her lap.

"It's morbid," Connie said for the millionth time, referring to the victims on Jazz's wall.

"It helped me figure out this guy's pattern," Jazz said.

"That doesn't make it any less morbid."

"Morbid, shmorbid," Howie chimed in. "It's just plain creeeeeeeepy!" He shot a rubber band and nailed victim number twenty-seven—Marsha Van Horn—between the eyes. "Oops."

Jazz rubbed his eyes. A rubber band to the forehead was the least of Marsha's problems.

"We need to figure this out," he said. "I need your help, guys."

"I aim to serve," Howie said, saluting.

Connie smoothed Jazz's hair back from his temples. "I, on the other hand, am here to tell you to chill out and forget all this nonsense."

"Can't forget it," Jazz said.

"Man's gotta do a man's work," Howie drawled in what was quite possibly the world's worst John Wayne impression. "Gotta strap on those six-guns and—"

"No one's carrying six-guns," Jazz told him. He didn't even have to look over; he knew Howie's expression would be crestfallen. "But I need to do this. I need to prove that I can do more than just mess people up with what Billy taught me. I can do some good with it, too."

Connie kissed his forehead. "Tanner's on the case. He

184

caught your dad—he can catch a guy doing an impression of your dad."

"G. William got lucky when he caught Billy," Jazz said. "He might not get lucky a second time. Besides, he's not a hundred percent convinced this guy will follow Billy's pattern."

"What *is* the pattern?" Howie asked, swiveling the chair and leaning forward to get a better look at the Wall of Victims. "Victim *numero* four-o—"

"*Cuatro*," said an exasperated Connie.

"—was Vanessa Dawes. Heh. VD. Venereal disease." He chortled.

"Grow *up*," Connie said.

"She was an actress," Jazz said, ignoring both of them, staring at the ceiling. He didn't need to look into a file for information on any of Billy's victims—they were hammered straight into his memory banks for good. "Came from Boise, Idaho—"

"Home of the Great Potato!"

"—and moved to New York when she was nineteen," Jazz went on, still ignoring Howie. "She was on a trip with friends, train-hopping down the East Coast, when Billy met up with her. It was in a deli. She was ordering a corned beef sandwich." Jazz swallowed. Suddenly, it was like he was there, living it as Billy had described it. He remembered the dance of obscene light in his father's eyes as he'd told Jazz how he had pretended to recognize Vanessa, then apologized profusely when he "realized" he didn't....

Even said to her, "You must think I'm some kind of crazy," Billy had said. *And she fell all over herself to tell me that wasn't the case, that she totally understood, that she got that a lot....*

"She was on some commercials," Jazz said now. "Nothing major. Nothing national. All local and regional. But enough that Billy could get a good hook into her ego, get her thinking he was harmless. And then it was just a matter of offering to buy her a drink, getting her alone."

"And *bang*—two cc's of Drano, please, nurse."

"Howie!" Connie punched the bed. "People are dead!"

Chastened, Howie swiveled the chair back to Jazz's desk and fiddled idly with the computer mouse.

"Billy had already killed a waitress in the same town. At that point, he stayed there for three weeks. Killed Vanessa, then two more before skipping out."

"So we think he's going to kill three more people in Lobo's Nod before moving on?"

Jazz sat up, nodding. He stared at the Wall, in particular at Vanessa Dawes. "All of the copycat's victims have been identical to Billy's—same occupations. Same hair colors. Same initials. Same ages. So we're looking for someone in the Nod who has black hair, the initials V.D., age twenty-two."

Howie snorted again, then stopped, as if he could feel Connie's eyes blasting death rays into the back of his head.

"The Nod isn't exactly Hollywood," Howie pointed out from the desk. "It's not like there are a lot of actresses in this town. How would we find them, anyway?"

"What if he goes a little farther afield?" Connie asked, her voice heavy and slightly hesitant with thought.

Jazz turned to her. "What? What are you thinking?"

"It might be nothing." She looked from Jazz to Howie, who had spun around in the chair again. "It's probably—"

"Tell us." Jazz gave her one tenth of his sternest voice.

"Reel Life," she said immediately. "Over in Tynan Ridge. You know it? Actors go there all the time."

The boys shook their heads, almost in unison.

"It's an acting school. Some guy...Can't remember his name. He used to be on that stupid TV show about the monkey that solved crimes—"

"Connie," Jazz said in his best "move along" tone.

"Anyway, he set up this acting school. Does summer camps, stuff like that. My parents and I looked into it when we moved here, but it was too expensive. But he would have actresses from all over. Including the Nod."

Jazz nodded. Yes, that made sense. But also...

"What about *The Crucible*?" Howie asked, reading Jazz's mind. "There are actors right here in Lobo's Nod, too."

"They're too young. Still in high school," Jazz said. "But age twenty-two...Maybe there's someone who used to be an actor in high school, but graduated—what?—four or five years ago, and still lives in town. We'll have to check that out."

He hopped out of bed and started barking orders. "Connie, you take Howie's car and go to Reel Life. Check with this monkey actor guy and see if he has anyone enrolled who meets our criteria. You've been there before, so the guy will know you. Howie and I will go to school and check the roster for the drama club and the plays from the last few years."

"We should just call the sheriff," Connie said doubtfully. "This is his territory, not ours."

187

"Yeah," Howie said, "and more important than that, why does she get to take my car?"

Facing resistance from both of them, Jazz did the only thing he could think of: He paused for just a moment, pretending to weigh their thoughts. Then he started to speak; stopped; looked down at the floor as though ashamed.

"Guys," he said hesitantly, wondering if the little hitch in his voice would work. When he looked back up, they were both staring at him, rapt, enthralled, and he felt a sick/good flip-flop in his stomach. A job well done already, and he wasn't even halfway there.

"This is really important to me," he said, forcing his voice into a hushed whisper, as if he could barely speak without weeping. "You don't understand. G. William won't listen to us, anyway. This way we can get some solid evidence and present it to him. And maybe ... Maybe I can actually make the Dent name stand for something good and decent for a change."

He knew he had them when Connie put her arms around him.

Moments later, they headed for the cars.

Jazz wasn't proud of himself for manipulating his girlfriend and his best friend—

No. Wait. That wasn't entirely true. If he was being honest with himself, Jazz had to admit that there was a part of him that positively preened at how adroitly he'd gotten Connie and Howie to do what he wanted. What he *needed*.

It was necessary, he told himself. They were holding him back, and the world was propelling him forward. He'd had no choice.

Besides, it had been kind of fun, using that particular talent. There was no harm in that, right? Just a little adrenaline rush, a glow of pure *yes!* suffusing his whole being. He hadn't killed anyone. He hadn't done any harm to anyone.

He accelerated, pushing the Jeep faster down the road to the school. It was dark, and the streets of Lobo's Nod were practically empty. Jazz goosed the Jeep to six miles over the speed limit. He knew from careful observation that the Lobo's Nod cops rarely bothered to pull anyone over unless they were doing seven or more miles over the limit.

"Is this the right way to do it?" Howie asked. "Like, is this how the real cops do things? Figure out who the victim is, instead of who the killer is?"

"Sometimes that's all you have to go on," Jazz said.

"What if I already have a theory about who the killer is?"

Jazz smirked. This should be good. "Go ahead."

"I think it's that creep Weathers."

Jazz opened his mouth to tear apart Howie's theory. Then he shut it again.

"That," he said slowly, "isn't totally stupid."

"Gee, thanks. You do wonders for my self-esteem."

"He knows Billy's crimes. He would want the media to go nuts in the Nod again."

"See? See?"

Jazz thought of Weathers and his ego. That he could be the killer was certainly more likely than Jazz's earlier rogue thought that G. William might be guilty. The memory of it made him squirm with guilt.

"It's possible," he admitted. "But our best bet is to find the next victim. That will lead us straight to this guy, whether he's Weathers or not."

Howie had his arm out the window, hand-surfing the wind currents. "I can't believe you talked me into this," Howie complained. "Actually, no. I take that back. I can totally believe you talked me into this. What I can't believe is that you talked *Connie* into this."

"Between the three of us, we're gonna figure this out," Jazz said. "This guy is done. He just doesn't know it yet."

"How many people did your pops kill?"

"A hundred twenty-four," Jazz said, adding—as always—his mother to the "official" tally.

"And you think we're gonna stop this guy after three?"

"He wants to get caught. Billy once told me that most of these guys want to get caught. This guy is practically waving a white flag of surrender, man."

Howie snorted. "If this works..."

"If this all works out, I'll get *two* tattoos, man."

Howie hooted and pumped his fist. "Yes, Virginia, there *is* a Santa Claus!"

Jazz grinned and shook his head. "You're way too ex—"

He broke off mid-word, staring straight ahead.

"Oh, crap," he said.

"Jazz!" Howie screamed at the top of his lungs, and Jazz blinked and cranked the wheel left just in time to avoid a car peeling around a corner. He stomped on the brakes and the Jeep skidded to a halt in the middle of the intersection. The other car's horn blared loud and angry, Dopplering into a whine as the driver accelerated ahead of them and out of sight.

"The light was red!" Howie said. "Redder than red! Red like Christmas! Aw, man, look!" He held out his right arm, bruised from where it had hit the side of the car.

"I missed it." Jazz was surprised to find that his heart wasn't beating any faster, that his breath was perfectly normal. He had nearly slammed the Jeep into the other car at top speed, and the result would not have been pretty. The Jeep was too old to have air bags, so Jazz probably would have been wearing the steering wheel halfway through his chest, and Howie... Well, the internal bleeding from jerking against the seat belt probably would have done Howie in.

"Are you trying to kill us?"

"Virginia," Jazz said. "You said Virginia, right?"

"So what?" Howie ranted. "I didn't know the word offended you so much that you were gonna try to—"

"We have to go." Jazz slammed his foot on the gas as he threw the Jeep into reverse. Tires squealing, he spun the Jeep around and then headed back the way they'd come.

"Where are you going? School is *that* way."

"I know. We're not going to school. We're going to Ginny's."

"Ginny's? You mean Ms. Davis? Why are we going there?"

Jazz focused on the road, now breaking the speed limit by significantly more than seven miles an hour. Howie wasn't stupid. He would figure it out.

"Oh, man," Howie said a moment later. "Ginny. Virginia Davis. And she's an actress with black hair...."

"I don't know how old she is, but she's right out of college. I bet she's twenty-two," Jazz said, leaning into the wheel, gripping it like a race-car driver, throttling it like a throat. "What are you doing?"

This last because Howie had fished his cell phone out of his pocket. "Calling the sheriff, man. This is his department. Like, literally."

Jazz risked taking one hand off the wheel long enough to snatch away the phone. "Hey!" Howie complained.

"You call G. William and one of two things will happen. One, he won't believe us and we're right back at square one. Two, he'll totally believe us and he'll send a million squad cars over, and that'll scare this guy off."

"Isn't scaring the guy off a *good* thing?" Howie asked, reaching for the phone, but Jazz dropped it between his legs on the seat.

"No. We want to stay one step ahead of him, but he has to stay on the same path. Get it?"

"So if he thinks we don't know about Ginny..."

"We get there. We ask her if she's noticed anything weird lately. Like some guy following her around. If she has, *then* we tell G. William what we think, and he can put some undercover guys on her or something. If not, we can still ask her about any other actresses with her initials in town. Faster than breaking in to school to check the records."

"Ah, and now the reason you brought me instead of Connie becomes clear," Howie grumbled. "Whenever it's illegal, there's good ol' Howie."

Jazz threw him a grin. "Your life would be so boring without me, and you know it."

"Yeah, well, if you don't want to scare this guy off, you should probably slow down. If we careen into Ms. Davis's parking lot like a bat outta hell, he's going to think something's up."

Good point. Jazz tapped the brakes, and by the time they'd gotten to Ginny's, the Jeep was moseying along like any other lazy car.

Right after casting for *The Crucible* had been finalized, Ginny had invited the whole cast and crew to her apartment for an informal read-through and getting-to-know-one-another session. Jazz had lurked around the kitchen, uncomfortable being crammed into the tiny apartment with so many other kids. He'd watched Connie as she effortlessly flitted from one small cluster to another, and by the end of the night he'd figured out how to mimic that behavior well enough to fit in. So the night had been a win for him, and now it was a double-win because he knew exactly where she lived: a small three-story apartment building inserted like a mismatched LEGO block between a dry cleaner and a car wash.

He pulled in to the parking lot and pointed through the windshield. "Her car," he told Howie. "She's home." He parked. Scanned the area quickly. Nothing weird in the parking lot that he could see. No cars with out-of-state plates. No big vans or sedans that would make it easy to sneak a body away.

"Let's get this done and over with," Howie said with a nervousness that made Jazz want to laugh.

Jazz handed Howie's cell over and killed the Jeep's engine. "Let's go."

Ginny lived on the third floor. There was no elevator; Howie beat Jazz by virtue of his ridiculously long legs, which ate up stairs three at a time.

"I win!" he chortled, knocking on the door.

"What exactly did you win?"

"Bragging rights."

Jazz let it go. They waited for Ginny to come to the door. Nothing.

"She probably didn't hear you," Jazz said. "Knock harder."

"I bruise easy," Howie said, as if Jazz needed reminding.

Jazz gently pushed Howie out of the way and knocked on the door—three quick, hard raps that couldn't be missed from inside.

"Maybe she's not home."

"Her car's in the parking lot. She— Wait."

Jazz put his ear to the door.

"What?"

"Shh!" He waved Howie into silence, concentrating. From within the apartment, he heard...something. "I hear—"

"Is she coming?"

Jazz backed up and his gaze drifted down. To the keyhole. His stomach twisted. Was that a glimmer of reflected light he spotted?

He leaned over and sniffed the doorknob, ignoring Howie, who wanted to know just what the hell he was doing.

Glue. Filled with superglue.

You need some alone time? Billy's voice whispered from the past. *You need some special, uninterrupted time? Well, then you gotta make sure you can't be interrupted in the first place, you know what I mean? Block the doors. Block the windows.*

Make it so no one else can get in. And hey—bonus! When the
cops come, they have to break in, and that makes a mess, and
a mess is our friend, Jasper. Evidence gets lost in a mess. Peo-
ple get confused by messes.

Jazz's heart raced. A high-pitched whine filled his ears.

"He's here," he whispered.

CHAPTER 19

"What?" Howie goggled at Jazz like a kid stuck on the Ferris wheel.

Jazz grabbed Howie by the neck and pulled his friend's ear to his lips. "He's. Here."

"Holy crap."

"Run, Howie. Get outside. Call the cops. Watch for him by the fire escape out in the alley, in case he tries to get away."

Howie stared straight ahead, fear and shock flickering in his eyes. Jazz pushed him, hard. "Go!" he whispered as loudly as he dared. "Now!"

Howie ran like hell for the stairs.

Jazz didn't think. He didn't *allow* himself to think. He'd heard the killer in there, he was sure. Maybe they weren't too late.

His heart no longer raced. His breath came slow and easy, and the world seemed doused in syrup—everything moving lethargically. He had all the time in the world.

In that strange, sudden fugue state, he backed up against

the opposite side of the narrow corridor and lunged forward, kicking out with his right foot, catching the door at doorknob height, just the way Billy had taught him. The door trembled. A shock wave of pain vibrated up to Jazz's groin. It felt like he'd pounded a sledgehammer against his thigh, and all he had to show for it was a little bowing around the doorknob.

And the unmistakable sound of rapid footfalls from within, as time returned to its normal flow, Jazz's heart thrumming like a timpani played by a spastic, his breath a harsh and hot wind in his throat.

"Don't you dare run!" Jazz yelled. "The cops are already surrounding the place!" And then he pushed through the throbbing pain in his leg and lashed out again; he was surprised when the door burst inward, the knob and lock clanging to the floor.

He ran, limping, as fast as he could, exploding into Ginny's entryway. The apartment was dark, but a rectangle of light spilled onto the floor halfway down a short hall. The living room, he remembered.

Jazz made for it, spinning into the open archway that led to the living room. He barely had time to adjust to the light before the scene assaulted his eyes: the sofa he'd sat on with Connie, holding hands, now pushed against the wall under the window, tilted crazily askew from the rest of the room, a figure climbing atop it. Another, slight figure lying on a white-and-red patterned throw rug.

The man on the sofa turned back. He wore a black ski mask, but that left the eyes open. Jazz's gaze met his for a bare second. Blue eyes. Crazy eyes.

And then the killer turned away as though blasted with sunlight, one arm coming up to protect his face as he darted out the window.

Jazz scrambled to the sofa, stopping when he felt the carpet squishing under his feet. The throw rug didn't have a white-and-red pattern. It was just white.

He froze for a moment. He could still go through the window, maybe grab the killer, hold him until the police arrived....

But Ginny.

She was trembling on the throw rug, shaking as the fibers soaked up her blood, which jetted from the five clinical, almost surgical, stumps on her right hand. Her eyes had rolled back in her head.

He couldn't move. He was paralyzed. Staring at her.

This was it. This was the moment he'd heard so much about. The moment Billy had apotheosized.

People say there's a light goes out in their eyes when someone dies, Billy whispered in Jazz's mind, in his memory. *But that ain't all. There's a sound, Jasper. A sound that goes quiet. It's beautiful and it's peaceful and it's sacred an' holy. You gotta get close to hear it go.*

The telltale pinprick on her neck told the story, as if he needed the help. Like Myerson had been and like the next two victims would be, she'd been injected with drain cleaner, which had wreaked havoc on the muscles of her heart. As if the shock trauma of her fingers being cut off weren't enough, she was also in incredible pain, and suffering a massive heart attack.

Jazz prayed that Howie had called 911. He shook himself

from his stupor and dropped to his knees next to Ginny. The sight and smell of the blood, the feel of it seeping through his jeans, made him dizzy. There was so much of it; you chop off five fingers while the victim's alive and struggling, and most likely you open up an artery or two. *First time I cut an artery,* Billy said, *I couldn't believe how much—*

Jazz stopped the voice. He felt the blood. He wanted more of it. He wanted to run his hands through the carpet. He wanted none of it. He wanted to run.

No! You can't run! Help her! You have to help her!

Did she recognize him? Or was she too far gone? He couldn't tell. Her expression was one of sheer panic, a terror that absorbed into every pore and every inch of flesh. If she did recognize him, what was she thinking? Was she thinking, *Oh, thank God, it's Jasper!*

Or *Oh, God, no—anyone but Jasper!*

He felt like he should say something to her, but he didn't trust his voice. He didn't trust anything about himself. All he wanted at that moment was to lean over, take her throat in his hands....

God! Goddamn it! Goddamn Billy Dent and goddamn his son, too. Tears sprang to Jazz's eyes. She was dying. Dying right in front of him, and he didn't trust himself to help her because he didn't trust his hands not to finish the job instead.

"Just do it!" he yelled to himself, his voice raw and bleak in the close quarters of the apartment. "Save her, you useless piece of—"

He didn't finish. As he watched, she hitched a breath, then gasped, then stopped breathing. She was in the full throes of cardiac arrest.

Jazz didn't think. He didn't torture himself. He tilted her head back and listened for breathing. Nothing. A moment of intense pleasure washed over him, followed by a revulsion so sickening that he almost threw himself headlong out the window.

Not yet. She's not dead yet.

With her head still tilted back, he pinched her nose shut and sealed his mouth over hers, exhaling hard into her until her chest rose. Then again.

She lay there, still.

His fingers probed her chest until he found the xiphoid process. He started chest compressions, pumping thirty times, then rocking back on his heels. Nothing. He blew into her mouth again, her chest rising and falling for him, but then going still again when he switched back to compressions.

"Don't do this, Ginny," he said to her. "Don't give him this. Don't give *me* this." Tears streamed down his face. He didn't know why. He didn't know if he was desperate to save her or just angry at himself for even trying. A voice in his head—it wasn't Billy's; Jazz was afraid it was his own—whispered that if she died, at least he would be here for it. At least he would witness it.

Breath-breath. And compressions. Breath-breath. And compressions. It felt like it went on forever. It felt like he'd aged years, grown old while trying to keep her alive, his arms and shoulders burning, his lips chapped and raw. The flow of blood from her fingers slowed and stopped. Clotting already? Or because the heart no longer beat to drive blood anywhere? He couldn't decide which. Didn't want to know which.

Finally, he rocked back on his heels, still kneeling in her blood. She was gone. There was nothing he could do. She'd probably been dead for entire minutes now.

And he felt...

He didn't know. He didn't know what he felt. A part of him had dreaded this day, this moment when he would encounter his first fresh kill. He'd been afraid it would awaken something that slumbered fitfully within him. But he'd also anticipated it, yearned for it. It would, he knew, answer the question one way or another: Did he lust for death like his father before him?

And yet here he was. Here he knelt, with a shattered, drained life before him. And nothing.

He had tried to save her, hadn't he? Did that mean anything? But she wasn't *his* victim. Maybe he'd only tried because he'd had no hand in her death. Or maybe he'd truly wanted her to live. He didn't know.

He'd tried and failed. Had he tried hard enough? Had some part of him held back? Had he only done it so that he could touch her as she died? Everything he'd done seemed so loaded now, the motions of CPR taking on a tawdry, lurid tenor in his mind—his lips on hers, his hands on her chest, between those same breasts that had been compressed against him so recently....

The silence was overpowering. Billy had been right. When she'd gone, some sound had gone with her. One moment, there'd been something *of* her, something along with his own hissing breath and his own grunts as he pounded at her still chest. In the next, that something was gone, dead, quiet. He listened to the silence. The emotions running through him made no sense: fear, hope, grief, joy, lust. They weren't Billy Dent's feelings, but they weren't a normal person's, either.

What the hell am I?

The silence ended as suddenly as it had begun—in the distance, sirens wailed, closing in. Howie had called 911 after all.

How much time had passed since he'd sent Howie rushing outside? The killer had gotten out the window, but how far had he gone? Could he still be caught?

Jazz leapt to his feet and scrambled over the sofa to the window. He looked down as the sirens grew louder.

Down in the alley, a long, thin figure lay in a pool of widening blood, illuminated by the lights from the car wash.

Howie!

CHAPTER 20

Jazz didn't think; he hurled himself through the window and clambered down the fire escape like a monkey on crystal meth, dropping the last six feet to the dirty alley pavement the way the killer must have. How long had it been? How long had he struggled with Ginny?

No sooner had his feet touched the ground than one of the sirens moaned to a halt, an ambulance jerking to a sudden stop right in front of him. Two paramedics practically fell out of the ambo, one carrying a black bag.

Jazz got to Howie before they did; he was still breathing, lying facedown on the asphalt. Where was all the blood coming from? He didn't want to move Howie and make it worse, but he had to know. In the background, he could still hear another siren—the police, pulling into the parking lot. Ginny lived— *had* lived, he reminded himself—closer to the hospital than to the police station.

"Howie, can you hear me? Howie? Come on, man. Howie?"

"Jumper?" the first paramedic said, running over and checking the distance from the roof at the same time. "What the hell? Call said third floor, but—"

"There's no time," Jazz said, taking control. "He's a type-A hemophiliac—"

"Hold on, kid," the second paramedic said. "Our call said third floor. Is this the same—"

"The woman on three is dead already," Jazz said, as composed as he could make himself. Which was, actually, very, *very* composed. "This one here is a type-A hemophiliac. He needs—"

"No bracelet," said the first one, already down on one knee next to Howie. The paramedic touched his neck. "Pulse is thready."

"He needs clotting factor VIII," Jazz said. He felt awash in blood—Ginny's, now Howie's. The second paramedic, standing doubtfully aside, pointed to Jazz's pants.

"Is that *your* blood? What's going on here?"

"Please." Howie had already lost a lot of blood, and he would lose more if these yahoos didn't get their acts together. Ten pints. Ten pints was all he had, and it gushed from him like a water cannon. As if to complicate things, a Lobo's Nod deputy came into the alleyway, barking into his shoulder mic, clearly communicating with another cop in the building. A moment later, another man followed—it was Deputy Erickson, out of uniform, dressed in jeans and a T-shirt. Great. Where the hell had *he* come from?

Jazz shook it off. Howie was all that mattered. "Please, just administer a dose of—"

"Kid, this guy's got no medical bracelet, and I'm not about to give him—"

"He forgets it all the time," Jazz told them. By now the second paramedic had decided that Jazz needed medical attention, too, and was preparing to wrap a blood-pressure cuff around his arm. Jazz shook him off. "He forgets the bracelet. Trust me; he's gonna bleed out if you don't—"

"We know our jobs. Who the hell do you think you are, kid?"

And Jazz snapped.

He didn't snap the way a normal person might snap. A normal person would fling his arms around and stomp his feet and rant at the top of his lungs, bellowing to the sky. There might be tears, from a normal person.

Jazz went quiet. He darted out one hand and grabbed the wrist of the paramedic who had been trying to cuff him and pulled the man close, holding his gaze.

In a moment, he channeled every last drop of Billy Dent.

"Who am I? I'll tell you. I'm the local psychopath, and if you don't save my best friend's life, I will hunt down everyone you've ever cared about in your life and make you watch while I do things to them that will have you begging me to kill them. *That's* who I am."

It was ridiculous. It was absurd. And yet...It was utterly believable. He left no doubt in the man's mind that Jazz could—and would—do exactly as he'd promised. Moreover, he left no doubt that Jazz would enjoy every last second of it.

"You, uh"—the EMT swallowed—"you said type-A?"

"Yes."

"We don't have, uh, clotting factor VIII on the bus, but

we can give him DDAVP to hold him until we get to the hospital."

"Then do it," Jazz ordered, shoving the paramedic away from him. Erickson, who had watched the whole thing, stood stunned for a moment, then approached Jazz and, without pre-amble, slapped handcuffs on him.

CHAPTER 21

Erickson shoved Jazz against the wall and started reading him his rights. As much as Jazz didn't like Erickson, he really couldn't blame the deputy. Jazz *had* threatened the paramedic, and the other cops on the scene were reporting over their mics that the third-floor apartment's door was kicked in, the window was open, and there was a dead woman on the floor. Jazz probably would have brought out the cuffs, too, if their positions had been flipped.

"Do you understand these rights?" Erickson asked as he finished. "Well?"

"Sure I do. Hey, do you always carry handcuffs when you're off-duty?" Jazz taunted. "Your girlfriends like that?"

"Shut up," Erickson said, frisking Jazz quickly but efficiently. Jazz stood mute as the deputy ran his hands up between his thighs. Howie would have had a smart-ass zinger ready; Jazz couldn't think of a single one.

Erickson spun him around and Jazz made a point of looking at the deputy's eyes. Blue.

Were they the same blue as the killer's? Jazz couldn't be sure. The lighting here in the alleyway was so different from the light in Ginny's apartment. He could hear G. William now: *Eye color ain't exactly evidence, Jazz.*

"Take a picture," Erickson growled as Jazz stared. "It'll last longer."

"Just happened to be in the area while off-duty, Erickson?" Jazz said sarcastically. "Like when you were the first one there to see Carla O'Donnelly and Helen Myerson?"

"I don't know what you're getting at, kid. I live two blocks away."

"What am I under arrest for?" Jazz asked. Behind Erickson, he could see the paramedics lifting Howie on a stretcher. An IV bag had already been hung. They were moving quickly, speaking in short, clipped sentences composed mostly of numbers and abbreviations. Howie's stats. Howie's meds. Howie's life, reduced to medical jargon.

"Pretty much anything I can think of," Erickson said. He gestured to another deputy, who had come back into the alleyway. "Take this kid to the station. I'll be along soon."

"What's the charge?" the other deputy asked.

"Yeah, I was just wondering the same thing," Jazz put in.

"Shut up," Erickson said again. "The charge right now is suspicion of being a pain in my ass. I'll put something formal down when I get to the station. For now, just get him out of my sight."

"Wait!" Jazz shouted. "Look, don't take me away yet. Let me go to the hospital with Howie."

"Are you nuts? For all I know, you're the one who killed him."

"Killed him? He's not—"

"Get him out of here," Erickson said.

Jazz struggled as the deputy dragged him away. He heard the ambulance doors slam, and then the ambulance engine revved. The siren wailed. Good. If Howie were dead, then they wouldn't be bothering with the siren.

Pulled out of the alley and into the parking lot of Ginny's building, Jazz saw his night go from miserable to nightmarish. Standing there in the parking lot was none other than Doug Weathers. What was *he* doing there?

It took Weathers a moment to realize what was happening, but Jazz could see the calculation in his eyes as he began to understand what was unfolding before him: Jazz in cuffs. Police on the scene. Ambulance roaring past. It all equaled a major story to Weathers, a story that could easily be grafted to the Billy Dent story and once again have CNN and the networks pointing their satellites at Doug Weathers.

Weathers quickly fumbled in his pocket and brought out his cell phone, raising it to eye level. Oh, great. He was going to take a picture as soon as Jazz got close enough.

Jazz couldn't let that happen.

"Hey, Jasper!" Weathers called out, naked glee in his voice. "Smile!"

Before Weathers could do anything, Jazz dropped his head and charged, breaking free from the deputy. His hands were cuffed behind him, so he collided with Weathers, his shoulder digging into the reporter's gut, knocking him off-kilter and sending the cell phone to the ground. The deputy shouted out from behind him, but Jazz just barreled ahead; Weathers fell backward and landed on his butt. Jazz staggered to one side, stepping on the cell phone with a satisfying *crack*.

Just to be sure, he ground his foot down, hard. Plastic crunched.

"Hey!" Weathers shouted, jumping up. "Hey! You can't do that!"

The deputy grabbed Jazz and pulled him away. The phone looked like someone had stepped on an enormous, high-tech cockroach, its wiry guts shooting out from the broken case.

"You son of a—!" Weathers got up in Jazz's face. "You just destroyed private property, kid. I'm gonna sue you. I'm gonna have you arrested for malicious—"

"Already arrested," Jazz said calmly. "And hey, you can't sue me for being clumsy."

"Clumsy!" Weathers's eyes went so wide that Jazz wondered if the man's sockets could hold them in. "Clumsy! You charged me."

"Nah, I tripped, man. I'm such a klutz. Sorry. I'll buy you a new cell."

Weathers lunged for Jazz, who tried to sidestep but found himself stuck between the reporter and the deputy. Jazz grunted as Weathers landed a weak blow on his shoulder.

"You gonna arrest this guy for battery?" Jazz asked the deputy.

"Oh, jeez," the deputy muttered as Weathers flailed again. This time, all three of them went down in a heap. Jazz winced as he landed on his side.

"Clumsy!" Weathers ranted. "I'll clumsy you, you little—"

And then Erickson came running up, shouting. He waded

into the fray, pulling Weathers off of Jazz, pushing Jazz to one side to free up the other deputy. He moved with ruthless efficiency and quiet strength, easily shoving Weathers aside as if the man weighed no more than a bag of sugar. Jazz kicked and shimmied a little to make Erickson's job tougher.

Suddenly, bright headlights stabbed at him. He couldn't shield his eyes with his hands, so he had to close them instead, sinking into the bright red world behind his eyelids. The car stopped nearby; a door opened.

A voice said, "What the hell is going on here?"

Jazz had never been so glad to hear G. William's voice.

Jazz's wrists still hurt a half hour later at the hospital—Erickson had put the cuffs on way too tight. With the cuffs off now, he sat in the waiting room at Lobo's Nod General Hospital, alternating between wrists, rubbing them back to life.

G. William had immediately demanded a report from Erickson, who ran down what he knew, including that Howie was on his way to the hospital. G. William had taken in the scene, including a beyond-irate Doug Weathers, and ordered Erickson to secure the area while he took Jazz to the hospital.

Jazz spoke little to G. William on the way to the hospital. A part of him—some intuitive, quiet part—wanted to warn G. William not to trust Erickson with the crime scene. But the larger part of him was worried about Howie. He was afraid that getting into an argument with the sheriff would delay his getting to the hospital.

Howie was still in surgery when Jazz arrived.

Once G. William was done with the crime scene at Ginny's, the sheriff would—Jazz knew—unload a world of hurt on Jazz for interfering. Worse yet, once Howie's parents returned from filling out the insurance forms, they were going to unload their own particular brand of hurt on him. Howie's mom had never approved of her son hanging out with Jazz, and she would never, ever let him forget this, even if Howie lived.

The door whispered open and Connie ran in, out of breath, her braids flying behind her. She launched herself into Jazz's arms as he rose from his chair. "What happened? Are you okay? Is Howie okay? What *happened*?" She'd been halfway to Tynan Ridge when Jazz, borrowing G. William's cell for a moment, had texted her to tell her to get to the hospital.

He gave her a truncated version of events: Ginny, the killer, Howie. "Looks like he was cut when he intercepted the guy in the alley," Jazz finished, "and then—"

"Ginny? Ginny's dead?" Connie went weak in his arms and it took all his strength to keep her from collapsing to the floor and guide her to the chair he'd just abandoned. He maneuvered her into it.

"I'm really sorry," he said. "It was—"

Connie started sobbing; heaving, violent sobs that wracked her body. Jazz stood before her, baffled, unsure what to do. In movies and books, the man always puts his arms around the crying woman, but he'd never understood what that was supposed to accomplish, and he couldn't see it now, either.

Still, it usually worked, so he bent over and folded Connie into his embrace, where her crying became muffled, the

212

rhythm of it a strange and sour chorus to the beating of his heart.

"It'll be okay," he said, feeling like an idiot for saying it. It would not be okay. It would most emphatically *not* be okay. Ginny was dead. Howie was in surgery. Worst of all, the killer was still at large. It was the exact *opposite* of okay.

Just then, the door hissed again, in that peculiar sibilance reserved for hospital doors. Howie's parents stumbled into the waiting room as though they'd both been shot. Mr. Gersten's face was as ashen as Howie's had been in the alleyway; Jazz couldn't see Mrs. Gersten's face, which was buried against her husband's shoulder.

"Should we—" Connie started, then stopped herself, remembering, no doubt, that Howie's parents had never liked Jazz much to begin with.

The Gerstens made their way to a sofa and collapsed onto it like some bizarre conjoined twins. Overhead, a voice said, "Dr. McDowell to Oncology. Dr. McDowell, Oncology," and when it went away, the air was populated only with the stereo effect of two people weeping.

"What if he doesn't..." Mrs. Gersten said.

"Shh. He will. He's strong," her husband answered in what Jazz thought was the least convincing tone of voice in history.

"He's *not* strong!" she yelled. "He's the *opposite* of strong! He can't even—" And then she lost all her words and just wept and wept.

Jazz forced himself not to look away, and Mr. Gersten met his eyes. A moment passed between them, as if they were respecting each other and their strangely male, stoic roles in this drama, but then Mr. Gersten broke down, too, and tears streamed down his face.

"And now it happens. . . ." Jazz murmured, figuring that this would be the moment where Mr. Gersten would come over and abuse him, verbally at the very least, but physically would be completely understandable. But the Gerstens didn't move, didn't speak, didn't glare, not even when Mrs. Gersten finally looked up from her husband's shoulder to reveal eyes bloodshot like a road map.

Relatively sure he wouldn't be assaulted, Jazz steered Connie to a largish chair and they both settled into it. "You ready to hear what happened?" he asked in a soft voice that would not cut through the churchlike quiet of the waiting room.

Connie wiped her eyes and nodded.

"This isn't going to be easy to hear," Jazz told her, already editing events in his mind; Connie didn't need to know all of it. "We remembered Ginny's real name was Virginia, making her a perfect match for the next victim," Jazz started, and then told her what had happened after that, leaving out the most gruesome details of Ginny's death and his own complicated reaction to it.

Time in the waiting room had no real meaning; even though Jazz was sure he must have spoken to Connie for hours, he was convinced no time had passed at all. Eventually, though, a doctor emerged through a different whispering, hissing door and approached the Gerstens.

"Mr. and Mrs. Gersten? I'm Dr. Mogelof. I'm the trauma surgeon who saw your son."

Jazz felt Connie stiffen next to him, but the doctor's body

language and tone of voice told Jazz everything he needed to know even before she said it: "Your son came through surgery much, much better than we would have expected. Given his condition and the amount of trauma, he's really in phenomenal shape. I think—"

She got no further. Mrs. Gersten collapsed against her husband, her tears now of joy. Mr. Gersten pumped the doctor's hand enthusiastically, and the surgeon's reserve cracked into a broad and relieved smile.

"He's in recovery right now and he needs to be alone while he sleeps, but he's going to be okay. He's going to live."

Connie sighed with relief as the Gerstens sank into the couch again. For Jazz, it was as though he'd been trapped underwater in a frozen lake, frantically swimming back and forth, pounding on the thick ice above, looking for a break, for a hole. Able to see the sunlight filtering through the ice, able to see the open air, but unable to breathe it, the air in his lungs already run out, his life measured not even in seconds, but in instants of no determinate length. When suddenly—just as the black of the water and the black of his own death had wrapped their tendrils around him and threatened to squeeze the last bits of life out of him— his questing hands found a break above and he launched himself through it and opened his mouth to the sweet, sweet—

Jazz dropped into a hard, sudden sleep in Connie's arms.

A hand gently nudged Jazz from a deep slumber
—*gotta wakey, wakey, Jasper, my boy*—

215

and he startled, waking Connie, who had drifted off with him. The Gerstens were nowhere to be seen, and G. William stood over him.

"You hearin' me, Jazz? You awake?"

Jazz grumbled, sitting up and wiping an embarrassing string of drool from his chin. It hadn't been the usual dream, with the knife. It had been Rusty this time. He blinked bleary sleep away.

—*gotta wakey*—

"I'm awake. Is Howie—"

"He's up. In the ICU. Dr. Mogelof says no visitors tonight, but she's making an exception, given the circumstances. Need to talk to the two of you. Put together some kind of timeline for what happened tonight." G. William checked his watch. "*Last* night, technically."

Connie disentangled herself from Jazz and stood up. "Let's go."

"Sorry." G. William seemed genuinely apologetic. "Family only back there. I got a need for Jazz—police business—but they won't let you in. Maybe tomorrow."

Connie took that as well as she usually took someone telling her what she couldn't do: She crossed her arms over her chest and cocked her left hip in what she called her Sassy Stance and fixed the sheriff with a glare that Jazz knew all too well.

He leapt up between them before Connie could start a fight. "Con, it'll be okay. You should go home. Get some real rest. We'll both come back tomorrow to see Howie together, okay?"

"He's my friend, too," she said, her jaw set, her eyes flashing with anger.

"I know." He hugged her, even though she didn't open her arms to him. He held her until she thawed, pecking him on the cheek and leaving without so much as a kind look in the sheriff's direction.

G. William adjusted his hat and grinned. "That one'll keep you on the straight and narrow, Jasper Francis. Don't let her go."

He clapped a hand on Jazz's shoulder and guided him through a door and down a corridor. The hospital was quiet, even the footfalls of nurses muffled by the gummy soles of their shoes. Jazz felt like he was walking down a dream hallway, where sounds were not allowed to exist. Sounds and, maybe, the living.

Breaking the unnerving silence, he said, "I have to ask.... This may seem stupid, but... Ginny. Ms. Davis. Is she really—"

"Sorry, Jazz. I know you tried your best. But yeah."

"Okay. I thought there was a chance maybe that I was wrong, that I didn't read her pulse right, or..."

—put your fingers right here and make sure, Jasper, make damn sure, 'cause the last thing you want is what's supposed to be a corpse gettin' up and tellin' the world what you done—

There was no chance. Of course not. But he'd hoped.

"I want to wrap this up fast," G. William said, moving. "I bet you're worried about your grandmom, and I want to get you home to her."

Gramma. In all the craziness, he'd forgotten about her, had completely lost track of time. He wasn't even sure what day

217

it was, or what year. Time had gone elastic and malleable and ductile.

Nighttime was the worst time of the day for Gramma, but the Benadryl should have kept her knocked out. He hated imagining what she would do if she woke up alone. Anything was possible, really, up to and including deciding that he'd been abducted and launching her own version of a commando raid on the nearest house.

Well, there was nothing to do about it for now. He had to help G. William, and then—

"Here we are," G. William said, gesturing to a door.

Somehow it wasn't fair. Beyond that door lay Jazz's best friend in the world, the best friend he'd put in harm's way, the best friend he had nearly killed as easily as if he'd wielded the knife himself. And yet the door looked like every other door along the corridor. There was nothing special about it, and there should have been.

"You ready for this?" G. William asked.

Jazz wasn't, but he nodded anyway and G. William pushed open the door.

It wasn't nearly as bad as Jazz had feared. That said, it was still bad enough.

"If I didn't have bad luck, I wouldn't have any luck at all," Howie said as soon as he saw Jazz, cracking a grin.

It was Howie and it wasn't Howie, all at once. His best friend lay in a hospital bed, covered to the chest with a blanket so faded blue that it was almost white. Stick-thin Howie looked even thinner under that blanket, a series of long wrinkles in the fabric that suggested a body more than revealed one. His skin was sallow, his eyes sunken above massive bags that drooped down like twin black eyes with something to prove. Bruises ran up and down both arms, radiating out from the points where tubes entered his body.

The tubes.

There were—Jazz counted—three of them. A saline drip for hydration. A line still transfusing blood. And a third one. Something else...

"Dinnertime," Howie joked, pointing to one bag, as if he could read Jazz's confusion over the air like a radio transmission.

Dextrose. Right. It had been hours since Howie had eaten, and he probably still wasn't up to taking solid food, what with the trauma, the anesthetics....

A duo of wires also hung limp between connection points on Howie's chest and a heart monitor beside the bed. The monitor's EKG line loped along at a steady, slow sixty beats per minute. Tolerable.

"Apparently," Howie said jovially, "he missed every vital organ and only nicked a blood vessel. You probably would have gotten up and chased the guy down. Me? I end up facedown in my own blood. Three cheers for low clotting factor! Next time *you* get to be the one who gets stabbed."

"You weren't stabbed," Jazz said after a moment's hesitation. "You were slashed. They're different."

"Okay, whatever." Howie grimaced as he adjusted his position in bed. "Can we at least do some *CSI* mojo on my wound and figure out what kind of knife he used and then, like, track him down where he bought it and totally go SWAT-style on his ass?"

G. William answered before Jazz could. "Doesn't work like that. Sorry. Slashing wounds don't, uh, betray any characteristic of the blade. Only stab wounds do that. If he'd stabbed you instead of slashing you, then maybe we could get some kind of forensic..." G. William realized he was rambling and drifted off into silence, clearing his throat. He settled into a chair next to the bed. "Anyway. The docs are saying you're gonna be fine. Glad to hear it."

Jazz still lingered by the door, unable to move closer. A crashing wave of guilt had broken over him as soon as he recognized Howie in the bed, and the force of that wave kept him from approaching. Guilt—this kind of guilt, at least—was unfamiliar to him. Guilt for manipulating people? Sure. All the time. But he dismissed that guilt as a matter of course, as a cost of doing business. This was different. He'd almost gotten someone killed.

He *had* gotten someone killed.

Howie raised a hand, even though it clearly took effort, and waved for Jazz to come closer. "You gonna guard the door all night? Don't you want to see my stitches? They're gross." He said "gross" with a whisper of delight.

Jazz went to the bed and stood opposite G. William. He had a powerful urge to *touch* Howie, almost to prove to himself that this paper-thin, transparent-skinned thing in bed was really his best friend and not a hallucination.

Howie leaned as close as he could, given his weakness and the tubes. His voice—already weak—wasn't getting any stronger as he spoke. "I have to own up, dawg; you can't see the stitches yet. They're still taped and gauzed."

Jazz played along. "Are you gonna have a scar?"

Howie frowned. "A little one. I wanted a nice big one, but no one asked me, on account of me being unconscious at the time. Can you believe it?"

"Bastards," Jazz intoned, and then he did it—he reached out and put his hand over Howie's where it lay on top of the blanket.

Something in that connection, something in that completed circuit—the taut vulnerability of Howie's skin, the reality of contact, *something*—shattered a vessel deep inside Jazz, and he found himself speaking before he could think.

"It's all my fault," he whispered. "It's my fault she's dead."

"It's not."

"It is. You wanted to call G. William from the car. If we had—"

"If we had"—Howie's voice floated from the bed, weak but resolved—"it would have gone down the same. Homeboy was already killing her."

"Howie's right, Jazz," G. William said gently. He rubbed his battered mass of a nose. "If you'd called, we wouldn't have gotten there any faster. And in the meantime, you made him deviate from his plan. You interrupted him. Scared him. He usually cuts the fingers off postmortem. This time he cut them off while she was still alive."

"Oh, yay." The bitterness lay heavy on Jazz's tongue. "A

victory for us. I'm sure Ginny will be glad to hear— Oh, wait, that's right: She's *dead*."

G. William gave him a moment to indulge his anger and guilt, then cleared his throat. "I need to know exactly what you guys did and saw. Gonna record this, okay?" He brandished his smartphone and aimed the camera at them.

They consented to being recorded and Jazz pulled up a chair, sinking into it next to Howie, leaving one hand brushing against Howie's, as if to make sure his friend wasn't going anywhere. Between the two of them, they recounted the logic that had taken them to Ginny's apartment, and what had happened afterward. Jazz surprised himself by recalling and describing Ginny's death in a voice entirely devoid of emotion, and as he recited the facts, he found those same facts bothering him less and less. Grief was replaced with anger— anger at himself for failing, but also anger at the man impersonating his father.

" . . . called nine-one-one," Howie was saying, "and then I heard something in the alleyway, so I went back there and"— Howie coughed—"and valiantly attacked his knife with my guts, to no avail."

"Did you get a good look at him? Could you describe him?"

Howie smiled wanly. "Yeah. He was about yay long"—he held up his hands, four inches apart—"thin, made of steel. Pointy. Sharp."

Jazz grinned despite himself.

"What about you, Jasper?"

Jazz shook his head. He'd been trying to recall the killer's face, his eyes, anything. But he'd had only that single instant before the man vanished through the window, heading for street level and Howie's gut. Those blue eyes. "All I can tell you is he's white, which I think we already assumed. Probably between five-eleven and six-one. Ish." He waggled a hand. "Blue eyes."

G. William thanked them and stood to leave, gesturing to Jazz that it was time for Howie to get some rest. But Jazz had to know: "Did you guys find props? In her apartment?"

The sheriff hesitated, then nodded. "Yeah. A toy bow and arrow, and some other stuff. You know."

During his phase as the Artist, Billy had posed his victims. For his fourth victim, he'd posed her like Cupid drawing a bow, matching her initials—V.D.—to Valentine's Day. Billy's first dozen or so killings had all taken place before Jazz was born, so he didn't know why Billy had done this. Probably one more in a highly successful string of distracting tactics that had kept the cops off his trail for decades.

"So I was right," Jazz said.

"Looks like it. Definitely mimicking Billy's career."

"What about the fingers?"

"Cut 'em premortem, not post-, but you knew that already. We're not assuming this is a change in MO. Just that he heard you guys coming and had to move quickly."

Quickly...No more than a minute had passed between Jazz pounding on and then crashing through the door. The Impressionist had cut off Ginny's fingers in record time.

"Left the middle finger, as per usual. We found it under the sofa."

Jazz wondered if he'd kicked it there when running into

223

the room. "You know what you have to do." He stared at G. William and did not let up.

The sheriff didn't even need to consult his smartphone. "Billy's next victim was named Isabella Hernandez. Maid at a hotel. Thirty-five. First thing in the morning, my crew is contacting every hotel in the area and asking if they have anyone with the initials I.H. working for them."

"Morning? What about now?"

"If he's following Billy's pattern, we have three days before he takes his next victim. Better to let my people go at it in the light of day."

"What about the victims after her? You have the whole chronology of Billy's career. You can start looking for all of them, not just the next one."

G. William shook his head. "Jazz, I can't do it that way. Have to put all of my manpower on the most imminent threat." He held up a hand to stop Jazz before he could interrupt. "How would you feel if your wife was the next victim and she got killed and then you found out that the cops hadn't put all their efforts into protecting her?"

Good point. "What about the feds? You have to be getting them involved, right?"

G. William snorted. "Not just yet. Still putting together the ViCAP report." Quickly, before Jazz could jump in, he added, "That thing's thirteen pages long, Jazz. A hundred eighty-some questions to answer. And it ain't worth doin' if we don't do it right. And right now there's nothing convincing. Right now it's just a pattern, but there's no MO, no signature that's common—"

"The pattern *is* the signature!" Jazz was up and out of his chair. "God, G. William!"

"Jazz, everything's inconclusive right now. I've made some calls to the feds, on the QT, but the first murder just didn't have enough unique characteristics—"

"A severed finger isn't a—"

"Hey, guys?" They broke off and looked down at Howie, who lay exhausted and weary between them. "You guys are totally harshing the killer buzz I've been working on, thanks to some amazing meds a very nice nurse gave me. It's bumming me out." He grinned lazily. "And I'm not gonna last much longer, anyway. Sleepy-time is totally strong-arming me."

"Sorry." G. William cleared his throat with a sound like a drowning child. "We'll let you get some rest." He jerked his head toward the door in a manner that tolerated no rebellion.

"Hang on. Wait a sec," Howie said.

Jazz turned back to the bed. Howie gestured him over.

G. William went out into the hall and Jazz stood by Howie. "You need something?" Jazz asked him. "More meds? Some water? A hot nurse and a stripper pole?"

Howie chuckled, then winced. "Don't make me laugh. And I'll take that nurse and stripper pole in, like, a week. But here. I wanted to give you this."

He fumbled with the nightstand drawer for a moment, then handed his cell phone over to Jazz. "I'm not gonna need it for a little while. So you might as well have it."

"Uh, thanks." Jazz stared at the thing. "But, um..."

Howie gripped Jazz's wrist with all his strength, which wasn't much. It was like a baby's clench, if a baby had had

Howie's absurdly long fingers. Still, the fact that Howie made the effort and the urgency in his eyes corralled Jazz's attention.

"Get this guy," Howie whispered with all that was left in him. "You'll need a cell when you're tracking him down. Take it."

"Howie, man, I'm done. You heard G. William—he's got it under control. He's on it."

"G. William isn't *you*, man. You're the guy. You're the one."

"No."

"Do it for me."

"Howie, I'm out. Seriously. This was too much. You almost..." He yanked his hand away. "I'm done."

"You think—" Howie swallowed hard. It seemed to take forever. "You think you need to stop because I have some stitches? Lost some blood?" He forced the phone back into Jazz's hands, as though his life depended on it. "Man, that's why you have to..." A long, slow blink. "That's why you *have* to..." He giggled. "Wow, this is some really good—"

Bang. He was out.

Jazz took a deep breath. Patted his best friend's hand.

Tucked the cell phone into his pocket and left.

CHAPTER 22

Connie still had Howie's car and had driven home with it, leaving Jazz stranded, the Jeep abandoned in Ginny's parking lot. G. William drove Jazz there, even though Ginny's apartment building was the very last thing in the world Jazz wanted to see.

From the street, you couldn't even tell anything had happened. There were two cruisers parked in the lot, but they had their lights out and engines off—they could have been two cops on patrol stopping to gossip or swap doughnut recipes. Down in the alley, he caught an occasional glimpse of a flashlight played along the walls. Crime-scene investigating to see if the killer had left any evidence. Footprints, maybe. Maybe he'd dropped the knife he'd used to—

Well, in any event, they'd be looking for evidence. A part of Jazz yearned to join them, but he had told Howie he was done. And he meant it. He was out of the profiling business.

It had been abstract and compelling and—in a way, he had to admit—fun when it had been Jane Doe. But Ginny died under his own hands. He had probably pushed her last breath out of her lungs. And Howie could have died so easily that . . .

"You all right?" G. William asked.

Jazz hesitated. He was out of the profiling business, true, but a part of him still felt compelled to help. As though the cops could never do this on their own.

But who was he to think he could crack this case? Profiling was an art, not a science. Sure, he thought he had some insight into the killer, but way back in 2002, the cops thought they had insight into the Beltway Sniper, too. They knew the guy was white, young, childless. So imagine their surprise when they caught John Allen Muhammad: black, forties, with a kid close to Jazz's age in tow.

"Jazz? I asked if—"

"Yep," he said, making a split-second decision. "I'm fine. Thanks for the ride."

He drove home a little faster than the law would favor. Now that he knew Howie was all right, he had to shift gears to the other person in his life who needed him: Gramma. He'd left her for—quick check of the in-dash clock—oh, Lord. More hours than he cared to imagine.

He was worried she'd done something stupid. Hurt herself. Hurt someone else. Done something that would make it easier for Melissa to yank him into foster care. Even if the Benadryl hadn't worn off yet, she could have rolled off the sofa and broken something.

The house was quiet and dark when he unlocked the front door. He usually left a light on so that Gramma wouldn't trip in the dark, but he'd forgotten when he and Connie and Howie had left the house a million years ago. He paused in the foyer for a moment, listening to the careful click of the lock as he shut the door. Something cold lingered in the air, something that set him on edge.

He had the feeling he was being watched.

That someone was in the house.

Well, of course someone's in the house. Gramma's in the—

He didn't even finish the thought. Absurd. Trying to rationalize away the fear.

Fear's okay, Billy had said to him once. It had surprised Jazz, who had always heard his father speak of fear as comedic, as something prospects evinced in a desperate, useless attempt to stay alive. Fear was something to laugh at in all its many, splendid forms, each one unique to the victim. *Fear can keep you alive. The trick is not to let it overwhelm you. Not to let it rule you. If you're afraid, that's the universe trying to tell you something. Get away. Don't run; don't panic. Just pick up and walk out, calm as you please. Panic makes you stupid.*

Should he call G. William? After all, he had Howie's cell, an unfamiliar but comforting brick in his pocket.

No. No, that was ridiculous. There was no one in the house.

He crept into the sitting room. Gramma slept on the sofa, her breath a light, snoring buzz. He sneaked closer to her and realized that she was covered with a blanket.

She hadn't been under a blanket when he'd left.

He turned slowly, his eyes adjusting to the dark, peering into the murk of the room. Empty.

She *might* have covered herself. The blanket was from the

chair a couple of feet away. She might have just gotten up, cold, groggily snatched up the blanket, and wrapped herself in it before succumbing to sleep again.

No one is in the house. It's just your nerves. After everything you've been through tonight, you're entitled.

He grinned. Here he was, son of the world's most notorious serial killer, afraid of the dark. What was next: the boogeyman? The monster in the closet? Gremlins under the bed?

Prowling the house like a burglar, he left the lights off, moving silently with touch and memory to guide him. If someone *was* in the house, he didn't want to let on that he was aware. He wanted to catch the intruder. He checked each room on the ground floor, including the little pantry, just in case. In a moment of paranoia so ridiculous it would have been funny if not for the circumstances, he even checked under the sink, imagining the killer tucked up in there like a hermit crab, waiting to strike. All that lurked beneath the sink, though, were a pile of sponges, a roll of paper towels, bottles of various cleaners, and an empty cigar box Gramma insisted belonged there.

He roamed the top floor, executed quick single push-ups to look under the beds, rifled through the closets, then went down to the basement, poking behind the furnace and the water heater (cobwebs, dust, desiccated spider shells, and a single pile of petrified mouse droppings that made him add *Buy mousetraps* to his mental to-do list). He even crawled into what Gramma called the "rut cellar," an old crawl space under the stairs that had once served as home to an archive of Billy's childhood and early adult years—notebooks, yearbooks, boxes of newspaper clippings, a lone swimming trophy

(*I figured why not?* Billy had said with a shrug), and more. All of it confiscated during the trial. Jazz could have had it back just by signing some papers, but he didn't want it. And, unlike the Jeep, he didn't need it.

Shimmying out of the crawl space, he allowed himself a small laugh at his own expense. *There. Can you go to bed now, you coward?*

He traipsed back upstairs. Checked on Gramma one last time. She was really out. Made sense just to leave her on the sofa. She'd be a bit disoriented in the morning, but he'd rather deal with her disoriented in the morning than in the middle of the night. So upstairs he went. Flicked on the first light of the evening, washed up, brushed his teeth.

In his bedroom, he groaned when he saw the clock. It was a quarter to four in the morning. He had to be up for school in less than three hours. Beyond the lack of sleep, the idea of walking those halls when everyone learned about Ginny...as the rumors spread that Jazz had been there...He knew how high school gossip worked: By the end of the day, half the school would be convinced Jazz had actually killed her and then covered it up. *His dad... You know, his dad taught him how to get away with it....*

His dad *had* taught him how to get away with it. That was the hell of it.

Stripping off his clothes, Jazz put Howie's cell on the nightstand and crawled into bed. Stared at the ceiling, at the rigid pattern of dark and gray etched there by the distant moon through the window grilles.

Had he made the right decision by bowing out? Yes. He was

convinced of it. Time to let G. William handle this. The sheriff was more than capable. And if he wanted Jazz's advice, well, Jazz would be happy to offer it. But only when asked.

Jazz sighed, sleepy, and rolled over to face the wall—then bolted out of bed, sleepy no more, fumbling for the light switch, his adrenaline pumping so hard and fast that he flicked the switch on, then off, then on again before he could stop himself.

The wall.

The wall of Billy's victims.

Someone had inscribed the first four pictures with a red marker, writing, "1, 2, 3, 4" on them and then coloring the eyes into demonic glares.

The fifth picture—Isabella Hernandez—was circled in thick red loops that wavered and skittered over one another. Written over Isabella's smiling face was this:

COMING SOON
COURTESY OF THE IMPRESSIONIST

CHAPTER 23

The cops were just wrapping up their processing of the crime scene (or, as Jazz thought of it, his house) by the time the sun came up.

Upon getting Jazz's call hours earlier, G. William had wasted no time and taken no chances, personally bringing a team of techs to the house. They searched the house thoroughly, scanned for listening devices, tromped through the surrounding area, questioned the nearest neighbors (no doubt thrilled to be awakened at five in the morning to be asked about "that Dent house"), and dropped roughly a metric ton of fingerprint dust on every conceivable surface.

Nothing.

Jazz sat in the kitchen, nursing a cup of extra-strength coffee with a truly obscene amount of sugar for an added boost of energy. Gramma had awakened before the cops arrived, groggy but somewhat lucid, though once the police got there, she decided it was 1957 and she was at a high school dance. She paraded around the house in her nightgown, coyly batting her eyelashes at the cops, who took the whole thing with good humor. One of them even danced a quick Charleston with her.

Now she was puttering around in her bedroom upstairs, no doubt changing her outfit or, perhaps, her entire mind. The cops were packing up their gear when G. William joined Jazz in the kitchen.

"About those pictures on the wall..."

Jazz sighed. He knew G. William had to confiscate the first five, the ones the "Impressionist" had written on.

"How long you had them up?"

"About a year, I guess."

"What about that screen saver on your computer? 'Remember Bobby Joe Long.' He was some kinda serial killer, wasn't he? What's that about?"

"He didn't do that. It's always been there. I put it there." Jazz shrugged. "He was a killer, yeah, but he let one victim go. Girl named Lisa McVey. He knew she would lead the cops back to him, but he let her go anyway. He couldn't help himself. It was a compulsion. I guess I just..." He shrugged again. "I like knowing that sometimes the impulses can go the other way. That maybe it's possible to have an impulse for good."

G. William clucked his tongue in a way that made Jazz want to fly across the table and rip that tongue out. He was on edge. He had been *invaded*. He was in no mood for anyone—even G. William—to condescend to him.

"You gotta let go, Jazz. Billy is Billy. He's not you. Let it go."

"Does that have anything to do with that guy breaking in here?" Jazz snarled.

"This isn't about you. Don't make it personal."

"Of course it's about me! Of course it's personal! He came into my house. He went into my bedroom. He left a message on *my* wall. This is all about me."

The sheriff looked like he was going to say something. Hesitated. Thought better of it. He consulted his smartphone.

"No prints. No fibers apparent, but we vacuumed the holy hell out of this place. It'll be a while before we can sort through that, though. Looks like he picked the lock with the usual tools—we have tool marks, but nothing exotic or interesting. And that's it."

"No. We have a name for him now."

" 'The Impressionist.' " G. William arched his back, thrusting out his belly like he was pregnant. "Yeah, that makes sense, I guess."

"You have to find him, G. William. Find him or find his next victim. I.H."

"I've already got people compiling a list of every hotel, motel, inn, and B-and-B within twenty miles of here. He's not getting a fifth victim, Jazz. I promise you."

Jazz wished he could believe that. The Impressionist had been one step ahead of them all along, even once they knew his pattern. There was something he was missing, he was sure. Something the Impressionist had done or would do that would make all their preparations moot.

"You oughtta stay home from school today. Get some rest."

"You need some rest, too, big man," Jazz said. G. William's eyes were carrying as much luggage as Howie's had in the hospital. God, Howie! That seemed so long ago now, but it had only been a couple of hours.

"I'll catch some *Z*'s in the office. I'm gonna leave a patrol car out front, so—"

"Ugh." Jazz groaned and dropped his head into his hands. "No. Please don't. People already treat this house like it's...like it was built over an Indian burial ground. You park a car out there and everyone's going to think I did something. 'That crazy Dent kid—'"

"The guy came here once." G. William's tone offered no room for disagreement. "He could come back. I'm not letting him come and go as he pleases. Maybe this is a game to him, but not to me. Got it?"

Before Jazz could answer, he heard the front door open and a pair of unmistakably high heels clicking on the hardwood foyer. Who could—?

He shot a look at G. William, who pretended innocence when Melissa's voice sounded out: "Jasper? Jasper, where are you?"

"You called *her*?" he demanded.

"Your gran's getting worse."

"She's always been a little—"

"Yeah, she's always been a *little*. Now she's a *lot*."

"You think I belong in foster care? Really?"

"Not my call to make. That's Melissa's."

They stared at each other in silence for a moment, until Melissa called out again.

"We're in the kitchen," G. William answered.

A moment later, Melissa entered the kitchen, nodding to the sheriff (who tipped his hat chivalrously) before putting her briefcase on the table. Even though it was five in the morning, Melissa had still put on a severely professional skirt suit and done her makeup. Her own personal brand of body armor.

"Are you willing to listen to reason?" she asked Jazz.

Too tired for the usual sparring and intimidation games, Jazz merely shrugged.

Melissa's lips pressed into a shiny red line. She wanted him to react. She *needed* him to react. He refused to give her the satisfaction.

Until she said . . .

"Jasper, I'm finishing up my report and filing it first thing on Monday. I wanted to give you a heads-up. Especially considering what just happened here. This environment . . . I'm suggesting you be removed to foster care and your grandmother placed in an assisted-living facility. If you want to add your own letter to the report, to counter what I have to say, you're welcome to, but I'll need it by Sunday night. You have my e-mail address, right?"

She said it all in a rush, as though afraid he would interrupt her. But he had no fight left in him. Not now.

People matter. People are real. People matter. He couldn't convince himself.

"Do what you have to do," he told her, not even looking at her, staring instead into the coffee cup on the table before him. "Whatever."

"This is really for the best—"

"If you're done, you can get out of my house," he said.

The kitchen went so silent that he imagined he could hear Melissa's blood pressure. Then she turned on her heel, snatched up her briefcase, and marched out of the kitchen. A moment later, the front door opened and closed.

"I know you're upset—"

"Leave it alone, G. William."

"I know you're upset," the sheriff tried again, "but that was uncalled for. You should call and apologize."

"Apologize?" He lurched out of his chair, shoving it back across the linoleum with a squeak and a stutter. "Apologize? She's gonna put me in some foster home, and my grand-mother'll end up strapped down to a bed twenty-three hours a day in some stack-'em-and-pack-'em old-age home! And I'm supposed to apologize to her?"

G. William shrugged. "Sorry, Jazz. I know it's not ideal, and I know it's not what you want, but she's probably right, you know?"

Jazz had nothing to say to that.

After the house was empty again, Jazz called Connie to let her know what had happened and to tell her that he wouldn't be at school that day. They agreed to meet in the afternoon to visit Howie in the hospital. Connie told him not to worry about the foster home.

"It might end up being a good thing," she said. "Getting out of that house. Taking care of yourself for once, not your grand-mother. And maybe it won't be a foster home. Maybe it'll be your aunt—"

"Yeah, and Billy's sister lives, like, three hundred miles away. What about that, Con? What about us?"

She had no comeback; he felt vaguely guilty for shutting her down like that, but only vaguely. He was tired of everyone telling him what was good for him.

He meant to rest on his day off, but being with Gramma during the day was like babysitting a toddler who thinks the height of fun is badgering you every single minute. She spent a feverish twenty minutes panicking after the police left, worried that she'd somehow offended them (still thinking they were all at a sock-hop in the fifties), and bawling her eyes out like a young girl. Then she stood in the kitchen, screaming out the window at the forlorn, lonesome birdbath, berating it for not attracting any birds. "You're a pathetic excuse for a birdbath!" she yelled. "I've seen birdbaths with dozens of birds, hundreds of birds, *thousands* of birds. You shouldn't even call yourself a birdbath! You're a bird-repellent. Why do you hate birds?"

She grabbed the shotgun and went outside and threatened the birdbath with it, yelling and waving the heavy gun around until she was exhausted. Then she came back inside and stumbled into the parlor.

"Good boy, Billy," she said, patting Jazz's cheek with one withered palm. "Good boy." And she planted a dry, lingering kiss on his forehead. "Good boy to take care of your mama."

Jazz shivered.

Upstairs, he tried to nap while Gramma watched a game show. He drifted off for a few minutes, minutes haunted by the knife, the voices, the flesh. *Just like cutting chicken*, Billy whispered from the past, or from his imagination. *Just like cutting . . .*

And Jazz woke up

—*wakey, wakey*—

thinking of Rusty, both nightmares converging now, oh joy, oh lovely, oh how wonderful. He stared at the blank spots on the wall where Billy's first victims had been. He printed out new pictures and tacked them into place, then stared at them for what seemed to be hours.

Who am I cutting? In the dream. Or who did I cut? Was it Mom? Did Billy make me—

No. He wouldn't go there again.

Eventually—still sleepless—he meandered downstairs. Gramma had vacated her place in front of the TV. Panicking, he checked the window and saw the cop still sitting there. Okay, so she was still inside, then.

He found her in what had once been the formal dining room. No one had eaten in there for years, and the china closet had been nearly empty for just as long. Gramma sat on the old dining table, cross-legged, her nightgown tucked up around her spindly thighs, her hands clasped in her lap. She glared at him with eyes at once cold and burning.

"Mom," he said with relief. "What are you doing in—"

"Why are you calling me 'Mom'?" she demanded, her voice low and gravelly. "Running around this house like a damn *baby*, crying for your *mommy*. You pathetic child."

Oh.

"*Mommy*," she whined, a cruel grin on her lips. "Mommy, where *are* you? Mommy! Mommy!"

"Okay, Gram—"

"Mommy! Mommy! Ha! Remember you as a boy, little

Jasper. Followin' your mama around like a puppy. Glued to her skirts."

Jazz swallowed.

"But your mommy ain't around no more, boy. Your mommy's gone. You hear? Gone." She cackled and her cruel grin grew wider. "Gone, gone, gone! Praise God, gone!"

Jazz's jaw tightened.

"Your mother was a *terrible* person. It's her fault, what happened to your daddy. He was just as fine as can be until she came along and she, you know . . ." Here she leaned back a bit, and the nightgown rose even farther. Jazz's stomach turned. "And she swallowed him with evil and made his soul black and ruined him."

It wasn't true. It wasn't even remotely true, and Jazz couldn't stand for it. "Watch what you say about my mother, Gramma," he warned her.

She licked her lips. "Mama's boy. Like I said. She was evil. She made your daddy evil. And you was born outta her evil. What d'you think that makes you?"

Jazz's temper flared and he lurched toward her, his fists clenched.

"You go ahead, Jasper," she whispered, a cunning light in her eyes. "You hit me. You go on and do it. Think it's the first time I been beat up? Do you?"

He growled and spun around and smacked the flat of his hand against the china closet instead. One of the remaining dishes toppled and cracked.

Gramma laughed. "Mama's boy!" she chortled. "Ain't got

the guts to smack me around, huh? Only one cure for a mama's boy, Jasper."

He spun around and stalked out of the dining room, but her voice followed him down the hall: "Only one cure! Gotta become just like your daddy! That's the only hope for you. You're gonna *become* your daddy...."

CHAPTER 24

Jazz spent a chunk of the day fantasizing about ways to kill his grandmother, plotting them and planning them in the most excruciating, gruesome detail his imagination would allow. It turned out his imagination allowed quite a bit.

He spent the rest of the day convincing himself—over and over—not to do it.

She was goofy and childlike so much of the time that sometimes it was easy to forget that her madness had a cunning dimension to it, too. She knew Jazz's weaknesses. She knew which buttons to push. And when the right synapses fired in the wrong order, she did it cruelly. Gleefully.

By the time Connie was free for the day, his grandmother had shifted into a young girl's persona, asking Jazz (whom she thought to be a priest of some sort, apparently) with a slight lisp if she could have some pudding, since she'd been such a good girl and said all her Hail Marys. Jazz resisted the urge to throttle her. There was some yogurt in the fridge, and it only took him a couple of minutes to convince her that it was actually pudding.

He bundled her up on the sofa with her blanket and an old teddy bear and Nickelodeon, then hopped in the Jeep to pick up Connie. She slid into the passenger seat and gave him a long, lingering kiss that warmed him all over.

"Are you all right?" she asked when they came up for air. "After last night and this morning and—"

"I'm fine," he said, surprised to hear himself say it. It might have even been the truth; he couldn't tell. His world had changed in ways he couldn't yet understand. In *The Crucible,* Reverend Hale says at one point, "Man, remember, until an hour before the Devil fell, God thought him beautiful in Heaven." It was that kind of change.

They made good time getting to the hospital, but were shocked to find Doug Weathers waiting for them in the lobby.

"Hey, kid, about last night—no hard feelings, right? I didn't know it was Gersten. Glad he's doing better."

"I have no comment," Jazz said.

Weathers laughed a big, expansive, fake laugh that earned him a scowl from the nurse at the registration desk. "Look, let's talk about this thing with Helen Myerson. You heard about it? Between her and your teacher and that other woman found in the Harrison field on Sunday, there's some real action in this town again."

"People are dead, you idiot!" Connie said.

"Whoa! Whoa!" Weathers raised his hands defensively. "I'm just describing the situation, is all. Now, what if these murders were all connected somehow?" A light danced like a cheap stripper in his eyes. "Wouldn't that be an interesting story?"

"What are you getting at?" Jazz asked.

"I'm just saying—maybe I write something up. Maybe you offer some commentary. As a sort of expert in the field, you know?" He licked his lips. "And everyone gets what they want."

Jazz wasn't tempted in the least, and he could feel Connie's agitation rising beside him. He was ready to push past Weathers when the man said, "I'll even give your buddy some glory. Run a piece about the kid who confronted the killer and got slashed for his troubles."

Jazz stopped halfway to the elevator, turning to Weathers. "What did you just say? Did you just say 'slashed'? How did you know he was slashed and not stabbed?"

Weathers grinned. "C'mon, Jasper. I have sources. I can't reveal them."

Jazz stared into Weathers's eyes—pale gray, with flecks of brown.

"Do you wear contacts?" he asked the reporter.

"What?"

"I'm watching you," Jazz said with as much menace as he could, then took Connie's hand and stepped into the elevator.

"What was that all about?" Connie asked when the doors closed and they were alone.

"Nothing. Maybe. I don't know." He shook his head. "Let's just see Howie. That's what matters right now."

In his room, Howie was in and out of sleep, heavily drugged and loopy. His parents had taken up a vigil at his bedside and neither of them looked ready to move. Connie offered to fetch something for them to eat, so Jazz was left alone with them, trying to melt into a corner, waiting for one or both of them to turn from Howie's bed and launch a fusillade of angry invective at him.

It never came. They seemed too relieved and exhausted to be angry. The day would come, though, he knew.

Howie surfaced briefly around dinnertime, clutching his mother's hand and asking for a glass of water. He noticed Jazz and winked at him, then said, "Man, these drugs are a-*mayzing*!" That was the extent of his conversational skills at that point, so Jazz and Connie left and scored sandwiches at a diner, sitting across from each other in a booth.

"Have you heard anything new from the police?" Connie asked, picking through her french fries for the crispiest ones. "Any leads?"

"No. Nothing yet. I guess they'll tell me when they do. Or not. I don't know." His BLT tasted slightly rotten; not enough that it was noticeable at first, but just tainted enough that the flavor mounted with each bite. "What was school like today?"

She stalled, sucking on her drink straw. "It was rough. Some people saw the news about Ginny on the Web this morning, so word had spread by homeroom. But the details were all jacked up and people were just babbling. A bunch of people weren't even sure it was real until they announced it over the PA. And there was a lot of crying, and it was just awful, Jazz. Really awful."

She laid one hand on the table between them. Jazz stared at it for a moment before realizing she wanted him to hold her hand. He squeezed it.

"All the *Crucible* people got together at lunch. We were trying to figure out something we could do. Like a memorial, you know?" She wiped at new tears beginning in her eyes. "We want to do *something*."

A memorial. The idea made Jazz slightly uneasy. It wasn't quite the same thing as a serial killer's trophy, not quite the same as the things Billy had taken from his victims. But it was close enough. Marking the dead seemed so maudlin. So obsessive. But that was what people did. They marked the dead.

"You'll think of something," he told her. "All of you guys."

"And you," she insisted. "You're a part of the cast, too. No one knows you were there," she said quickly, knowing what he was about to say. "No one knows you saw her die."

"They will." There would be something on the Web, and eventually on TV, with more details about the murder of a young, pretty, popular teacher. There would be a report that eyewitnesses had seen the killer flee. That one of them had been injured. And Howie was in the hospital, and people in Lobo's Nod knew how to add one and one; they came to two every single time.

"Can we go?" he asked. A headache had begun to test the tender nerves threading through his right temple.

"You've hardly touched your sandwich."

"Leave it." He fumbled for money and left several bills on the table. "Let's go."

Gramma made up for her rotten behavior earlier in the day; by the time Jazz got home, she had passed out on the floor in front of the TV (which she had switched over to the Speed

Channel at some point) and was gently snoring there, the teddy bear serving as a makeshift pillow.

How on earth, he wondered, looking down at her, could such a peaceful, contented-looking woman be such a lunatic monster? How could she give birth to a force of pure evil, suckle it, raise it to its own grotesque brand of perfection?

Lacking the strength to carry her upstairs, he left her on the floor. The cop was still parked outside—another detail soon to be entered into the local gossip database, he knew—but he double-checked the front door, the kitchen door, and all the windows before slinking upstairs. By now the headache was done testing and had decided to kick up a fuss. His head was lopsided with pain.

Nonetheless, he had things to do. It was almost the weekend. Melissa's report would be filed on Monday, and he needed his rebuttal letter to accompany it. He couldn't let her report go unanswered for any length of time if he wanted to stay in the house.

Remember Bobby Joe Long scrolled across his computer screen.

"Are you sure you *want* to stay in the house?" he mumbled to himself as he slumped at the desk, his computer's monitor too painful and too harsh for him to look at it directly. "A foster home might be a vacation. Samantha's house might be a blessing."

It was tempting to look at it that way, but he knew that once he was out of the house and in the system, he'd have no way back. He'd fooled Social Services into thinking that his grandmother was taking care of him for the past four years, when the opposite was closer to the truth. And he'd never even met his aunt Samantha. There was no guarantee she'd even want him. Now he had to find a way to at least stall the process until he turned eighteen. Then he could do whatever he wanted, and no one could stop him.

I do whatever I want, Billy had said once, grinning over his trophy collection. With one hand, he fondled a necklace he'd taken from a victim. With the other, he stroked Jazz's hair. *And no one can stop me. I'm their God. I say if they live or die. Greatest feeling in the world.*

Jazz's fingers trembled on the keyboard. Maybe he should let them take him away. Maybe that would be best.

CHAPTER 25

The Impressionist had the TV on for background noise as he went over the plans for his next piece of action. Everything was ready; there was no more preparation to be done. He only had to execute the plan.

Something on the screen distracted him for a moment—a commercial, with two puppets pretending to run across a field.

He thought for a moment. About puppets.

About being controlled.

Everyone was controlled by something, the Impressionist knew. By a spouse. A parent. A boss. A friend. By one's own impulses, be they dark or light.

Everyone was a puppet to something.

Most people just couldn't see the strings, is all. And so they didn't believe they were puppets in the first place.

The Impressionist could see his strings. He knew how long they were. He knew their tensile strength. How much slack they had.

He knew who pulled them.

But he wondered.

He wondered about a puppet that can see its strings.

He wondered... What if a puppet could cut its own strings?

Physics and logic dictated that the puppet would collapse, lifeless.

But what if that didn't happen?

What if a puppet could cut its own strings, and in that act of defiance and strength of will become truly alive? Become its own puppetmaster?

What if, indeed?

The Impressionist was not supposed to engage with Jasper Dent. He had broken that rule.

He couldn't help himself. The Impressionist knew himself to be a strong-willed individual, but when it came to Jasper Dent... Every rational part of him screamed to avoid the kid. But something deeper and more primal urged him forward, wanted him hurtling in Dent's direction.

The Impressionist wondered: *Is this what it's like to be in love? Is this what people in love experience?*

He flicked through his phone until he found a picture of Dent. What, he wondered, did other people see when they saw Jasper Dent? They probably saw nothing more than a teenager. A boy. A student. They didn't know—not really— what walked among them.

We do what we want, the Impressionist thought. *And no one can stop us.*

CHAPTER 26

The next day, school was practically silent. There was none of the usual boisterous shouting and jibing in the halls before homeroom; the buzz of conversation had been replaced with the occasional sound of a hiccupping sob.

Jazz wondered how they would all feel if they knew that Ginny's death—as devastating as it had been to them—was only one pearl in a bloody strand. In two more days, a woman with the initials I.H. would die. She would be sexually assaulted, invaded both vaginally and rectally, then injected with drain cleaner (the penultimate victim to be so injected) and posed via a system of nails and fishing line so that she stood in a hotel shower as though washing. That's what Billy had done as the Artist, and that's what the Impressionist would do, down to a T, adding only the subtraction of six fingers for his own sick reasons.

Waiting for the first bell in homeroom, Jazz flipped open a notebook to a fresh page and started scribbling names and facts, hoping that his writing hand would figure out what his brain could not. But nothing connected. Nothing worked. He had only two real suspects: Erickson and Weathers. It could be either one, but neither of them fit exactly. He didn't even bother writing down G. William's name, his cheeks again flushing briefly with the embarrassing memory of suspecting the sheriff.

He thought, too, of Jeff Fulton, Harriet Klein's father, but quickly discarded him. It was possible—in theory—that the man's grief had pushed him over the edge, but grief usually didn't take that sort of form. If Fulton had been driven *that* crazy, he'd be more likely to try to kill Jazz or Billy, not to replicate Billy's crimes.

In addition, he realized there was no reason the killer should be someone Jazz knew—the odds were that it was a complete stranger. Which meant that he had a lot of information and no conclusions. As usual.

"All classes," the principal's voice boomed over the PA, "please observe a moment of silence for Ms. Davis."

Other than a stifled sob, Jazz's homeroom went utterly silent.

Two days. Two days until another murder. The Impressionist was stalking Lobo's Nod, and Jazz couldn't think of a single thing to do to stop him. He texted G. William—*any updates????*—surreptitiously using Howie's cell under his desk, but the moment of silence ended and classes began with no response.

It went that way all day. He checked the phone obsessively, certain that he'd missed some sort of notification due to his unfamiliarity with the gadget, but no matter how he tapped, poked, swiped, or manhandled the thing, no message from G. William came up.

He suffered the school day in silence and solitude, keeping to himself even more than usual, avoiding eye contact. By now, everyone knew that he'd been present at Ginny's death. As he'd predicted, that bit of news had been deduced and spread overnight. The only thing they didn't know was that Ginny's death was connected to others. G. William was still waiting for the ViCAP report to come back from the FBI. That would officially connect the first murder in Lindenberg to the others—then he would go public. So the cops were pretending that the body in the field and the dead waitress and the dead teacher had nothing to do with one another.

That was a lot of murders for little Lobo's Nod. A lot of suspicion.

Jazz wore the heavy cloak of that suspicion all day.

He'd been an idiot to think that he could just be a normal kid. The past four years, he'd been fooling himself in the worst possible way. First, when Billy was arrested, there'd been sympathy. Then that had withered away, and now only suspicion remained.

It would never change. It would never go away. People didn't trust him; they would never trust him, and he could scarcely blame them. Someone else would have been able to save Ginny, he knew. Or at least wouldn't have had some sick part of him enjoying her death...

Since Ginny's death, of course there hadn't been a play rehearsal. But Connie dragged Jazz to Eddie Viggaro's house right after school for a meeting of the cast and crew. He stood in a corner and said nothing, certain that no one in the room could abide his presence.

It took a long time before anyone could speak; there were too many tears. Jazz wished he could join them. Wished he could cry. Wished he could tell them all about Ginny's last moments in some way that would help them and not seem morbid.

"We need to honor her," Connie said. "She meant so much to us."

Everyone agreed and tears gave way to words spoken with the urgency of the desperate and the mourning.

"A plaque," someone suggested, and Jazz flinched despite himself.

"That's lame," the girl playing Abigail scoffed. "We should build a *statue*—"

Jazz fidgeted. A plaque. A statue. *Trophies*.

"Maybe a whole series of statues," said the kid playing Giles Corey. "Like, for each role she played in college or some thing."

That generated an excited babble among the cast and crew, a babble that stilled only when a strong voice cut in: "Do you really want to honor her memory?"

Everyone looked at Jazz in surprise.

He hadn't meant to speak, but he couldn't help himself. And now he had to keep going because they were all staring.

"Look," he said, hesitant at first, but gaining confidence with each word, "if you want to memorialize her, you don't do it with a...with a *thing*. That's not what life is about. Life isn't about"—*gloves, an iPod, a driver's license, a lipstick*—

"the things we own. If you want to honor someone, you don't do it with things. You do it with action."

They were still staring, but the stares were no longer of surprise. They were of curiosity.

He told them his idea.

There was a candlelight vigil on the school football field at sundown that evening. Connie insisted that Jazz attend, although the last thing in the world he wanted was to attend a celebration of a life he had failed to preserve. It felt somehow ghoulish and hypocritical.

"They're all looking at me," he whispered to her as they settled into their spots in the crowd. Around them, it seemed as though every warm body in the school had gathered, jockeying for position in near-silence. And it wasn't just kids—half the town had come out for the vigil. "Didn't you notice?"

"No one's looking."

"They are."

"Because they know you tried to save her. Because they know you found her."

"They blame me," he said.

"No one blames you."

They should, he did not say.

"Your idea was brilliant," she said, leaning in close and hugging him. "I'm so proud of you."

"It'll be a lot of work," he cautioned. "We'll see if we can pull it off."

"We can. I know we— Oh, they're starting."

The vigil began with Principal Jeffries making some remarks about hiring Ginny, how it had felt like a risk, this young, dynamic teacher fresh out of school, with all sorts of crazy ideas about teaching. But in the end, the real risk, he claimed, would have been *not* to hire her. . . .

He droned on. Jazz wondered what the point was. Was telling him how wonderful Ginny had been supposed to somehow make him feel better about her being dead? That didn't make any sense.

All around him, he was surrounded by tears and outright weeping. Kids and adults alike.

Principal Jeffries opened up the podium to anyone who wanted to speak. A few students mumbled into the microphone. A college friend of Ginny's said a few words.

And then there—to Jazz's surprise—was Jeff Fulton.

"I'm sorry. I hope I'm not intruding on your town's grief. But I feel, in a small way, as though maybe God brought me here for this purpose. You see, a few years ago, a man from Lobo's Nod killed my daughter, Harriet." Fulton didn't say Billy's name; he didn't need to. "And when I found that my business would take me near your town, I felt like I had to come here, to see the place where the man who killed my child lived. I don't know why. Maybe I felt like I'd get some closure." He chuckled ruefully. " 'Closure.' That's a real popular word, isn't it? I came here looking for it, and what I realized was that I had it in my own heart all along. I can't forgive the man who killed my daughter, but I can stop letting him run my life. I can move on. And that's what I need to do. And that's what I want to tell all of you to do. You, and you, and you." He pointed out into the crowd. "We humans have the capacity to wreak horrors on each other. But we also have the capacity to survive those horrors.

"You know, I wasn't fortunate enough to know your Ms. Davis. But listening to everyone speak, I like to think…" He hesitated, and for a moment it seemed that he might just walk away from the microphone. But instead, he gripped the lectern and went on. "I like to think that maybe she would have been friends with my Harriet." Tears streamed down Fulton's face, and his voice caught. "So maybe now they both have a new friend in heaven. Thank you. Thank you, all of you."

Fulton staggered away from the podium to applause. Connie's cheeks were smeared with dampness that shifted in the flickering light of her candle, and she clutched Jazz's hand as speaker after speaker extolled the virtues and wonderment that had once been Virginia Davis. Jazz tried to be sympathetic, but the truth was, the crying and the wailing made him numb. Crying, he knew, was useless. An important lesson learned so young…

—wakey, wakey, Jasper, my boy—

And then:

I'm doing Rusty tonight. You don't gotta help, but you gotta watch.

Rusty had been Jazz's companion for the first eight years of his life, a mix of cocker spaniel and retriever the perfect color of soft caramel. They'd romped and played in the backyard together, and zoned out on the sofa watching TV together, and then one night, Jazz had watched as Billy gutted and flayed Rusty alive.

Looking back, he was shocked at just how long the poor beast had lived, and in such unrelenting pain, but at the time he knew only that his dog was dying, was hurting, and there was nothing he could do about it. He'd cried; cried early and long and hard, the whole time Billy patiently stripped away Rusty's life with his knives.

When Rusty was well and truly dead, nothing more than a wet, slick hump of muscle and bone with a second pile of flesh and intestines glistening in the corner, Billy came to him and knelt down next to his bawling son. He folded his arms around Jazz and whispered, "It's okay, it's okay," in a soothing, paternal tone, until Jazz had quieted enough to listen and understand what he said next. Which was: "You go on crying. You keep crying. It's all right."

Jazz had needed no further encouragement. The tears kept coming, an endless gush of them, like a deepwater well under pressure spewing its contents out into the world. He leaned into his father—yes, he was a killer and a torturer, but he was Jazz's father, and some biological imperative made his presence comforting—and Billy said, "Close your eyes," and Jazz did, still weeping, the tears leaking out from his shut eyelids, and Billy held him, and when Jazz's sobs began to slow, Billy said, in a voice that was almost kind, "You need to open your eyes now, son. You need to see something," and Jazz did so, thinking magical, childish thoughts, but all he still saw was the two piles, and then Billy—his voice jovial with a sinister undercurrent—said, "See, Jasper?

All that crying, and what did you accomplish? Nothing. And nothing."

He looked around the football field. Every eye was aimed at the makeshift dais set up on the fifty-yard line. Even Deputy Erickson was rapt by the testimonials, standing to one side near a still visibly overcome Jeff Fulton.

Every eye but one.

Jazz couldn't believe it—there was Doug Weathers, looking directly at Jazz. And now he was making his way through the crowd toward him.

God, that guy was everywhere! Was nothing sacred to him? Nothing at all?

A rage more powerful than any he'd ever known before bubbled up inside Jazz. He wanted to do horrible, unspeakable things to Weathers, things that culminated in Weathers begging for his own death. Jazz let those fantasies range free in his imagination, and it felt *good*.

Serial killers often went to the funerals and memorials of their victims, Jazz knew. Billy had done so on more than one occasion, always taking care to be in disguise. It was a compulsion with many of them, a way of extending their perceived ownership of the victim even beyond the act of murder.

"Ow," Connie whispered. "Jazz."

He was crushing her hand. He loosened his grip and whispered an apology, then let go of her hand completely and mumbled something lame about needing to get some fresh air. He pushed through the crowd, heading for the exit.

Weathers changed direction, pressing through the crowd in Jazz's wake. Soon, Jazz emerged from the throng of mourners into one of the field's end zones. The tunnel path out of the football field wasn't far away.

He didn't make it. Instead, he saw G. William and two deputies appear in the exit. The sheriff did a double take when he saw Jazz, then made a beeline for him.

Jazz checked over his shoulder. Weathers had vanished. Great.

"Jazz," G. William said, "we got a problem. We got a body. Two days early, we got a body."

CHAPTER 27

Her name was, or had been—Jazz wasn't sure which way it went, once they were dead; did names survive death?—Irene Heller. Jazz gazed at her body, tucked into a shower, positioned exactly as he'd predicted. She hadn't been moved or touched since being found.

G. William handed him a photo of the Isabella Hernandez crime scene, not that Jazz needed one. Except for the difference in the shower tiles and the obvious differences between Isabella and Irene, it could have been a picture of the very crime scene before Jazz.

"She wasn't a maid at a hotel," G. William said miserably. "We checked them all. She's a stay-at-home mom. Kids go to school now, so she cleans houses during the day to supplement her husband's income."

"Technically a maid," Jazz murmured. He was only mildly surprised to find that Irene Heller's corpse did not bother him. He scrutinized it, looking for any clue that might lead him to the Impressionist. She was partly into rigor mortis—she'd been killed and posed hours ago.

G. William, at the end of his rope, had asked Jazz to come look at the fresh crime scene. "I'm ready to try just about anything," he had confessed in the end zone. "I know I didn't want to do this to you, but...Look, I don't know if you can help or not, but can you try?"

Of course, Jazz had said yes. He had used Howie's cell to call Connie and tell her what had happened, then followed G. William to a smallish split-level house in a shabby but clean neighborhood just off the main highway on the east side of Lobo's Nod. And now it was him and G. William in the bathroom of Irene's home, where her husband had found the body after coming home from work. Her kids, ironically enough, had gone straight from an after-school event to the Ginny Davis vigil.

"I don't see any differences between what he did here and what Billy did to Hernandez," Jazz said. "Except for the fingers, of course."

Irene Heller's right hand was fingerless, like Ginny's. Her left hand's middle finger lay on the floor of the shower, near the drain.

"Sexually assaulted?" he asked.

G. William cleared his throat. "Tough to say until we get her on the slab. But the ME thinks so. No obvious fluids."

"There wouldn't be. Billy was always careful. Used a condom. But..." Jazz crouched down, getting a worm's-eye view of the crime scene. "I don't know. I have a suspicion that he didn't actually rape her. Not with his own...you know. I bet he used a, a, you know, a sex toy or something."

"Why?"

Jazz shrugged. He felt...good. He felt powerful and confident. Maybe it was being needed by G. William. More likely, it was because he was doing something he was good at.

"This guy calls himself the Impressionist. He's aping Billy's crimes. He has no originality, no self. No personality. He's an imprint of someone else. Billy raped women as a way of showing his dominance and control."

And because it's fun, Jasper, Billy's voice whispered. *Don't forget that part. You'll know, someday.*

Jazz shivered uncontrollably. G. William, alarmed, grabbed his arm and pulled him to a standing position. "C'mon, kid. Let's get—"

"No. No. I'm okay." He shook off G. William and leaned closer to Irene Heller. "This guy...He's *not* in control. He's *under* control. He's subordinated his entire personality to this idea in his head of who and what Billy is. Worships Billy's memory and legacy. I mean, he's obviously studied everything there is to study about Billy. He might even think he *is* Billy, on some level."

The sheriff grunted. Jazz paused, but G. William nodded for him to continue.

"He's probably impotent," Jazz went on. "He doesn't have the triggers Billy had. Has, I mean. Billy was compelled to rape. But rape isn't just something you do. It's not an easy thing. This guy...He wants to be able to rape, but he can't. Because he's just pretending to be Billy. He couldn't rape her with his penis if you put a gun to his head and threatened to kill him. He used something else."

G. William cleared his throat and made a note on his smartphone. "Anything else?"

Jazz looked around the tiny bathroom. "He's accelerating his timetable. It took Billy two more days to kill Isabella Hernandez. The Impressionist is moving faster. He might know we're on to him. Figures he needs to start stacking up the bodies." Jazz thought for a moment. "His next will be number six. I wonder if he'll stop there?"

"Well, if he sticks to fingers, he can only go to nine, since he leaves one behind. But six would coincide with the last murder Billy did as the Artist," the sheriff mused, "before he switched over to, uh..."

"Green Jack," Jazz supplied.

Jazz turned to G. William. The sheriff looked utterly deflated, as though someone had pulled a tab on his back and let all the air and all the life run out of his insides. The big red nose supplied the only color in his otherwise pallid, drawn face.

"I'll make sure you get a copy of the final report," he told Jazz, "assuming you think it'll help."

"Yeah. Do that," Jazz said distractedly. An idea had begun to form in the back of his mind, nagging at him, gnawing through the boundary between subconscious and conscious. He tried to ignore it, tried to push it away. No good. It was coming. Whether he wanted it or not. "I'm going to think a bit more," he said.

As they left the bathroom and entered the master bedroom, Jazz heard a familiar voice. He looked over to see Deputy Erickson instructing one of the crime-scene techs to dust the bedroom window. When Erickson noticed Jazz looking at him, he sneered.

Jazz wasn't about to let that go. "Hey, Erickson! Did

you just happen to be the first guy on the scene this time, too?"

The entire room went silent. Every cop in the room turned to look at Erickson. The deputy had gone bright red; his lips moved and his throat bobbed, but no sound came out.

G. William grabbed Jazz by the elbow and yanked him out into the hallway. Jazz heard Erickson finally squawk, "I don't have to listen to that kind of—" before the sheriff slammed the door.

"What the hell was that just now?" he demanded, shaking Jazz. "Do you suspect Erickson? Is that what you're getting at? Because for your information, he was *not* first on the scene tonight. Hanson was."

Of course, of course. Jazz had seen Erickson at Ginny's memorial with his own two eyes. He couldn't have been first on the scene this time.

Jazz stared into G. William's darting, feverish eyes. "I'm sorry. I'm just dead tired. And he just rubs me the wrong way."

"The whole world rubs you the wrong way, Jasper Francis."

"Should I go apologize to him?" The very thought made Jazz's guts squirm.

"No, no. Let it blow over." G. William guided him to the front door. "Sorry I got a little physical there."

"It's okay."

"I'm juggling a lot. And I have to tell you ... Jazz, I've been trying to keep a lid on this, but I can't do that anymore. The feds are sending some people from Quantico tomorrow morning, and Atlanta PD is sending someone, too. There's gonna be an interagency task force. I have to hold a press conference.

Tonight. Already got my guys setting it up. I have to put the word out. Warn whoever the next victim is."

The next victim...A blond, aged twenty-six. A secretary. Initials would be B.Q. Injected with drain cleaner again, sexually assaulted again, posed in a kitchen...

"I understand," Jazz said.

"I'll leave the squad car at your house. In case things get, you know, ugly."

Translation: In case a vigilante mob decides that the return of Billy Dent's crimes can only be exorcised by eliminating the descendant of Billy Dent himself. The old Dent house would burn pretty well.

"Got it."

"You want to be there? At the press conference?"

Jazz stared at G. William as if the man had turned blue and grown a third nipple in the center of his forehead.

"I can say that you're not on the suspect list. I can say you're helping us."

"No. I appreciate it, G. William, I really do. But..." The spotlight. The center of attention. One more thing he shared with Billy: an aversion to public attention.

"I got it, Jazz. I understand. I'll do what I can to keep the heat down."

They shook hands. In the sheriff's grip, Jazz felt not strength, but desperation. Then he hopped in the Jeep. He needed to be alone with his thoughts.

He headed for the Hideout.

CHAPTER 28

Halfway to the Hideout, the Jeep's radio—tuned to a local hard-rock station—broke in for a news brief, and Jazz heard G. William's voice. He pictured the sheriff standing at a hastily arranged podium on the steps outside the sheriff's office, probably wiping sweat from his brow with one of those special handkerchiefs, even though it wasn't remotely hot out. Lights would flash; there would be a babble of voices from the reporters present, as G. William announced...

"...the disturbing news that the recent murders in Lobo's Nod—and one more out of state—have been conclusively linked..."

Jazz bit his bottom lip. More flashes of cameras now. The babble transmutes to an excited undercurrent. Did he just say—?

"...believe these crimes to be the work of one man, going by the name 'the Impressionist.' This Impressionist is duplicating crimes originally perpetrated many years ago by William Cornelius Dent...."

And that was it. The crowd, as the old saying promises, goes wild. An endless strobe effect of camera flashes, a sonic hodgepodge of shouted questions, demands for clarification, G. William struggling to make himself not only heard, but also understood above the sudden, crazed din. Doug Weathers at the head of the crowd, chortling with glee, already imagining himself being made up for his next appearance on national television, dusting off his anecdotes about Billy, maybe adding in a bit about the time he tussled with Billy's son, who was handcuffed.

Jazz switched off the radio with a savage jab at the power button. That was it, then. It was a done deal. The name Billy Dent had been invoked and, like a magic spell from some dusty old tome, it had conjured visions of past degradations from modern history's vilest serial killer. The demons of press coverage and the attention of the mob would ride the spell's effects into the real world, and Jazz's life—never normal to begin with—would be upended yet again.

He didn't know if this time he was strong enough to survive it.

Piloting the Jeep through the trees that lined the dirt road to the Hideout, Jazz caught a glimpse of Howie's little electric-blue Honda parked up ahead. It couldn't be Howie—it had to be Connie, still taking advantage of having Howie's car in her possession.

He parked the Jeep and took a few deep breaths. The image of Irene Heller posed in her shower like that, her limbs arrayed and propped through a careful arrangement of counterweights and nearly invisible monofilament, wouldn't go away. Her entire body was an accusation.

He'd seen much worse in his life. The Impressionist was a killer, true, but the crime scene was meticulous, and almost neat. A pinprick in the neck where the drain cleaner had been injected. And the severed fingers. No other violence done to the bodies. Sure, it was painful, but it was quick. Clean. If you had to be killed by a serial killer, having the Impressionist as your killer wasn't the worst way to go, Jazz decided. Especially if you wanted an open casket at your funeral.

Still. Irene Heller. Positioned naked in the shower.

This was not your fault, G. William had told him, and for a moment, Jazz had believed him.

But it wasn't true. If Jazz had been smarter or more insightful or ... or ... more *something*, then Irene Heller would not be dead, and her husband would not be telling their two kids that, hey, you know how you just went to a vigil for that teacher? Well, funny thing, that. Guess what? Mommy's got something in common with that teacher now.

He slowly climbed out of the Jeep and went to the Hideout. "Hi, honey!" he announced with fake cheer. "I'm home!"

Connie sat on the beanbag chair, her long legs tucked up under her. The only light came through the milky plastic over the one window. In the near-dark, she looked like a statue carved out of walnut.

She crossed her arms over her chest and stared at him. "Let's talk about it."

His smile did not falter. "About what? There's nothing to

talk about. Hey, if Howie suddenly takes a turn for the worse, you think his parents'll let you keep the car?"

Connie's jaw dropped at his cruel humor. "What did you say?"

"Just thinking out loud," he said lightly.

She pushed herself up out of the chair and slapped him across the face before he could react. They stared at each other.

"I'm sorry," he murmured, wrapping his arms around her and pulling her close. He kissed her forehead and rocked her back and forth. "I'm a jerk," he whispered.

"No, you're not," she said, her voice muffled against his chest.

"Yeah, I am."

"No, you're..." She tensed up in his arms and then pulled away. "You're not a jerk," she whispered, but her expression said otherwise. "You're *not* a jerk," she said again, once more folding her arms over her chest, her stance defensive. "So you're just *acting* like a jerk. You're Billying me!"

"Con—"

"Yeah, *con* is right! You're conning me! You got me all pissed off about your little joke so that I wouldn't think about what happened tonight. Jesus!"

"I'm sorry."

He reached for her, but she moved away. "I can't believe you pulled that on me. I left the vigil early, and I've been sitting here, waiting for you to come, because I knew you would be upset about that woman dying, and I was going to be here for you, and you act like I'm a...like I'm a, a—what's the word he used?—a *prospect*, and you Billy me. Me!"

"I didn't mean to," he said. "It was just reflex."

"I just wanted to be here for you," she said. "Why the hell do you have to turn that against me?"

"I know." He opened his arms again, and she came to him. She felt good against him, the warmth of her, the pounding of her heart against his body as he held her tight. "I know," he said, pressing his lips to the top of her head, careful to avoid her hair as he kissed her scalp between the intricate sculpting of cornrows. "I don't want to Billy you," he said, and she squeezed him back.

They snuggled on the beanbag chair, Connie occasionally shivering. He tightened his arms around her and leaned in, speaking softly in her ear. "I bet I could warm you up."

She twisted around to glare at him. "Nice try, smooth talker. But these legs are closed for business." As if to drive the point home, she shifted, locking her ankles together.

He felt pretty confident he could convince her otherwise. Before Connie had come into his life, he'd come perilously close to sweet-talking girls into his bed, some of them much older than he was. He thought of Lana, for example. She could be his, and that was nothing that any other teenage boy wouldn't do.

But he wasn't any other teenage boy. Schooled by Billy Dent, Jazz had an advantage the average teen could never have: a sociopath's ability to fake absolutely any emotion with utterly convincing authority. He had always backed out at the last minute, never sure why until one day it all clicked for him, and he realized that backing off was a self-preservation instinct. That sex could lead to horror for him, and he couldn't risk it. Ever since that realization, he'd been careful. He remained—like so many other boys—a virgin desperate not to be. Unlike so many other boys, he was also terrified not to be.

Connie was safe. With Connie, things were different. He could be with her without fear because he didn't feel Billy's presence looming over them. Because...

He knew why. He felt uncomfortable admitting it, but maybe it was just Connie herself. Maybe he'd resisted convincing her to unlock those ankles *not* for fear of sex, but due to his sneaking suspicion that, even though she'd never used the words, she loved him, and he couldn't bear the thought of seducing her virginity away.

Or, simpler than that, was it because *he* loved *her*?

He wasn't sure. He just knew that he didn't want to talk her into doing anything she wasn't ready to do, no matter how badly he wanted to do it.

He chuckled. At least in this he was a normal teenager—*any* straight male snuggling with Connie would be desperate to get those jeans off.

"What's so funny?" she asked.

"Nothing."

"Share."

He rummaged around and found an old space blanket he'd stashed here against the coming colder weather. "Really, it was nothing."

She let it go for a moment as they arranged the blanket around themselves, then said, "Tell me about the woman."

Jazz sighed. "Her name was Irene Heller...." He told her everything he knew—the things G. William had told him at the house and the things he'd figured out on his own just by observing the Impressionist's work.

She craned her neck and planted a kiss on his jawline. "You can't blame yourself. It's not like you could have known."

"I could have done better. I could have narrowed it down more. I could have convinced G. William to put out an alert to the media—"

"Do something useful, then. Stop complaining about it and figure it out. And if you can't figure it out, then realize that that's not your fault—no one made you the Grand High Poobah of Lobo's Nod."

He let her kiss the side of his neck. Her lips were soft, plush. He closed his eyes, but when he did that, he saw not just Irene Heller, but also the whole roster of his father's victims, all of them accusing him: *Why didn't you save us, Jazz? You knew what your father was. Why didn't you save us?*

"Think about it logically," Connie went on after a moment. "Who could it be? Do you have any thoughts?"

He cast his mind back to his scribbled notebook pages. "A few. But none of them totally gel for me. Not yet. And the big thing"—he hesitated for a moment—"I guess the thing that really worries me is that I've only considered people I know about. Which makes sense, but you know, it's not like there's a *rule* or something that says the killer has to be someone I know or someone I met. Even in a little town like the

Nod, there's a lot of people I don't know. And people passing through. Anybody could be the killer.

"I have to do better," he said, a frightening idea already forming in his head. He tried not to let it out. "I have to stop him—"

"Jazz." She pulled at him, rolling him over so that they were face-to-face. "Stop it. It's *not* your fault. You didn't kill that woman. You didn't kill Ginny."

"I might as well have."

"That's—"

"No. No, listen. If I could stop it and I didn't, then it's like I killed her myself, right? Isn't that true?"

"But you couldn't stop it. You—"

He stared at the ceiling. "What if I could have, Con? What if I could have done something more and some part of me, something deep down, some *Billy* part of me, didn't? What if I let her die?"

She stroked his arm, squeezing his shoulder, then working down to his wrist, then back up, soothing him. "That's not how it works. You told me it's not about killing just any random person. Serial killers have a type, right?"

He flinched. He didn't want to go down this particular road. The fact was, yes, serial killers generally had a specific kind of victim they felt compelled to kill. Billy had been so damn hard to catch because his victim profile was broad and loose— a whole range of women fit into it, with one notable exception: Not a single one of his victims had been African American.

Jazz looked at Connie, at her lustrous skin. He couldn't tell her that however he felt about her now, he'd originally been drawn to her because she was one of the few girls he could be certain Billy hadn't programmed him to want to kill.

He'd fallen for her because, as best he could tell, she was safe.

"They have types," he said eventually. "But Billy broke a lot of those rules. And he..." He thought of Dr. Shinkeski from the TV show, who suddenly no longer seemed pathetic and laughable. "What if I'm a new kind of serial killer? Billy always said he wanted me to be something new. Something special."

"Don't talk like that. You're more than what your father wants you to be. You're *you*. He doesn't control you."

Jazz wished that were true. Connie was brilliant and wonderful and empathetic, but no matter how amazing she was, she couldn't understand what it had been like to grow up as Billy Dent's son. Billy didn't have supernatural powers that allowed him to control people, but it sure felt like he did. To his victims, he was a seductive force, an apparently sympathetic, compassionate resource that promised succor and aid, only to turn into a hellhound. He was a pitcher plant, luring in prey with sweet promises, only to devour it.

And to his son...

To his son, he had been a god. A war god, a god of love, the two of them intertwined in a sick hybrid. Billy Dent excelled at alternating brute force with tender love, then blending the two together until Jazz thought that being forced to mop up blood spatter was just a natural way to show love to his dad. Watching Rusty die was just something his father needed him to see, is all.

Just like cutting chicken.

But it hadn't been Rusty in the dream. He'd cut a person in the dream. Human flesh. Human blood. At Billy's command. And yet still Jazz had loved his father. Somehow.

It was natural for sons to worship their fathers, anyway. And when the father in question was a charismatic dragon who taught his child that society's rules did not apply to him, that other people were either chattel or prey, that the world had been made for the two of them and no one else...

That was the worst sort of control. A sort of brainwashing that Jazz had only managed to throw off when Billy's arrest approached. It was as though he'd been helpless to rebel against his upbringing, until the world itself put the lie to Billy's promise that the world's laws didn't matter. And then, slowly—so damn slowly—Jazz came to realize that his father was a devil, not a god.

"He made me what I am," Jazz said. "Bad and good alike. You can't deny that, Con."

"And my parents made me what I am. So what? We get stuff from our parents, but we also get stuff from the world around us. From the people around us. And at the end of the day, we're us." She leaned up on her elbows and loomed over him, her braids dangling. "Sons aren't their fathers. Not the good, not the bad. Sons get second chances. You don't have to be what your dad is." She stared into his eyes for so long that Jazz thought he'd somehow hypnotized her with his gaze. "You told me you hated his eyes. Ice blue. Like your grandmother's. But they're not yours. You don't have his eyes, and you don't have to have his life." She suddenly stiffened in his arms. "Did you hear that?"

"Hear what?"

"A sound." She was on alert. "Someone's out there."

"Raccoon," he said. "They're always scavenging out there."

"Are you sure?"

"I'll protect you from the big, bad rodents," Jazz told her.

She chuckled and snuggled into him. "You will, won't you?"

"Yeah. Even from me."

"I don't need protection from you." She giggled.

"Don't say that."

A poke to his ribs. "I'm not afraid of you. I know you."

"I don't want to hurt you," he whispered.

"You won't."

"You don't know that. You can't."

"I do."

That makes one of us. Jazz closed his eyes tight. He didn't want to say what was in his head, but he couldn't stop himself. He owed it to Connie. He owed her this honesty.

"You know I could kill you, right?" he said quietly, his voice measured and calm. "I could do it right now. Right now. And there's nothing you could do to stop me. Even though I've told you."

She went still against him. "But you won't."

He exploded. "How do you know that?" He pushed her away. "How? Tell me! Jesus!" Tears came from nowhere, shocking him as they streamed down his cheeks. He didn't know what the hell these fresh tears were for, and he didn't care; he swiped at them with his palms, pressing them into flesh gone suddenly hot.

"Why aren't you running? Why aren't you terrified? How do you know, Connie?" he whispered. "Even I don't know that I won't kill you. How the hell can *you* know?"

All his strength left him and he collapsed against her. Without hesitation, her arms went around him, drawing him in, his head nestled against her breasts as sobs wracked his body.

"I know because—"

"Damn it!" He scrambled away, escaping her grasp. "Damn it, Connie! Don't fall for this crap! I'm trying to help you!" He paced the Hideout, his body vibrating with anger, with fear. Words spilled out of him, stumbling over one another like people running in an earthquake. "This is how we do it. We lure you in, sucker you, rely on your compassion, your empathy. And if you're lucky, you're dead before you realize it. And we...We—"

He ran out of words. He stood in the darkness, his breath heaving, staring down at her as she huddled against the wall under the space blanket, which now appeared alien and too bright in the close confines of the Hideout. It was a chunk of the modern world that did not belong there, where he could only speak of ancient impulses, biblical rage, medieval torment. The natural, original state of man: savagery.

She would get up. She would leave. She would be on her cell phone to G. William before she even got into the car, and every fiber of Jazz cried out to delve into his bag of sociopath's tricks, to cozen and coddle her, persuade her not to go. Because once she left and told G. William what he'd said, it was all over. G. William would accept no more help with the Impressionist, and the Impressionist would just keep on killing, and Jazz would end up in an institution somewhere, looking for the last scraps of his soul in a padded cell.

But some part of him...

Some part of him *yearned* for her to go. To flee him.

And that was when Jazz realized that he was in love with Connie. Because for the first time in his life, there was someone more important than himself.

She stood.

She stared at him.

"So do it," she said with a quiet, confident intensity that almost—almost—frightened him. "I'm so sick of this," she went on, urgency and heat gathering like friction in her voice. "So sick of this constant pity party you throw for yourself. I *love* you, you moron. I try to be understanding and supportive, but you keep acting like I don't get you. And you keep trying to scare me, or push me away."

"Con—"

"Shut up! It's my turn. If you want me to stop talking, then you'll have to kill me, which you *claim* you could do. And I'll say it again: Do it. Stop threatening it and stop whining about it and just do it. But if you don't, then shut the hell up about it and let me be there for you and let me help you. Because if you don't, then your crazy father really has won, and *my* crazy father gets his wish and I stop dating the white guy. But either way, figure out your crap and stop dumping it on me!"

Jazz stared at her. Did she have any idea what she was saying? What she was *provoking*? "I—"

"Ah!" She raised a hand to stop him. "Think carefully here,

Jazz. What are you going to say? Because if it's more of this 'I'm too dangerous for you' BS, I might just kill myself to get away from it. And then where would you be?"

He threw his hands in the air, wanting desperately to hit something, to hit some*one*, wanting and needing to bring pain, to feel pain. But only Connie stood before him, and while a part of him—a big part, he could tell—knew exactly what to do to her, exactly how to do it, some other part (small, but strong) wrestled with him and with the voice of his father that lived inside him.

With a cry of anger and frustration, he pushed past her and barged outside, running to the edge of the clearing, where he dropped to his knees in a pile of leaves and scattered grasses, his mind whirling with images of Connie blended with the Impressionist's victims—Connie in the field, Connie in the Heller shower, Connie on Ginny's once-white carpet, her blood and her life running out as Jazz put his lips to hers, only this time he sucked out her last breaths, inhaled her very soul.

Is this what I am? Is this what I have to be? Or is it like Connie says? Is it all just drama? And how do I tell? How do I figure it out?

He knelt there on the cold ground, the images battering at his mind, until he heard the door to the Hideout open, heard the crunch of her tread on dried leaves.

He waited for her to come up behind him, to touch his shoulder. For the slightly sweet scent of chemical detangler that followed her.

And waited.

Until he heard Howie's car start.

Yes. He hung his head. Exactly what he deserved.

He stayed in that position for a long time. He thought that maybe he could stay there forever.

If not for the image of Irene Heller, suddenly before him.

Of her eyelids, closed by the Impressionist, as though he was worried about getting shampoo in her eyes.

But he knew what was under those eyelids. He knew the blank stare of the dead.

He'd seen it in his father's victims. In Fiona Goodling.

In Ginny Davis.

It was something he could never forget.

No one would hold Irene Heller tonight.

No one would hold Irene, and somewhere someone was missing the holding.

Connie was right. This wasn't about him and his problems, his past. It was about Irene and Fiona and Carla and poor, poor Ginny. He had to do everything in his power to avenge them.

And there was one more thing he could do.

He stood and stared up at the night sky. Took in a deep breath and then blew it out in a long, lazy cloud.

And then he said it out loud, to the night, to himself. To make it real.

"I have to see my father."

CHAPTER 29

Connie didn't call that night or the next morning. Not that Jazz really expected her to. He wanted desperately to call her, but every time his hand strayed to the phone, he snatched it back. What would he say to her?

Gramma was in a shrieking state of high dudgeon as reporters clustered down the driveway at the very boundary where the public road abutted her private property. She didn't see them as the press—she was convinced they were an army of enemy warriors, come to pillage and burn the house, then rape her and make her give birth to a new generation of soldiers. The presence of several black and Hispanic reporters among the throng did nothing to assuage her fears.

Melissa Hoover would have an absolute field day with her report if she could see Gramma now.

"You'd probably be better off pillaged than with reporters," Jazz muttered, watching them through a peeled-back curtain. He resented the press for the way it had turned his life into a spectacle. "At least then it'd be over quickly."

"They're coming! Oh, they're coming!" Gramma was belly-crawling across the kitchen floor, a long, sharp barbecue fork in one hand and a deadly gleam in her eye. If she hadn't reminded him so much of his father in that moment, Jazz might have laughed.

"I think they're hanging back for now," he reported.

Predictably, Doug Weathers was at the head of the crowd. He'd been the first to arrive, in fact, beating the TV crew out of Tynan Ridge by a good half hour. Right now everyone was focused on the house, but Jazz knew that soon enough they would get bored with waiting. And that's when the media would start doing that crazy thing where they interviewed one another about the story that they didn't have any facts on. Weathers would be in his glory.

G. William had promised to send a couple of deputies to help the poor cop stuck in the driveway and keep the press in line. So far, no one had crossed onto private property, but it was just a matter of time. Serial killer in Lobo's Nod? Again? A bonus to the first sleazebag to get a picture of the son of the local sociopath!

"They're gonna rape mongrel babies into me! Mongrel babies to kill white folks! And they're gonna give me the AIDS to kill me off!" Gramma ranted.

Jazz sighed and rested his forehead against the window. He had to get out of here.

Gramma had a prescription for a powerful tranquilizer. Jazz hated to use it—it was really strong stuff, and while Gramma had a lot of hate and crazy to keep her going, she was still a frail old woman—but in this case he didn't have much choice.

He couldn't leave her here while he visited Billy. Not with the press outside like that. She would probably charge them with the useless shotgun at some point, racing down the driveway, screaming, her nightgown flapping around her like bat wings....

So he'd dropped one of the tranqs into her morning oatmeal twenty minutes earlier. He didn't know how long he'd be gone, and with the press outside, he didn't want to rely on the Benadryl. He wanted her *out*.

After a few more minutes of ranting and raving, she drifted off to sleep on the floor, still clutching the barbecue fork. Jazz pried it from her fingers and put it on top of the TV, then gathered her up in his arms and struggled up the stairs. He made sure all the blinds and curtains in her room were closed and left her tucked safely in bed. She would be out for most of the day.

I have to see my father, he'd said the night before. The light of day hadn't changed the necessity of it at all.

Too bad.

He put on his darkest sunglasses and most nondescript clothing, then walked straight out the front door and marched to the Jeep without looking in any direction other than right in front of him. The press vultures went nuts.

"Hey, Jasper!"

"—look over here—"

"—kid, you can't—"

"Jasper!"

"—comment?"

"Mr. Dent!"

"—think your father's—"

"—right here at the camera, okay?"

"You need to give a—"

"—*gotta* have a comment!"

"—says you're not a suspect, but—"

"—over *here*!"

He hopped into the Jeep, gunned the engine, and pulled out of the driveway. The lone cop did his best to move the reporters away from the road; Jazz's threatening revving of the engine did the rest. Reporters pressed against the Jeep as he oozed through them. Cameras flashed. Videotape rolled. At some point, someone would make the connection that Billy Dent's kid was driving the vehicle the monster himself had driven when murdering people, and that tape loop would play endlessly on cable channels and the Internet.

Jazz resisted the urge to flip them all the bird, to roll down the window and yell at them. He didn't allow himself to even look at them. Though he yearned to find Doug Weathers, he didn't trust himself not to run the guy over. He just pushed through the crowd and zoomed off before anyone could gather the presence of mind to hop in a car and follow him.

The scene was nearly identical at his destination: The sheriff's office was surrounded four deep by reporters and news crews. Jazz slyly parked next door at the funeral home and slipped in through the connecting corridor before anyone realized who he was.

Inside, G. William's homey little police station looked like a madcap scene from a Wall Street trading floor. Suited strangers—FBI, Jazz wagered—barked orders at one another and into telephones. More deputies and staties than Jazz had ever seen gathered in one place shared cramped desk space and argued over the placement of large whiteboards. Lana did her best to prevent sheer chaos, but it was like wrestling a Teflon-coated tiger. The acrid smell of burned, stale coffee hung over the room, intermingled with body odor and gun oil. Telephones rang constantly, overlapping so that the individual rings blended into a single blare of sound.

No one noticed Jazz. Except for Deputy Erickson. Who stood—alone, of course—in a corner, flipping through a thick binder. He followed Jazz with his eyes, his expression unreadable. Unreadable even to Jazz, who could read anyone.

Jazz did his best to ignore Erickson as he pushed through the helter-skelter of cops. *'Scuse me*, he thought. *Pardon me. Serial killer's kid coming through.*

G. William's office was an oasis of normalcy in the desert of lunacy. The only change to it was a new corkboard mounted behind the desk, pinned with photos from the Impressionist's various crime scenes.

"How d'you like our circus?" the sheriff asked coolly when Jazz came in and closed the door.

"Needs more clowns."

"Clowns we got plenty of. Want to hear the latest?"

"Sure."

"Toxicology on Helen Myerson came back—takes time, you know." Lobo's Nod was too small to have its own full-scale

287

crime lab, so most tests had to be done elsewhere. Which took time. It wasn't like on TV, where test results were available in a matter of hours. "Checked blood and liver, just to be sure. Confirms drain cleaner, not that that's a big surprise. Crime-scene guys vacuumed some good hairs at Heller's place that don't match her or the kids or the hubby. Could be our guy, but—"

"But they're meaningless without something to compare them to."

"If we ever get a suspect, we'll at least be able to place him at Heller's house, but that's about it. Still, it's the first time he's left us anything at all. That's something. At least, that's what I tell myself."

Unspoken between them was the fact that they had even less evidence because Jazz's behavior at Ginny's apartment had made it nearly impossible to collect anything worthwhile. He'd walked in her blood and spread it around, ruined any possible footprints on the carpet, touched the body and the window and other surfaces the killer had touched....

G. William smiled sadly and rubbed his eyes. "To what do I owe this visit? What can I do you for, Jazz?"

He expected G. William to fight him on the idea of seeing Billy, but the sheriff instead nodded thoughtfully, tilted his head to stare at the ceiling, and made a popping sound with his lips as he considered it. Then G. William snatched up the phone on his desk.

"I can get the warden on the line and have you in to see Billy this afternoon," he said.

Jazz did a double take. "Aren't you the guy who's been

telling me for four years to forget about him, not to have anything to do with him, to pretend he's dead?"

G. William pointed with the phone receiver. "Hey. Jazz. If this was just about you and your well-being, I wouldn't be pullin' no strings for you, okay? Your biggest problem these days oughtta be figuring out where you want to go to college and scraping together the money for your car insurance. But this is bigger than you or me or what we want. We got a lunatic killing people. If he follows your dad's pattern perfectly, he'll kill one more in Lobo's Nod, then disappear for three months and pop up somewhere else with a totally different MO and signature. We'll never catch him. We got this one chance. We know everything about his next victim except for who it is. I got descriptions and warnings out. I got a task force out there taking panicky calls from every blond secretary in a fifty-mile radius. So, yeah, if you talking to your daddy even *might* get us something we can use, I'm all for it."

Jazz said nothing. What was there to say?

G. William made the call. Jazz settled into a chair and watched the sheriff glad-hand the warden for a few minutes. When he hung up, he was smiling a grim little smile under his bushy mustache.

"Billy will see you. The warden's arranging it for this afternoon. I'll have a cruiser take you up to Wammaket with the siren going."

"Not Erickson," Jazz said, perhaps a little too quickly.

G. William pursed his lips, but didn't ask any questions. He just nodded and then bellowed "HANSON!" at the top of his lungs.

"I need to stop by the hospital first," Jazz said.

G. William nodded. "Yeah, you do what you need to do."

Deputy Hanson poked his head into the office. "What's up, chief?"

"First, how many times I gotta tell you? I'm a sheriff, not a chief. Second, take Jasper here to the hospital, then to Wammaket. Sirens all the way. This matters more than your momma and your little baby girl, Hanson."

Hanson stared, mentally adding Jazz's presence to Wammaket State Penitentiary and coming up with the only obvious solution. "Oh, wow," he whispered.

"Save your *oh, wow* for your memoirs, Hanson. Get going."

Jazz wanted to see Howie before he left for Wammaket. He couldn't say why, just that it mattered that he see his best friend and know his condition.

Three surprises waited for him at the hospital. First, Howie's parents were off getting lunch.

Second, Connie was in Howie's room, keeping him company while his parents got a meal and some rest. Third, Howie was sitting up in bed, looking like a pale(r) version of himself—but at least looking like himself.

"The doctors say I can go home tonight," he told Jazz. "I'll have to take it easy, but when has *that* not been true?"

Jazz was genuinely glad to hear it. "That's great, man." He pulled up a chair. "Try to keep the blood on the inside from now on, okay?"

"Doing my best. You owe me some big-time tats." Howie tilted his head, concerned. "What's up with you guys, anyway?"

Jazz and Connie shared a brief glance. "What do you mean?" Connie asked.

"I'm a bleeder, not a moron," Howie said. "And I think the drugs they've pumped into me have, like, sent me to a higher plane of consciousness. You guys are fighting."

"No we're not," Connie said, surprising Jazz.

"We're not?"

"Oh, this is gonna be good," Howie said.

Ignoring Howie, Connie said, "No, you idiot."

"But you left last night—"

"I was pissed. We weren't getting anywhere. So yeah, I left. Not the end of the world. I told you last night: I love you. A little argument isn't going to get in the way of that."

Jazz didn't know what to say. Fortunately, Howie filled in the gap: "Dude, get up off your butt and stick your tongue down her throat."

They settled on a lingering kiss on the lips. Howie graded it an 8.5.

Now, holding Connie's hand, Jazz suddenly felt stronger, able to reveal what he'd come here to tell. "Guys"—he drew in a deep breath—"I'm going to see my father."

Connie's eyes went wide, and she squeezed Jazz's hand so hard it went numb. She opened her mouth to speak, but nothing came out.

"Yo, dawg, you sure about that?" Howie asked in an accent that could have been street-talk, Irish, or something in between.

"Yeah. I'm going. Now. G. William set it up."

Howie laughed weakly. "Tell your pops I said 'hi.'"

"Seriously?"

"God, no! Are you nuts? Tell him I'm already dead. Tell him I've *been* dead." Howie shivered.

They fist-bumped—gently—and then Connie joined Jazz in the hallway to say good-bye.

"Are you really doing this?" she asked.

"It's the last thing I haven't tried."

"I thought you were afraid of letting him into your head."

"Yeah, well, last night someone told me to figure out my crap and challenged me to be a little stronger than usual, and it turned out all right. So, y'know." He grinned at her.

"I'm proud of you," she said. "I'm serious."

"You took a hell of a risk," he told her. "Last night. Saying what you said."

"I know. Paid off, too." She flashed him a dazzling smile.

"Look," he told her, "I don't know if I'm crazy or what, but I need you to promise me that you'll stay away from Doug Weathers while I'm gone."

Connie blinked in surprise. "Why on earth would I even go near that bottom-feeder in the first place?"

"And stay away from that new deputy, Erickson. If you need to call the cops, call G. William direct, okay? And don't let him send Erickson."

She touched his cheek. "Is something going on? Do you think Erickson or Weathers—"

"I don't know what I think," he admitted. "It could all be

coincidence. And I'm probably wrong, but better safe than sorry."

"You think one of them is...?" She didn't want to voice it.

"Maybe. That's my best guess." He paused. "Or maybe both of them. Together."

Connie gasped. "Oh my God."

"I'm sure I'm wrong. I mean, like I said before, there's no reason the killer should be someone I know. It's not like there are rules. But just be safe, okay? I'll be back soon enough."

"Are you sure about seeing your dad?" she asked again as they enfolded each other in a hug.

"You're the one who said I should do this. Remember? Back when this all started."

"I was talking about you getting closure from him, not opening up old wounds."

"There's no such thing as closure when it comes to Dear Old Dad. But maybe I can learn something, or get some kind of information out of him. Something that will save the next victim. Something to stop the Impressionist."

"Do you really think so?"

He hated to smash her hope to bits, but he had to be honest. "No, not really. But I have to at least try."

CHAPTER 30

Wammaket State Penitentiary rose against the horizon like a cement factory from hell. Two concentric fences ten feet high surrounded the property, topped by razor-sharp loops of concertina wire that sparkled prettily and dangerously in the sunlight. A year earlier, some prisoners on an outdoor work detail had started a brushfire, and the building's exterior still bore streaks and leaping shadows charred into its surface, giving it a mottled, medieval appearance.

Even with the siren going and Hanson ignoring every speed limit to indulge his inner Andretti, it had taken them almost two hours to get to Wammaket from Lobo's Nod. There were no closer prisons that could handle an inmate of Billy Dent's caliber.

Billy had cut several deals with the prosecutors. Most of them had to do with keeping the state or federal government from injecting a lethal dose of chemicals into his bloodstream as due punishment for his crimes. But his last deal had guaranteed that he would serve his time—and die behind bars of old age—at Wammaket, the closest penitentiary to Lobo's Nod. "So my boy can visit," he'd told the lawyers.

Jazz hadn't bothered. And now…

"So," Hanson said, speaking for the first time since they'd left G. William's office. Wammaket loomed ahead of them, growing larger. "So. Uh."

Jazz was in no mood for small talk. "Want to join me?" he asked Hanson.

"Jesus, no!" the deputy blurted out. Then he recovered and said, "Uh, I mean, that's probably not a good idea."

Outside the penitentiary, a group of three people—two women and a man—stood together, hoisting protest signs and stomping their feet rhythmically. As Hanson pulled the cruiser closer, Jazz realized that the signs and the trio's matching T-shirts all said the same thing:

FREE BILLY DENT!

So. Here were the lunatics who thought Billy had been framed, his confessions coerced. Jazz had read about them on the Internet, but he'd never actually seen any of them. It was a nationwide movement, apparently. Jazz was grateful they could only muster three morons at a time.

"Idiots," Hanson muttered under his breath.

A corrections officer waved them through the two fences and guided them to a small parking lot against a cinder-block wall that still bore a peaked tattoo from last year's fire. Another corrections officer met them at the entrance and pointed out a lounge to Hanson. Jazz was escorted directly to the warden's office.

"You're sure about this?" the warden asked. He had a tall, thick build that made Jazz think, for some reason, of a rhinoceros. He seemed like he was clenching all of his muscles, all the time. Constantly on alert.

And he regarded Jazz with suspicion. Did he think Jazz was Billy's conspirator in the Impressionist's crimes? Or was it just a matter of suspicion-as-survival, surrounded as he was daily by some of the most dangerous men in the state?

"I'm sure," Jazz said.

The warden shook his head. "Billy hasn't agreed to see anyone in the four years we've had him. Last person he saw was one of his lawyers. I didn't think he would agree to see even you, but he surprised me. I can't stop you from seeing him, but I can do everything possible to warn you."

"Billy won't hurt me," Jazz said with more confidence than he actually felt. He didn't know what Billy might do, truthfully. And besides, Billy had ways of hurting that went beyond the physical. He could cause pain without a touch.

"You need to be careful around this guy," the warden said. "He's a master manipulator, and one of the best liars I've ever seen. A real PhD in slinging high-grade horse manure, you catch me?"

If Jazz had been in a better mood, he might have appreciated the comedy in the very thought of the warden warning him, of all people, of the dangers of Billy Dent.

"If Billy Dent told me so much as his name," the warden went on, "I'd check his birth certificate to be sure."

He gazed at Jazz for an amount of time that would have intimidated or spooked most people. But Jazz wasn't "most people." He just stared back. He admitted a grudging respect for the fact that the warden didn't back down. He'd been taught his stare by Dear Old Dad, and very few people could stand it for long without becoming flustered at the very least.

"I'll ask again: You sure you want to do this, kid?"

Jazz shrugged lazily. Inside, he had swallowed a potent cocktail of terror and thrill—the thought of seeing his father again scared the hell out of him, but also made him feel somehow more alive. He supposed this was what skydivers felt just before they pulled the rip cord. But he wasn't about to let anyone, least of all the warden, know that.

The warden snorted. "Fine. Let's do 'er."

Moments later, Jazz found himself with the warden and a couple of corrections officers in a small gray room, sitting at a metal table that was bolted to the concrete floor. The chairs, he noticed, were also bolted down. The walls were made of unpainted cinder blocks. Jazz remembered reading about a prison where they had painted the walls in pastels, thinking the colors would calm the inmates.

Instead, the inmates had peeled the paint off the walls. And eaten it.

There were two doors, dull metal affairs set into perpendicular walls. Jazz had come through one, and he knew what would be coming through the other.

A single, narrow, barred window would have let in sunlight from up near the ceiling had the day not been overcast and gray. Instead, the only light came from a naked bulb dangling from the high ceiling. Jazz calculated quickly—if he stood on the table, he could probably snatch the bulb. Could he break it into a serviceable weapon before anyone could stop him?

He thought he could.

He was pretty damn sure he could.

Jazz tightened his grip on the edge of the table until the blood drained from his fingers. *You don't need a weapon*, he told himself. *You don't need—*

—wakey, wakey—

—do it!

"Don't be nervous, kid," the warden said, mistaking Jazz's white knuckles for nerves, not restraint. "My men'll make sure you're safe."

"I'm fine," he replied. "You always accompany your prisoners' guests?"

The warden burst out laughing—for such a big, impressive man, he had a surprisingly high and trembly laugh. Jazz found himself wanting to rip out the man's larynx. Kill that girlie laugh.

Instead, he smiled his best, most polite smile and pretended that he didn't want to kill the guy.

A buzzer sounded. Through a barred slot at eye level in the second door, Jazz saw a CO's face. "Prisoner!" the man barked.

The warden nodded and one of the COs in the room opened

that door. The barking CO entered the room and stepped aside.

Jazz laid his eyes on his father, in the flesh, for the first time in four years.

Billy Dent looked...

He looked happy.

His mouth was twisted in a wry grin, his eyes wide and alight with what some people—none of them in this room— might mistake for an impish glee. He carried himself with a loose swagger, as if he expected music to strike up at any moment and he was trying to decide if he would dance or not. He wore bright orange prison-issue pants and a matching shirt, unbuttoned, with a clean white T-shirt underneath.

Jazz had somehow expected Billy to be grimy. Filthy. Covered with soot and cinder and dust. Instead, he was disappointed to see that Billy looked like he'd just come from a shower to a wardrobe of fresh laundry. His sandy-blond hair, no longer shaved and a bit longer than Jazz had ever seen it, was clean and combed back.

"Welcome, Billy," the warden said with a sneer. "This here's the visitors' room. Figure I need to introduce it to you, since you haven't had any use for it."

Billy shuffled in. He was shackled, hand and foot. He had roughly three inches of play between his wrists, maybe five inches between his ankles. A longer chain ran between the ones binding his limbs, just short enough that he had to stoop an inch. He jangled and clanked. Another CO stood behind him. So, two had come in with him, two were already here, and there was the warden. Five men between Billy and Jazz, and

Jazz still felt like Billy was in control of the room. His father stared straight at him, that smile still twisting his lips, that light in his eyes never dimming.

"Read him the riot act," the warden said to the lead CO, and then he left the room.

"Now it's fun-time, Billy," the CO said, his voice no-nonsense. "I'm only gonna tell you this once, so y'all listen careful, okay? Here's how it's gonna be. You're gonna sit in this here seat. I'm gonna shackle you to the table. Me and my men'll be on the other side of that there door."

He pointed. Jazz watched his father's eyes. They didn't move at all; Billy was still staring at him. It was as though Jazz were the only other person in the room.

"The door ain't gonna be locked. I want you to pretend there's an invisible fence halfway down that table. Right smack in the middle. You touch that fence, you lean forward too much, and we're gonna come through that door and we're gonna hurt you, Billy. Now, I don't mean we're gonna hit you with the clubs or give you the Taser. It's gonna be a big hurt, Billy. A bad hurt. It's gonna go on a long time. Your boy here will be home in bed and it'll still be going on, see? I'm trying to impress upon y'all how serious this hurtin' is gonna be. Do we understand each other?"

Without removing his gaze from Jazz, Billy Dent nodded once.

The lead guard looked over at Jazz again. "You sure about this, kid?"

Jazz didn't trust his voice all of a sudden. He nodded exactly like his father had, realized what he was doing, nodded a second time just to be different, then cursed himself for showing weakness to Dear Old Dad.

The guards sat Billy down and locked his wrist chain to the table. Billy folded his hands in front of him.

And then Jazz was alone with his father, the two of them staring at each other across the table, separated by no more than two foot of empty air and an imaginary fence.

"Is it Father's Day already?" Billy asked jovially, as if no time at all had passed, as if it hadn't been four years.

Jazz weighed his words carefully. Billy Dent came across like some sort of bumpkin or redneck idiot, but nothing could be further from the truth. His IQ had tested off the charts; he had driven two psychiatrists (one with the FBI, one with a victims' rights group) to quit their profession. He was pure brilliance and pure evil in one package, and woe be to anyone who forgot this when talking to him.

"So this is funny to you?" Jazz asked, keeping his tone even, bland. "You're amused?"

Billy craned his neck left, then right, producing an audible crack. "*Life* amuses me, Jasper. Until it don't no more." He grinned. "When you're a happy guy, you find amusement in all kinds of places. Even in here."

"There was a shrink on TV once," Jazz said evenly. "Said you would probably kill yourself in prison."

Billy chuckled. "Kill myself? And destroy all of this?" He couldn't gesture well with his shackled hands, so he nodded his head around the room. The state. The universe.

"Still, I'm surprised you're in one piece. I thought there was a pecking order in prison."

"There sure is!" Billy leaned back and guffawed. "Oh, there's one hell of a pecking order! And your dear old daddy sits right up around the top. You got triple digits next to your name, they sorta king you in here. Like in checkers, you follow?"

"I figured someone would shank you. Try to prove he's a big man by knocking off Billy Dent."

"Well, now"—Billy's slow drawl became even more syrupy—"I ain't sayin' there ain't been no—whatchacallem?—*altercations* in the past couple years. There's definitely been what I'd call a, well, a *breakin'-in* period."

He produced a smile that—to anyone else—would have seemed full of genuine warmth. Jazz remembered it from the night Billy had shown him how to saw through a knee joint in under five minutes. (*First you gotta get under the kneecap, what your doctors an' such call the patella, see?*)

"But now me an' the folks in here get along just fine. They get me and I get them. Prison ain't so bad for people like us, Jasper."

Too late, Jazz tried to keep his spine from stiffening at the comment, but he'd reacted already, and Billy had seen it, had seen that he'd crawled right under Jazz's skin. Jazz bit back the expected retort—*I'm nothing like you*—because he knew Billy already had a counterattack ready.

"I'm glad you're doing well," he said instead, and pretended to mean it.

Billy paused, trying to decide whether or not to believe him. "I don't think you'd be wanting me dead, anyway. Know what set me off on my prospecting? My own daddy died.

God, I loved that man. When he died, I just went and did as I pleased. Happens to a lot like us: Gein and Speck and de Rais. And me. And maybe you. How about that? Wouldn't that be a kick, if you got your wish and I died and all it did was..." He trailed off and stared. "But enough of that morbid talk." He smiled. "When a man's done his life's work—and done it well, Jasper—he can go into his retirement a happy man."

Jazz snorted laughter. Billy could gas about "retirement" all he wanted, but they both knew the old man would be infinitely happier on the outside. Prospecting.

"Is that what this is to you? Retirement? Came a little earlier than you expected, didn't it?"

Billy smiled that warm killer's smile again. "Did it?"

For long moments, they gazed at each other across the table and through the imaginary fence. Billy unfolded his hands and rested his fists on the table. Jazz could see new prison tats on his father's knuckles—fresh, from the looks of them. Raw.

L-O-V-E spelled out on his right fist. F-E-A-R spelled on the left.

"Nice ink," Jazz said.

A shrug. "Brand-new. Glad you like 'em. Look here: You ain't gotta worry about anyone killin' your daddy in here, Jasper. Ain't gonna happen. I guaran-damn-tee it. I got respect in here. You talked about that 'pecking order.' Well, it don't peck me. They save that for the real bastards. It's not like I hurt *kids*."

Jazz bristled. That liar! That hypocrite! He was probably giving Billy exactly what he wanted, but he couldn't help it. He didn't care what kind of mind game Billy Dent was playing; he couldn't let a comment like that go.

"No kids? What about George Harper?"

"George Harper..." Billy stared at the ceiling as if trying to place the name. Which was bull, because Billy had a photographic memory and total recall. "Oh. Right," he said after a moment or two of pretense. "Hell, son—that kid looked nineteen, twenty, easy. You saw the pictures. You know he didn't look fifteen." He shook his head, clearly pleased with the reaction he'd managed to provoke in Jazz. "They grow up so fast, you know? Like you did, Jasper-boy. You ever think of having kids, Jasper? Giving me a grandbaby? Something for me to live for? I know I got a bunch of life sentences, but with science the way it is, hell, maybe I'll live 'em all. What do you think?"

The idea of having children nauseated Jazz. To pass down the genetic *mistake* that was his grandmother's madness, his father's madness, his own madness... No. That would not happen. He would not create the next generation's Billy Dent.

"I bet I know what you're thinking, Jasper," Billy said, his voice low and seductive and knowing. It was the perfect sociopath's voice, and Jazz hated it because it was so like his own. He'd heard himself use it with teachers who needed to be persuaded of things. With G. William and Melissa Hoover. Hell, he might as well just admit it—with *everyone*. It was as natural as blinking, as natural as falling asleep.

"You're thinking you ain't gonna give the world no more Dents. I hear that. I understand. But it ain't always your decision. You got a little piece of tail you like to bang? Handsome boy like you, all silver-tongued, those little girls don't stand a chance, Jasper. They line up for a taste of your dick, don't they? Don't they?"

Jazz shook his head before he could stop himself. Damn it! He had sworn to himself that he would give his father neither information nor satisfaction, and now, with one movement, he'd surrendered both.

"You ain't lookin' at the line, then. That's good. You got one girl. One special girl. That's good, Jasper. Men like us, we like our consistency, you know what I mean? Fewer surprises that way. You plow a lotta fields, you never know where there's gonna be a stone. You stick to one field, you get to know it. You know the stones and the ruts and the pits.

"But here's the thing, Jasper. I bet you're a nice, responsible kid, 'cause I raised you that way, but are you always the one buyin' the rubbers? Hmm? Or maybe she's on that pill? 'Cause you can't always trust 'em, Jasper. You look at them rubbers real close-like, see? You watch her take that pill, Jasper. Hell"—he roared with laughter—"how you think *you* was born?

"Oh, yeah, that's right," Billy went on, leaning forward, leaning in so far that Jazz thought for sure that he must have crossed the imaginary fence—he *must* have!—but the door stayed closed and no one came in to rescue him. "You were the biggest surprise of my life, Jasper. I was so angry at your momma. At first. Won't tell you the things I considered doing to her because they might disturb you, boy, and I ain't gonna do that. I know how sensitive you are. But then you were born, Jasper. You came sliding out easy as you please, didn't cause your momma any pain, hardly any labor. Just come sliding

305

right out, practically into my arms, my boy, my son, my future. So I forgave your momma for what she done, for her deception."

"What did you do to Mom?" Jazz asked, his voice strangled, his throat tight. He didn't mean to ask it. He didn't *want* to ask it, but he was helpless, wrapped up in Billy Dent's spell, just like all of Billy's other victims, for surely Jazz was as much a victim as the rest of them. Surely that was true?

"Do? What did I do to your mother?" A shrug. "Nothing."

—just like cutting—

—good boy—

"What did you make *me* do?" Jazz whispered.

Billy grinned.

"What did you make me do? Did you make me kill my mother?"

Billy laughed. "Don't you remember?"

But he didn't. He couldn't. His memory—his poor, abused, fragmented memory. He could remember Billy skinning Rusty, could remember the quicklime lessons, could remember so much horror, but couldn't remember the most important thing of all. He couldn't remember—

—do it!

—cut—

the knife

It was Mom. I cut Mom with the knife. Billy made me.

Jazz felt the room spinning around him. This was crazy. A mistake. A huge one. He was insane to have come here. Billy Dent was the master of manipulation, the king of not just the penitentiary, but also of the psychic spaces between father and son. He was lord of Jazz's own mind. After all, hadn't Billy built that mind? Hadn't he sired Jazz, raised him, shaped and guided him like any father would? Wasn't Jazz his father's creature?

Billy. Billy in the past, urging Jazz with the knife. Billy in the present, grinning still, now whispering: "What's her name, Jasper? Tell Dear Old Dad your little pussy's name. I want to think of how happy you are, and I need to have a name to go with it. Tell me her name."

Connie, Jazz thought, but he would not let himself say it. He couldn't sully her name by letting it anywhere near Billy Dent's ears and brain. He couldn't bear the thought of Billy Dent knowing that name, much less speaking it out loud.

"Tell me her name, son."

Connie ...

And that brought to mind what she'd said before. About how he didn't have to be his dad, how he could rise above his own upbringing. *Sons aren't their fathers. Not the good, not the bad. Sons get second chances. You don't have to be what your dad is. You don't have his eyes, and you don't have to have his life.*

"I'm a virgin," he told Billy.

Billy snorted with disgust and leaned back. Jazz felt as though the room had suddenly been flooded with pure oxygen—he could breathe so much more easily now.

"No. No, you ain't. You gonna lie to me, we ain't got nothing to discuss," Billy said.

Jazz didn't care that Billy thought it was a lie. It didn't matter. What mattered was that it had broken the spell, made it possible for Jazz to think again.

It had put power back on Jazz's side of the imaginary fence.

"I'm sorry," he said with as much contrition as he could muster. "I shouldn't have lied. I'm not a virgin. Her name's"— *Heidi Linda Rae Delores Juanita Chelsea Tonya*—"Tonya."

"Tonya?" Billy frowned. "Killed me a Tonya once. Perfect little titties. Fake redhead. Hate that."

"I remember," Jazz said. "I remember the trophy."

Pleased, Billy leaned forward again. "Tell me."

"Leather gloves," Jazz said. "Kid gloves. So brown they were almost red. They were so smooth and soft. I remember imagining that was what a woman felt like."

Billy chuckled. "You got my memory, that's for sure, Jasper. But you got your momma's way with words. Damn, I miss her."

"I used to put them on. In the rumpus room. I never told you because I thought you'd be mad."

"Playing with your daddy's toys."

"I would wear the gloves and touch my cheek. My lips. I would imagine that's what it would feel like—"

"To be with a woman," Billy finished, his eyes dancing. "And now? Now that you've been with a woman? Is that what it was like?"

"No. It's better. Better. But not as good as it can be. I know. I remember that from what you taught me. Sometimes, when I'm with"—*Connie*—"Tonya, I want to see what you told me about: the fear."

"It'll come, son," Billy whispered. "In time, it'll come. I promise you."

They stared at each other across the table for long, long moments. Jazz wondered how long he could keep it up. How long could he pretend to be in Billy's thrall? How long could he pretend to be aroused by these thoughts? Worst of all—*was* he pretending? Could anyone really fake this?

"Anyway, Jasper," Billy said, breaking the suspense. "I'm glad you're gettin' your dick wet. I should've brought you a girl a long time ago. That was neglectful of me, and I apologize for it. For that and nothing else."

"That's fine."

"What brings you to see Dear Old Dad, kiddo?" Billy leaned as far back as he could, given that he was tethered to the table and to his own ankle chain. Somehow, he managed to look relaxed and at peace. "I raised you to think of yourself; first, last, and always. So you gotta want something from me."

"I do."

"Spit it out."

"I..." Was this the right thing to do? He'd managed to build up a rapport of sorts with Billy over the past few minutes. As soon as he asked for help in catching the Impressionist... wouldn't Billy realize he'd been had? Wouldn't he— enraged—lunge for Jazz across the table, imaginary fence be damned?

Well, maybe. And in that case, Jazz would see his father beaten to within an inch of his life. So it was really a win-win scenario.

"I need your help. To find someone."

"Really?" Billy actually seemed interested. "Who?"

"This might sound a little strange. So hear me out, okay? I'm sort of... I'm sort of trying to find a serial killer."

Jazz had expected either a burst of laughter or a snarl of rage. He got neither. Billy's grin just widened. "You don't say."

"Do you watch the news in here at all? Do you know about the Impressionist?"

"The Impressionist." Billy said the name slowly, drawing it out to infinite syllables. "Can't say as I do."

"He's copying your first kills. Right down to the drain cleaner. Right down to the initials of the victims."

Jazz watched his father carefully for his reaction, but Billy's face remained placidly—sociopathically—still.

Billy nodded slowly. "Why are you looking for this gentleman?"

To save my soul. If I have one in the first place. "Honestly? I'm helping the cops."

Now would come the rage.

"Interesting," Billy mused. "Very interesting."

"That's all you have to say? I'm trying to help the cops catch someone like you and you think it's *interesting*?"

"Nah. That part's boring. Totally natural for you to be checkin' out the other side of the equation. Perfect sense. Hell, I spent three weeks at the police academy when I was a little older than you, Jasper. I get it."

"Oh?" Jazz forced himself to show nothing but casual, impassive interest, while inside he fumed. Billy had been researching the cops, trying to learn their secrets. Jazz was doing something else entirely—trying to figure out how a killer's mind worked. Trying to figure out if it was the same as his own.

"What's interesting is that you ain't tellin' me the whole truth. You ain't doin' this to help the cops. You don't give a

310

damn about them. You're doing this for *you*. To figure yourself out. To see what makes you tick."

"No."

"More important, Jasper, you're doing this because you *have to*. Dog gotta hunt, son. You go find yourself a three-legged bird dog and then take it out hunting and you watch it fall over trying to point out the bird. It'll happen every time, damn sure. You're a hunter, born and bred. You got the scent. You want your prey, boy. You want to go prospecting. You need it."

"No."

Billy said, "It waits inside you. It lurks, you see? It waits and it pads around like a big cat, and when you least expect it, it comes up behind you. So don't kid yourself. It's there all along. It's there. It's just waiting, is all."

"I'm not a killer."

"Sure you are. You just ain't killed no one yet."

"Are you going to help me or not?"

"Heh. I should send you on your way empty-handed. No one held *my* hand and taught me how to play. No, sir. But I know how kids are today. Gotta have their parents doing everything for them. Helicopter parents, right?" He chuckled. "Read about that in *Newsweek*, same issue with my picture in it. So, yeah, I'll help you, Jasper. But you're going to help me, too."

Jazz felt despair wash over him. A sociopath never gives anything away for free, and Jazz couldn't unleash Billy Dent on the world.

"Forget it," Jazz said, the bitter tang of regret gathering in his mouth with each syllable. "I won't help you get out of here. I'm not doing that."

"Who said I wanted you to?" Billy looked mortified by the very thought of it. "I told you, Jasper—I'm a king in here. Why would a king forsake his throne and his subjects? I ain't going anywhere. Well"—he paused, considering—"except probably in a body bag, but that's a ways off, I think."

"Then what do you want? I'm not smuggling stuff in here for you—"

"Don't want you to."

"Then what?" Jazz threw up his hands in frustration. "What *do* you want?"

And Billy told him.

CHAPTER 31

Jazz told his father as much about the Impressionist as he could, leaving out no details. He watched Billy carefully, wary of his reaction. Billy might be flattered that someone had decided to "honor" him in this fashion, or he might be enraged that another killer dared to walk in his footsteps. It could go either way.

But Billy gave no indication of how the information impacted him. He simply leaned back as far as the manacles would allow and closed his eyes, a slight, almost beatific smile on his lips, a smile that did not waver a micron as Jazz recounted the events of the last week.

When he finished, Billy took in a deep breath and exhaled through flaring nostrils, his eyes still closed. "Well, now," he said quietly, "this is sure an interestin' dilemma. And an interestin' gentleman, that's for sure." His eyes popped open and he yawned, as though he'd just had a relaxing, refreshing nap. "Not sure what I can do for you, though."

"You know. You have admirers out there." He thought of

the FREE BILLY DENT! conspiracy theorists outside Wammaket's walls. "Sociopath groupies. Junkies for this stuff. I know. Women want to marry you. There's websites dedicated to you. People write you fan mail."

"That they do," Billy agreed. "I don't read most of it. It's all the same junk: 'Billy, I pray to you every night to give me the strength to do what you done.' 'Mr. Dent, my blood is your blood.' 'Oh, Billy, you're the only real man on the planet.' Hell, I know that. Don't need letters to tell me. Some of them, they say they want to be like me. They say they want to learn from me. Be my protégé. You know what? I don't need a protégé. Already got one. You."

Jazz ignored that last bit. "He's obviously an admirer of yours. If I could look at the letters…"

"Got rid of 'em. Like I said—I don't care."

Jazz seethed, but he forced himself to remain calm. "Maybe you remember one in particular—"

"Guarantee you he ain't been in touch with me." Billy stroked his jaw with FEAR. "He's thinkin' he's his own man. He's doin' a whatchacallit—a theme and variation. Like jazz musicians, playin' the same melody but makin' it their own tune."

"Like rappers, sampling old rock songs?"

Billy snorted. "Whatever it takes for you to understand. Sure, like them hip-hop idiots. And he's doin' a fine job. No one's got away from him. Not easy, you know. Most of those jackasses—guys like Gacy and Bundy and even that pecker-head Dahmer—most of 'em, at some point they let someone go. Either on purpose or by accident, someone gets away, and

314

that's when the downfall starts. Not me, though." His eyes glittered, the coldest sapphires in the world. "Not me. Never let a one of 'em get away. Never screwed up."

"Like this guy," Jazz said, dragging the conversation back to the topic at hand.

"Well, he's just starting out. Any fool can kill—what?—five people and get away with it. If he's still out there batting a thousand after twenty or thirty, then come talk to me. I'll be appropriately impressed. Bake him a cake or something." Billy lit up. "There's your answer, Jasper. You don't gotta catch this guy. Just wait. He'll trip on his own feet at some point, and then you got him."

"That's hardly an acceptable solution," Jazz said calmly.

Billy shrugged. "Why not? Five dead, fifteen dead, fifty dead...Everyone dies. That's a fact. The timing of it is just a detail."

"I don't want any more people to die."

"Really?" Billy leaned in close, almost touching the invisible fence again. "Really, Jasper? 'Cause let me tell you something. I think you don't really care about these people. And you know how I know that?"

"Tell me," Jazz said tonelessly. But inside, his heart pounded at the idea of being psychoanalyzed by the man who knew him best.

"Because these people, these...these *mythical* people 'out there' somewhere, the ones he ain't killed yet...You don't know them, Jasper. They ain't nothing to you. So why should you care if he kills them? Right now, someone's dyin'." Billy thumped the table lightly with his fist, the LOVE moving down, then up. "And

315

now." *Thump* went LOVE again. "And now." *Thump.* "Some beggar in India, some Mexican on the border, some girl in New York City thinkin' she's gonna be a model but just got turned out to whoring instead. All of them dyin' now"—*thump*—"and now"—*thump*—"and now"—*thump*—"and now"—*thump*—"and what do you care? What do I care?"

"Just because they're abstract doesn't mean they don't matter," Jazz said, forcing his voice not to quake or tremble or otherwise betray emotion. Because Billy was right. To a degree. People died all the time. He didn't know them or even know about them. So did they matter?

People matter. People are real.

"You don't care about savin' his prospects. You care about yourself. About makin' sure no one thinks you were involved. About provin' you can be a regular citizen like all the others. That's what you care about, Jasper."

It was the truth—not a truth he wanted or needed to hear, but a truth nonetheless. But maybe it wasn't the whole truth. Maybe there was more to the truth than Billy's cynicism.

"My motives don't matter," he told Billy. "You agreed to help. Are you gonna help or not?"

Billy clucked his tongue. "So impatient. I ain't seen my boy in years. Can you blame me for dragging things out a little?" He flashed a full-on angelic grin, like a child caught swiping a cookie.

Jazz would have none of it. He stared at his father.

"Oh, all right," Billy said, slumping in his chair. "You ain't no fun. Look, you got to learn how to think like this guy. Shouldn't be hard for you, Jasper. He's thinking like me, and

316

you're part of me. He's an Impressionist. Don't you know anything about Impressionism?"

Jazz shook his head.

"What *are* they teaching you in school these days?" Billy
said in his best parody of a concerned parent. Jazz had the
feeling that Billy would—if he could—kill every last teacher
in Lobo's Nod just to make his point. "Impressionism ain't
about what *is*. It's about the overall *impression* of things, see?
It's about the effect of something on the eye, not the exact details. You follow?"

"I guess."

"Now this last, poor victim, this poor Heller woman..."
Billy did a passable job of sounding mournful about her pass-
ing. "She wasn't exactly a maid, but she was close enough, see?
That's what mattered to him."

"He also killed her too soon. You had a delay between your
fourth and fifth."

"So? Go to a museum sometime, son, and look at a Monet.
Get real close, as close as they'll let you, and then you tell me
what day it was when good ol' Claude painted one brushstroke
as opposed to another. Timing don't matter. Not to this guy.
He cares about the overall effect."

That made sense. But it didn't resolve the essential problem.

"How does that help us figure out who his next victim is?"

Billy sighed and looked skyward, as if asking the Good Lord
why he had to do all the work himself. "Look at ways he
can twist the details, son, but still keep the overall effect. Like
your teacher—she wasn't *exactly* an actress, but close enough.
Same thing here: He's not going after some blond piece of tail

317

in an office building. He's looking for the secretary of the Rotary Club, or the gal who makes coffee at the PTA meetings."

"But—"

"But nothing!" Billy said, showing some heat for the first time. "This guy's being *accurate*, Jasper. Not *precise*. He bumped off some two-bit coffee-and-hash slinger from the local grease pit. My girl, she was a waitress at a fancy bistro right near the beach. Lot of tourist trade. Made more in tips in one night than this guy's girl made in a week." Billy spoke possessively, as if he owned his prospects. In a way, maybe he did. His contempt for the Impressionist was suddenly all too obvious. "I killed Vanessa Dawes. Beautiful Vanessa." He sighed and leaned back, his expression that of a man remembering a gourmet meal. "She was an actress. Just starting out, sure, but she'd been on TV, and she had promise. This guy, who'd he kill? Your drama teacher? Your *drama teacher*? And that's supposed to be the same thing? Are you kidding me?"

Excitement and anger both coursed through Jazz at the same time, and he struggled not to let either one show. This was it—what he'd been looking for. He should have seen it all along: The Impressionist was sticking to the spirit of Billy's crimes, changing the letter to suit his own needs. Each victim was so close to Billy's that Jazz hadn't seen the differences. How had he missed that?

"Find the victim and we find him," Jazz said.

"Maybe. But you also have to figure out how to identify this guy. He's a part of our little hometown, sonny boy." Billy grinned. "He's gettin' his breakfast at the Coff-E-Shop and probably checkin' books outta the library. He feels comfortable in Lobo's Nod. Killin' so many there . . . Yeah, he feels comfortable there."

A thought buzzed along the back of Jazz's mind. "You think he's a native? Someone from town who knew you, maybe? Or from nearby?"

Billy shrugged again. "Don't really matter. What matters is, he fits in. Doesn't stand out. That's our biggest and best skill, Jasper. People think it's knowing how to cut up a body or seducing a pretty little thing into your car. Nah. That's bull. That's stuff you can learn on the Internet. Our real skill is *blending in*. That's what we're good at." He flashed a grin. "They never see us comin', son, 'cause we look just like they do. We look human."

Jazz's mind was spinning. This was it—the key to catching the Impressionist.

He had to tell G. William right away. He stood up. "Are we done already?" Billy asked, hurt. "I ain't had time to ask you about your Little League games and your soccer practice."

Jazz looked down at his father's hands. LOVE. FEAR.

"I have to go." With great difficulty, he said, "Thanks for your help. I really appreciate it." He called to the CO at the door.

"Don't forget our agreement, Jasper," his father said as the COs came in. "Don't you dare forget."

"I won't," Jazz promised. As he made for the door, the COs unshackled Billy from the table and hoisted him to his feet by his elbows.

"Jasper."

Jazz was out the door, but he turned to look back at his

319

father—manacled, surrounded by trained, armed men. And still utterly in charge.

"Yeah?"

"The way you came in here... Wearing your armor, the coldest, baddest son of a bitch on the planet. The way you agreed with me about things. Slinging that line of bull-puckey about the kid gloves and all that. You were manipulating me. And did a damn fine job of it, too."

The words and the sincerity behind them slid down Jazz's spine like an icicle threading his vertebrae. "I'm not you."

"You're better," Billy said.

"I'm not evil." Saying that to anyone else, under any other circumstances, would have felt hyperbolic. Here and now and to Billy, it felt like not enough.

Billy's lips curled in a smirk. "Want to know the difference between good and evil, Jasper?" Without waiting for an answer, Billy raised his right hand—LOVE—and snapped his fingers.

"That's it, kid. That's the difference. You won't even know you've crossed the line until it's way back in your rearview mirror."

"That's enough, Billy," one of the COs growled, and they dragged him through the other door. If Jazz expected his father to shout out one last parting shot, he was disappointed: Billy Dent vanished—silent but for the rattle and clank of his chains—into the depths of Wammaket State Penitentiary.

Deputy Hanson said nothing the whole way home, once again letting his lead foot and the siren do all the speaking for him. The constant wail and blare sledgehammered their way into Jazz's skull and bred a nice little headache there. He tried to ignore it, focusing instead on making himself heard over the shriek as he talked to G. William on Howie's phone.

"...and he thinks she won't be what we think of as a traditional secretary," he went on, "maybe not even in a position that goes by the title of secretary, but something that could be *construed* as, you know, secretarial."

G. William's relief was palpable, even over the phone. "You just gave us a whole hell of a lot more work," he told Jazz, "but it's the kind of work I can get behind."

He shut his eyes and tried to exorcise the ghost of Billy's presence, but the rhythm of the siren somehow merged with Billy's voice and kept howling at him over and over:

I think you don't really care about these people.

You won't even know you've crossed the line until it's way back in your rearview mirror.

I don't need a protégé. Already got one.

Sure you are. You just ain't killed no one yet.

Jazz swallowed hard. Maybe that meant he hadn't killed his own mother.

Or maybe Billy was just playing with him. He remembered what he'd told Connie: *You show any weakness to a serial killer and they live inside you after that.*

The sky had gone the hard blue of a new bruise by the time Hanson got him back to the police station and sneaked him in through a rear entrance. Jazz checked in with G. William, who was too busy to talk, coordinating a whole new effort to find the Impressionist's next victim. So he slipped out through the funeral home to avoid the press and drove home in the Jeep.

A great sense of relief washed over him as he drove. He'd done it. He'd bearded the lion—the dragon—in his den and come away not only alive, but with valuable treasure: the information that would stop the Impressionist. Jazz felt newly alive. Like a whole new human being, with a whole new life ahead of him.

He noticed something in the center console of the Jeep and reached for it at a red light. It was Jeff Fulton's business card. Jazz thought of Fulton's impassioned speech at Ginny's service and sighed. Would it really hurt anyone to spend five minutes with the guy? Jazz didn't want to establish a precedent for talking to the grieving families of his father's victims, but there was no reason he couldn't show a little kindness to the man. He would call Fulton in the morning. It was something no serial killer would ever do, something no sociopath would ever imagine doing. Just thinking of it made Jazz feel good.

At home, he was surprised to find the crowds of reporters gone. A lone cop still sat in a cruiser in the driveway, and Jazz approached to ask what had happened to the mob.

"Tanner sent over a bunch of guys a couple of hours ago. Told everyone you and your gramma were in protective custody because there'd been some threats against you."

"Have there been?"

"I don't know." The cop was clearly uncomfortable with the whole conversation. "Anyway, everyone cleared out. Welcome home."

Jazz went inside and locked up. He checked on Gramma, who was still off in sleepland, maybe dreaming that she was sane. His stomach lurched and rumbled, and he realized he hadn't eaten anything all day.

Down in the kitchen, all he could find to eat were some ice cream that had sprouted a fuzz of crystals, and two sad-looking drumsticks from the bucket of chicken Melissa had brought for Gramma days ago. He settled in at the table with the drumsticks and ate them cold, then scraped the top off the ice cream and ate the stuff underneath, which was stale, but edible.

As he ate, he stared through the kitchen door into Gramma's backyard. During spring and summer, it was a night-mare of weeds, thistles, and overgrown grass that went on for two acres. But now, in autumn, it was just dead and flat all the way out to the toolshed.

Except for the birdbath.

There was nothing special about the birdbath. Cracked con-crete base. A sculpted fish at the center, spewing water from its mouth into the basin. In a couple of weeks, it would be too cold for the birdbath and Jazz would disconnect it from the water line.

But right now, it sat there, happily gurgling away. Birdless.

So, yeah, Billy had said, *I'll help you, Jasper. But you're go-ing to help me, too.*

Then what? Jazz remembered throwing up his hands in frus-tration. *What do you want?*

He got up from the table, dumped the remaining ice cream in the trash, and walked out to the birdbath.

You know that old birdbath my momma's got in her back-yard?

Yeah. Yeah, I know it. What are you—

Hush and listen, Jasper. I listened to you, now you listen to me. That damned thing... She's had it since I was a kid. And I've been tellin' her for forty years: She ain't gettin' birds in it 'cause she's got it placed wrong.

What? What does this have to do with—

I said hush and listen, Jasper! For the first time, Billy had seemed agitated. Not in control.

Over a birdbath.

She's got it oriented to a western exposure. See? It's not gettin' the morning light, and that's what them birds want. It needs to be moved to the opposite edge of the lawn. I tried gettin' her to move it, but she never listens. And then she bitches and complains that she don't got no birds to watch during the day.

So... Jazz had thought carefully. *So, in exchange for your help, you—what? Want me to convince Gramma to move the—*

No. I don't want you to convince her of anything. Just move the damn thing. Go when she's asleep and just move it. You know, where that big ol' sycamore sits. Once she sees all her birdie friends, she won't care what you've done. And if she complains or asks, just tell her it's always been there. She's already batty like a belfry; she won't remember.

And this, Jazz had said with incredulity, *is the price of your help?*

Billy had sighed and placed LOVE over FEAR. *Indulge your*

old man, Jasper. You're the only one who can take care of my momma while I'm locked up in here.

And so Jazz had agreed, and now he stared down at the birdbath.

The whole thing was ridiculous. It was insane.

So is Dear Old Dad.

Still, Billy was right. Gramma *did* always complain about the lack of birds for her to watch. And moving the birdbath probably *would* help.

He disconnected the water line and tilted the birdbath. It was lighter than he'd expected—it looked like the whole thing was made of concrete, but only the base was.

It couldn't be as simple as moving it, he thought. Billy must have buried something under it.

But when he tilted the birdbath, all he saw underneath was a ring of dead, light brown grass that had been there forever.

Well . . . Why not?

He grunted and rolled the thing on the edge of its base. It wasn't too heavy for him, but it was unwieldy, so it took him a while to wrestle it into its new position. From here the hose wouldn't reach, so he had to go inside and find a longer hose. He reconnected everything and the birdbath started burbling again.

"I guess we'll see what we see in the morning," he said to it.

Inside, he caught the tail end of a chime of some sort coming from Howie's cell phone, which was sitting on the kitchen table.

He tapped and poked at the screen until he found a text message from the sheriff:

think we found her. thx 4 yr help.—gwt

Jazz grinned. Now that the cops had the next victim in their sights, they could sit on her and wait for the killer to show up. Not bad for a day's work. Not bad at all.

He went upstairs, tired beyond all belief. A note stuck to his computer reminded him that he needed to work on his rebuttal to Melissa Hoover's recommendation, but his sleep-deprived brain couldn't even entertain the idea. *Tomorrow*, he promised himself. *Tomorrow I'll write it. Take care of everything. Tomorrow.*

Even though it was still early, he stripped down to his boxers and crawled into bed.

For the first time since Fiona Goodling had been found in Harrison's field, he drifted into an untroubled, un-dreaming sleep.

CHAPTER 32

The Impressionist cursed under his breath and took a quick step back, positioning himself behind a tree. It was dark out and a street lamp was busted, so he had plenty of shadows.

He also had plenty of cops.

Cops!

Brenda Quimby. Mid-thirties. Blond. Kept the minutes for her husband's monthly Masons meetings. Which, as far as the Impressionist was concerned, made her a secretary, even though her actual job was data analyst for a computer help desk.

It had taken him a while to find her, and he'd been keeping tabs on her for days. Tonight was the night he planned to abduct her and create his next artistic masterpiece, his final homage to Billy Dent's career as the Artist before moving on to the next phase in his personal evolution.

But her apartment was surrounded by cops.

Oh, they thought they were clever, these particular cops. Thought they were hiding in plain sight, thought their undercover disguises would fool him.

The Impressionist was no idiot. He could see right through their deception.

How had they known? How had they figured it out? How had they beaten him to the punch?

The answer came to him in a flash of insight: the Dent kid. It *had* to be the Dent kid. There was no other possible answer. No other way. The Impressionist had underestimated young Dent, the only mistake he'd made so far in Lobo's Nod.

Well, it would also be the last mistake.

The Impressionist strode calmly up the driveway toward the Dent house. The sun was down, the night black and starless. A police car was parked there, and the man inside had already noticed him coming. The Impressionist waved cheerfully. *See? Nothing to worry about here. Why, if I were a serial killer, I would hardly call attention to myself with a wave, would I?*

He came up alongside the car and crouched down to look at the cop through the open window. "Is there something wrong, Officer?" he asked, feigning worry as he pulled a silenced pistol from his pocket and shot the cop right through the temple. The pistol made a small coughing sound; the cop made a strangled hiccupping sound. They sounded nice together.

Well, that was easy.

CHAPTER 33

Jazz blinked awake at the sound of the doorbell. He checked the clock on his nightstand. It was just past nine. He'd only been asleep a half hour.

The bell rang again.

"Hang on!" Jazz shouted, rolling out of bed. He pawed around in the dark, found his jeans and T-shirt by touch, and dressed on his way to the stairs. Before going down, he poked his head into Gramma's room. Still asleep. Good. Who was bothering him, anyway? Couldn't be a reporter—there was still a cop positioned in the driveway, after all.

Maybe it was G. William, come to deliver some good news in person.

He raced down the stairs and threw open the front door.

Oh.

"Hi," he said, slightly annoyed, but also—in an odd way— grateful. "I was just thinking about you."

"Really? Can I come in?"

"Sure."

Jazz stepped aside and ushered Jeff Fulton into the house.

CHAPTER 34

The Impressionist took in the foyer. He'd been here before, but he'd been in a hurry. Now he could truly take it in. The house where Billy Dent had grown up. Somehow, he'd expected more. He wrinkled his nose.

"I guess this isn't ideal," the boy was saying, "but I'm glad you came over. I was going to call you in the morning."

"My business kept me here a little longer than I thought," the Impressionist said. "But I'll be leaving soon." He wanted to grin—wanted quite badly to grin—but instead forced himself to maintain Jeff Fulton's air of agony and depression.

"Can I get you some coffee? Or something else?"

"Coffee would be great," the Impressionist said. Billy Dent's child was about to serve him coffee! What an amazing day.

He followed the boy into the kitchen—peeling paint on the cabinets, old appliances in harvest gold and avocado green. Leftover remnants from Billy Dent's childhood. Billy Dent might have run to that refrigerator for an afternoon snack. He might have stored the severed head of a dead cat in the freezer.

The boy turned away from the Impressionist, reaching into one of the shadowy cabinets for a coffee mug.

And the Impressionist reached into his jacket pocket.

Jazz sensed more than felt Jeff Fulton come up behind him, stepping closer than usual propriety or politeness would dictate. For a single moment, he did not question their proximity.

That single moment was one moment too long.

Before he could turn, before he could move at all, the cool, unmistakable ring of a pistol muzzle pressed into the back of his neck.

"What—" he began, breaking off the instant he felt something sharp and thin press against the side of his neck and then break the skin.

"Don't worry," Fulton said in a tone of voice that Jazz thought was intended to be comforting. It wasn't.

Fulton probably had more to say, but Jazz never heard it.

CHAPTER 35

Jazz's head throbbed, and there was a harsh rushing in his ears. He thought he heard something else, something above and beyond the rushing, but he couldn't be sure.

dond whirrrr e

He tried to focus.

nahhhhhhd rain clee nar

His eyelids were weighed down with lead blocks, or so it felt. He didn't even try to open them. He focused on the words (if they were words at all) in and among the vicious thrum filling his ears:

rain clee narrrr

He was bound, he realized. His limbs, numb until this moment, had come back online and reported that he was shackled. And—oh, what a pleasant surprise—gagged.

He had no choice. He had to open his eyes.

unnerstan meee?

He pried open his eyes. It took forever. Or at least much longer than it should have. Spots danced before him, sparkles flashing in the air, and he half expected to see Billy standing there, with Rusty's leash in his hand.

A figure sat before him, elbows on knees, leaning forward. The lips moved in slow motion, and Jazz tried to match the shapes they made to what his ears were picking up a second later.

Drugged. I've been—

"—understand me?" Jeff Fulton said. "I said, 'Don't worry. It wasn't drain cleaner.' Just a mild sedative."

Jazz blinked rapidly, clearing his vision. The room snapped into shape: He was in his own bedroom. Handcuffed to a chair at the wrists. His ankles were also cuffed. He was, he realized, manacled just as Billy had been earlier in the day. Fulton was sitting on the edge of the desk.

"Awake now, eh?" Fulton said. "Good. Good." He stood up and walked over to Jazz. "I'm gonna take off your gag now. If you feel like yelling or screaming, go right ahead and do it. Won't bother me at all. No one's around to hear you. Closest house is . . . Well, I guess you know where that is, right? And the cop outside is, well, not terribly attentive right now."

He slipped the gag off. Jazz drew in a huge breath. He wanted to scream at the top of his lungs, but he knew that Fulton had told the truth.

So instead of screaming, he said, "What do you want?"

Fulton's eyes glittered. He spoke without rancor. "What do I want? Oh, I want a great many things, Jasper Francis Dent. For one thing, I want that pretty little girlfriend of yours dead. I want her gutted and her innards in a heap on the floor in front of you."

Jazz's jaw tightened. "Is that what this is about? Vengeance for your daughter? Kill Connie, kill me, to make Billy pay? That won't bring your daughter back."

Fulton looked surprised. "My daughter? What are...? Oh." He lit up. "Oh, oh!" He laughed. "Oh, this is delicious! You still think I'm Fulton!" He produced a handkerchief from his pocket and wiped at his face, smearing some theatrical makeup, which made him look a little younger, a little less tired. Then he pawed around in his eyes and removed a pair of contact lenses. He fixed Jazz with a new gaze, this one bright blue.

Jazz blinked rapidly a few more times, chasing away the last of the drug-induced blurriness. He knew those eyes. He'd glimpsed them oh-so-briefly as the Impressionist jumped onto Ginny's sofa, heading out the window.

The Impressionist laughed again, raucously. "You know something, Jasper? I wasn't a hundred percent sure it was even gonna work. Even with the contacts. I thought for sure you'd see right through me. You, of all people. But then, after that first time I confronted you, I knew I had you. Because you could barely look at me. I could have had THE IMPRESSIONIST tattooed on my forehead and you wouldn't have noticed.

"My God," he went on. "I gave you every chance. I flew so close to the sun for you. When I got up to speak at that woman's memorial..." He drew in a deep, satisfied breath. "When I spoke at her memorial, Jasper—God, I thought I was going to explode right there. I thought I would just combust from the sheer joy of it all. All of them looking at me. None of them knowing. It was glorious. *Glorious.*"

Jazz's guts clenched, and for a perilous moment he thought he would soil himself, like a baby. The Impressionist had been under his nose the whole time. Playing with him. Manipulating him. Jazz's failure was complete—he could have stopped the killer after Fiona Goodling died if only he'd done something as simple as looking for a picture of Jeff Fulton online.

The Impressionist returned to his chair, now sitting more confidently, as if by removing the elements of his disguise he'd also cleaned away the last dregs of Jeff Fulton's sad, downtrodden personality. "Now do you get it?" he asked. "Now do you understand?"

"Yeah," Jazz said, thinking quickly. He was physically restrained, so all he had on his side was psychology. He knew how sociopaths thought. Especially this one. This one, who had mimicked his own father. "You're trying to take me off the board. You think Billy doesn't need another protégé because he has me. But if you get rid of me, you can have that spot."

The Impressionist didn't honor that with a laugh. He just snorted. "You don't get it at all. You have no idea *what* this is about. You can't begin to imagine. You're Billy Dent's son, the heir apparent, and you haven't killed a single person yet! Not even an animal!"

He stood up and advanced on Jazz, coming around behind him. Jazz tensed, remembering the pistol at his neck, the needle. But the Impressionist simply leaned over, his lips close to Jazz's ear, and whispered, "You've forsaken your birthright. I've decided to make sure you accept it, Jasper Francis Dent. I'm here to help you learn the ways of blood and bone."

Jazz closed his eyes. No. He would not.

"You know you want to," the Impressionist said, his voice soft and low. "You've always wanted to."

—*do it*—

"You've always wanted to be like Daddy, deep down inside."

—*good boy, good boy*—

"Stop it," Jazz said in a voice so quiet it was almost silent. "Stop."

"Too much?" the Impressionist asked. He came around Jazz's left side and sat on the edge of the desk again. "Too much for you? I know. It's tough, isn't it? At first, when you first realize what you are...It isn't easy."

"And what are you?" Jazz asked. He realized that he had to keep the Impressionist talking. As long as he kept him talking, there was always the chance that the man would reveal something—some weakness or quirk—that Jazz could exploit.

The Impressionist grinned. "What am I? I think you mean 'What are *we*?' You and I, we're the same. We could have been brothers, Jasper. I'll tell you what we're not: We're not sheep. We're not mere humans. We're not *prospects*. Oh, no. And we are not lords or kings or emperors. We're *gods*, Jasper." He leaned in toward Jazz again, his face lit with rapture. "You are the child of divinity. I came here to honor your father in my own way, you know. And I was never supposed to talk to you or see you, but I couldn't resist. Who could resist meeting the child of Billy Dent?" He stroked Jazz's cheek like a small child touching the softness of a rabbit for the first time. "Who could resist?" He leapt up from the desk, suddenly outraged and offended. "Imagine my disappointment in you. Imagine it!" he roared. "Pretending to be one of them! Acting—and yes, I know it's an act—like any other child, forsaking your rightful place as king of the murderers. Well, all of that will change. I could not be here and watch you stumble through your life like a new toddler. Oh, no. I will birth you into the world you richly deserve."

He turned to Jazz's desk, where the contents of Jazz's pockets lay: wallet, keys, Howie's cell phone.

"We won't need these things," the Impressionist said, sweeping them all to the floor with his arm. "This, however..."

And he placed on the table the largest of the kitchen knives from the block on Gramma's counter.

He grinned wickedly. "This, we will definitely need."

Jazz swallowed. "You can't kill me," he said. He wanted to blurt it out, to scream it, to cry, but he knew that human weakness was like an aphrodisiac to a sociopath such as the Impressionist. "If you try, you'll fail. I'm Billy Dent's son. I can't be killed." A bluff. An insane bluff that wouldn't work on anyone with even a shred of intact brainpower, but the Impressionist was a madman who believed he was a god. So...

The Impressionist blinked and in a moment his wicked expression fell into abject innocence, an innocence so real that for a moment Jazz felt guilty for accusing the man at all.

"Kill you? Why on earth...Is that what you think? That I want to kill you? No! Of course not! I would *never*..." He dropped to his knees in front of Jazz and gazed earnestly into his eyes. "I want to *improve* you. I want you to stride this earth like the murder god you're meant to be, like the creature your father wanted to create. I'm not going to kill you. I'm going to help you.

"I'm going to help you fulfill your first kill."

And with that, the Impressionist turned the chair so that Jazz could see his bed.

Lying on it was his grandmother.

She was still alive—Jazz could hear the slight susurration of her breathing. The tranq he'd given her would have kept her out for hours, and who knew if the Impressionist had given her a booster shot from his own stash?

"I killed my father when I was fifteen," the Impressionist said. "Trust me when I say, Jasper, that you have no idea how liberating it is to cut—literally—your ties to your past. It's a glorious thing."

"I won't do it," Jazz said.

"Of course you will. If Billy Dent were here, he would *want* you to do it. He would gladly let you kill *him*, knowing that it would ignite your path to glory."

Jazz thought of Billy in prison, gesturing to the universe and saying, *And destroy all of this?* when asked why he hadn't committed suicide. "You don't know anything about my father," he said, and then some strange combination of panic and fear and guilt and—he couldn't believe it—filial honor took him over, and he blurted out, "You don't know anything about him. You're some psychopathic *fanboy* who's such a loser that he has to pretend to be my father in order to give meaning to his life. You're nothing. You're not a god. You're nothing. You couldn't even get it up to rape Irene Heller."

He scored. The Impressionist's left eyelid twitched, though the rest of his face remained serene even as he backhanded Jazz across the face with a blow so powerful that Jazz wouldn't have been surprised if he'd lost a molar.

"I'm not afraid of you," the Impressionist said, leaning in close. "I could worship you, but I will never fear you. Do you understand?" He held up the knife between them. Jazz caught his reflection in the blade and was astonished to see that he did not look in the least bit afraid.

"Then I'm one up on you," Jazz said, his head spinning from the force of the blow and the taste of his own blood. "Because I'm also not afraid of you, and I'll *never* worship you."

With a strangled cry, the Impressionist grabbed Jazz's collar with his free hand, jerking him forward. But the shirt was thin and old—it split down the middle from the force of the tug. The Impressionist laughed and twisted his arm, ripping the shirt apart, so that it hung in three big folds down around Jazz's waist.

"Get your kicks like this?" Jazz taunted. "Is that why you couldn't rape Irene Heller?"

But the Impressionist wasn't paying attention. He'd caught notice of something and, after craning his neck to look behind Jazz, moved around the chair so that he had a view of Jazz's back.

"Yosemite Sam?" he said in a perplexed voice. "Don't you think it's time to grow up?"

It could have been worse. Howie wanted SpongeBob

SquarePants, but I talked him into something at least a little bit tough.

"This has all been fun." The Impressionist came back around to face Jazz. "But we have much to do before the night is over. And we need to start now."

The Impressionist came at Jazz, and Jazz tensed, ready for the knife blade. But all the man did was unlock Jazz's ankles from the chair, then quickly cuff them together. He did the same with his hands, first unshackling the right wrist from the chair, then recuffing it to the left before unshackling that one.

Jazz was free to stand. To hobble. Could he escape?

Impossible. He couldn't move more than six inches at a time. His hands were practically glued together.

The Impressionist hauled him out of the chair and half marched, half dragged him over to Gramma. Jazz's head spun. Still dizzy from the drugs.

Jazz felt the knife forced into his hands—

—hold it tight—

—and then his hands pressed around the grip. The Impressionist's strength was impressive. With one hand, he was keeping Jazz's grip tight on the knife handle, and preventing Jazz from jerking the knife into the Impressionist.

A knife.

Another knife.

So familiar.

And Jazz knew in that moment: It wasn't just a dream.

It was a memory.

He'd held a knife before. Like this.

Exactly like this. Hands on his own. Guiding him.

But it was his own hands on the handle. Just like before.

The Impressionist maneuvered Jazz with his other hand on his back, forcing him closer to Gramma, who snored and twitched, unaware. "This is your first one," the Impressionist said, "so I want it to be easy on you. She's not waking up anytime soon. Hell"—he chuckled—"she's not waking up, period. So. Here we go."

He positioned Jazz so that he was leaning toward Gramma, the point of the knife dimpling her dress between and slightly under her deflated breasts. "All you need to do," the Impressionist whispered, "is put your weight into it. The knife will slip right under the sternum and slide into her heart. She's old. Weak. Frail. It'll be quick. She won't even really feel it, if that's what you're worried about. After this, you'll feel so much better. Then we can go get your girlfriend."

"No," Jazz whispered. There was still a very dark, very disturbed, and very real part of him that wanted his grandmother dead, but he would be damned if he would let this man force him to do it. He would be damned if he would allow it to happen like this. "I won't."

"You will," the Impressionist whispered, his voice more seductive than any siren. "You want to. You will." His breath, warm and gentle, in Jazz's ear. His words soft. "You will. And if you don't..."

And if I don't...

If he didn't, she would be dead soon, anyway. She was an old woman. In poor health. With a brain that hardly worked. And her only help was a grandson who frequently drugged her and left her unattended.

Would it really hurt anyone if he did it? If he removed her from the world? Who would miss her? No one, that's who.

He was about to be taken from her, anyway, thanks to Melissa Hoover and Social Services. And Gramma would prefer death to an old-age home.

Right?

—*like chicken, like cutting into chicken, that's all it is, like chicken*—

She would die soon, anyway, he reminded himself. And once he killed her, the Impressionist would unlock the cuffs, would trust him, and Jazz could . . .

He could . . .

He *would* take advantage of that trust. Keep the knife. Let the Impressionist think he'd won. And then . . .

Kill the Impressionist.

Yes. Jazz's heartbeat accelerated, as though someone had stomped on the gas pedal connected to his heart. Yes, that would work. He could see it now. Gramma wouldn't even be finished bleeding out when he would turn on the Impressionist, who wouldn't see it coming, and do exactly as Billy had taught him—one quick thrust into the heart. A twist to the left. Or, if the angles were wrong, slash across the carotid where it pulsed fat and juicy on the side of the neck, so tempting, so easy, *Like God wants us to cut it*, Billy used to say. That—

No. He blinked fiercely until he no longer saw a useless old woman in front of him, but rather his grandmother. What had happened to him? No. No!

Had he really just been contemplating—anticipating, joy-fully!—committing two murders in a matter of minutes?

"I won't." Jazz was more trying to convince himself than deny the Impressionist.

"If you don't, Jazz, then I will." The words hard now, the once-gentle breath coming fast and harsh. "I'll let her wake up, and I'll start with the eyes. For her, I'll be the Artist *and* Green Jack *and* Gentle Killer *and* Hand-in-Glove all rolled into one, and we'll see how long Granny can last when I start taking pieces and parts away, won't we?"

Just then Jazz saw something. Something the Impressionist couldn't see because he was staring at Jazz.

Shadows.

Shadows moving in the light spilling under the door from the hallway.

Someone was out there.

"Help!" Jazz cried before he could change his mind. "Help me!"

The Impressionist snickered. "I told you before: No one can—"

He broke off as someone from the hallway thumped against the door.

"What the hell?" He looked over at the door, his hands still tight on Jazz, leaving him no room to maneuver.

Then a familiar voice said "Try again!" in a high note of panic, and Jazz found that he could twist just enough. The knife point dragged and caught, slicing Gramma's dress open, but then it came free and up as Jazz pivoted. He missed the Impressionist with the knife but managed to land a double-handed blow against the man's jaw, which rocked him back on his heels and made him take a step away.

343

Jazz hopped backward, looking for a better angle to slash with the knife, but he tripped over his own feet and fell, the knife clattering from his hands. It bounced once and landed a couple of feet away. He lunged for it, corkscrewing his body, straining against his bonds to reach out with both hands just as the Impressionist pounced on him and pinned him to the carpet.

"Don't even—" the Impressionist started, and then broke off with a howl of pain as Jazz craned his neck and bit deep into the man's wrist. His teeth scraped against bone and the taste of blood filled his mouth.

The door thumped again and then exploded open. Out of the corner of his eye, Jazz saw Connie and Howie spill into the room. Howie, unbelievably, wielded a shotgun, looking like the world's most improbable action hero.

Still entangled with Jazz, the Impressionist ripped his arm out of Jazz's mouth. Blood spurted. The Impressionist twisted and reached for the knife.

Connie kicked it away.

And then suddenly Howie stood over them, the shotgun leveled without so much as a tremble at the Impressionist's head.

"Watch it, man," Howie snarled. "If you're not careful, I will bleed *all over you*."

Jazz couldn't help it; he started laughing.

Jazz rubbed feeling back into his wrists and ankles. Connie was wrapping a hand towel from the bathroom around the Impressionist's wound. The Impressionist—shackled to the same chair he'd bound Jazz to, and with the same cuffs he'd used on Jazz—stared straight ahead, impassively. Howie stood guard with the shotgun.

"He's really bleeding," Connie said. "We should call nine-one-one again and tell them we need an ambulance, too."

"Let him bleed," Howie said in a stone-cold tone Jazz had never heard from him before.

"Watch him," Jazz said, heading for the bedroom door. "I want a couple of minutes with him before the cops get here."

Jazz disappeared down the hall into the bathroom and slurped water from the sink, then spit it out. No matter what he did, he could still taste the Impressionist's flesh and blood on his tongue. He wondered how long it would take to lose that taste. He felt infected.

He went back to the bedroom. Howie and Connie still stood guard over the Impressionist, who simply stared straight ahead.

"How did you guys get here, anyway?"

Connie stepped back from the Impressionist and shrugged, as though she knew her makeshift bandage wasn't the best, but didn't really care. "Howie couldn't sleep at home. Called and made me come get him. Or else he says he would have walked the whole way."

"We got here and the cop was—" Howie broke off, swallowing hard.

"Not doing his job very well," the Impressionist said.

Howie surprised Jazz with a savage swing of the shotgun. It was poorly aimed—he missed the killer's face and clipped his shoulder instead—but it was a solid hit, and the Impressionist nearly toppled over in the chair.

"Shut up!" Howie screamed. "Shut up! You killed him! You almost killed me!"

"I'll cut deeper next time, bleeder."

Jazz snatched away the shotgun before Howie could brain the Impressionist into a coma. He needed the man alive. For now.

Howie retreated to the other side of the room, breathing hard.

"We tried G. William, but couldn't get him. So we called nine-one-one," Connie said, picking up from where Howie had left off, "and they promised to hurry, but dispatch is all screwed up and everyone's all crazy."

"Because of the task force," Howie continued. "And because everyone's scrambled to snap up this guy"—he jerked his head at the Impressionist—"at the next victim's house."

"Right. So we came inside...."

"Found the shotgun..."

"Right near the grandfather clock," Connie said, nodding.

Jazz grinned. The Impressionist didn't know that he'd been held at bay with a harmless shotgun.

"And when we realized you were in here," Howie said, calmer now, "we kicked in the door."

"What do you mean, 'we'?" Connie said.

"I meant to say, *Connie* kicked it down. I supervised."

The Impressionist blinked. "I just wanted to make you strong," he said. "That's what it's all about. Making you strong. Making you worthy of your name."

He shifted in the chair and something in the way he moved made Jazz think back to moments earlier, when the two of them had struggled on the floor. Something had brushed against him, he was sure. He'd been too busy fighting for his life to think about it, but now...

"What did you do with the fingers?" he asked the Impressionist. "What was that about?"

"That's not for you to know!" the Impressionist shouted, as though terrified. "You can't know! You're not ready."

The Impressionist wore a loose-fitting golf shirt—perfect camouflage for his Jeff Fulton disguise. No one would give it a second thought. But now Jazz thought of something. Wondered something.

Ignoring Howie and Connie, who asked what he was doing, Jazz approached the Impressionist.

Something told Jazz not to lift the shirt, but he ignored that, too.

The Impressionist flinched and twisted, but couldn't stop Jazz from tugging up on the shirttail.

Oh. Wait. Oh, God...

Nice ink.

The ring of Howie's cell phone sounded distant and alien.

"Hello?" Howie said, as Jazz stared at the Impressionist's exposed midsection.

"What the—" said Connie.

It was a belt. A belt worn under the shirt and against the skin—a thick leather cord from which dangled severed fingers, trophies from the Impressionist's victims. And on each finger...

347

Oh, God!

"Nice ink," Jazz said.

A shrug. "Brand-new. Glad you like 'em."

"Hey, Jazz," Howie said. "It's the sheriff. He says it's important."

Jazz took the phone, unable to tear his eyes away from the belt of fingers encircling the Impressionist's waist. Each finger was inscribed with a rough tattoo on the knuckle so that they spelled words as they looped around him. Fifteen fingers in total, so the words repeated.

"Jazz?" G. William said. "Jazz, that you?"

LOVE, the tattoos said. FEAR, they said.

"Oh, God," Jazz whispered.

"Jazz, buddy, I don't know quite how to tell you this," G. William went on, his voice papery and thin. "But your daddy, he...Your daddy broke outta prison a couple hours ago."

"I know," Jazz said.

CHAPTER 36

Free for the first time in four years, Billy Dent needed only an hour to find and kill his first victim. The sheriff sent two cars to the Dent house—one to secure the Impressionist and tend to Gramma, the other to pick up Jazz, Connie, and Howie. The second car had them on the scene in under twenty minutes.

Melissa Hoover lay dead on the coffee table in her own living room, barely recognizable as herself. Or as a female human being at all.

Jazz took one look at the crime scene and spun around, pushing Howie and Connie out the door.

"Jazz!"

"You can't see this," he said. "You'll have nightmares for the rest of your lives."

Billy's appetites had gone unsated after his arrest and during his years in prison; Melissa Hoover had been the banquet he'd ravaged on first sight. There were seasoned cops at the crime scene—federal agents and locals handpicked by G. William for this kind of work—and every last one of them looked more than ill. They looked haunted. Jazz imagined they were watching him with something like contempt as he mingled among them, asking themselves how long they could possibly endure near a creature like Jazz in the midst of Billy's handiwork. At least, he hoped he was imagining it.

Deputy Erickson was in the room, standing off to one side, as usual. But for the first time, Jazz really *saw* the man. What he'd thought was belligerence and meanness was actually deep pain at the senseless murders he'd been forced to see one after the other after the other. He'd just transferred to what was supposed to be a quiet little town, only to find a bloodbath. Jazz felt like he owed Erickson an apology for everything he'd thought, every accusation he'd harbored.

Maybe later. Right now, there were more important things to do.

Melissa had been a royal pain in the ass, but she didn't deserve what Billy had done to her. And that, Jazz knew, was precisely Billy's point. Her body was devastated. Her surroundings had become a cathedral of pain and degradation. Jazz knew she had begged and pleaded for her life. Billy hadn't cared.

"Still getting all the stories straight," G. William said as Jazz picked his way through the crime scene, careful not to disturb anything or bother the cops. "Billy cut his own neck open to get into the infirmary. Knew just how to make it look bad, but it wasn't, of course. Looks like some protestors were involved as a diversion. Three people killed in a firefight while Billy escaped, we think with someone else. Not really sure yet. We figure someone on the outside was keeping in touch with him.

Communicating with him, feeding him information through some kind of code in his fan mail. What we can't figure out is how he communicated back. He never wrote to anyone, never made phone calls."

Jazz thought of the favor he'd done for Billy. Moving the birdbath. A signal?

A few hours after he did it, Billy was free. It couldn't be a coincidence. Billy must have had his escape plan set up long in advance.

And then Jazz pulled the trigger.

"When? When did it happen?" Jazz asked.

"He escaped at around two this morning."

Jazz checked his watch. It was past five. He'd been drugged and with the Impressionist for hours.

"Then it wasn't the Impressionist. He was with me the whole time."

"You sure this guy was working with Billy? Not just inspired by him?"

"He had the prison tats on the fingers, G. William." Jazz shivered. "Billy just got them yesterday. It had to be coordinated. Some kind of communication. Or..." A new thought occurred to him. A new link. He didn't want to think it; he pushed it away, deep into his brain. But it wouldn't go into the darkness. It flashed at him.

G. William had some more details on Billy's escape, but Jazz couldn't listen to them just then. The details didn't really matter, anyway. What mattered was the flashing thought, the one that wouldn't be ignored: Billy must have set all of this up before he ever went to prison. He had admirers out there, after all. Crazies all over the country who worshipped him. Any combination of them could be out there on his behalf.

He thought of the protestors outside Wammaket. Thought of a nationwide movement. How many true believers were there? How many people would help his father?

"The penitentiary logged every piece of mail he got," G. William said, "but there's a lot of it. U.S. Marshals are helping us, but it'll take a long time."

Jazz nodded, gnawing on his bottom lip. One of the cops had given him a blue Windbreaker with POLICE stenciled on the back to cover up his naked torso, and he pulled it tighter around himself as he watched the crime-scene techs scurry about the house.

Billy had left all kinds of evidence: hair, fiber, fingerprints. Some saliva, of course. Probably semen, once the rape kit was done.

Not that it mattered.

"He signed this," Jazz said. "Literally."

G. William nodded. "Yeah. Pretty much. He *knows* we know it's him. And it doesn't matter. He doesn't care. He's not trying to hide."

Of all the personas his father had taken on—the Artist, Green Jack, Hand-in-Glove, Gentle Killer—this one, this pure Billy, frightened Jazz the most.

"He trashed her computer, wrecked her files."

You're the only one who can take care of my momma while I'm locked up in here, Billy had said. And now he had seen to it that the only person who could have taken Jazz away from Gramma...couldn't.

"He also left this." G. William held up a plastic evidence bag. Within was a sheet of paper filled with cramped writing. Jazz took it from the sheriff.

Up close, he could see a bloody thumbprint on it, too.

The stationery was FROM THE DESK OF MELISSA HOOVER. The word DESK was crossed out and replaced with DEATH.

The note read:

Dear Jasper,

I can't begin to tell you what a pleasure it was to see you at Wammaket. You've grown into such a strong and powerful young man. I am so proud of what you will accomplish in this life. I already know you are destined for great things. I dream of the things we'll do together. Someday.

For now, though, I have to leave you with this. Never let it be said your old man doesn't know how to repay a debt.

Love,
Dear Old Dad

And there was a postscript that made Jazz want to kill everyone in the room, himself included:

PS Maybe one of these days we'll get together and talk about what you did to your mother.

The police insisted on Gramma going to the hospital, and the doctors wanted to keep her for observation. Jazz stayed with her. He knew he needed to sleep, but he couldn't. He was responsible for Billy's escape. For the death of a corrections officer, the wounding of two more. For the horrors visited upon Melissa Hoover.

And, if Billy could be believed, maybe for his own mother's death.

G. William had asked about that bit in the letter about "repaying a debt." Jazz made a split-second decision not to tell G. William about the birdbath. He didn't know why—he just knew that he couldn't handle a lecture from G. William at the moment. So he pled ignorance, and G. William—overwhelmed by the crime scene—accepted it.

Finally, exhaustion overtook Jazz, wrestled him down. He slept fitfully in a chair near Gramma's bed.

He awoke to his grandmother shrieking at the top of her lungs, screaming that the young Latina nurse was trying to suck out her soul through the saline IV line.

So, things were back to normal.

And then Jazz woke up fully, and remembered that his father was out of prison. On the loose.

Nothing was normal. Nothing would ever be normal again.

Everyone expected Billy to go after the people who testified against him. And the jury. And the shrinks who'd examined him. Bodyguards were hired, police escorts were paid over-time, then double overtime. Across the state and across the country, anyone who had ever had anything to do with Billy Dent went on high alert.

In Lobo's Nod, Sheriff G. William Tanner insisted on police protection for Connie, Howie, and their families. The Impres-sionist had known about Connie; maybe Billy did, too. Some-how.

Jazz knew it was a waste of time. Billy might come for Connie or Howie someday, but it wouldn't be anytime soon. And he would most likely never go after his prosecutors, his jury, his witnesses, or even G. William, the one man who'd bested him. He wanted everyone to think he would, of course. Wanted them all to think he was predictable. Wanted them to waste time and resources protecting people he wouldn't touch.

In the meantime, Billy would be out there. Blending in to the world.

Making his way back into society.

Looking for his next victim.

Prospecting.

CHAPTER 37

By the time Jazz got to the sheriff's office later that day, it was nearly dinnertime. Jazz was disoriented—he'd missed a big part of the day—but determined.

He bulled his way through the remains of the Impressionist task force and into G. William's office, where he utterly demeaned himself, begging, *imploring* G. William to allow him just five minutes. "No more," he promised. "Five minutes down to the second. I swear."

Eventually G. William relented, but only after a thorough search of Jazz's body that included one meaty hand uncomfortably close to the family jewels. Jazz bore it stoically. He needed these five minutes.

G. William unlocked the door and let Jazz into the holding area. There were three cells in the Lobo's Nod Municipal Police Building, two of them empty. The Impressionist was in the third, calmly lounging on the bunk, staring at the ceiling. He looked up as Jazz entered the holding area and swung his feet to the floor.

"Five minutes," G. William said. "And don't put your hands or anything else through the bars. Either of you."

Then he left.

Jazz stared at the Impressionist. The killer stared back. Jazz became aware that he was staring not at a person, but at something pretending to be a person. It was a look he'd seen on Billy's face for years, but he had forgotten its power and intensity once it was gone, the way one can remember that a food is spicy, but cannot relive the heat of it without eating it again.

"Hello, Jasper," the Impressionist said. "Or... wait. You prefer 'Jazz,' don't you? And now you'll tell me, 'Only my friends call me Jazz.' But we're much closer than friends, you and I. I've broken all the rules for you. I cut my own strings. Became my own puppet."

What in the world was he talking about?

"You're a blank," Jazz told him. "A nothing. Clay to be imprinted, and Billy imprinted you. You're like every other sociopath living; there's nothing inside."

Nothing except, perhaps, information.

The Impressionist chuckled an empty chuckle. "You'd like to think that. I *defied* for you. All to make you better. I could have gone on killing. I could have been as successful as your father. But I deviated from my path. Because I saw promise in you. I still do." He leaned closer. "I'll tell you nothing. Nothing but this: Embrace your destiny. I did, and I have no regrets. Even though I ended up here."

Enough of the faux psychological crap. "You had a letter," Jazz said. "In your pocket. The police found it when they searched you."

He held out a photocopy of the note, which listed each victim's profile. It also said, at the very end:

UNDER NO CIRCUMSTANCES ARE YOU TO
GO NEAR THE DENT BOY.
LEAVE HIM ALONE.
YOU ARE NOT TO ENGAGE HIM.
JASPER DENT IS OFF-LIMITS.

The Impressionist shrugged.

"It's not in your handwriting, and it's not in Billy's. Someone else is out there. I know my father has his sick groupies. Tell me who was working with you. Who helped him escape? How many of you are there? How many of you sick bastards are out there doing his work?"

Nothing.

Jazz heard his father's voice, as he always did: *You won't even know you've crossed the line until it's way back in your rearview mirror.*

Maybe so.

"Do you have a way to contact my father?" Jazz asked. "No, wait, never mind. Don't answer. You'd only lie."

Still nothing. A true believer. A true freak. The Impressionist would die before he would betray Billy Dent.

"Listen to me," Jazz said, leaning against the bars, his heart skipping a thrilled beat when the Impressionist pulled back in sudden fear. "Listen closely. If you *can* contact my father, I want you to send him a message for me. I want you to tell him that I'm on to him. That I'm hunting him. Tell him that I'm using every trick he ever taught me, that I won't rest until I've run him to ground. And tell him this, too: He once said that I was already a killer, I just hadn't killed anyone yet.

"Well, tell him that once I catch him...I *will*."

CHAPTER 38

ONE WEEK LATER

"When do I get mine?" Howie whined.

"Later," Jazz told him, settling in. "Okay, you can start."

"You sure about this, man?" the tattoo artist asked.

"Yeah."

"But no one's gonna be able to read it. Unless they hold a mirror up to you."

"It's not for anyone else," Jazz said. "It's for me. To remind me."

The tattoo artist shot a look at Howie and Connie, as if he needed approval from them. Howie folded his arms over his chest and looked away. Connie just sighed and gave a resigned nod.

The artist bent to his work. Jazz hissed in a breath and held it as long as he could as the man inked him.

Later, it was done. A total of twelve letters, in two-inch-high black Gothic script, inked along the broad V of his clavicle. The letters were flipped, but when Jazz looked in the mirror, he could read them just fine:

I hunt killers

EPILOGUE

FIVE WEEKS LATER

Just before Thanksgiving—after the headlines about Billy Dent's escape and the Impressionist's arrest had faded—the community of Lobo's Nod gathered at the high school in what would someday be christened the Virginia F. Davis Memorial Performing Auditorium. They gathered for the first and last performance of *The Crucible*, directed and stage-produced by the students themselves at Jazz's suggestion, dedicated to her memory and performed in her honor.

In the very back of the auditorium, a figure in a trench coat and cap stood in a convenient intersection of shadows, watching, hands thrust deep into the coat's pockets.

Toward the play's culmination, Reverend Hale screamed to the rafters as the figure in the rear watched: "There is blood on my head! Can you not see the blood on my head!!"

And there was.

Oh, and there would be so much more....

ACKNOWLEDGMENTS

As always, a big thank-you to my agent, Kathy Anderson, for dealing with the stuff I can't (or won't) wrap my brain around.

Thanks to the gang at Little, Brown for welcoming this sordid, bloody tale and making it fun, especially Alvina Ling, Megan Tingley, Jennifer Hunt, Connie Hsu, Andrew Smith, Victoria Stapleton, Alison Impey, and JoAnna Kremer. And a special shout-out to Bethany Strout, Amy Habayeb, and Allison Moore.

My early readers deserve extra-special thanks: Eric Lyga, Mary Kole, Lisa McMann, and the mighty, mighty Libba Bray.

Last but not least, thanks to Dr. Deborah Mogelof, who answered my questions about emergency room medicine and hemophilia. Please do not hold her responsible for any literary license I may have invoked.

An Interview with Barry Lyga

with Questions from Printz Award–Winning Author Libba Bray

Libba Bray: So, Barry, who would you say are some of your writing influences? And don't say me, because that gets tired.

Barry Lyga: Oh man.

L.B.: Think. Reach deep.

B.L.: Honestly, this is strange because he's not a novelist, but Bruce Springsteen was a huge influence on me when I was a kid. I can't say Bruce Springsteen made me *want* to write, because I wanted to write long before I discovered him, but he made me want to be a *good* writer. I think listening to his music and seeing how different it was from the other music that I was listening to at the time made me realize there are levels of quality. You can do this well, or you can do it not so well. And he tells stories in his music. It's not just "Oh, girl, I love you. Why don't you love me?" He tells these epic stories in his music.

L.B.: And then somebody gets in a car.

B.L.: And then somebody gets in a car and drives to a river. There's always a river. But what I really just love about it is he does it all in a five-minute song. It takes me five hundred pages to do what he does in a five-minute song. So someday, if I can ever get it down to five minutes, I'll feel like I've accomplished something. But he was definitely one of my biggest influences. In the comic-book world, guys like Alan Moore and Paul Levitz were big influences on me. And then in terms of people who actually write prose, it's just such an eclectic group: Joe Haldeman, brilliant science-fiction author; Edgar Allan Poe, just because he's so macabre; John Milton, because I'm a huge English nerd and I love epic poetry. It's really just a strange mix of influences.

L.B.: What kinds of books did you like reading as a teen, and what are you reading now?

B.L.: Well, you know, I'm an old man, so when I was a teenager, the books that were for teenagers really sucked. They were just not good books. There was not a young adult market the way there is today. So I went from reading comic books straight into adult fiction. I read a lot of Joe Haldeman, who I mentioned before. I read a lot of Stephen King, which could explain a lot. Nowadays, I'm reading everything. When I was working on *I Hunt Killers*, I read a lot of nonfiction. I read a lot of books about the pathology of serial killers.

L.B.: Like you do.

B.L.: Like you do.

L.B.: Can you tell us a little bit about *I Hunt Killers*?

B.L.: I sure can.

L.B.: That would be awesome. That's why we're here.

B.L.: It's the story of a kid. His father happens to be the world's most notorious serial killer. As the book opens, Dad's been in jail for four years, and Jazz is just trying to figure out how to get through life—because when you're raised by a serial killer to go into the family business, that messes with your head. And he's constantly worried that he's going to snap someday and turn out to be just like his father. And then bodies start piling up in town.

L.B.: In a Jenga kind of way?

B.L.: No, not even in an organized way at all! It's very chaotic and random. They're just all over the place. And he thinks, "You know, everyone's going to be pointing the finger at me eventually." So he decides he's going to go figure out who's doing this, to prove to the world, "Hey, look, it wasn't me." But more importantly to prove to *himself*, "Hey, look, it wasn't me." He's looking for his soul. It's a thriller, it's got some gruesome stuff in there, I'm not going to lie. But it's very much a book about him and the struggles that he's going through despite all the thriller elements to it.

L.B.: I loved the book, and I think one of the things I really loved about it is the character of Jazz. He's such a fascinating character. He's so conflicted and keeps you really guessing. So that poses the question: What if your dad *were* America's most notorious serial killer? What made you want to focus on the son?

B.L.: Well, the way this whole project came about was that I was talking with my editor and she commented that she thought it would be great if someone would write a book about a teenage serial killer—which horrified me. The idea of writing a book about a teenager killing people...I just didn't know how to make that character sympathetic and interesting. But I've always enjoyed thrillers. I think a lot of people enjoy a good serial-killer story. They're sort of the boogeymen of the twentieth and twenty-first centuries. And I kept thinking about it. And I woke up the next day and went, "Wait, the *kid's* not the killer, his father is the killer." And once that occurred to me, I realized there was a lot of fertile ground there to play with.

A lot of young adult fiction is about relationships with parents. And when we're teenagers, we all hate our parents. We all think our parents are horrible human beings. But what if, objectively, your parent *was* the worst human being alive? And I thought, "Well, that's kind of cool to play with." On top of that, I looked at it from the parent's point of view, and you know, they always want the best for you, and they want you to grow up like them. And this guy's a serial killer, and he wants his kid to grow up to be like him.

L.B.: Family values!

B.L.: Yes, family values! And once all of that jelled for me, this whole big story occurred to me about parental relationships and murder and growing up to disappoint your parents and growing up to make your parents proud and what parents do for their kids. I had to do it at that point.

L.B.: Let's talk murder scenes.

B.L.: Ah, yes, murder scenes.

L.B.: They're pretty gruesome! How did you come up with them?

B.L.: Are they? That to me...

L.B.: Are you going to say something to me that's going to make me move my chair?

B.L.: This is going to make you move your chair. This is why people don't want to be alone with me anymore! I actually don't think they're all that gruesome. This is going to sound terrible. Someday this will be used against me in a court of law. I wrote the book and I finished it and I looked at it and I said to myself, "Wow, I'm really proud of myself. I restrained myself. I wasn't too bloody or gory or anything." And then I turned it in and I heard from my editor and copy editor who said, "Whoa! This part is way gory!" People who have read it have said, "Oh my god, it's so gruesome." And I guess my blood dial is turned way down compared to other people. I guess I've been desensitized.

L.B.: So you thought you were writing the Little Black Dress—the Audrey Hepburn—of murders, and it turned out you were doing Dolly Parton?

B.L.: First of all, gore doesn't terribly interest me that much. The most interesting and gruesome things are what goes on in somebody's head. To me, the most horrifying thing in the book isn't what Billy has done to his victims, isn't what this new serial killer is doing to his victims. To me, the most horrifying thing is the flashbacks Jazz has to being a kid, the things Billy told him as a child, and the things Jazz remembers from being the child of a serial killer. A lot of those things don't even involve a single drop of blood. A lot of it is just Billy's attitude toward the rest of the world. That was the stuff I focused on that was really horrific. So when people read it and went, "Oh my god, it's so bloody," I thought, "Really?" Because I can be much bloodier. Trust me, I can be really, really gory and gruesome. That's nothing.

Turn the page for a sneak peek of
the sequel to

I Hunt KILLers

BODIES ARE PILING UP. AGAIN.

Game

THE SEQUEL TO I HuntKILLers

BARRY LYGA

CHAPTER 1

She had screamed, but she had not cried.

That's what he would remember about this one, he thought. Not the color of her hair or her eyes. Not the tilt of her hips, the curve of her lips. None of those things. Not even her name.

She had screamed. Screamed to an uncaring, star-pocked sky. They all screamed. Everyone screamed.

But she had not cried.

Not that crying would have helped. He was going to kill her no matter what, so her behavior was moot. And yet it stuck with him: No tears. No weeping. Women always cried. It was their last, best weapon. It made boyfriends apologize and husbands fold them in their arms. It made Daddy spend the extra money on the prom dress.

She screamed. Her screaming was beautiful.

But, truth be told, he missed the crying.

Later, when he was finished, he looked down on her. The early morning—so early the sun had yet to rise—was warm and the air held the slight tang of motor oil. Now that she was silent and dead and still, he could no longer remember why he had killed her. For a brief moment, he wondered if that was strange, but dismissed the doubt immediately. She was one of what would be many. There had been others, and there would be more.

Kneeling next to her, he unsheathed a short, sharp knife. Ran his fingertips over her for a moment.

He decided on the left hip. He began to carve.

CHAPTER 2

The dying man's name was...

Well, it didn't matter. Not anymore. Not right now. Names were labels for *things*, the killer knew. Nouns. Person, place, thing, idea—just like you learned in school. See this thing I drink from? I give it the label of "cup," and so what? See this thing I cover my body with? I give it the label of "shirt," and so what? See this thing I have opened to the darkening sky, allowing beautiful moonlight to shine within? I give it the label of "Jerome Herrington," and so what?

The killer stood and stretched, arching his back. Carrying the thing labeled Jerome Herrington up five flights of stairs hadn't been easy; his muscles were sore. Fortunately, he wouldn't have to carry the thing labeled Jerome Herrington back down.

The thing's head twisted left and right, the eyes staring straight ahead, unblinking. Unblinking because they had no choice—the killer had removed the eyelids first. Always first. Very important.

The killer crouched down near the thing's head and whispered, "We're very close now. Very close. I've opened your gut, and I have to say—you're beautiful in the moonlight. So very beautiful."

The thing labeled Jerome Herrington said nothing, which the killer found rude. And yet the killer was not angry. The killer knew what anger was, but had never experienced it. Anger was a waste of time and energy. Anger was useless. "Anger" was the label given to an emotion that accomplished nothing.

Maybe the thing labeled Jerome Herrington simply did not and could not appreciate its own beauty. The killer pondered a moment, then reached down and lifted a blood-slippery mass of intestines from the thing's open cavity. Moonlight glinted on the shiny, gray-red loops.

The thing labeled Jerome Herrington groaned with deep and abiding agony. It raised its head, straining as though to escape, barely able to keep its head aloft.

The thing blubbered. Tears streamed down its cheeks and it tried to speak.

The killer beamed. The thing sounded happy. That was good.

"Almost done," the killer promised, dropping the guts. At the same moment, the thing's neck gave out and its head dropped. *Kunk!* went one. *Splet!* went the other.

The killer slid a small, sharp knife from his boot. "I think the forehead," he said, and began to carve.

CHAPTER 3

Billy Dent stared in the mirror. He didn't quite recognize himself, but that was nothing new. Billy had almost always seen a stranger in mirrors, ever since childhood. At first he had hated and feared the figure that seemed to pursue him everywhere, stalking him through mirrors and store windows. But eventually Billy came to understand that what he saw in the mirror was what other people saw when they looked at him.

Other people somehow did not see the real Billy. They saw something that looked like them. Something that looked human and mortal. Something that looked like a prospect.

From outside came the grinding, mechanical sound of a trash compactor. Billy parted the curtains and looked out. Three stories down, a trash truck was smashing recycled cans and bottles.

Billy grinned. "Oh, New York," he whispered. "We're gonna have so much fun."

CHAPTER 4

It was a cold, clear January day when they gathered to bury Jazz's mother.

Bury was probably the wrong word; there was no body. Janice Dent had disappeared more than nine years ago, when Jazz was eight, and hadn't been seen since. The world knew she was dead; the courts had declared her dead after the requisite seven-year waiting period. Jazz just hadn't been able to bring himself to take the final step.

A funeral.

As the only child of the world's most notorious serial killer, he'd grown up with an intimate understanding of the mechanisms and the causes of death. But, strangely enough, he'd never attended a funeral until now.

This was poetic justice, in a way: Many of his father's victims had had funerals without bodies, too. They would have had more mourners, of course. For Janice Dent, wife of Billy, there were fewer than a dozen people. The press, fortunately, was held back at the cemetery gate.

No one would cry for Janice Dent. Not today. Her parents were long dead, and she'd been an only child. She had no friends left in Lobo's Nod that Jazz knew of, at least no one who had come forth when the funeral had been announced. Jazz figured this was fitting; she had vanished alone, and now she would be buried alone.

Next to him, his girlfriend, Connie, squeezed his hand tightly. On the other side of him stood G. William Tanner, the sheriff of Lobo's Nod and the man who had brought Billy Dent to justice more than four years ago. He was the closest thing Jazz had to a father figure, an irony that Billy would probably have laughed at. That was just Billy's sense of humor.

"Dear Lord," the priest said, "we ask that you continue to look over our beloved sister Janice in your kingdom. She has been gone from us for a while, O Lord, and we know you have watched over her in that time. Now we ask you to watch over us, as well, as we grieve for her."

Jazz found himself in the strange position of wanting this to be over as quickly as possible, for the priest to wrap things up and let them all go. Ever since Lobo's Nod's assault by the Impressionist—a Billy Dent wannabe—and then Billy's escape from prison into the wide world a couple of months ago, Jazz had felt a burning need to close off as much of his past as possible. He knew the future portended a brutal reckoning (Billy had been quiet, but that wouldn't last), so he wanted his past put to rest. Finally acknowledging his mother's death was the biggest step he'd taken so far.

Jazz hadn't cared which faith buried his mother; Father McKane at the local church had been the most willing to perform the service, so Jazz had gone Catholic. Now, as the priest droned on and on, Jazz wondered if he should have held out for a less verbose brand of religion. He sighed and gripped Connie's hand and stared straight ahead at the casket. It contained a bunch of brand-new stuffed animals, similar to the ones Jazz remembered his mother buying him as a child. It also contained a batch of lemon-frosted cupcakes Jazz had baked. That was his strongest memory of his mother—the lemon-frosted cupcakes she used to bake. He could have just had a service and a stone, but he'd wanted the whole experience, the totality of the funeral ritual. He wanted to witness the literal expression of burying his past.

Sentimental? Probably. And what of it? Bury it all. Bury the memories and the sentiment and move on.

Arrayed around the cemetery, he knew, were more than a dozen police officers and federal agents. Once the authorities had gotten wind of Jazz's plan to hold a funeral service for his mother, they had insisted on staking it out, certain (or maybe just hopeful) that Billy wouldn't be able to resist this opportunity to emerge from hiding. It was a waste of time, Jazz had told them, his insistence as useless as a sledgehammer against a tidal wave.

Billy would never reveal himself for something as prosaic and predictable as a funeral. He had occasionally attended the funerals of his victims, but that was before cable news had splashed his face on HD screens all around the world. "Butcher Billy" was too smart to show that famous face here, of all places.

"We're going to make a go of it, anyway," an FBI agent had

told Jazz, who had shrugged and said, "You want to waste tax dollars, I guess that's your prerogative."

Finally the priest finished up. He asked if anyone would like to say anything at the grave, looking pointedly at Jazz. But Jazz had nothing to say. Nothing to say in public, at least. He'd come to terms with his mother's death years ago. There was nothing *left* to say.

To his surprise, though, the priest nodded and pointed just over Jazz's shoulder. Jazz and Connie both turned—he caught the shock of her expression, too—and watched as Howie Gersten, Jazz's best friend, threaded carefully between G. William and Jazz, studiously avoiding meeting Jazz's eyes. Dressed in a black suit with a somber olive tie, six foot seven at the age of seventeen, Howie looked like a white-boy version of the images Jazz had seen of Baron Samedi, the skeletal voodoo god of the dead. The suit jacket was slightly too short for Howie's ridiculously long limbs, and a good two inches of white shirt cuff and pale wrist jutted out.

"My name is Howie Gersten," Howie said once he'd gotten to the gravestone. Jazz almost burst out laughing. Everyone here knew who Howie was already. "I didn't know Mrs. Dent. But I just really feel like when you bury someone, when you say good-bye, that someone should say something. And I figure that's my job as Jazz's best friend." Howie cleared his throat and glanced at Jazz for the first time. "Don't be pissed, dude," he stage-whispered.

A ripple of laughter washed over the attendees. Connie shook her head. "That boy..."

"Anyway," Howie went on, "here's the thing: When I was a

kid, I used to get pushed around a lot. I'm a hemophiliac, so I have to be careful all the time, and when you combine that with being a gangly string bean, it's like you're just asking for trouble, you know? And I wish I could tell you that Mrs. Dent was nice to me and used to say kind and encouraging things to me when I was going through all of that, but like I said, I didn't know her. By the time I met Jazz, she was already, y'know, not around.

"But here's the thing. Here's the thing. And I think it's an obvious thing, but someone needs to say it. We all know that, uh, Jazz's dad wasn't, isn't, exactly a great role model. But there I was one day when I was like ten or something and these kids were having a fine old time poking bruises into my arms. And Jazz came along. He was smaller than them and outnumbered, and let's face it—I wasn't going to be much help—"

Another ripple of laughter.

"But Jazz just waded into those douchebags—um, sorry, Father. He just waded into them and kicked their, um, rears, which I know isn't terribly Christian or anything, but I'll tell you, it looked pretty good from where I was standing. And I guess the thing is—the obvious thing that I mentioned before is—that I never met Mrs. Dent, but I know she must have been a good person because I'm pretty sure Billy Dent didn't raise Jazz to rescue helpless hemophiliacs from bullies. And that's all I have to say. I'll miss you, Mrs. Dent, even though I never met you. I wish I had." He started to walk back to the group of mourners, then stopped and said, "Um, God bless you and amen and stuff," before hustling back to his spot.

And then they lowered the casket into the ground. The

stone said JANICE DENT, MOTHER. No dates, because Jazz couldn't be sure exactly when Billy had killed her.

He took the small spade from the priest and shoveled some dirt into the grave. It rattled.

G. William and Connie and Howie followed suit. Then they backed away so that the cemetery workers could do the real shoveling.

Jazz became aware that he was staring at the shovels as they heaved dirt on top of the casket that did not hold his mother's body, snapping out of it only when Connie poked him to get his attention. She held a tissue out for him.

"What's this for?" he asked, taking it automatically.

"Your eyes," she said, and Jazz realized that—much to his surprise—he was crying.